The See

Kelly,
It was great
meeting you!
All the best.
Lisa

First Edition Design Publishing

The Seeds of Sorrow
Copyright ©2014 Lisa Brown

ISBN 978-1622-876-68-6 PRINT
ISBN 978-1622-876-67-9 EBOOK

LCCN 2014944290

July 2014

Published and Distributed by
First Edition Design Publishing, Inc.
P.O. Box 20217, Sarasota, FL 34276-3217
www.firsteditiondesignpublishing.com

This book is dedicated to the women who fill its pages, the strong and determined women whose lives moulded each generation that came after—including that of this author. Agnes and Sarah died before my time, but their indelible spirit continues to live on. I was blessed to know my Grandma Dorothy, an incredibly special woman who gracefully endured her own difficulties in life ... perhaps this story is not quite finished yet!

The Seeds of Sorrow

By

Lisa Brown

Prologue

1944

The breeze announced itself with a whisper, infusing the stale air with the sweet smell of rain. It was one of Dorothy's favourites, but today the scent went unnoticed. Today the breeze offered only a damp chill that she felt deep within her bones.

It was a day like any other, a day in which certainty and uncertainty were bound together in an unbreakable bond. All that had come before weighed heavily, like a ghost whose constant presence was undeniable and inescapable. And yet, in the moment's circumstance, there was a glimmer of hope, hope for a life that was deserved, but had long been denied.

Mary bent down and kissed her niece on the cheek. Dorothy's smile was broad and her excitement undeniable, but there was a lingering sadness in her eyes. Dorothy's sadness became Mary's. It always had. She loved Dorothy as her own daughter, and the helplessness she felt over her life's circumstance was overwhelming.

"Where is your mother?" Mary asked.

"I'm not certain," Dorothy answered. Her face dropped slightly as she toyed with a button on her jacket. Its silky covering felt good on her fingers and provided some of the comfort that she so desperately needed.

"Soon you will be a beautiful bride, and you will start your life anew with the man you love. I couldn't be happier for you both." Mary rested her hand on Dorothy's shoulder, squeezing it ever so slightly.

"Thank you, Aunty Mary."

Dorothy looked up at her aunt and cousin in the mirror and did her best to release them of their concern, but they did not oblige. How could they? Dorothy's existence had been fractured and the pieces that weren't broken were missing. They created a void that could not be filled, not even by the man she was about to marry.

"Do not be nervous, my dear girl. Your groom awaits. That is all you need occupy your mind with."

But it was of no use. Trepidation was as woven into the fibres of Dorothy's being as was the constancy of her countenance.

"There, all done," Margaret said as she finished spraying Dorothy's hair in place. Dorothy's chestnut curls were swept back loosely behind her head, revealing her exquisite, porcelain skin.

"Absolutely perfect. Just like you," Mary said as she winked at her niece.

Dorothy glanced at the open door before her eyes moved to the clock on the wall. The second hand swept around its face, turning and turning and slowing for nothing.

"I need to find Mum," Dorothy said anxiously. "We must get to City Hall. Tom will be waiting."

"I will find her. Finish getting yourself ready, my dear. We will leave in five minutes."

Mary left the room in search of her sister. She tried so desperately to understand her, but it was not possible. How could she? Mary had only been an observer of her sister's life, and now Agnes was buried in a deep and unending darkness and could not find her way out.

Mary came upon her quickly. She stood at the living room window, enraptured by the sole focus of her attention. At that moment nothing else existed for her but that tiny bird.

"There you are. It is time to leave. Dorothy is ready."

"Art loved birds," Agnes said, her gaze unaffected and unmoved. "He loved the sounds they made. He used to say it was nature's symphony."

"I know, Agnes," Mary said, sighing deeply. "We must leave now. It is time to go."

Agnes turned and walked toward Mary's outstretched hand and took it in hers. Together they went to the front door where the others were waiting.

"You look lovely, darling," Agnes said to her daughter.

Agnes's smile was warm, but she embodied a childlike innocence that was incapable of acknowledging the importance of the occasion. She truly loved her daughter, but she could only mother her as well as she was capable, and it wasn't nearly as much as Dorothy needed.

"Thank you, Mum. So do you. Are you ready to go?"

Dorothy was relieved to see her mother, and her expression revealed as much.

"Dorothy, you need only think of yourself. This is your wedding day," Mary said. Mary was looking at her sister as she spoke, hopeful for some spark of acknowledgement and understanding. There was none.

Mary tensed as she thought of all that could go wrong. But in her prayers she had bargained some of her happiness for her niece's. She only hoped that God had listened.

Chapter 1

1919

October had always been a glum month for Agnes. It heralded in a sombre transition, bringing chilling arctic winds to assault the last of the Winnipeg summer, and it thrust wide open the door to another long and arduous winter. Bright, beautiful flowers became a mess of wilted, rotting stems, and trees, dressed with a thick blanket of foliage, suddenly found themselves naked, barren, and exposed. Summer suited Agnes, with its outdoor picnics and parties, sunshine, and laughter. It suited her infinitely better.

October typically brought unwelcome changes for Agnes, but not so far that year. That year early October held winter at bay, giving all that lived in its midst an unexpected gift. Winter would soon come, but until then it was nowhere to be seen.

"Agnes! Stop fidgeting, would you? How do you expect me to finish your hair if you keep moving about in your seat like a two year old?"

"Mary, you sound like a grumpy old woman. Relax."

Mary was exasperated. "And, you … you, Agnes, should act your age. You are getting married in an hour's time. Does Art know he is marrying a child?"

"You *both* sound like children," Sarah said, rolling her eyes and sighing heavily as she entered the room. "How are we coming along?"

"I am almost done with Agnes's hair, Mum. It is perfect, if I do say so myself." Agnes turned to look in the mirror but was promptly stopped by Mary's hand. "Not until I am finished."

Agnes grunted but obeyed her sister.

"Agnes, your dress is on my bed. It is all ready for you. You are going to be the most beautiful bride," Sarah said, beaming with pride.

"Thank you, Mum." Agnes blushed. "Has Art arrived yet?"

In her daughter's tone, Sarah caught a glimpse of nervousness. "Do not fret. He is downstairs and looking as handsome as has ever been seen. Percy is right at his side, as any good best man should be. And your sister and John are handling the food brilliantly."

The warm, autumn breeze continued to fill the room, carrying with it the joyous sounds of pending celebration from the yard outside. Chatter and laughter filled the air, as did a grand feast's assembly.

"My, my, this weather is simply outstanding," Sarah exclaimed as she looked toward the window. "I imagined a church wedding and reception indoors, away from the cold. This is lovely. I'd say it is a very good sign."

Sarah held her hand out for her daughter. "Come, Agnes, you must dress for your groom." Agnes accepted her mother's hand with every bit of the excitement she felt.

As Agnes approached her mother's bed, she stopped and took a deep breath. She became overwhelmed by the magnitude of the moment, by the sheer oneness of the life experience. It had not come before, and God willing, it would not come again.

Agnes stepped into her dress and Sarah was overcome with emotion. She was not one to give in to the overdramatic fancies of women. She was of a more practical nature, and despite that she fully surrendered.

"Come now, I am not the first of your daughters to be married. You are well practiced. You stood in this position a few short years ago with Margaret."

Sarah nodded but did not speak for she feared the consequences. It was true. Sarah had been through this experience before, but this time it was different.

When Agnes was born, she was named Sarah Agnes, but she was always more than just her mother's namesake. She *was* Sarah. She was practical, hard headed, driven to make rules, and even more driven to follow them.

"Yes, I did. But a mother loves her daughters equally. How could I be any less affected by this?" Sarah said as she touched her daughter's dress. "One day you will have a daughter and you will understand. You will cherish her as I cherish you."

Agnes kissed her mother softly on the cheek. "Thank you, Mum."

A knock on the door brought an abrupt end to the tender exchange. Sam opened the door but did not enter. He kept his eyes focused elsewhere.

"Am I free to gaze upon the beauty of the bride or is it still a work in progress?"

Agnes giggled. "Yes, I believe I am as good as I will ever be."

Sam walked out from behind the door and took a deep breath. He became overwhelmed at the sight of her. Agnes was not his flesh and blood, but she was his daughter in every way that mattered.

"You look exquisite. You truly do. I'm sorry your father could not be here for you, but I am very grateful that I have the opportunity to be."

Agnes wrapped her arms around Sam. She loved him as her father. She had known him longer than her father had been in her life. The memories of him were very distant, and the ones that persisted were of sickness and sadness. Sam had always been a bright light, and she loved him with all her heart.

"Thank you, Pa. I would want no one other than you to be standing beside me today."

Agnes turned and looked at herself in the mirror. She was pleased. The smooth, ivory silk hung delicately on her long and slender body. From her hips to just below her knees, flowing ruffles decorated the dress like ribbons of icing on a perfectly decorated cake. The dress was elegant and demure. The hat, which was covered in silk roses and lace, was the perfect finishing touch.

"You did a splendid job on the dress, my love," Sam said as he kissed his wife.

Agnes loved to see Sam and her mother together. Sam was so in love with her, as was Sarah in return. Not a moment passed between them that went unnoticed or unacknowledged. Agnes prayed for such an everlasting love.

"Mary, you look lovely as well. What a fine maid of honour you make." Sam loved all of Sarah's girls as his own. "Are we ready?"

"I will go on ahead and take my seat," Sarah said as she walked toward the door. "I will let the pastor know we are ready."

Sarah turned and took one last look at her daughter. It was as though every scrape, every tear, every smile, every laugh was there before her eyes. A lifetime of memories came flooding back in one crushing blow.

Suddenly joy became pain, the pain of loss, the pain of emptiness. The woman who stood before Sarah had been a child up to that point, a child bound by maternal dependence. And from that moment forward, that dependence would be no more. From that moment on, Sarah would be replaced by a husband and relegated to a role that felt entirely inconsequential. But Sarah knew it was a mother's pain to bear.

As Sarah left the room and Mary took her place in front of Agnes, beautiful music began to fill the air. A quartet of instruments—a violin, a cello, a clarinet and a flute—began to play Vivaldi's "The Four Seasons." Agnes took Sam's arm and together they made their way downstairs.

As Mary stepped through the door and into the yard, the quartet continued to play Vivaldi but changed pace and moved from "Winter" to "Spring," Agnes's favourite. Guests stood at their seats awaiting the entrance of the bride. And when she appeared, she did not disappoint. Agnes was absolutely incandescent.

Upon the stone path that led the bride to her groom, Agnes held tightly on to Sam's arm. It was not for fear or nervousness but for an overwhelming love for a man who had provided the same to Agnes throughout most of her life. She was organized and steadfast because of her mother, but she loved without reserve because of Sam.

As Agnes walked up the pathway, she locked eyes with Art. He stood before her grinning widely, seeming as though his sole life's purpose was being fulfilled. He looked so dapper and debonair in his cream coloured suit and tie. She felt a surge of emotion that almost brought her to her knees.

Art gazed upon his bride and found he was unable to grasp the depths of his feelings. Love was simply a word, as was beauty, and neither sufficed. Agnes was his soul and, with every breath he took, and for the rest of his life, he would strive to prove his devotion to her.

Agnes kissed Sam's cheek and took Art's hand. Together they turned to face the pastor who would bring them together in the eyes of God. There were no second thoughts, no misgivings, only a wave of impatience for all that was to follow. And as Art and Agnes sealed the union with a deep and passionate kiss, their friends and family cheered wildly. Sarah was shocked at the impropriety of such a display, but that shock was quickly swept aside as she realized that her very own husband was the loudest of the lot.

As the couple turned to face their guests, the bride and groom were showered with confetti by the younger siblings who were not as taken by the poignancy of the promise as they were the excitement of the celebration. They were all too happy to throw brightly coloured paper at the newlyweds. Creating such a mess rarely came without consequences, and they took full advantage while they could.

"Let us partake in this amazing feast and enjoy this incredible weather. Thank you all for coming and celebrating with us." Art was ready to share his contentment with his guests.

"Yes, please indulge yourselves in this delicious feast that Margaret and John have prepared for us," Sam said, motioning toward the tables of food. "Harold, Cliff, and William, you may remove the chairs now."

Agnes's younger siblings promptly began moving the chairs to the perimeter of the yard, placing them around the tables that awaited them. As they did, the early afternoon sun continued to warm from high in the cobalt sky. The day was the very definition of perfection and showed no signs of dulling.

"May I have your attention, please?" Sam requested. "I would now like to take this opportunity to introduce Mr. and Mrs. William Arthur Craig."

Sam stepped aside, and Agnes and Art made their way to the newly cleared dance floor. Both were walking on air, feeling as though every step was a step further into a dream. The crowd continued to clap and whistle as they stood front and centre.

"May I have this dance, Mrs. Craig?" Art asked as he bowed deeply to his new bride. Agnes blushed as she nodded and took her husband's hand. The quartet began to play the first few notes of the song and Art took his wife in his arms.

At Art's insistence, Agnes had relinquished control of the wedding waltz music. Agnes had planned and executed every other aspect of the wedding and to lose control over something so important had not been easy for her. But Art's impassioned plea moved Agnes, and she could not refuse him this.

As the music continued to play, Agnes quickly recognized *"If You Were the Only Girl in the World"* and it brought a smile to her face. But her smile quickly turned to surprise as Art began to sing.

> *Sometimes when I feel bad*
> *and things look blue,*
> *I wish a pal I had ... say one like you.*
> *Someone within my heart to build a throne,*
> *Someone who'd never part, to call my own.*

Tears that had been held at bay began to flow down Agnes's cheeks. Art smiled lovingly at her as he removed his hand from the small of her back and wiped the tears away.

> *If you were the only girl in the world*
> *and I were the only boy....*

Together they moved in perfect unison, and not during one single word did Art take his eyes off his beautiful bride. They shut out the world and nothing existed but the two of them.

The song reached its end, and for a brief moment bride and groom stood in silence, unmoving, eyes fixated on one another. Their guests held their collective breath, for the romantic crescendo proved unbearable. Not a dry eye existed among them. Art cradled his bride's face in his hands and kissed her as though heaven was his.

"Now it's time to speed things up a bit and get this party started," Art said enthusiastically, lightening the air. "Mary, Percy, get on out here. Time to foxtrot."

The quartet picked up speed and played a tune perfect for the energetic dance. Mary and Percy took to the dance floor with Art and Agnes, and together they began to shake it up, much to the excitement of all present.

The ground was hard and compact after a long, dry summer, and it made for the perfect dancing base. The couples kicked it up, moving about with abundant enthusiasm. All four had taken dancing lessons specifically for the occasion. Their excitement was contagious, and as Art invited everyone else to join them, the dance floor began to fill quickly.

Art and Agnes took a break from the dancing and started to mingle with their guests. It wasn't a large wedding, only forty of their closest friends and family. They had desperately wanted it to be fun and intimate, not large and impersonal, and they succeeded handily. It had the ambiance of a summer barbeque, despite the more formal attire.

Agnes made a beeline for her sister when she spied her through the crowd. Agnes hugged Margaret so forcefully that they almost lost their footing, and they laughed childishly as they regained their balance.

"You are an exquisite bride, Agnes. It is hard to believe someone who was such a pest can look so pretty," Margaret said in jest. Agnes pushed her sister away and laughed.

"The food looks absolutely delicious," Agnes said. "Thank you so much for doing this for us."

And it did. Agnes had specifically instructed a casual and fun menu, not a traditional silver and china one. There were tables of perfectly crispy fried chicken, creamy gourmet potato salad and coleslaw, belly-warming chili con carne and slow-roasted ribs with Ember's famous chili mustard sauce. Margaret and John's restaurant specialized in a wood-fired grill menu and Margaret's sauces ... well, no words could describe how incredibly delicious they were.

Margaret and John met while they were both employed at The Fort Garry Hotel. Margaret had been a kitchen assistant and prepared meals for the staff. Chef Nicolas Bertrand's written recommendation was all that was required. Margaret had learned under his guidance while at Amberley House back in England when she was just a girl. Chef Nicolas had long had his own restaurant in Paris, and Bertrand's was known internationally for its traditional French country roasting and braising. His recommendation could have put any restaurant in *The Michelin Guide*.

After impressing The Fort Garry's master chef with her saucing skills, Margaret was often invited to work with the sous chefs, including John, the roast and grill chef who became her husband. She should have been hired as one of the sous chefs at the outset, but she was still fighting discrimination in a man's world. It made no sense to Margaret ... women cooked most meals in the home, yet in a restaurant all the top chefs were men. *Utterly ridiculous*, she thought! So, Margaret did the only thing she could after John returned home from war; she persuaded her husband to join her in starting their own restaurant. Sam and Sarah were the major investors in this new venture. Sam had said, "I've eaten your cooking. I would be a fool not to."

"You have been such a wonderful help in the restaurant. We wouldn't have let anyone else do it for you," Margaret said as she turned quickly. Out of the corner of her eye, she saw one of her three-year-old twin girls standing on a chair, her hands wrist deep in the bread pudding. Agnes turned to see where her sister was running and began to laugh heartily. *Only a mother wouldn't find that utterly amusing*, Agnes thought.

But Eileen saw her mother coming and she jumped down and ran in the opposite direction, squealing with delight as she did. Eileen managed to run through the crowd and back toward her Aunt Agnes, who did not see her coming. Margaret, absolutely horrified, caught her daughter just in time to avoid a messy disaster.

"Aren't you a little chocolate monster?" Agnes teased. She squeezed Eileen's face and gave her a big kiss. Then it was Betty's turn.

Eileen's sister emerged from the crowd with a mouthful of chocolate creampuff. What remained of the creampuff, besides what was in her mouth, was painted all over her face.

"It would appear my granddaughters have their mother's love of food, although they haven't quite mastered the art of actually eating it," Sam quipped. He arrived with a wet cloth and began to wipe little hands and faces.

"Thank you, Sam," Margaret said appreciatively. "Sometimes I believe these girls conspire to drive me over the edge."

"Words spoken by every parent from the beginning of time. From what I hear, your mother ran around a table a time or two in pursuit of you."

"I was an angel, I'll have you know," Margaret said with a cheeky grin.

"They are just children being children. They grow up fast enough, and really, in the grand scheme, no harm done." Sam looked on lovingly at the girls as they ran off in search of more mischief. "Agnes, you will know yourself soon enough."

Agnes blushed at the thought.

Chapter 2

Art and Agnes were on a cloud as they sat in the back of the Model T. The afternoon festivities were already a blur, and their thoughts were now focused on the evening to come. Art whispered into Agnes's ear, bringing about a girlish giggle. It was a short, ten minute drive and Sam focused on the road ahead, trying to provide the newlyweds with as much privacy as he could.

Quickly The Fort Garry came into view, its steep roofline and turrets rising up majestically above Broadway. It was elegant and stately, a stark contrast to the railway yard that lay not far beyond the tree-lined boulevard. While it appeared out of place and out of time, to those who lived in Winnipeg, and even more so to those who had been fortunate enough to have stood in its grand lobby, it was a source of fierce pride and a welcome distraction to the inevitable fallout of war. It was a jewel in the prairie landscape, and it rivaled any hotel in New York or Paris.

As Sam pulled the car up to the hotel entrance, the arriving guests were greeted like royalty. A sharply dressed valet helped Agnes out of the car while another took the overnight bag from Art and carried it inside. Sam walked around the car to say good-bye to the blissful couple.

"Pa, thank you so much for helping to make this such a glorious day for Art and me. I could not have imagined it any better. And this," Agnes said pointing to The Fort Garry, "is the best gift in the world." Agnes wrapped her arms around Sam and kissed his cheek.

"You do not have to thank me, my dear. Your happiness is all I need. I hope you enjoy your evening tonight. The hotel car will bring you home, and your mother will have brunch ready. Now I have a yard full of guests to get back to, and you have the beginning of the rest of your lives awaiting you beyond those doors. Congratulations, you two." Sam shook Art's hand, gave Agnes one final kiss on the cheek, and was on his way.

Art and Agnes entered through the gold and glass revolving door. It was as though they passed into a fairy tale. Inside they stood mesmerized by the grandeur that lay before them. It was the first time they had seen it, and it was a sight to behold.

A spectacular floral arrangement, taller than either of them had ever seen, sat gloriously as the lobby's centrepiece. Its fragrance permeated the room, bringing the presence of an English garden indoors. It was framed by a square of black marble inlayed into the grey marble floor, and it was illuminated by an intricately designed chandelier that glittered from overhead.

A valet directed them to the front desk where their overnight bag was waiting. A gentleman, perfectly pressed without a wrinkle, appeared behind the long, marble countertop. "Welcome to The Fort Garry Hotel. May I have your name, please?" he asked of Art.

"Certainly. Mr. and Mrs. Art Craig," Art said as Agnes giggled quietly. Mrs. Art Craig sounded marvelous but so foreign in its newness.

The employee flipped through a stack of cards and pulled out their reservation. He scanned it briefly and then excused himself. He exited through a door to his rear, returning with another gentleman.

"Mr. and Mrs. Craig, what a pleasure it is to host you on your wedding night. Heartfelt congratulations on the wonderful event," he offered. "We have a special room selected for you, which I hope will be to your liking. Your dinner reservations are at half-past six in The Factor's Table Dining Room. Is that time still desirable for you?" Agnes turned to look at the entrance to the dining room, which even from a distance looked magnificent.

"Thank you. We look forward to it."

"Excellent. Would you like help with your bag, Mr. Craig?"

"No, thank you. I believe I can manage." Art wanted only to be alone with his bride.

Art was handed the key to their room and directed to the elevators, but his wife had something else in mind.

"Oh, Art. Let us walk up that magnificent staircase. It reminds me of Amberley House. I was just a girl when I visited, but my memories are as strong as if it were just yesterday. Please indulge me, my darling," Agnes implored lovingly.

"How can I refuse you anything?" Art asked, knowing he couldn't. It gave him great pleasure to indulge her.

Agnes ran her hand up the brass railing as they ascended the staircase. Halfway up she stopped and turned back, looking down at the foyer as though she were the lady of the manor. The look of awe and wonder on his wife's face grabbed at Art.

"My darling, as long as I draw breath I will not stop until I have built you your own castle."

Agnes caressed Art's arm affectionately. "My castle is wherever I am with you. I have my prince. What more do I need?" Art could do nothing but smile.

The brass elevator doors glistened, casting the flawless reflection of a happy couple. It revealed a perfect fluid moment, one whose permanency would only be born in their minds, for reflections are more dreams than etches in time, frames to be stored away in the imagination of one's life and remembered in some exalted form as the years bear down. Agnes noted the reflection and acknowledged her blessings.

As the door to the room opened, both felt a surge of nervous excitement. What lay beyond was irreversible. Their commitment to each other would soon become eternal. Until then they were husband and wife in name and ceremony only. Agnes gasped as she walked into the room. It was a suite fit for royalty. They were overcome by the massive living room, with its ten foot ceiling and elaborately draped window.

"They must have made a mistake. I doubt this was the room that Sam and your mother intended. I can't even imagine the cost."

A formal dining table sat directly in front of the window. On it was a bottle of sparkling cider that was chilling in an elegant, crystal ice bucket. Beside it was a tray of strawberries, which had been drizzled with sumptuously rich, chocolate swirls.

"Look, Art. If it was a mistake, this would not be here," Agnes said full of hope. She did not want to give up this grand room.

There was a note, which Agnes took out of the envelope and read aloud. *Mr. and Mrs. Craig, congratulations on your marriage. We hope you enjoy your stay with us. Sincerely, the staff at The Fort Garry Hotel.*

"Well, that does it then. It couldn't possibly be a mistake," Art conceded.

"Let us have some cider and strawberries. How utterly decadent and exciting," Agnes gushed.

Agnes picked up a strawberry from the tray and held it up to Art's mouth. He took a bite and then held Agnes's hand to her own mouth. She took a slow, sensuous bite and as she swallowed, Art pulled his wife forcefully against him, making her swoon.

"Perhaps we can skip dinner and just have the dessert. What do you say?" Art asked playfully.

"Patience, my darling. Dinner is part of our wedding gift, and they would be disappointed if we didn't enjoy it too."

Art acted wounded, as though an arrow had just pierced his heart.

"I suppose we have waited this long. What're a few more hours?"

Art pulled the bottle out of the ice bucket and wiped it off with the towel. As he untwisted the metal caging from the cork, Agnes's excitement mounted. With the loud pop, Agnes shrieked and then laughed. The cork hit the ceiling and then landed in between the two of them. Agnes picked it up and placed it in her purse.

Art poured the cider, bubbles overflowing onto the table. Art handed his bride a glass, and they both held up their glasses as he said a toast.

"To the most magnificent bride who has ever walked this earth. I love you with all my heart, and I promise to be your prince, to take care of you, to make you happy, all the days of our lives. And I won't forget about that castle either," he said as he winked at his bride.

Agnes laughed at Art's light-heartedness. She so loved his sense of humour. "And I promise to love you back, to make you deliriously happy, and to keep our castle sparkling clean."

"Cheers," they both said as they clanked their glasses in unison. The bubbles brought tears to Agnes's eyes.

"I am hungry. I could eat this entire tray of strawberries."

"I am hungry as well," Art teased as he pulled his wife into him again. He placed his glass on the table and then cupped his wife's face in his hands and kissed her passionately.

"Is it just me or is it getting warm in here?" Agnes said as she started to fan herself with her hand.

Art filled Agnes's glass again. "This will cool you down. Let's pretend we are in Paris and this is real champagne, not sparkling cider, and we are celebrating as we should. The French would never conceive of the notion of banning alcohol. How utterly preposterous."

Agnes nodded. It made no sense to her either. Free will and the right to choose was the foundation of democracy. What was next to go, free thought?

"I would like to freshen up before we go to dinner. Why don't you finish your cider and I will be out in a moment?" Agnes retrieved her purse and made her way to the washroom. She dabbed some powder on her face to remove the shine and then freshened her lipstick. Her lips popped with the crimson hue. She studied herself in the mirror. Through her eyes she looked different—more mature, no longer a child. It was exhilarating, but the emotional chasm she was about to leap over was suddenly daunting.

Art stood to greet his returning wife. "I did not think it possible for you to be more beautiful than you were just a breath ago, but alas, here you are. My heart burns ... it yearns for you. What is a mere mortal such as me to do?" Art asked as he held his hand to his heart and bowed his head.

"My dear, should you choose to change occupations, you could always find yourself in theatre. You have an unmatched flair for the dramatic, and I do love you so for it."

They both laughed. Art took his wife's arm and they made their way downstairs. As they passed the Musician's Gallery in the lobby, the sound of strings filled the air, adding a refined sophistication that was not lost on Agnes.

"How utterly captivating. I could just melt into that glorious sound, couldn't you?" Art nodded in agreement, thrilled that his new bride was enjoying herself so.

The Factor's Table Dining Room was as grand as the lobby, extending two stories in height. From the panelled gold and cream ceiling hung antique silver electroliers which radiated an amber hue that resembled a harvest sunset. The large, ornate windows, which were draped in an elegant yet earthy, forest green brocade, let little light in from the setting sun. Table top candlelight amplified the contrast of the twilight.

The maître d'hotel showed Art and Agnes to their table. "Art, this is simply wonderful." Agnes continued to look over the room. It was filled with splendidly dressed people, deep in conversation, unaffected by her scanning eyes.

"Your waiter will be with you shortly. May I offer you a sparkling raspberry cocktail to start?"

"That sounds divine. Yes, please. Darling, would you care for one?"

"Raspberry cocktails for two it is. Thank you."

The food was superb—mouth-watering chateaubriand, a cheese platter with a caramelized apple jelly worthy of the best French restaurant, and a luscious lemon soufflé. It was definitely a meal to remember.

"I could not eat another morsel. I need to stand up or I will burst." Agnes wiped her mouth with her napkin and let out a contented sigh.

"Why don't you explore the lobby, my dear? I will square things away in here and join you shortly."

Agnes agreed. She decided on a replication Louis XIV settee opposite the Musician's Gallery so that she could sit and watch the musicians as she enjoyed their heavenly music. Strings were Agnes's favourites, and that night she was able to drench herself in the euphonious sounds of violin, cello, and harp.

"There you are, my dear," Art said as he approached his wife.

"Yes. This sound is breathtaking," Agnes said as she closed her eyes and welcomed the music into her soul. "I wish it would not end."

"It doesn't have to end. Come," Art said as he held out his hand.

As the door to their suite opened, the sound of music filled the air. Agnes walked into the room and looked for its source. On a bureau, there was a tabletop Edison phonograph spinning a fantastically exotic classical tune. Agnes looked at Art with as broad a smile as her mouth would allow. Art grinned and walked over to the phonograph. In the bureau drawer, he pulled out another record and replaced the one that had been playing. He cranked the handle a few times and *If You Were the Only Girl in the World* began to play.

"How on earth…" she whispered, astonished.

"A man cannot give away all his secrets. He must maintain an air of mystery. Now let us dance." Art closed the door, took his wife in his arms, and swung her around gently.

Agnes settled her head into the curve of Art's neck, and the two melted into each other. When the song was over, they stayed as they were, swaying to the sound of crackle and static. Art was the first to pull back. He looked deeply into his bride's eyes and placed his lips on hers. The soft, slow kiss became more impatient, their lips pressing hard against each other. Their passion mounted and Art, breathing heavily, lead his wife to the bedroom.

Art unbuttoned Agnes's jacket, slowly and deliberately, each button more dramatically than the last. As she stood there with only her lace camisole, Art gazed upon his wife in awe. Agnes unbuttoned Art's jacket and eased it off his shoulders until it fell to the floor. She covered his neck with sensuous kisses as she unbuttoned his shirt.

Both stood before each other without pretense, the cloak of vanity stripped away. Raw and pure, they teetered on the precipice of bliss. Art gently led his bride to the bed. He kissed her tenderly as he ran his hands down the length of her willowy body. The outside world melted away and Art and Agnes, at the beginning of their journey together, became one, body and soul, in perfect love for eternity.

They lay in a haze, silent in their own thoughts. Art's arm was wrapped safely around his bride as she lay with her head on his chest. The cadence of his breathing was hypnotic. As his chest rose and fell, they passed into a single, indistinguishable rhythm.

Agnes covered up her sleeping groom, switched off the light, and settled in. It had been a day full of activity and emotion, and they both succumbed to exhaustion. However, the peace that embraced Agnes was not to be for long.

A thundering, guttural boom filled the room, thrusting Agnes from the unconscious. Art was sitting up, flailing his arms with terrifying intensity, as though he were fending off an enemy. But there was no enemy, only his wife. Art continued to fight for his life, the fear in his voice as clear as the moonlight that showered the room.

Agnes reached out to her husband and placed her hand on his arm, and in one sudden and powerful blow, his elbow met Agnes's eye, the force of which sent Agnes flying from their bed. Agnes lay on the floor as she landed. Pain seared through her face as the dusty smell of the carpet permeated her nose. The shock of the explosion left her paralyzed.

How can this be? Her mind raced. After a few moments, she managed to pull herself up to her feet. Her husband was sleeping soundly now, no trace of crisis, nothing to indicate all wasn't as it should be, that is, with the exception of the throbbing in her eye.

Agnes closed the door to the washroom and turned on the light. She stood before the mirror, naked and alone. Overwhelming fear and insecurity engulfed her. And for an instant, she feared her new husband.

The morning brought sunshine. Art awoke, stretched his arms, and let out a sound of contentment. He rolled over and placed his arm around his wife.

"You dressed," Art observed, disappointed. He kissed the back of her neck and then her shoulder. He gently rolled her over on her back and kissed her lips. He pulled back so he could look at her.

"What on earth happened to your eye?" he gasped. Art was genuinely troubled.

Agnes lay there, unsure of what to say. Clearly he had no recollection. It was obvious to her it had not been intentional. The look of concern on Art's face was an emotional blow to Agnes, one more painful than the physical blow she had received. Suddenly she felt protective, no longer afraid.

"That will teach me for not turning a light on in the dark. I slipped and fell on the way to the toilet and hit my eye on the door handle. How utterly clumsy of me."

"My dear, we should call a doctor. Are you all right?"

"I am fine. Nothing that a bit of powder won't cover up. How did you sleep?" Agnes asked hesitantly.

"Fairly well. A bad dream, but other than that I slept like a baby."

"What did you dream about?" Agnes probed, hoping it would provide some clarity.

"Nothing for you to worry your pretty little head about. Winnipeg is far from France. And thanks to the grace of God, I am here with you." Despite his attempt to brush it all aside with the nonchalant response, the memory of the dream surfaced an anxiety that Agnes had not witnessed in him before.

"All right," Agnes said agreeably, not wanting to take it any further.

Art and Agnes made passionate love again, as though nothing had happened, as though there had been no war and no blackened eye.

Chapter 3

An enticing aroma filled the air. Sarah emerged from the kitchen with a bowl of cornmeal muffins and placed them on the table. She saw the front door was open and hurried to greet her daughter and new son-in-law.

"Hello, you two. I hope you had a wonderful evening," Sarah said with her arms outstretched toward her daughter. She embraced her as though it was a long awaited homecoming. "Here, let me look at you," Sarah said as she stepped back, hands still firmly on her daughter's shoulders.

"We have only been gone one night, Mum," Agnes teased.

Sarah took another look at her daughter and noticed what was not quite right.

"Goodness, what happened to your eye?" Agnes placed her hand over her eye as she exhaled loudly.

"Your silly, clumsy daughter lost her footing on the way to the toilet. I took the worst end of it. I think the door handle got off rather easily."

"She was as quiet as a mouse. She didn't even wake me when it happened. I didn't know until this morning. The powder has covered up most of it. It was quite puffy and red earlier." Art put his arm around his wife's shoulder and pulled her in protectively.

Sarah looped her arm through her daughter's free arm and led her in the direction of the living room; she couldn't help herself. Sam smiled at his wife's boldness. Not wanting to leave Art standing in the hallway alone, Sam slapped him jovially on the back and led him in the same direction.

Margaret and John, Art's father and brother Percy, and Agnes's sister Mary were all seated and in mid-conversation. Mary was the first to notice their arrival.

"Agnes, what happened to your eye?" She could barely get the words out before she was inches from the bruise.

Agnes braced herself for the inevitable. So far the people who knew her best saw no deception. There was no reason to believe the others wouldn't be any less easy.

"I fell in the dark on the way to the toilet. No harm done, really. It looks worse than it is."

Mary sensed her sister did not want to talk about it, so she left it alone. She was more anxious to hear about the hotel and the dinner. It was a luxury that they weren't accustomed to. The war had all but swallowed up extravagance, and the very definitions of need and want had changed for good; but as mighty as the sacrifice of pleasure had been, the burden of loss had been far greater. A grenade blast took James fresh into his tour of duty, and the brevity of his absence had not yet allowed Sarah the opportunity to grow accustomed to the void that her son's loss had created. It was as though her son had left for work in the morning and simply never returned home for dinner.

Constant reminders of James helped ease the pain. His carvings filled corners and spaces, and the spirit that radiated from them was palpable. Samuel was more fortunate. He had made it home safely and seemed no worse for wear.

"Please tell us about The Fort Garry. Is it as grand as you imagined?" Mary begged.

Agnes was glowing. "Even more so. It is grand beyond words."

"What about dinner? Was is delicious? What did you have?" Agnes laughed as Mary peppered her with questions.

"It was delightful. We had chateaubriand and a sinful lemon soufflé for dessert. But the best part was the chocolate covered strawberries and sparkling cider waiting for us in the room. And the room ... oh, what a room. It was a suite. It was grander than anything I have ever seen. And it was ours for the entire night," Agnes said, engrossed in the memory.

"How romantic," Mary swooned.

"The world moves so fast. I can't quite keep up," Art's father, Bill, interjected. His tone was light-hearted, but his discomfort was evident. "Nothing like that existed when I was your age. Gosh, there wasn't even a train to Winnipeg. I was ten when the family came from Drummond with nothing more than what we could load onto an ox cart. Thirteen hundred miles it was. Took us close to six months."

It was a story that Agnes had heard many times, and each time she indulged her father-in-law and listened intently. It was a difficult journey, and one made even more so because his mother and younger sister didn't survive it. Ironically, retelling the tale seemed cathartic for him.

Bill didn't mean to dampen the mood. His inability to relate to such extravagance, and to the pace of change, was overwhelming. His own wife, Art's mother, had also passed away when Art was only fifteen and female softness and sensitivity had been void in Bill's life for a long time. His only remaining daughter had long lived in Vancouver. Bill had aunts and cousins close by, all of whom had made the same journey at some point; but after his mother died and his father remarried so quickly, the interactions all but stopped. For Bill, Agnes was a very welcome addition to their family.

"It seems not so many who live here were born here. Most have come from somewhere else, as did we. Art tells me you were born in Canada," Sarah said to Bill.

"My children are third generation Canadian. My mother was born in Lanark County, Ontario, as was I. Her parents came over from Ireland close to a hundred years ago now. The Irish in us is all but gone," he said with a chuckle. "And that is fine with me. I am happy to be Canadian. It doesn't matter that you weren't born here. Your James gave his life for this country. We are all Canadian and I'm damn proud of it. My grandfather fought in the American War of 1812. My three boys all fought in France." Bill stopped himself. His eyes started to tear, and he was not going to let himself go. He was fiercely proud but staunchly private.

Bill's passion was moving, and in the moment Sarah's own feelings of pride were greater than her feelings of pain and loss.

"Thank you, Bill. You are absolutely right," Sarah said. Everyone in the room nodded. Sarah took advantage of the lull in conversation to announce brunch.

"Let us pray," Sam said as everyone gathered around the table and bowed their heads. "We are so grateful to God for the opportunity to come together and welcome Agnes and Art home as husband and wife. We pray for your gracious blessings upon them and for strength and guidance to help them through the challenges you will place before them. And we thank you for our new family—Art, Bill, and Percy. May you bless them always. And finally, thank you for the food that you have so generously provided for us. We know we are fortunate, and we ask that you show mercy on those less fortunate. Amen."

After the meal was finished, Art and Agnes got up to leave. It had been a busy few days, and they simply wanted to be alone to revel in marital bliss. There was to be no honeymoon, at least not yet. Money did not permit anything extravagant. They talked about visiting Uncle Bertie in California, but nothing definite had been decided.

"Are you sure you don't want us to drive you?" Percy asked. "It is a bit far to walk."

Art tried to maintain Percy's straight tone but was unsuccessful. His grin turned into a laugh. "I am confident we can manage. But I do thank you for the offer."

"Thank you, everyone, for all that you have done. Our wedding will hold very special memories for us, and having you all here this morning means the world to us. *You all* mean the world to us." Art nodded in agreement and took his wife's arm.

The walk to their new home was a short one. From the front door, they walked down the driveway and up the carriage house stairs. It was one of the few homes in the area that was large enough to fit a driveway that extended from the front of the property to the back; most accessed a garage from the alley.

"No threshold is too difficult that I could not carry my beautiful bride across, no effort too arduous. I would carry you to the ends of the earth, my sweetheart. I am, after all, your prince."

Agnes giggled and let her husband carry her over the doorstep. It was the same carriage house that Sam had lived in when he had first moved to Norwood. Grandma and Grandpa Warman, Sam's parents, had since passed on, and Sam and Sarah now lived in the main house with the children. The lower part of the carriage house had since been converted to an auto garage, and the apartment above had been updated with a fresh coat of paint and some new pieces of furniture.

While perfectly comfortable, their new abode was spartan. It lacked any trace of colour or lives lived. It was merely a foundation but one they were excited to build upon.

"Look at the gifts." Agnes felt like a young girl at Christmas time as she gazed upon the mountain of colour on the table. "They are so beautifully wrapped. How can we open them?"

"Come, my love, sit with me and let's breathe in our new life." Art led his wife to the chesterfield.

Agnes sat down and melted into her husband. For the first time, she felt settled and complete. It was as though her purpose and reason for being had been discovered and defined. She was now a wife, and she would do everything in her power to ensure she was the best wife that Art could ever wish for.

"Darling, did you see the way your brother was looking at Mary? If I saw what I think I saw, I am guessing there will be another wedding within a year's time," Agnes said cheekily.

"I believe your perception may be spot on," Art said as he kissed his wife's cheek. "Percy told me that he has been sweet on her for some time."

Agnes mockingly punched her husband in the shoulder. "You knew this, and you didn't share it with me? I'm hurt," she said with a forced pout.

"I'm not one to gossip. It wasn't my place to say anything." Art was trying to excuse his lack of disclosure. "It is premature. I didn't want to break Cupid's arrow. I think they would be smashing together. However, my brother is shy, and it may take him a while to gather the nerve."

Art's explanation seemed to satisfy his wife. She did not pursue it further, as difficult as it was, for the thought brought her immense joy.

Chapter 4

There was little autumn that year. The winter reprieve that Winnipeg had enjoyed into early October had ended abruptly. Temperatures were below average for most of November, but it was early December that brought on the paralyzing cold. The frigid air hovered around minus twenty-two degrees Fahrenheit for the better part of two weeks. Those who did not have to leave home did not, and if they did, they could not be out in the icy Arctic air for long. However, just as people were beginning to go mad, the freeze lifted, bringing a welcome warmth to the city.

Agnes and Art met the rest of the family at the foot of the driveway. It was a lovely day to walk to church. The sun, so long obscured by the dull, grey cloud that had marred the skyscape, hung brilliant and blazing in the clear, winter sky. With the exception of the roads and the sidewalks, snow blanketed the ground. Nearly a foot had fallen on a single day in November, and so it remained.

"Hello, you two. What a splendid day," Sarah exclaimed.

The walk to church was a short one, a mere three blocks. It was the same church that they had been attending since they arrived from England fifteen years earlier. From the churchyard they could see directly to Uncle Bertie's old house, where they first lived when they arrived. Bertie, Jane, and cousin Florence had left for California a few years earlier and the house had been sold. It was still odd to think of strangers living in the house that they had shared so many wonderful memories in.

As they did every Sunday, the entire family gathered at church. And as they also did every Sunday, the whole family gathered for brunch afterwards. More often than not, it was at Sam and Sarah's, but on occasion it was at Margaret and John's restaurant. It had become a beloved weekly ritual.

"Art, you look tired today. Are you feeling well?" Sarah asked.

"I'm fine. Just a bit of trouble sleeping lately. Nothing to worry about."

Agnes nudged her husband, whose face turned a dozen shades of red. He cleared his throat in nervous reaction, and it succeeded in directing everyone's attention to the two of them.

The moment of silence felt like an eternity for Agnes as she waited for her husband to speak. He sat up, shuffling his hands. No one spoke, sensing an announcement. It came and it did not disappoint.

"It appears as though there will be a new addition to the family soon." He managed to get the words out before he had to clear his throat again.

"Oh, my darling girl. How absolutely wonderful. I will have another grandbaby. When are you due?" Sarah was ecstatic. She could not hold herself back from touching her daughter's belly.

"I believe the doctor said the end of June, beginning of July. They are never quite sure about these things, it seems," Agnes explained.

"Congratulations, you two." Margaret offered them both a hug. "I have a crib and bassinette that you will be able to put to good use." John and Margaret had tried for more children but had been unsuccessful, and she had been saving her baby things for her sisters.

The reality of the situation hit home for both of them as they told their family. It was a nervous excitement unlike any they had experienced before. It surpassed marriage handily.

Agnes toyed with her food. Her morning sickness had been tolerable, but it was strong enough to tamper with her appetite. She drew sympathy from her mother and sister, clearly both of whom had been through it.

"John, how is the restaurant?" Sam asked.

"Business is good … all things considered. We are still trying to make up for our losses during the strike. And the Temperance Committee continues to stick their noses where they don't belong. They are more obsessed with the power they possess than the moral code that they supposedly stand behind. We have followed the laws fully and will continue to do so, yet they choose to harass us at every turn." John was noticeably riled. Everyone knew his opinions to be strong and they let him express them.

"We are still digging ourselves out of the same hole. The strike was such a counterproductive exercise. I understand a worker's desire to increase wages to catch up with the inflation that the war caused, but that was not the way to go about it. History has proven time and time again that mass demonstrations of worker solidarity are never successful in the long run. This strike proved no different. Many had no job to go back to after the strike because business owners could no longer afford them, and if they could, they didn't trust them. Our biggest threat is, and always will be, those who don't follow the rules. In order to sell to the public, I must have a permit and that permit comes at a cost. Some of the slaughterhouses in St. Boniface and Winnipeg don't follow the rules. They secretly sell to the public without licenses and without paying the fees that I must. That puts me at a disadvantage. But I will demonstrate my frustration within the confines of the law, and I believe I will be successful." Sam was working hard to educate the local politicians on the abattoirs' illegal activities and they were listening. And why shouldn't they? It was directly affecting their coffers.

"I too believe that we should follow the rules. I just don't believe all rules are good rules. They are not always well thought out. Typically they are made for the benefit of the maker and not necessarily the people for whom they are written to govern. You cannot legislate abstinence. How can you legislate away free will? When you do, you become no better than the communists. I do agree that alcohol can be a vice if not consumed responsibly, but forcibly removing it only makes some want it more. We see it every day. All you have to do is read the newspaper. Crime is at an all-time high, and Alex McCurdy is not willing to recognize the root cause. He and the rest of the morality squad see it as a moral issue and not a result of asinine laws." This was a subject that John and Art completely agreed on. Art was passionate about democracy. He fought a war for freedom and he came home to oppression.

John and Art nodded at Sam in agreement but then turned their eyes to each other and grinned ever so slightly. They believed in peaceful demonstration, but there were limits to a man's patience.

"Yes, sadly, not all rules are good rules, but we must work for change in a lawful and peaceful manner. Aggression and coercion only work to undermine the very foundation of the democracy that we work so hard to maintain. If we practise them, we will turn into nothing more than a police state," Sam continued.

"Enough of this dispiriting conversation," Sarah chastised. "We have a baby to plan for."

"Agnes, what do you think you are having? I hope it is another girl," Mary said excitedly.

"There are enough girls in this family," John said mockingly. "We need some boys."

"Whatever you have, it will be just as it should be," Sarah said. "And you must make sure you get plenty of rest. Babies can be very exhausting as they are growing."

"Yes, Mum, Art won't let me lift a finger. If he had his way, I would not get out of bed until the baby is born."

Chapter 5

Art switched on the bedside lantern to illuminate the cold, dark January morning. The floor was frigid and he rushed to put his slippers on. As he dressed for a morning of deliveries, he looked upon his wife.

"What are your plans for the day? Are you helping your mother with her cutting again?"

"I believe all the material has been cut and pinned for this batch, but I will check with her. I think I may lie here a bit longer this morning. I am feeling a bit under the weather today."

Art kneeled on the bed and leaned in over his wife. He felt her forehead and then kissed it affectionately.

"Do you need to see a doctor? I'm sure Sam wouldn't mind if I took some time to take you to a physician."

"Heavens, no need for a fuss. I will be fine. I am just tired," Agnes said reassuringly.

"All right. If you need anything, your mother is just a few feet away. You can ring me too and I will come immediately."

"Be a darling and grab yourself one of yesterday's cornmeal muffins for breakfast. Your lunch is in the refrigerator. I made it last night," Agnes instructed.

Art looked on protectively. There was a nagging in him that wouldn't go away. Agnes had no fever, and she assured him she would be fine, but he was not convinced.

"Please stop worrying, Art. I am fine. I am simply tired. It comes with the territory."

Agnes lay in bed in a haze of unwellness. She couldn't pinpoint the exact cause—it was just an overall feeling of malaise. The morning sickness had abated and she assumed it had returned. She knew of women who were debilitated throughout their entire pregnancy, so it wasn't entirely troubling to Agnes.

After a short nap, Agnes gathered the energy to get herself out of bed. She had no appetite but forced herself to eat a piece of toast. It didn't sit well, and she was at the toilet within minutes. She retched until her belly hurt. When the retching stopped, she wiped her mouth and sat on the toilet. As she looked down, she noticed spotting in her knickers. A sense of dread engulfed her, and she slumped over in a fit of tears.

Agnes dressed herself and walked up to the house. The boys had all left for school and Mary was at work. Sarah greeted her daughter as she walked through the door and she stopped in her tracks.

"What on earth is the matter? You are as white as a sheet. Here, come sit down," she said as she took her daughter's arm.

Agnes sat in silence, unsure of what to say. The tears came before the words did. Sarah became startled and began to fear the worst.

"I'm spotting and I don't feel well at all, Mum." Sarah let the words settle and then jumped up and rang the operator. She was placed through to the shop within seconds.

"Sam, I'm taking Agnes to the hospital. Please tell Art so he can meet us there ... I don't know. She is not feeling well ... I'll ring you when we return."

Sarah helped her daughter up and walked her to the car. Sam had driven the delivery truck to the shop and left the car at home for Sarah.

"Mum, I am scared. What if something is wrong?" Agnes asked, tears welling in her eyes.

"Let's not worry yet. So many changes happen to a body, and it is difficult to keep up with all of them. Let's let a doctor tell us exactly what he thinks." Sarah tried to reassure her daughter, but Sarah too was deeply concerned. She knew the signs. She had seen them before.

The drive to St. Boniface Hospital was a short one. They were there within minutes. Sarah parked in the west parking lot, closest to the emergency room doors. Sarah sat Agnes down in the waiting room and then spoke with a nurse. The room was quite full and they were forced to wait.

Eventually Agnes's name was called and they both went into the examination room. It was very sterile smelling and the odour caused Agnes to gag.

An academic-looking, middle-aged man with salt and pepper hair entered the room, his stethoscope dangling from his neck. Agnes felt a sense of relief at the sight of him, and even more of one when he agreed to allow Sarah to remain during the examination.

"Mrs. Craig, I understand you are having some difficulty with your pregnancy. The nurse tells me you are about sixteen weeks along. What you are experiencing?" he probed.

Agnes described her symptoms, and the doctor explained that he would need to examine her. He returned once she was undressed, covered in the gown, and lying on the examining table. Agnes focused on the ceiling tiles, and the black dots that splattered across them like stars in the sky. Agnes could feel the constant beat in her wrist as the doctor gripped it firmly. The blood pressure cuff tightened around her arm with each whoosh, and as the pressure abated the sensation did not. It reminded Agnes of her mother's stern hand, clasped firmly around her adolescent arm. The doctor navigated a Pinard horn around the full area of her abdomen, listening intently and uttering a distinct "hmmm" when he was done. Sarah knew something was horribly wrong.

The doctor asked Agnes to slide farther down the table so that she could place her heels in the stirrups. As she did, the paper beneath her crinkled noisily. The doctor inserted his hand deep inside Agnes. The shock of the cold and pressure caused her to stiffen her legs and push hard against the stirrups. Sarah winced at her daughter's discomfort.

Agnes stared at the doctor, her eyes focused on his furrowed brow. She braced herself for what was to come.

"Mrs. Craig, I am very sorry, but it is my opinion that your fetus is no longer viable. I did not find a heartbeat, although at your stage of pregnancy that isn't definitive, but you are beginning to dilate. I believe it will only be a matter of time before you enter full contraction and your body expels the fetus. I am very sorry, Mrs. Craig. Please take as much time as you need." The doctor said nothing further and left Sarah and Agnes in the room.

Agnes sat in silence, her head down. Sarah put her arms around her daughter to comfort her. She wished she could take her pain away because she knew the worst was yet to come. Sarah had never miscarried, but she had lost children and she knew the pain was unimaginable.

"Let's get you home," Sarah said as she helped her daughter dress.

Agnes was drained of all feeling. Her mind was awash with nothingness, her movements mechanical. As they left the room, Art appeared.

"I'm sorry I took so long. I was on a delivery and got here as soon as Sam was able to reach me. Are you all right, my darling?" Art became more panicked as his wife's ghastly appearance intensified. "Please tell me. What did the doctor say?" Art continued to grow more frenzied.

"Come, let's talk in the examination room," Sarah suggested. Agnes was in no position to explain.

Sarah closed the door behind Art. "Art, sit down."

"I do not need to sit down. I need to know what is going on," Art said, raising his voice.

"Art, I am so sorry. There will be other babies," Sarah said.

"What are you talking about ... other babies? What is wrong with *this* one?"

Agnes began to cry and Art sat down. He ran his fingers through his hair and then stood back up. He paced the room a few times and then looked at his wife.

"Did you lose the baby?" he asked slowly, trying desperately to remain calm.

Agnes could only nod, her eyes red and swollen. Art embraced his wife and offered her every comfort and reassurance he could. His heart too was breaking, but he stifled his pain to focus on his wife.

"Art, there is nothing any of us can do. Agnes needs to rest and take care of herself over the next few days so nature can run its course. I will take her home and stay with her. You will need to get the truck back to the shop. Go. Agnes will be fine with me. We'll see you when you get home."

Art was in a state of disbelief and could do nothing other than nod. He was a wounded animal searching for a place to die. Sarah didn't begrudge him this time. In fact, she really hadn't given him a choice.

Sarah put her daughter to bed when they arrived home, and she stayed with her until Art walked through the door. Art didn't leave his wife's side. On the second day, their son was delivered in bed, and Art scooped him up from the mess of blood and matter and wrapped him in a blanket before Agnes could see him. He was tiny, the size of a large apple. He had a full head of dark fuzz, and his eyelashes swept out from his closed eyes. Art choked at the sight of him. He was buried a few hours later. Art never told Agnes where. He carried that burden himself. He only wanted her to forget.

Agnes never spoke of her grief. She remained in bed for the remainder of the day and then awoke the next morning as though nothing out of the ordinary had happened. She had been exhausted, both physically and mentally, and had slept as though she hadn't slept in weeks. Art was not as fortunate. He lay awake in bed for most of the night, and when the sight of the ceiling became unbearable he retreated to the chesterfield. It was there that Agnes found her husband, uncovered and curled up.

Agnes bent down and kissed Art's lips. He awoke abruptly and sat up as if his body were a spring. Agnes jumped back in surprise.

"My darling, why did you sleep on the chesterfield?"

Art cleared the morning phlegm from his throat and explained himself. "I couldn't sleep and I didn't want to disturb you."

"That was thoughtful. I hope you weren't too uncomfortable. You must have been terribly cold. It is freezing in here," Agnes said. "Let me make you some breakfast. That will warm your belly at least."

Art didn't know what to expect when he awoke, but he knew he wasn't expecting what was before him. Agnes began moving in a flurry of activity, singularly focused, as though nothing in the world was more important than what she was doing.

"How are you feeling, my love?" Art asked tentatively.

Agnes looked at her husband and simply smiled.

Art thought Agnes's behavior odd, but he was reticent to push the matter. Everyone reacted to trauma differently, as he was well aware, and Agnes's pain would reveal itself in some way and at some time. He knew his wife well enough to know she would not allow him to fuss over her. Her mother was there to do that. As Art looked up from putting his boots on, Agnes was on her knees scrubbing the floor furiously.

"I love you, my darling," he said, but she did not hear him. Her focus remained where it was. Art sighed deeply as he left the house.

Chapter 6

The gamey smell of lamb filled Art's nose as he walked through the door, and it overpowered his thoughts. Agnes was setting the table, but she paused long enough to greet her husband with a kiss.

"How was your day?" she asked. She held out her hands to take his coat.

"Something smells marvelous."

"Shepherd's Pie. Mum brought some ground lamb from the shop. Come, sit. It's ready. You must be hungry." Agnes pulled out her husband's chair and patted it invitingly.

The casserole was piping hot, steam billowing out from the delicately browned top. Art watched his wife fill glasses with iced tea, and he couldn't help but acknowledge his good fortune to himself. She was a beautiful woman, but some days she looked extraordinary. He saw no sadness in her, no stress or fatigue, just the bright and vibrant woman he married. He thought to question, but he chose to be grateful instead.

"How was your day?" Agnes asked as she filled the plates.

"Busy. I had a day of deliveries. I didn't spend any time in the shop." Art took a bite of his meal, but it was much hotter than he had expected and he frantically reached for his drink.

"I should have let it sit. It just came out of the oven," Agnes said apologetically.

"It looked so good, I couldn't wait," Art said, amused by his own impatience. "I was at John and Margaret's this afternoon. John asked if I would like to join him and his friends for a game of cards tonight, which was quite nice of him. I told him that I would rather spend the evening with my gorgeous wife."

Agnes's look turned stern, and Art knew she was about to speak her mind.

"Nonsense. I am perfectly fine here. You should go spend time with the boys. You worry too much, really. Besides, I have been meaning to spend some time with Mary. I haven't seen much of her lately."

"If you insist, then I will accept. I won't be far. I believe this time it is at Tom Martin's house. He just lives a couple of blocks over."

"Tom was at John and Margaret's wedding. I seem to recall that he was a police officer," Agnes said, half asking.

After they'd had their tea, they walked up the driveway together. "I'm not sure what to expect of the evening. John tells me they can get quite carried away with the time. I'll try not to, but please don't wait up for me, just in case," Art said as he kissed his wife good-bye. "I hope you have a nice time with your sister."

Art walked the two blocks to Tom Martin's house and knocked on the door. The white clapboard house was comfortable looking but quite unremarkable in feature. He introduced himself to Tom's wife, who let him in and showed him to the dining room.

"Art, this is a surprise," John announced. "I thought you were staying home with your lovely bride."

"She insisted on it. I think she was trying to get rid of me," Art joked.

"Well, aren't you a lucky man?" one of the men said. "I wish my wife would try to get rid of me every so often." The men all laughed and nodded in unison. Tom's wife rolled her eyes and walked out of the room.

"Art, let me introduce you to the boys." Pointing to his right he said, "This here is Tom. He's the man of the house. Tom is a copper so you better behave yourself or you'll end up in the poky." Moving around the table he continued, "That's Phil, then there's Seamus, Pete, and finally Morty."

"Nice to meet you all. Hopefully I am not crashing your party."

"Nonsense," Seamus said. "More money for me to win tonight." The others all guffawed and waved their hand in dismissal.

"As long as you brought your keep, we're happy to have you," Tom said. "Now let's get on with the slaughter," he continued with a laugh.

John pulled back the empty chair beside him and Art took a seat. As the cards were being dealt, Tom filled a glass from a ceramic pitcher and pushed it in front of Art. Art nodded in appreciation. Five cards were dealt to each player, and the bonds of friendship were temporarily severed. Light-hearted banter was replaced by a screaming silence as dogged determination began to rage throughout the room. Pride and bravado were on the line and no one was prepared to lose.

The first round of bets was placed and Art felt pressure building in his throat. He was not an experienced gambler. In fact, he had only played poker a couple of times when he was stationed overseas. Over there, no money was won or lost. Used shell casings were the currency of choice. They were plentiful, but dangerous to gather, and it became the ultimate high stakes game.

After Art anteed up, he grabbed the water glass to moisten his dry throat. He coughed and sputtered as he took a generous drink. The seriousness that had filled the room was replaced with raucous laughter.

"Art, you have to go easy on that stuff. It'll strip paint off the walls." The laughter continued.

"Sorry, should have warned you, but I couldn't help myself," John said half-apologetically. "Seamus here has a license to brew the stuff for the local pharmacies. All perfectly legit. He keeps a little for himself. OK, that part's not so legit." The laughter continued.

Art moved his glance from John to Tom. Tom could read his thoughts; they were as apparent as the shock on Art's face.

"Don't worry about me. I'm anti-Prohibition. Just like every guy in this room. Seamus has a legal permit to make the stuff. We are drinking it in a private residence, which is also perfectly legal. How it gets from where it is made to here, now that's a bit fuzzy. No harm, no foul, I say. Most guys on the force say the same thing. We have more important things to do than stopping a little harmless fun."

Art was stunned. Seamus raised his glass and the others followed. They kept their glasses raised until Art joined them. "To the best brew in Manitoba, and to the best bunch of guys to drink it with." They all clanked their glasses to a boisterous "hear, hear" and then took a convivial drink.

"Lads, it is time to get back to the business at hand. My pot awaits me," John declared.

As the evening progressed, pots were won and lost. In the end, it was Phil Epps who took home the final one. "To the victor go the spoils," he smugly stated as he raked in his winnings. "Well, boys, it has been fun, but I must be on my way. Early morning tomorrow."

"You have enough dough here. Don't think you need to make any more," John joked. Phil owned the bakery on Marion, and John was quite amused with himself for his play on words.

Art was surprised to see it was half-past midnight. The evening had run away from him. Despite losing what little money he came with, he had enjoyed himself. It had been a long while since he had consumed alcohol, and he enjoyed the camaraderie. He wasn't wholly inebriated but was sufficiently anaesthetized to insulate himself from the harsh cold on the walk home.

The living room light was on as he let himself in. He quietly undressed so he wouldn't disturb Agnes, and as he slipped into bed she didn't stir. He lay there, unable to fall asleep. Her soft snore sounded like a cat's purr, and it brought a smile to his face. Eventually sleep did overtake him, but it was to be neither lengthy nor peaceful.

Art's face was pressed up against the wall of the foxhole as the blasts rang out. He could taste the earth. His teeth felt like glass paper as the dirty grit coated them. Smoke filled his nostrils and burned his eyes. Art stayed down. He was scared to move. His foxhole mate had his gun cocked and was ready to fire. As his mate began to stand up, Art tried to pull him down. He pulled as hard as he could, but his uniform slipped through

Art's fingers. Art screamed, but there was no sound. All went white from the blast. Colour vanished. It was as though the world had been erased. But it hadn't. Art could see his mate fall backwards. He could feel the crushing impact as he landed directly on top of him.

Art shot up in bed as he gasped for breath. His brow was thick with sweat and his body trembled uncontrollably. Agnes was awakened by the commotion. She saw her husband sitting up in the dark. The sound of his breathing frightened her. Without thinking she leapt out of bed, the memory of her wedding night still fresh in her mind. The movement woke Art, and he began to look around the room.

"Art, are you awake?" she asked in a whisper.

Art was silent as his conscious mind caught up. "Yes. I'm sorry if I frightened you. It was just a bad dream."

Agnes turned the bedside light on and sat down beside her husband. She ran her hand over his sweat-soaked cheek. "You are drenched. Let me get a cloth." Agnes retrieved a cloth and wiped his cheek. She manoeuvered herself around him so that she could rest his head against her chest. She stroked his hair and kissed the back of his head.

"Please tell me what was so horrible that you woke up in such a state. It must have been absolutely frightful."

Art sat up and turned to face his wife. He thought of dismissing the dream, explaining it as a singular experience, but he thought better of it. He wanted to explain himself.

Art took a deep breath. Agnes stroked his arm. She couldn't imagine what was causing his anxiety, but she could certainly feel its effect. Her heart ached as she watched his demons torment him. What could be causing it?

"In France I witnessed horrible things, things I wouldn't wish upon anyone. I'm not saying I was in a worse way than anybody else. I wasn't. I came home and I am forever grateful to God for that, but war leaves you with a darkness." Art took a deep breath before continuing. "It's a dream. I keep having a dream, a dreadful one. It keeps repeating itself. Over and over. It is always the same. The same sounds, the same smells, the same panic. It never changes."

Agnes could see Art's pain. He appeared as a child awoken from a traumatizing nightmare—inconsolable and fearful. She felt impotent.

"I cannot imagine the horror. But I know your strength. I know the strength that God has given you, and you will see through this. I am right here with you."

Art loved his wife so deeply that it rendered him silent. Agnes turned off the light and cradled her husband in her arms. Sleep overcame them both quickly, and eventually they awoke as they had drifted off. They didn't speak of the dream, and Art's disclosure conceived a sense of optimism for a panacea that would wash away the memories.

"Darling, Tom thought it might be nice if you got to know his wife, Janie. They married last summer. She has been here only a couple of years from Regina and still doesn't know many people. Tom says she is a bit shy. I met her and she seems like a great gal. Tom would like to have us over for dinner on Saturday. What do you think?"

Agnes quite liked the idea. She had been feeling a bit bored lately and thought it would be nice to make a new friend.

"That sounds splendid. I'll bake a pie to take with us. Hopefully they like pumpkin."

"Well, if they don't, they will after they eat yours," Art reassured her.

Chapter 7

Saturday brought a clear, brisk day. The temperature had dropped suddenly, bringing a bone numbing chill that even a hot cup of tea could not remedy. The newspaper said to expect the temperature to continue to drop to forty below and advised people to stay indoors.

As Agnes began to bake, she realized she was missing some of what she needed. She could call Art, but he would not be home in time, and she decided to brave the cold and go it on foot. She put on her long wool coat, the one with the fur collar, and buttoned it up to the very top. She wrapped her wool scarf tightly around her neck and up over her face. It was itchy against her bare skin, but it was the only one that provided enough protection against the frozen air. She put her fur lined hat on and pulled it down so that it was snug over her ears. She laughed at the sight of herself; only her eyes could be seen.

It was not a long walk, but the wind kicked up, making the cold seem even colder. Agnes lowered her head to keep her face from the wind. She focused on each square of concrete, knowing each step placed her one step closer to warmth. Her eyes stung. She blinked rapidly to break the seal that was beginning to form from her freezing tears. As she reached the street corner, she looked up for approaching traffic. The wind gusted through the intersection, stinging her eyes even more. For a moment she was blinded. She pressed her fingers against her closed eyes and covered her face with her gloves until the stinging subsided.

She was relieved as she approached the market. It sat right before Sam's butcher shop, but those few feet between bitter cold and warmth made her decision a simple one. Once inside Agnes massaged her frozen fingers, bringing them back to life. Painful tingling filled them as they warmed and Agnes slowly gathered the supplies she needed. She was in no rush. She was just beginning to thaw, and the thought of jumping right back into the Arctic air was not a pleasant one.

"Hello, Mrs. Craig. Mighty cold day for you to be out and about," the market owner said. "Here, have a cup of hot cider to warm your insides. I made some for those silly enough to go out in this cold," he said as he winked at her.

"Mr. Fuller, you are a wonderful man," Agnes said. "It has been sixteen years, and I still cannot get accustomed to these winters. Manchester was cold and damp, but your nose was never at risk of freezing and falling off."

Agnes wrapped her fingers around the warm cup. She could feel the cider going down her throat, like cold butter melting on a hot muffin. As it hit her stomach, she felt the warmth radiate from within. It was enough to give her the resolve to venture out into the cold once again.

The wind gusted against the storefront as Agnes stepped outside the market. The shop was directly next door, just a few steps away. Inside, the smell of oven-roasted chicken filled the air. Sam had built a wood-fired oven during the war. His roasted chickens became a big seller when women started leaving the home to work. Husbands were now back from the war, but many women continued working and didn't have the time or the inclination to cook. The tantalizing aroma certainly didn't hurt.

"Agnes, this is a surprise," Sam said as he stepped out from behind the glass case.

"Hello, Pa. I was next door getting some things at the market. Art and I are having dinner with some new friends tonight, and I am baking a pumpkin pie."

"Pumpkin pie. My favourite," Sam said before licking his lips.

"I shall make two then and bring one for brunch tomorrow," Agnes offered. Agnes gave Sam a hug and kiss and was on her way.

Agnes held the paper bag tightly against her chest, and there were no free hands to shield her face from the cold. When the wind whipped up and her eyes welled with tears, she tried to adjust the bag in her left hand so she could cover her eyes with her right. As she did, the bag fell from her arms onto the sidewalk, ripping open and sending her groceries rolling in every direction. The jar of cream cracked open onto the sidewalk, and its contents froze against the frigid concrete before Agnes could finish her cuss. She attempted to pick up the shards of glass, but she had nowhere to put them. She kicked them off to the side of the sidewalk with her boot. She quickly gathered the other items, laying them on the ripped bag and wrapping the tattered edges around them the best she could. She endured the remaining block and landed on her mother's doorstep, exhausted and terribly cold.

Agnes could not extricate her arms from the bag and had to resort to kicking the door with her foot.

"Good Lord, Agnes, what on earth?" Sarah asked.

"My bag broke. The cream is all over the sidewalk. I carried my groceries home like this," Agnes said, flustered.

"Come in and put the bag down on the table. We'll get you a new one."

"Mum, do you have any cream I could use? I need a half cup for my pies. I don't want to go back out there."

"Yes, of course. I'll have your father bring some more home this evening."

"Thank you, Mum. We'll see you tomorrow for church." Sarah waved at Agnes as she closed the door behind her.

By the time Art arrived home, the pies were baked and cooling on the counter, and Agnes was dressed and ready to go. In fact, she had been dressed and ready to go for an hour. Her nerves were getting the best of her, and she had changed outfits three times.

"Your sister may be the official chef in the family, but you, my dear, are equally as gifted. Yum."

Art hugged his wife and gave her derrière a playful pinch. He pulled her tightly against him and kissed her neck slowly and passionately.

"Art, stop it," Agnes said, giggling. "We have to leave shortly."

He stopped and exhaled a defeated moan.

"As always, you are right." Art would have gladly traded the evening out to have his wife right then and there, but her better judgement prevailed. "How was your day?" he asked, changing the subject.

Agnes recounted the mishap. "Darling, you should have rung the shop. I would have come and retrieved you."

"I know. You were busy, and I didn't want to trouble you. All is fine. But it is supposed to be a frightfully cold night tonight. We'd better bundle up."

"Well, I *was* quite warm and I know how we can get warm again," Art said playfully. Sadly for Art, Agnes was not taking the bait, so he ended his flirtatious coaxing. "Sam said we can take the shop truck tonight. It's only two blocks, but that is two blocks too many as far as I am concerned."

Agnes breathed a sigh of relief. She was not looking forward to that journey, even though it was only a short one.

Outside, their breath hung in the air like a cloud of factory smoke. The air was perfectly still and thick and confining. They could only take quick, shallow breaths or their lungs would burn. The air inside the truck was no warmer. Agnes sat in the passenger seat holding the pie while Art started the truck. It took a few attempts before the engine turned over in the cold.

"Come in, come in," Tom said as he ushered them in. "Just when you think it can't get any colder, Mother Nature has other ideas." Agnes handed the pie to Art so Tom could help her with her coat. "I don't know what is underneath that towel, but it smells wonderful."

"Here, let me take that from you," Janie said to Art. "That was very kind of you to bring it."

Art removed his coat and handed it to Tom. "Wait until you taste Agnes's pumpkin pie. It's the best. And that's not just a proud husband talking."

Agnes's face turned many shades of red. She was never one to enjoy attention, but the attention of strangers was particularly torturous.

"Please come in," Janie directed. "I'm Janie and this is Tom." She held her hand out and Agnes shook it politely. Janie was a tiny woman, about five inches shorter than Agnes's statuesque five foot nine inches. She was quite pretty, Agnes thought, but in a simple sort of way. Her blonde hair was pulled back in loose finger waves and her cheeks brightened with a bit of rouge.

"Pleased to meet you. I'm Agnes."

"Agnes, why don't you join me in the kitchen? I'm just finishing up. The men can talk manly things or whatever else it is that they do," Janie said through her wide smile.

Agnes followed behind as the men retreated to the living room. The house was tiny, but average by Norwood standards, and certainly apropos for a police officer's salary. The kitchen was filled with the aroma of cinnamon and maple, and it made Agnes's mouth water.

"Mmm, it smells heavenly in here," Agnes complimented.

"It's an old family recipe. Pork loin with roasted apples. It is Tom's favourite. I'm a bit of a horrible cook, really. I can follow directions and make a few things well, but beyond that I'm not going to win any blue ribbons. I swear I don't have a creative bone in my body."

"My sister is a chef. She says creativity in the kitchen is simply a matter of confidence and loads of practice." Agnes stopped herself. She was concerned that had sounded like an insult. "I'm not saying that you have no confidence. It took me a long while to feel comfortable trying new things. I made a lot of meals not fit for the alley cat, but I got better. I do enjoy cooking now. It is quite fun."

"That's all right," Janie said, giving no hint of offence. "I didn't take it that way. Perhaps you can teach me. A girl can always use more confidence."

Agnes instantly liked Janie. She had a very pleasant quality about her and lacked the simplemindedness that so many girls seemed to be plagued with. Agnes wasn't sure if it was her eyes or the way she lowered her head ever so slightly when she spoke, but there was a depth to her, a timidness, that Agnes was fascinated by.

"Tom, how do you know John?" Agnes asked as they sat down to dine. "I remember you from the wedding, but I recall you were single then."

"Yes, Janie and I had not yet met. We married last September, not much before you both, I believe. And I knew Margaret before John. I used to work at The Fort Garry as a bellman. She kept us well fed. There was a group of us that became fast friends. I went overseas right after the wedding, and as luck would have it John and I were stationed together."

"I didn't know that. Thankfully you made it back safe and sound. John left before he knew Margaret was pregnant. He came home to twin girls. That certainly was a tough time for her ... well, for everybody, really. War is a nasty business," Agnes said to collective nods. "I certainly hope that was the last of it."

"Janie, this is fantastic," Art praised.

"It's my favourite," Tom said. "I'd have it every day if Janie'd make it." His admiration was endearing to Agnes.

The seeds of everlasting friendship were sowed that evening. There was an unmistakable magnetism, a beautiful familiarity that drew them in. It was an affinity not born of effort or plan but of something deeper, and it seemed to satisfy some need in each of them.

Art had lost his two closest friends in the war and time had not yet healed those wounds. Grief held dominion over him, and the desire to rebuild what was lost had remained buried until that night. It was not a dramatic evolution, not a bellowing from the rooftops, but more an unconscious awakening, a subtle stirring of his soul.

"Well, I think that went smashingly," Agnes said as she lay in Art's arms. "Janie is absolutely lovely."

Sleep embraced them both that evening, and they drifted off peacefully and completely.

Chapter 8

"March certainly came in like a lion this year, but it appears she may go out like a lamb. It is quite pleasant out there today," Sam observed.

"It would be nice to have a proper spring this year," Sarah added. "We haven't had much of one the past few years. All that work in the garden, and for only a few short weeks of colour. We say that every year, and every year winter hits us with a wallop just when we thought it was gone for good."

The temperature was a notch above freezing during the day, and the sun's warmth managed to erode the snow that still covered the ground. There had not been fresh snow for a fortnight, and the snow that remained was reduced to a wet and sloppy mess during the daytime. But when the sun was gone from the spring sky, the temperatures plummeted and the wet snow froze into a slick and treacherous surface. It was a cycle that was not permanently broken until early May.

"You will read about it in the papers tomorrow. I just found out myself on Friday from a friend who is a member of the city council. It looks like Police Inspector Doiron was fired by the police chief. It supposedly goes much deeper than that, though. Council has told all members of the police department that they will not have employment after June. It seems all officers will be required to reapply for their jobs," Sam said.

There was a hush in the room. The firing of a single person was interesting conversation, especially when it was the chief inspector, but the entire police department … that was shocking.

"Really? That can't be right. How can they fire the entire police force? There will be no law enforcement. That is absolutely ludicrous. What is the reason?" John was incredulous.

"He tells me it is because of massive misconduct, not the least of which involves bribery. Several officers, including the police inspector, were witnessed taking bribes, supposedly in return for turning a blind eye to bootlegging and other infractions. I understand they also participated in the unlawful manufacturing and consumption of alcohol. I hear there will be a full scale investigation, and only those cleared of wrongdoing will be rehired."

John and Art looked at each other in disbelief. What would become of Tom? They could not imagine he would ever participate in any bribes. He was too honest and he took his job to heart. He simply didn't agree with the ridiculous temperance laws, and he wasn't alone in his beliefs. Most of the officers believed that imbibing in a few harmless drinks would not aggravate the ills of society. However, it was not the consumption of liquor that was at issue. It was the way it was obtained that fell outside the confines of the law. Sadly, it could be argued that Tom turned a blind eye to Seamus's breach of permit, which he clearly did, and therefore it could be conceived that he was derelict in his duties. John and Art were worried for him.

"What will become of Tom?" Agnes asked. "Janie is expecting a child. This will be not be helpful at all."

Art looked surprised. "I had no idea."

"Janie told me at church just this morning. She is three months along."

"Let's pray this all works out for them. They are a lovely couple," Sarah said affectionately.

For the remainder of the day, Agnes could not get her thoughts off Janie and Tom. Janie was a brooder and would take this news poorly. The timing couldn't be worse. This was such a vulnerable point in a pregnancy; Agnes knew that firsthand.

"I came bearing gifts," Agnes declared as she held her arms out.

"How thoughtful," Janie said as she stepped aside to let Agnes in. "To what do I owe this kind gesture?"

Agnes placed one of Sam's roasted chickens on the table and then turned to face her friend. She hesitated for only a moment, but that moment was enough to raise suspicion.

"What is the matter? Are you all right?" Janie asked, now concerned.

Agnes was confused. Janie seemed no worse for wear. Agnes was certain she would be distraught over her husband's fate, yet it appeared to be anything but the case. Nothing seemed out of place.

"I am fine. I was concerned about you, especially in your current state. You must not worry. It is not good for the baby."

"Worried? Agnes, whatever for?" Janie appeared confused. She believed Agnes's concern to be entirely misguided.

Agnes was taken aback. *Why is Janie not concerned?* Agnes wondered. *Is she taking it in stride, simply being positive?* That seemed unlikely to Agnes. Janie was timid, unsure, neutral at best, certainly not optimistic. That was Agnes. Perhaps Tom had been spared, which would have been an answered prayer. However, that also seemed unlikely so soon. Then a thought occurred to Agnes, and the ensuing panic tightened her chest in a single agonizing squeeze ... Janie simply didn't know yet, and it was too late for Agnes to backtrack.

"Agnes, why should I be worried? Please tell me. You are frightening me." Janie was beginning to panic, and Agnes felt terrible for bringing her friend to such a state.

"I'm so sorry. I thought you would have known."

"Known what? Agnes, you are making no sense."

"My father's friend is a city councilman, and he told him that the entire police force was relieved of their positions on Friday. Something about misconduct." Agnes was slow and unemotional as she spoke, not wanting Janie to become agitated.

"I don't understand. He must be mistaken. Tom never said anything. He would never hold something like that back from me." Janie's eyes darted around the room as her thoughts raced. She rubbed her hands furiously. Then suddenly she stopped. Agnes held her breath waiting for the pause to end.

"He didn't want to worry me," Janie blurted. "I told him about the baby Friday morning. He was so excited. And then to find this out the same day. He didn't want to worry me. Oh, poor Tom. He has had to live with it since." Janie's sole focus was her husband ... until her thoughts shifted to the baby. "Oh, Agnes, what will we do? How will we live? We will have a baby to take care of." Janie began to hyperventilate and Agnes sat her down.

"You mustn't worry, Janie. Here, have a drink of water." Agnes placed a glass in front of Janie and she took a sip. Janie took a deep breath and began to calm down.

"My father tells me the entire force was given notice that June would be their last month. The good news is that they will have the opportunity to reapply for their positions. So, all is not lost. Tom has nothing to worry about. I am certain of it. I cannot imagine he has participated in any of the misconduct that they speak of."

Janie smiled through her tears and nodded vigorously. Agnes's optimism was filling her with hope.

"Yes, Tom is a good officer. He believes in his work and always does the right thing," Janie said, reassuring herself. "What is this misconduct that they speak of?" she wondered out loud.

"Of what I was told, bribery was the worst of it." Janie continued to brighten. The husband she knew would never sink to such levels. Never.

"Bribery goes against everything that Tom believes in. What other offences did your father speak of?"

"He said that the bribery was to turn a blind eye to offences such as prostitution, bootlegging, and other unlawful liquor offences."

Janie went white. It was as though the life had drained out of her.

"Janie, what is it? What is wrong?" Agnes asked, troubled by her sudden change.

Janie took a deep breath and swallowed dramatically. Agnes could see something was amiss, and she had no idea why.

"Has Art spoken of the liquor?" Janie asked.

It was Agnes's turn to be confused. Liquor? She had no idea what Janie was speaking of. Agnes had not seen liquor in years.

"Liquor? What liquor?"

Janie swallowed hard as her throat continued to dry up. "When they get together for their boy's night they play cards, which I know you know, but they also drink liquor, which I am assuming you didn't."

Janie watched Agnes closely for her reaction. Agnes's blank stare confirmed Janie's suspicions. It appeared it was a day of enlightenment for them both.

Agnes was shocked. Art never spoke of this. She felt silly for not knowing. She felt betrayed for being kept in the dark.

"Where did this liquor come from? Art never mentioned anything."

"You know that Seamus produces alcohol for the local pharmacies," Janie said to Agnes's nods. "It seems he produces a little extra on the side for friendly consumption too. And Pete's doctor is all too happy to prescribe whisky for his rheumatism. Lots of it. Supposedly, it happens all the time. Tom says it drives McCurdy and his crew stark raving mad."

Agnes narrowed her look to a squint. Janie couldn't be right. Art would have mentioned this. He wouldn't do anything that could be questioned under the law, she was certain. It was Agnes's turn to pause and think. A thought entered her mind that hit her like a freight train ... John and Art spoke of their disdain for Prohibition and how they would disavow any laws that they were strongly opposed to. Agnes shook her head in disbelief. *This can't be happening*, she thought. *He can't be caught up in something illegal, and something so public.*

"We can be disagreeable with the laws as they are written, but the fact is they are written, and the behaviours that are contrary to them can and should be punished," Agnes said. Janie began to fret once again.

"Art did nothing illegal. There is no law against consuming alcohol in a private residence. But there is a law against acquiring it or providing it outside of legitimate dispensaries. Tom tells me the violations that he enforces invoke mere fines. I can only imagine what the failure to enforce them as an officer does. Clearly it will mean his position. Tom, what have you done?" Janie asked herself as she pondered their fate.

As Agnes placed her arm around her friend's shoulder to comfort her, the door opened. It was Tom. He looked pale and preoccupied, and he quickly found he had walked into piercing silence.

"There is no need to tell me. Agnes has already," Janie said flatly.

Agnes could not discern Tom's expression from horror or relief. He spoke not a word, waiting for Agnes to speak first.

"Tom, I am so sorry," she said. "I thought Janie knew."

Tom appeared contrite. He knew in that instance that withholding the news was an unpardonable offence. He kept his eyes on his wife as Agnes walked by him and through the door.

Chapter 9

Agnes lay awake in bed, her head filled with the sound of whistling wind and pelting rain. The warm prairie air was at war with its Arctic cousin, and a battle raged in the dark May sky. The boisterous boom of thunder amplified and dulled and then amplified again, a constant cycle of aggravation made more dramatic by the incredible bursts of light that transformed the panorama into a palette of white. But it was not the storm that had a hold on her thoughts; her mind was elsewhere.

As Art slept, Agnes lay alone in her grief, her pain for her alone to bear. She went to bed the previous night with a rekindled hope, with the blessing of the life that filled her womb. She tried desperately to ignore the dull aching that penetrated her body, but as the night progressed she learned her fate. This child was not to be either. Her body had betrayed her once again, and the emptiness she felt was all consuming.

Art stirred and rolled over to find his wife already awake. "Good morning, darling. How did you sleep?" he asked as he wrapped his arm around her waist and nuzzled his face into her neck.

Agnes put on her brave face, kissed her husband on the cheek, and slipped out of bed. Art pouted like a child, hoping his wife would linger with him in bed a bit longer.

"Where are you going? It is so much nicer in here," he said as he patted the empty space that Agnes had left.

"I promised to help Mum with some fittings this morning. And besides, we need to get you off to work." Agnes was happy with the excuses. She was not in the mood to be affectionate. She could not explain to her husband why. She had not told him she was pregnant to begin with.

"You are right, as always ... but it doesn't mean I have to like it."

By the time Art emerged from the bedroom, Agnes was completely occupied with her chores. He sensed that she was as she wanted to be, focused on her tasks and not in a conversational mood; so he let her be. He ate his breakfast in silence and then left for work.

Agnes meticulously wiped and scrubbed until their home was sterile within an inch of its foundation. She was never completely satisfied and only acquiesced when other duties called. She was not one comfortable with sitting still. Idle hands led to an idle mind and an idle mind led to contemplation. Motion was Agnes's friend.

The gusting wind knocked Agnes about with incredible force as she ran up the driveway to the house. She pulled down her rain hat to protect her face from the moisture, but the wind and rain were coming in all directions, and there was nowhere she could look to avoid being in the direct line of fire. Inside the house, she removed her plastic hat and shook off the wetness, sending beads of water through the air.

"And now it is raining inside," Sarah teased.

"Sorry, Mum, it is really wet out there," Agnes said apologetically as she hung her coat and hat in the closet. "I'll wipe up the mess."

"Do not fret. It is just water. No harm done." Sarah put her arm around her daughter's shoulder and led her toward the kitchen. "Come, let me get you a cup of tea. Mrs. Pottle won't be here for another half hour."

Agnes sat at the table while her mother put the kettle on. It was always striking to Agnes how empty the house seemed when the boys weren't home. When they were there, you couldn't hear yourself think for the constant noise they made, but when they weren't there it was so quiet the silence was almost deafening. A drop of water from the tap could sound like an explosion in the sink. A whistle of a kettle could replace a locomotive's. Everything was sharper, brighter, louder, and at times it distressed Agnes to her core.

Sarah placed the cup of tea in front of her daughter and sat down. Sarah's intuition was screaming and she tried to determine why. But Agnes was not helping. She said nothing.

"How are you on this delightful morning?" Sarah asked, the sarcasm going unnoticed.

"Fine, Mum, and you?" Agnes's expression was empty as she looked down at her cup of tea.

"What's wrong, Agnes? You don't seem yourself."

"I'm fine," Agnes answered.

"You can say that and think that I might even believe you, but you would be mistaken. I am your mother, and I know when your mind is elsewhere," Sarah explained, very matter-of-factly.

Agnes looked at her mother, unsure of how to respond. "Really, Mum, I am fine. It is just the weather. It is quite depressing."

Sarah didn't believe her daughter, but she wasn't about to push her if she didn't want to talk. Pushing Agnes was like pushing a porcupine. Nothing good could come from it.

Agnes continued to stare at her cup, running her finger over the handle. She sighed repeatedly, unaware she had done so. It was not long before she broke her silence.

"Did you always know you wanted to be a mother?" Agnes asked.

The question took Sarah by surprise. "I always saw myself as a mother. It never occurred to me that I might not be one. Why do you ask?" Sarah wondered.

"What if I can't have a child? What else will I do? I have no skills like you and Margaret do. Margaret is a chef. You are a seamstress. I am nothing but a housewife." Sarah could see that Agnes was upset, and it broke her heart.

"It has only been six months, Agnes. Every woman is different. It takes some longer than others. There is no need to worry yet. And what is this nonsense about having no skills? You are a wonderful wife and your husband loves you very much," Sarah said, trying to reassure her daughter.

"He loves me now. But what if I cannot give him a child? What then?" Agnes's anxiety was palpable. "I believe he worries about me. He has such trouble sleeping. I often wake to find him staring at the ceiling. He tells me he is fine, but he gets so tired. I can see it. And he often has such dreadful nightmares."

Agnes was deeply troubled. There was nothing Sarah could say to reassure her, and it tore at her. There was only one thing that would ease her mind, and only time would tell if that destiny would be fulfilled.

"You take on the world," Sarah said, sighing deeply. "He loves you for who you are and how you make him feel, not for any child that you may give him. It is entirely in God's hands and you cannot change His will. Worrying about it will only make it more difficult. It will all happen as it should."

Sarah's words of support had the opposite effect from what she intended. Agnes felt helpless and hopeless. Sarah could do nothing but change the subject.

"Did Janie tell you that the city council concluded their investigation and have decided to keep Police Chief Marcel and the entire police department in their positions? It appears that Tom's employment will remain unchanged. I am sure that he must be quite relieved. They both must be."

Agnes lit up like fireworks against the evening sky.

"Marvelous. There couldn't be better news," she enthused. "I must go offer my congratulations after we are done with Mrs. Pottle. When did you hear?"

"Sam mentioned it last evening. Charles Townley told him of the decision after he was called upon by the investigation panel to offer an accounting of his dealings with the police department. It does help to have friends in high places, I suppose. It would appear that Sam's testimony helped validate that the department, in most part, was composed of honest, upstanding officers who were acting as they should. Sam told them that when Tom was asked to respond to the vandalism at the shop the previous summer, Tom had been nothing but earnest and steadfast in his duties. Sam was more than happy to say so. It certainly helped that Sam is so well-respected in this community," Sarah said proudly.

A sense of relief overcame Agnes. Sam had no knowledge of the liquor. Sam would have only spoken the truth as he knew it, and that truth would have portrayed Tom as exemplary and above suspicion. As such, his record would remain unsullied. Agnes was unsure of how far Sam would go to protect a friend and she was thankful they did not have to find out.

By the afternoon, the inclement weather had cleared and the sun was beginning to peak through the ceiling of wispy, white clouds. It had turned into a beautiful afternoon. As Agnes rounded the street corner, she stopped, closed her eyes, and soaked in the warmth of the sun.

Agnes's attention was diverted to a familiar and welcome sound. A tiny finch sang out as it sat perched atop a fence in front of her. It was striking in appearance, its black-capped head and pink beak a contrast to its vibrant, yellow body. Its melody was captivating. The timid creature was startled by Agnes's movement and flew to the grass behind the fence. But it wasn't any closer to safety; a house sparrow swooped out of a tree and dove directly at the finch. As the sparrow plunged, the finch spread its black and white wings and flew off to safety, and Agnes was glad for it. Agnes loved birds but had no affection for house sparrows.

Janie was mending a skirt when Agnes arrived.

"Agnes, how wonderfully unexpected. I was going to come by tomorrow. As you can see, I have some mending to do. I am busting out of all my seams." Janie was about five months along and her pregnant belly was unmistakably present.

"I just heard the good news from my mother. I am so happy for you both. You must be relieved," Agnes said with a broad smile.

"Yes, quite relieved. Tom found out just yesterday, so it is still fresh. I don't feel as though it has settled in yet." Janie seemed frazzled, despite the admission of relief.

"How about we get out and enjoy the sunshine? Now that Tom's position is secure, you can afford to get yourself a new skirt. No need to rip apart any seams. What do you think?" Agnes asked.

Janie paused as she pondered Agnes's suggestion. She looked at her skirt, which was only half repaired, and nodded in agreement.

"If I poke myself with the needle one more time, I think I will go mad. Sewing has never been one of my strengths. Yes, let's do it."

"Marvellous. We'll have you back by five."

Agnes and Janie took the streetcar from Marion. They crossed the Norwood Bridge, which had been newly marked "use at your own risk." It was in a horrible state of disrepair—the sidewalks and pavement were badly worn, and the main structure of the bridge vibrated to a considerable degree when streetcars passed over. It was a disaster waiting to happen; but despite the risk, its use was not hindered while it was determined what to do with it.

They soon disembarked at Main and Portage and decided to walk the remaining four blocks to Eaton's. The scene was bustling. Organized chaos permeated the streets and sidewalks. People dodged oncoming streetcars and each other as they moved haphazardly about. The pleasant weather always brought out the crowds.

It was an eclectic blend of cityscape. There were tall buildings, short buildings, buildings with domed tops, buildings with simple and sleek perpendicular edges, buildings with columns, buildings with bland façades, and just when the eye became bored with mundane repetition, a vividly coloured awning emerged to disrupt the monotony.

At Donald, the Clarendon Hotel stood out, but not for the reason it would have liked to. In years past, it had been striking, but it had fallen into a terrible state of disrepair and now sat as nothing more than an eyesore. Its mansard roof, with its steeply pitched roofline, was perched atop the five storeys of unkempt stone and brick. It had lived most of its life as the belle of the Portage ball, but as other buildings grew up alongside it, it lost its brilliance. It was due to be demolished in a month's time, and there were very few sad for it.

In contrast, the Eaton's store, which stood on the opposite corner, was far more modern in design. It had no visual architectural merit, but it was sleek and simple, which seemed to be all the rage in newer buildings. It now stood three stories taller than it had originally, an insatiable retail demand driving it upward. It exemplified Winnipeg's boom time, and some argued it was the most successful department store in the world. Regardless of the accuracy of that claim, Winnipeggers were proud of it and loved *The Big Store*.

Agnes and Janie browsed the store for an hour before deciding to remedy their thirst and tired feet at the café. The café was full and humming with conversation. Agnes loved visiting it. It felt wonderfully cosmopolitan to her. There was no better place to watch people.

"Here you go," Agnes said as she placed a cup of tea in front of Janie. "I thought these looked good as well. I couldn't resist."

Janie looked upon the blueberry scones and grinned. "You take such good care of me. You will be a brilliant mother."

The well-intentioned compliment stung Agnes. She tried desperately to hide the pain from Janie. Talking about it was the last thing that she wanted to do.

"What was Regina like?" Agnes asked, changing the subject. "Do you miss it?"

It was Janie's turn to feel a sting. She too tried desperately to hide it, but she was not as successful as Agnes.

"I much prefer Winnipeg," was all she offered.

Janie was a very private person, even with Agnes, and Agnes was determined to learn more about her.

"Do you still have family there?"

Janie hesitated as she decided how she would answer. "No, my family have all passed away."

Agnes did not expect such a disclosure. It was hard to imagine that anyone could lose their entire family. Even with the admission, Janie was still not volunteering any details, and it made Agnes all the more curious.

"My father died of tuberculosis when I was not yet six. I have only a vague memory of him. I don't remember what he looks like. We haven't any photographs. I had a sister who died when she was two, and my brother James died in the war. I miss James very much. He was such a good brother," Agnes said sullenly. James's death was still raw and she couldn't pretend otherwise.

"My mother and..." Janie said, hesitating, "brother died of scarlet fever about five years ago. I had no other siblings. My father died a few years before that."

Agnes was at a loss for words. Janie had never shared such intimate details of her life before, and her revelation left Agnes saddened.

"How did you meet Tom?" Agnes asked, again diverting the conversation.

Janie smiled and relief flooded Agnes. Tom was a happy topic for Janie, and the subtle sadness that had transformed her face disappeared.

"I spilled coffee on him," she recalled, giggling. "I was working in the coffee shop at Union Station when he returned home from the war. I was filling his coffee cup and accidentally poured some on his lap. He was flirting with me. He distracted me. It was entirely his fault. Served him right," she said as she continued to giggle.

"Well, if someone that handsome was flirting with me, I dare say I would become distracted as well," Agnes teased.

Chapter 10

The summer heat had been undeniably uncomfortable. But with only the slightest rainfall over the summer months, it had been far more tolerable than in years past. However, as August pushed into September, the humidity soared, layering a moist stickiness on every surface. Without any reprieve from the oppressive heat, the days became unbearable.

"Wake up, sleepy-head," Agnes said as she kissed Art's cheek. "We can't keep the others waiting."

Art's eyes were closed, but he had been awake most of the night as he waited for sleep to overtake him. It was a constant battle.

Art's eyes were red and puffy as he opened them, and he fought to focus on his surroundings.

"You look exhausted. Are you ill?" Agnes asked, concerned.

"I am fine. It must be the heat. It has been difficult to sleep in it."

"Are you certain you want to go to the lake? I can tell the others that you are ill. There's always another time."

Not a day went by that he didn't thank God for her. As he pondered his good fortune, he fixated on her face.

"What?" she asked as she questioned his determined focus.

"Why *what?* Can I not appreciate the beauty that lies before me," he said as he rolled over and wrapped his arm around his wife. "You asked if I was ill. Can an ill man do this?" he asked as he ran his hand down her thigh and under her nightgown.

Agnes giggled and pulled back. She enjoyed playing hard to get.

"Art, we must get ready."

"I *am* getting ready. Part of getting ready is *getting up,* if you know what I mean," he said as he grinned and rolled against her. He kissed her neck and ran his hand up and down her thighs.

Agnes was no match for Art's kisses. They turned her to a mass of jelly and made every single hair on her body stand at attention. She could do nothing but surrender to the overpowering passion that engulfed her. It was inescapable. His allure was inescapable.

As Art rolled on his back and wiped the sweat from his brow, his smile was unbreakable and he sighed a deep and utter contentment.

"Now, my darling, it is time to get up. Let me rephrase that … it is time to get out of bed," Agnes teased.

As Art stood in the shower, his fatigue became overwhelming. His head became a heavy mass of cloud and fog and he fought to keep his eyes open. He couldn't remember the last time he had slept through the night. No, he could ... it was before the war. That thought sent shivers through his spine, and even the warm water couldn't overpower the chill. He felt adrift, with no clear path to return. He was lost, alone in the dark and fighting a war that he was not winning. The past was absolute, and the memories of it were indelibly seared into his mind.

"Hurry up, Poky," Agnes playfully chided. "Tom and Janie will be here any...."

"Speak of the devil," Art said, cutting Agnes off.

"Hello, you two. Are you ready for a day in the sun?" Agnes asked. "How are you feeling today, Janie? Are you sure you are up for the trip?"

"You have no idea. These last few weeks have been dragging on terribly. Something to take my mind off my big belly is what I need right now."

"Fantastic. That baby will keep you busy soon enough."

Agnes grabbed her beach bag, which was filled with all they would need for the day. On their way, they stopped at the house and added Mary to the group.

"Percy will meet us at Union Station," Art added.

"We're so happy your brother can join us," Agnes said to Art, but her gaze never left her sister. "Aren't we, Mary?" Agnes's meddling was undisguised and Mary could only blush.

They took the streetcar the one mile to Union Station. Save for a few wispy clouds, the sky was clear and incredibly blue, and the humidity was as thick as a Finnish steam bath.

Percy watched the group of five bounce happily into the station. They all caught sight of Percy at the same time he caught sight of them. Art held out his hand to greet his brother, while Mary hid shyly behind Agnes. Agnes, who had long ago bored of the shyness between the two, was having no part of any timidity. It was clear some interference was required and she was not hesitant in providing it, directly or otherwise.

"Hello, dear brother-in-law," Agnes said as she embraced Percy. "We are all so glad that you could join us today. Aren't we, Mary?" Agnes exclaimed, again none too discreetly.

"I am happy to be invited. I have felt like a cooking turkey in my house these past weeks. My windows face south and there is no hiding from the sun."

"We can be thankful it is a few degrees cooler today. I believe it was almost a hundred last week and there was no breeze, which certainly didn't help. There should be a nice breeze at the lake today," Agnes offered. "And if anyone has a right to complain about this incessant heat, it is Janie. Janie, you poor girl, you must be so hot."

Janie could only nod and continue to cool herself with her paper fan. She was a petite-framed girl, and at three weeks from her delivery date was as round around the middle as a laundry basket.

The six kept engaged in lively conversation as the train rolled toward Winnipeg Beach. They didn't pay any attention to the fields of canola, with their brown and withered flowers stretching on as far as the eye could see. Harvest was near. Only a few weeks before, they had been awash in bright yellow, a seemingly endless sea of sunshine.

The hour and a half trip passed much more quickly than the clock would have indicated. It was not so for the children on board, all of whom began to jump from their seats as the train pulled into the station. The train all but emptied at the Winnipeg Beach stop, with only a few passengers remaining to continue the short distance to Gimli.

The couples walked arm in arm, with Mary and Percy each flanking their siblings. It was a short walk to the Midway, and by a quarter of ten its boardwalk was already bustling with activity. The smell of corn dogs and popcorn and cotton candy filled the air and sent olfactory senses into a frenzy.

"I can hear the water calling us. Wait … can you hear it?" Agnes said as she cupped her hand over her ear.

Agnes jumped off the boardwalk and ran through the trees toward the lake. Mary went running after her, and Art and Percy soon followed. Tom stayed back with his wife and walked at her pregnant pace.

Agnes and Mary ran up the beach a distance before staking out their home for the day. They found a nice patch of beach close to the water, not far from the trees which they could hide amongst for shade later. They were close to the New Dips rollercoaster, which sat at the opposite end of the beach from the dancing pavilion and pier, the busiest area of the beach. For the daytime, they chose quiet; they knew they would have enough activity at the dancing pavilion that night.

"Janie, your blanket awaits," Agnes said, patting the one she had just laid out. "You mustn't overexert yourself today. That is an order."

"My dear, you have been ordered," Tom said, coaxing his wife.

"Yes, I would advise you listen. My wife doesn't generally take 'no' for an answer. Trust me, I have tried." Mary laughed out loud and Agnes rolled her eyes at her sister.

Janie parked her derrière on the blanket as the others settled in. It was a brilliant day, hot and steamy, but a quenching breeze blew off Lake Winnipeg to temper the sting. It really was heaven, and they were all delighted for the carefree day that lay before them. There was to be no work, no worry; only good friends, good fun, and enough joviality to light up all of Winnipeg Beach.

"Who wants to join me for a swim?" Agnes asked. "I think I am ready to cool off."

"Sure, but I can read the headlines now: 'Whale Sighted in Lake Winnipeg,'" Janie joked. "I will have everyone running for the fields."

"If you are a whale, then other women should wish to be one as well because you are the most beautiful whale that has ever existed," Tom returned.

Mary and Agnes "aww'd" collectively, while Art and Percy smirked at each other, amused by Tom's blatant attempt to impress his wife. Janie could only laugh.

As the men walked toward the changing room, Tom blew his wife a kiss.

"Boy, he is sure trying hard to gain favour. What did he do?" Mary wondered.

"Actually, nothing. I think his guilt over not being able to share in my misery is getting the best of him. Yesterday I woke up from a nap to a foot rub."

"Well, I say let him feel guilty a bit longer. You deserve it," Agnes added.

As welcome as the thought of the cool water was, in actuality it was a jolt to the system. Goosebumps covered their legs, and the hot sun didn't seem as hot anymore. All three walked in to waist level, and Agnes was the first to take the plunge, submerging herself to her neck.

"Brrrrr!" she shrieked, shivering. Mary and Janie took their time.

As the water hit Janie's belly, she let out a faint groan.

"Are you all right?" Agnes asked.

"Yes, I don't think the baby likes the cool water."

"Did it kick?" Mary asked, intrigued.

"No, my belly contracted."

"What does that mean? Are you going into labour?" Agnes asked, startled.

"No, it is just false labour. It has happened a few times since yesterday. They don't hurt; they are just uncomfortable, like someone is squeezing me too tightly. My midwife tells me they are normal and not to worry."

"Well, if you aren't worried, then neither are we. Right, Mary?"

"Right!"

As the girls were acclimating themselves to the chilly water, the men joined them. They ran in like horses through a stream, spraying water in their wake. As they approached the girls, they dove under, encircling them before coming up for air.

"Come on, Mary. Let's go for a walk and give the lovebirds some privacy." As Percy and Mary waded through the water, they looked back at the couples; they were each lost in their own worlds.

It was a few minutes before Agnes noticed her sister was gone. She looked in all directions before spotting Mary and Percy sitting in the water, deep in conversation.

"Look, darling, I think something may happen after all. And it is about darn time!" Agnes quipped.

The blazing sun continued to rise in the sky. As the morning dissolved into noon, sunbathers stood shoulder to shoulder, fighting to maintain their tiny place in paradise. And paradise it was, a welcome retreat from the ails of daily life, and only a stone's throw from the city.

"Who wants a hot dog?" Tom asked.

"I would love to walk up the boardwalk." Agnes jumped at the idea. "Mary, Percy!" she yelled, motioning to her sister. We're going for lunch."

Mary and Percy returned, their faces betraying the private pleasure they had just shared. A look of repressed longing passed between them. It was unmistakable to Agnes, and it gave her hope. In her eyes they were perfectly matched and she so wanted them to see it as well.

For young couples, the boardwalk was the best part of Winnipeg Beach. It was the place for declaration, *the* place to announce coupledom to the world. New couples strolled arm in arm, while the lingering rules of proper Canadian society remained at home. At Winnipeg Beach, things were different. Perhaps it was a sign of changing times. Certainly attitudes were more liberal. Some viewed it as an evolution. Others viewed it as demoralization. Regardless of the perceptions, the young flocked there in droves, happy to participate in their newfound freedom.

At the Midway, merchants lined the boardwalk. The sights, the smells, the sounds ... it was Winnipeg's World's Fair. Amusement park food of all types abounded, as did games of chance for young men wanting to impress their girls.

"I think my darling needs a teddy bear," Art said as he laid down his coins on the counter.

The game attendant handed Art three baseballs and Art tossed them, one at a time, at baskets that lay tilted on a table a few feet away. One by one, they bounced back out.

"That was good of you to leave the prizes for the others, old boy," Tom teased.

"I think my brother's skills lie elsewhere," Percy continued to taunt.

"Well, dear brother, if you think it is so easy, why don't you give it a shot? Here, I'll even pay."

Art placed more coins on the counter and stood back, extending his arm toward the counter. The attendant placed the balls on the counter and Percy stepped forward. He paused, anticipating the embarrassment of defeat. Miss ... miss ... bull's eye!

Percy shot his arms up in victory. "Take that, Art!"

Art laughed at his loss and the incessant teasing that followed in order to hide the crushing blow to his ego. Percy revelled in the win until he realized he was now the owner of a large stuffed giraffe.

"Well, aren't you cute?" Agnes said as she tugged on the giraffe.

Percy's face blushed crimson. He was embarrassed, much more so than usual. All eyes were on him and he did the only thing he could ... he handed the prize to Mary.

"Here you go, Mary. I think it is more your style." Percy was nervous, and his cheeks continued to redden.

"Just what every girl needs, wouldn't you say, Janie?"

It was Mary's turn to blush. She smiled shyly at Percy, and his eyes begged forgiveness back. It was all he could do to not run away.

Next they passed a palm reader who was gesturing wildly, her bright purple turban teetering atop her head. She was putting on a show, her free hand motioning a comical tale of some kind and it made them all laugh.

"What fun," Agnes said as she contemplated getting hers done.

Suddenly and unexpectedly, a loud shot pierced the air. It made the girls jump back and shriek. Without hesitation or thought, Art dropped to the ground, belly-down on the boardwalk with his hands covering the back of his head. They quickly realized the loud boom was from a target shooting game, and they laughed at their own reactions, but Art remained down. Agnes reached down and touched his back and he flinched.

"Art, darling, are you all right?" Agnes got down on her knees and touched his back again. There was no reaction. Bewildered eyes began to fall upon Art as he lay on the wooden walk.

Percy's heart sank. He understood far too well.

"All clear!" he yelled, his only concern being his brother. On Percy's signal, Art got up. He was visibly shaken, but in an instant he transitioned back to Winnipeg Beach. The sudden realization of what had happened brought a self-consciousness that was only amplified by the gawkers.

"That was impressive. Your reflexes were always far superior to mine." Percy tried to make light of it.

Agnes couldn't hide her worry. The sleepless nights, the bad dreams, the reactions, they were increasing in frequency and intensity. Time was not being kind to the memories and Agnes felt helpless, but she was determined to not make this a public spectacle. It was private, and privately she would handle it.

"Let's say we grab a drink and go sit down at the beach. I'm feeling a bit tired," Janie said. "I think I overestimated my energy level today."

Janie was brilliant, Agnes thought. In fact, they all thought so. And, while Janie's diversion may have helped the mood settle, there was significant truth in her admission.

The afternoon wasted away and the incident was soon forgotten. Thoughts had moved beyond it toward the Pavilion. They hadn't danced since their wedding night, and they were overcome with anticipation for the music, the lights, and the people.

"Agnes, I think we are going to go back on the 6:45. I'm feeling a bit tired."

"Is everything all right? Are you still having those pains? Are they getting worse?"

"They aren't getting worse. They are just as they have been."

"Perhaps we should get a doctor," Agnes suggested.

"No, I am fine. I will be fine. I am just tired."

Agnes couldn't tell if there was more, but she sensed there was. She hadn't known Janie long enough to know if she was being truthful or not.

Janie reassured her all was fine. It was a nagging that would not go away for Agnes, and she simply could not drop it.

"Let's spend the afternoon together tomorrow. How does that sound? I've been meaning to make a few pies. How about we do it together at your house?"

Janie was touched by Agnes's concern. "I would like that. Thank you."

"I'm not working tomorrow. I'd love to join you both if it isn't too rude to invite myself," Mary asked.

"Fantastic! The more hands, the better," Agnes said.

The group was suddenly and unexpectedly one couple short, and the mood shifted from jovial to intimate with the departure of that single train. Percy and Mary both felt a rush of adrenaline as they anticipated the opportunity that the evening presented. They were ready to take the next step; Percy's shyness had been the only impediment.

The Pavilion filled quickly. It was the last big weekend of summer, and it was as though the entire city of Winnipeg filled the dance hall for one final taste of it. Beachwear was replaced by dancewear—the men in the freshly pressed suits they rode the train in and the women in brightly coloured summer dresses, all of which added a rainbow of colour to the dimly lit hall.

The band started up at dusk and would play on until just before midnight, breaking only a few times. Agnes and Art lit the floor on fire, stopping only when the band did. Percy and Mary danced as enthusiastically as their siblings, but they stopped when the slow songs played, when Percy nervously used a visit to the toilet as an excuse for a break.

Art and Agnes shimmied their way over to Mary and Percy, dancing a few songs side by side. The band played a foxtrot, and Art let go of his wife's hand and grabbed Mary's. Percy did the same with Agnes, rekindling the fond memories of their wedding night.

The band leader spoke into his microphone, thanking everyone for coming out for such a great night. He announced the next song would be the last of the evening and a collective moan of disappointment filled the room. The music slowed down and the floor filled. For most, the finality of it all was enough to overcome deep-seated fear. For others it was not.

Percy waffled, his body betraying his heart. Mary did not. She reached out for Percy's hand and placed it on her waist, rolling her eyes and releasing a sigh of frustration. She was having no more of this ridiculous shyness. Enough was enough.

Agnes grinned and looked away. That was the Mary she knew and loved. Agnes was only surprised that Mary had maintained her patience for as long as she did.

Percy was so relieved the dam had been broken that he wasn't bothered that Mary had been the one to break it. It would all be easy for him now.

Percy held Mary at a respectable distance, but as the song progressed he pulled her in closer, bit by bit. Mary settled in comfortably, overjoyed with the immediacy and because Percy was finally taking charge. As the song ended, they joined the others in clapping for the band, looking at each other as they did. For the first time, Percy did not look away and instead gazed at Mary with an unapologetic intensity that made her weak. Mary was in love, and she could not hide it from herself any longer.

The whistle on the train sounded. There was always a rush to make the last train; the only alternative was a cold night on the beach. By Labour Day, the nighttime temperatures were dropping and the prospect was not an entertaining one.

The mood on that last train was inevitably more sedate. There was very little conversation, and oftentimes snoring was the most raucous sound in the darkened cars.

The train was full for the ride back so the four were forced to split up two and two. Mary and Percy sat two cars back, both happy for some time away. Percy found self-confidence in the anonymity. Within five minutes of the train station, Percy was holding Mary's hand, and within ten Mary's head was resting comfortably on Percy's shoulder. Percy decided he was not going to waste any more time. He was ready.

Chapter 11

Agnes arrived at the main house with a bag loaded with baking ingredients. It was one o'clock, another glorious day, and Mary waited impatiently for her sister.

"How are you on this fabulous, September afternoon?"

Mary's cheerfulness caught Agnes off guard, and not just a little. It wasn't that Mary was usually negative; it was more a case that sarcastic sibling humour was the usual tone between them.

"My, it looks like someone picked some happy flowers today?"

Agnes's sarcasm didn't even register with Mary. That day she was untouchable. She was on a cloud and nothing could bring her off it.

"So are you going to tell me, or do I have to pretend I have no idea why you are so chipper and pry it out of you?"

"Pry what?" Mary asked coyly.

"Do not play dumb with me, Mary. It is not becoming," Agnes shot back in frustration.

Mary only laughed. She loved to torment her sister when she had the chance. In her mind, it wasn't nearly often enough because the barbs were usually flying in the opposite direction.

"We should leave. Janie will be waiting for us," Mary said defiantly, as pleased as Punch. She didn't leave her sister in a state for long.

'It was wonderful. It really was." Mary was as giddy as a schoolgirl.

"Details. I need details."

As they walked to Janie's house, Mary told her of the last dance, the train ride home, and the kiss. Agnes squealed at the revelation of a kiss. *This is just perfect*, she thought.

It was another sultry morning. Darkened storm clouds floated along the horizon, framing the blue sky and creating the illusion of mountains. At that point, it wasn't clear which way the weather would go.

After they entered the yard, Mary closed Tom and Janie's gate behind them. Halfway up the short path to the front door, a dreadful sound filled the air. Both Agnes and Mary stopped in their tracks, listening for a recurrence. They didn't have to wait long; it came again a few seconds later. It was a sound born of intense agony, and it was coming from Janie's house.

Agnes darted up the stairs. The sound continued. Agnes tried frantically to turn the door knob, but it was locked. She looked in the window and could see Janie on the chesterfield, lying on her side and clutching at her belly. Agnes banged on the door.

"I can't get up. The baby's coming!" Janie screamed. Another moan escaped her mouth and past her tightly clenched jaw.

"The door is locked!" Agnes was panicked. She had to get in, but how?

Agnes looked around as she searched for a way in. She spied the garden gnome at the base of the stairs and grabbed it. Without pause she smashed the glass pane beside the door. She reached in, turned the lock, opened the door, and ran to Janie.

"Agnes, the baby's coming!" Janie sounded terrified.

"Mary, go get Delores. She lives four houses down—the yellow house with the brown shutters. Hurry, please!"

Mary left the house as Janie let out another moan.

"Janie, you have to try and relax. I know it hurts, but panicking will only make it hurt more. This is your first. You should still have a bit of time."

"This is not my first!" Janie yelled through another contraction. "The baby is coming now!"

Janie adjusted herself on the chesterfield as Agnes became locked in a look of surprise. Agnes's stupor was broken by another moan, this one deeper and more insistent than the last. Mary was nowhere in sight, and the realization that this baby might appear before Mary returned with Delores hit her like a brick.

"Oh God, it's coming." Janie reached under her skirt and into her bloomers. "Agnes, I can feel the head. I can't stop it."

Janie curled upward as she pushed. Agnes positioned herself at Janie's feet and pulled down her bloomers. Agnes looked down between Janie's legs and could see the baby's head crowning. It was covered in a blonde fuzz that was wet and matted.

Janie curled up again for another push. This time the baby's head fully emerged. Agnes looked around, hoping to see Delores, but she and Mary were nowhere to be seen. Agnes had never been more frightened or felt more helpless in her life. All Agnes could do was hold out her hands to catch the baby.

"You are doing wonderfully, Janie. It's going to be just fine. The baby is almost here."

Agnes wasn't sure if Janie heard her. It didn't really matter, though; she was speaking more to calm herself down than anything.

A bloodcurdling scream followed the next push. One of the shoulders emerged, followed by the other. Agnes had her hands under the baby's head and shoulders as the remainder of the baby was delivered from Janie's womb. Agnes placed a hand under the baby's buttocks to balance the support. The umbilical cord was tethered to the placenta, which remained inside. The baby was not crying.

"What is wrong?" Janie whimpered through her tears.

Agnes remembered her mother telling her that babies sometimes need their airways cleared, especially if they are born quickly.

Agnes turned the baby over, resting the baby on her forearm and placing her fingers around the baby's throat to secure its head. She gently slapped the baby's back twice as she tipped it forward. Still nothing. Agnes couldn't breathe herself either.

Slap. Slap. Slap. On the fifth slap, the baby let out a loud scream, and it continued to cry for its life, stopping only to draw a breath. It was the most incredibly wonderful sound that Agnes had ever heard.

Before Janie could savour motherhood, she experienced another contraction, this one expelling the afterbirth. Child and placenta had both been delivered, but Agnes remained terrified, unsure of what to do next. The umbilical cord needed to be cut at some point, *but where and with what*? Agnes's panic mounted.

Agnes did the only thing she could think of. She placed the baby on Janie's belly. As she did, the door opened and Mary and Sarah entered.

"Mum! Thank heavens. Mary, where is Delores?"

"She wasn't home. I didn't know what else to do."

"Mum, the baby came," Agnes said. She quickly realized she had never paid attention to whether it was a boy or girl.

"Let's see what we have here," Sarah said, clearly unfazed. "What a beautiful little girl."

"A girl," Janie whispered as her head finally caught up to her heart.

"Agnes, get two towels and a wet washcloth. The baby will need to be wrapped up. I'll need one of you to cut a few strips off a sheet and boil them in water for at least fifteen minutes. Wash scissors well with soap and water and then put them in the boiling water as well. We'll also need a bucket or bag for the afterbirth."

Agnes retrieved what she was instructed to. Sarah laid out the towel and placed the baby on it. She wiped the baby's face and head, cleaning her as well as she could. Mary returned with the sterilized strips of sheeting and scissors, and Sarah tied the umbilical cord and cut it just above where she tied it. Then she snugly swaddled Janie's crying daughter and handed her to her mother.

Janie was overcome with emotion and relief, her chest heaving with each sob. She had been frightened at the prospect of giving birth, and in her most wild imaginings she could have never conceived of this scenario. She was so grateful for Agnes and her family.

Sarah sensed Janie's trepidation. "You are going to be a wonderful mother. There is no need to be concerned. We are all here to help you."

Janie had no parents, and Sarah's presence could not have been more comforting to her.

Agnes chastised herself for not listening to her intuition. If things had turned out differently, she would have never forgiven herself.

The baby began to make sucking sounds.

"I think your little girl is ready for her first meal. Let's get you comfortable first. Why don't you let Agnes hold your daughter and we'll get you out of these soiled clothes?" Janie still felt disoriented and followed Sarah's lead without question.

Agnes took the baby and drowned in a surge of maternal emotion. This precious little child made her heart ache with love. Agnes kissed her forehead; her skin was as soft as silk. The light blonde fuzz that covered her head was no longer matted. It was as delightfully soft as her round, chubby cheeks. But it was her perfectly pink, doll-like lips that made Agnes cry. They made her seem so tiny and vulnerable, and Agnes wanted to hold her forever and protect her from the world.

"What happened?"

Agnes turned to Tom, who stood in the doorway staring at the broken glass. When Agnes didn't answer, he looked up at her. Agnes had positioned herself so Tom would notice his daughter.

Tom's protectiveness over the broken window disappeared in a blink. He was now overcome by the realization that he was a father.

"Hello, Papa. Come meet your new daughter."

Tom moved toward Agnes slowly, as if frightened his excitement would somehow make it all vanish. Tom looked at his daughter and then at Agnes, waiting for validation that she was real. His entire being was transformed with that first glance.

"Congratulations, Tom. She is an angel." Agnes held the girl out in front of her father, inviting him to hold her. Agnes gently placed the baby in her father's outstretched arms. Agnes could feel him tense up.

Tom looked around the room and Agnes could see the tears in his eyes. It brought tears to her own.

"Where is my wife?" Tom asked with concern.

"My mother is helping her get cleaned up. She'll be right out."

He looked over and saw Mary attempting to clean the chesterfield. "I am happy Janie was not alone, but I should have been here with her. I was only gone a few hours. I came back to check on her because she wasn't feeling well this morning. She promised me she was just tired. She said Delores was just a few doors away. I would not have left her if I had known." Tom was feeling as though he had failed his wife, and he was wearing his guilt for all to see.

"Of course you wouldn't have. It all came on very quickly."

The baby began to cry and Tom's rocking had no effect. Her high-pitched cries erupted in a frenzy of unspoken need and Tom was helpless to soothe her.

"Your daughter wants something only your wife can provide," Sarah explained.

Janie entered the room and Tom lit up. Janie walked over to her husband and kissed him tenderly. She was as relieved to see him.

"Are you all right? I was worried when I saw the broken glass," he asked protectively.

"I am sorry about that," Agnes responded. "That was me."

"Your daughter was determined to come precisely when she did. There was no stopping her. Thankfully Agnes and Mary arrived in the nick of time," Janie said as she kissed her daughter and took her from her father.

A knock at the door came soon thereafter.

"I am so sorry. I was delivering another baby. I just returned home, and my neighbour told me someone was frantically knocking on my door. Janie is my only other mother at full term; I knew it had to be her. Where is she?"

"She just went into the bedroom to feed the baby," Agnes informed her.

"The baby? She had the baby already?" Delores asked, not sure she had heard properly.

"Yes, we came just in time. The baby arrived a few minutes later."

Delores was in a state of disbelief. She completely missed a birth that she had prepared six months for. It was as embarrassing as it was distressing.

"Please excuse me. I need to go check on mother and child." Delores continued to sound apologetic.

Tom looked distressed and it broke Agnes's heart. This was supposed to be a joyous occasion, not a fretful one. As much as Agnes wanted to continue reassuring him, she knew the only thing he needed to soothe his conscience was time alone with his wife and baby girl.

After twenty minutes, Janie appeared. The baby was sleeping peacefully in her mother's arms.

"How are you?" Agnes asked, eager to hear more. It had been an intensely emotional experience for her, and she craved details.

"It appears my daughter knows how to eat," Janie said with a chuckle. "I think those jaws could crack a walnut." From the sparkle in her eyes, it was evident Janie liked the sound of "my daughter."

"Mother and baby are both in good health. Baby has successfully had her first feeding and is sleeping. Now what Mum needs is some well-deserved rest."

Delores's tone was almost curt. She was trying to gain some control in a situation where she had none, one where she was no longer required. At this point, it wasn't a midwife that Janie needed. She needed a mother, and the irony wasn't lost on Janie. As unpleasant as the circumstances had been that had led her to this moment, it was clear they had been divinely directed. She could not have conceived of the magnitude of the void that her mother's death had left in her life, certainly never more painfully felt than at this time, or how much of a comfort Sarah had been in her absence. Janie's faith had always been strong, but her trust in God's will was now unshakable.

"Delores is right. Rest is exactly what Janie needs. There will be plenty of time for visits." Nobody could disagree with Sarah, not even Agnes, who desperately wanted to.

"I cannot thank you all enough for everything. I'll never be able to. I shudder to think what would have happened if you hadn't been here."

"And to think, all it cost me was a broken window," Tom joked.

"What can I say? I like to make an entrance," Agnes said, giving it back. "It was either that or knock the door down, and I don't think your garden gnome would have been fierce enough."

"In all seriousness, thank you." No humour could hide Tom's heartfelt sentiment.

"There is no need for thanks. You are like family now," Sarah said. Janie looked down at the baby to redirect her eyes, which were welling with tears.

Agnes gave Janie and Tom a hug and kissed the baby gently so she wouldn't wake her.

"Please come back tomorrow, Agnes. Tom will be working and I would love the company."

There is nothing Janie could have said that would have made Agnes happier. If she couldn't have her own child, then she would love Janie's.

Chapter 12

Agnes arrived home to find Art asleep on the chesterfield. Sam's shop was closed for Labour Day, as were most businesses. She was happy he was getting rest; he hadn't had much of it lately.

Agnes knew better than to wake him. Startling him never ended well. He looked so peaceful and Agnes felt compelled to watch him. She could never begin to understand the demons he was fighting, and she wished from a place so deep that it took her breath away that she could make it better. But she couldn't. She loved him unendingly, but it was an understanding born of common experience, one that they didn't share. It broke her heart that she could not help him, and she felt she would never be connected to him at the deepest level, the one that existed beyond all fears and insecurities. It appeared only Percy could reach him through the fog.

"Mmm, what smells so good?" Art asked as he sat up from his sleep.

"So far, chicken casserole. Next it will be fried chicken and then potato salad."

"What time is the party?"

"No party. It is for Tom and Janie."

"Getting ready for the baby?"

Agnes let out a laugh.

"More like feeding the new parents."

"New parents? Did they have the baby?"

Agnes replayed the afternoon's events as Art listened, stunned. He was astonished by what had happened, and all while he slept. He waited for Agnes to tell him the joke was on him, but she didn't.

"Did you talk with your brother today?"

"Well, judging from your tone, you must know something that I do not."

"You didn't answer my question." She was becoming as frustrated as she had been with Mary earlier.

"No, I didn't speak with him. I'm assuming he finally made a move."

The nonchalant attitude that men possessed over matters of romantic significance drove Agnes crazy. It was as though they were born without hearts.

"Yes, he finally made a move, but only after my sister made the first one. Sound familiar?"

Agnes walked into it headfirst; she couldn't help herself.

Art laughed. "Yes, you made the first move, my darling, but I would say it was well played on my part, wouldn't you? You like to be wooed, so long as you are in control. I love that about you. You are a take-charge gal. Your sister is no different than you are. You are both cut from the same feisty cloth."

Agnes wasn't sure if she should be offended or not, but she certainly wasn't going to give him the satisfaction of responding.

"Is any of that amazing food for dinner?"

"We are going to Mum and Sam's Labour Day barbeque. Did you forget? John and Margaret and the girls are coming as well. John is grilling something—I'm not sure what. I'll be taking this over before dinner so poor Tom doesn't starve."

"Clearly, nap-induced memory loss. John's grilling … excellent! I will try to not make a hog of myself."

John was rotating a hind quarter of lamb over the coals when Art and Agnes arrived. The succulent smell was beginning to permeate the yard, wafting up in a steady plume of herb-infused smoke.

"This day is certainly shaping up nicely," Art said, inhaling deeply.

"I hear you had an eventful day." Agnes turned around to see Margaret standing there. "I thought Janie might be able to use these. The bassinette and pram are in the house."

"She will be so pleased, Margaret. Thank you! We were going to go shopping together this week, but the baby had other plans." Agnes took two large bags of baby clothes from Margaret.

Agnes looked up the driveway to see Percy and Bill walking toward the group. It hadn't even occurred to her to invite them, and her conscience burned with the oversight. She had not invited them, *but then who did*? It wasn't Art; he hadn't even remembered there was to be a barbeque.

"Percy, Bill, how nice to see you both. Percy, I thought you might be tired of us after seeing us just yesterday."

"I could never be tired of my favourite sister-in-law."

Percy's face blushed with red, eliciting curiosity in Agnes. He excused himself and walked off and Agnes looked over to see where, or more precisely to whom, but she knew before she did.

Mary stood by the backdoor looking as though she had primped all day. Her hair was set with perfect waves and her cheeks were rouged. Mary never wore makeup and it made Agnes giggle out loud.

"Did you say something, Agnes?" Bill asked.

"I was just about to say how tremendous the roast smells. I hope you like lamb."

"I certainly do. It is a rare treat." Bill seemed so happy to be there and

Agnes's guilt did not subside.

"Now, where is that husband of mine?" Agnes asked as she looked around the yard. The blue jay that had captured Art's attention was high enough in the tree that it was not bothered by the activity, yet low enough for its cobalt, black, and white feathers to stand out amongst the red maple leaves. It sat perched alone, squawking noisily as it surveyed the yard.

Agnes walked up behind her husband and placed her hand on his shoulder. He flinched and jumped forward.

"Sorry, my darling. You startled me." Art looked embarrassed.

Agnes was startled herself but not surprised. She knew better than to touch him before announcing herself. Agnes looked around to see if anyone had noticed, and the only eyes that were upon her were Percy's. Agnes's sad eyes left Percy feeling powerless. She was lost for understanding and lost for a cure, but she at least had someone to share in her sorrow. Percy was the only one who understood.

As Agnes lay in bed that night, she attempted to compose the words that would persuade her husband to seek help, but they were escaping her. He needed help to expel the memories that tormented his soul. As long as they remained, he would never be at peace.

Agnes awoke to find herself alone in the bed. She went to the living room anticipating Art to be asleep on the chesterfield. It was empty. He was nowhere to be found, and there was no note to indicate where he could have gone. Agnes could only assume he had gone to work early, but it was not like him to leave without a note.

Agnes showered and dressed to go to Janie's. It was only half-past eight, probably too early, she thought.

Agnes instead sifted through the baby clothes again. She had taken them out of the bags and held them against her one by one, as though her own baby filled them. The delicious smell had not been entirely erased by the wash and Agnes became consumed by it. As she folded the clothes, the longing tugged at her again, but this time she resisted.

Outside the sun was still low in the sky, low enough to have had no effect on the dew that was laid down throughout the night. As Agnes walked toward the main house, something caught her eye and she turned toward it. At first Agnes couldn't tell what it was; it was partially hidden by the gazebo trellis. Then she noticed the hand dangling toward the gazebo floor. She stood, frozen in place. She focused intently on the shape, its body slumped back in the chair and head tipped backwards. Agnes recognized the head. It was Art's.

Agnes dropped her bags. Her mind was frozen in disbelief, but her body managed to carry her slowly toward him.

His mouth was wide open, as if there was no life left to hold it in place. Fear consumed her, crushing her heart against her chest. She could not speak. She could do nothing but look.

"Agnes, what are you doing back there?" Agnes turned to see her mother standing alongside the pram. But Agnes couldn't respond, her mouth unable to form words.

"I must have fallen asleep." Agnes turned back to find Art sitting up and rubbing his neck. "What's wrong, my love? You look as though you have seen a ghost."

"Why are you out here? I woke up and you weren't there. No note. Nothing." It was clear to Art his wife was not pleased.

"I'm sorry. I couldn't sleep. The birds woke up just before dawn, and I thought listening to them out here might be more pleasant than staring at the ceiling. I fell asleep, I guess. I am sorry. I didn't mean to frighten you."

"You are late for your deliveries. You had better get going. Pa will wonder where you are." Agnes's mood remained unpleasant, and she had no desire to begin a conversation now. Art didn't understand that it was the totality of events, not just this morning's, that had her so riled.

"I have to go to Janie's now," Agnes said as she turned to leave. "Goodbye, Mum. Thank you for bringing me the rest of the things."

Agnes walked off, leaving her mother and husband where they stood. Art started to follow his wife, but Sarah grabbed his arm. She knew well enough to let her daughter go.

Agnes arrived at Janie's to the sound of crying. She tried the handle and this time it was not locked. The cries were coming from the bedroom.

"Janie, it's me, Agnes." Agnes walked toward the bedroom.

"Back here, Agnes."

Agnes entered the bedroom as Janie was beginning to feed her daughter. "I'll wait for you out here," Agnes said as she turned her head away.

"Agnes, there is nothing of mine that you haven't seen already," Janie said with a laugh.

Agnes reluctantly turned back and sat on the edge of the bed. The baby stopped crying as she took to the breast. Agnes could hear her sweet sucking sounds, and they gave her such pleasure.

"You look like you have done this before," Agnes complimented before realizing what she had said. She kicked herself for it. Janie was unaffected, too content with the maternal rush to feel anything but euphoric.

"My sister brought over a few baby clothes, a bassinette, and a pram. Her girls have outgrown them, and she thought you could put them to good use."

Janie got so excited she startled the baby off her breast, and the baby started to cry. Janie adjusted herself and then began to giggle.

"I couldn't imagine shopping this week. Even if I had the energy, which I definitely do not, I couldn't without a pram. I hadn't even thought that far out. Please thank your sister for me. I so appreciate her kindness."

Janie finished feeding the baby and then held her out for Agnes.

"Would you like to hold your goddaughter?"

Agnes looked at Janie in wonder. "Did you say 'goddaughter'?"

"I did. Tom and I would be honoured if you and Art would be her godparents ... if you would like to, of course. We would have liked to ask you together, but I have never been one for keeping secrets."

"I can answer for both of us. Absolutely. Without question. We would be delighted." Agnes planted kisses all over the baby's face. "Your godmother loves you very much, little one."

"Elizabeth Agnes is very fortunate," Janie said.

"Elizabeth Agnes?" Agnes asked with a look of surprise that was becoming fixed.

"Yes, Elizabeth Agnes. She is named after her grandmother and godmother."

"I don't know what to say. I cannot tell you how much this means to me."

"You needn't. I can see it plain as day. I knew we made the right choice," she said. "Now I need to explain something. I am sure you are quite curious."

"Please don't feel that you need to tell me." Agnes felt as though she was prying, even though she hadn't asked. Even wondering made her feel invasive. She understood the pain of a failed pregnancy and couldn't fathom losing a child.

"No, I want to. I need to, really. Next to Tom, you are the closest person in the world to me. I don't want to have any secrets from you. I have held it in for far too long."

Agnes felt a lump forming in her throat, and not because of the sentiment, which Agnes too felt, but because she was anticipating Janie's pain and she knew that pain all too well herself.

Agnes placed Elizabeth in her crib and followed Janie out to the living room.

"How on earth did you get the cushions so clean?"

"The cushions were easy. Just don't turn them over," Janie said with a smirk.

Janie sat down in the chair. She adjusted her skirt and then smoothed it out. Nervous, she cleared her throat and managed an exaggerated Mona Lisa smile that grieved Agnes, and despite Agnes's own discomfort she didn't rush Janie.

"When I was fourteen years old, I was raped."

Agnes gasped and clutched at her chest.

"Sorry if that shocked you." Janie spoke flatly, as though she were talking about the weather. "There's really no way to dress it up."

Agnes's revelation was entirely unexpected and beyond horrifying. Agnes was still reeling as Janie continued to speak.

"It was our neighbour. He had worked for my father. When my father found out, he confronted him. They fought and he died."

"The man killed your father?!" Agnes was incredulous. She couldn't believe what she was hearing.

"My father was so angry when he found out. He didn't scream or shout, but it was clear. His face got so red and I was so scared. My mother tried to stop him, but he kept walking."

Janie was no longer looking at Agnes. She was looking at the floor, her voice no longer flat. She was reliving every terrifying moment.

"They fought and my father died."

Janie was still not looking up, but Agnes could see the tears staining her skirt. Agnes went over to her and kneeled down beside her to offer her comfort.

"The man wasn't charged with any crime. He raped me and killed my father, and he got nothing. The police said it was self-defence."

"What about what he did to you? Surely, that couldn't go unpunished."

"It is hard to prove rape, apparently, especially when you have police officers as friends." Janie looked up at Agnes and laughed slightly, acknowledging the absurdity of it all. Janie's anger had not diminished in all the years since, and she sat before Agnes looking as angry as Agnes imagined Janie's father had.

"I found out I was pregnant soon after. My son was born and my mother raised him as her own. My son became my brother."

Agnes knew that Janie had said she had no family, so she knew there was still more to come. She was numb with empathy for her dear friend.

"The monster left before the baby was born. I came upon him when I was far enough along to tell. The look on his face was unforgettable ... he was gone right after that. I'll never forget his name. Jasper. Jasper Flincher. What a vile name." Janie's face contorted in disgust.

Agnes had never heard Janie speak with such anger and passion. She exhaled a fiery mien. What had lain dormant was now awakened. What had long been repressed was now free.

"My mother and Patrick died when Patrick was only a few years old. Tuberculosis. Both of them. I don't know how I survived. I was sick as the dickens too, but God spared me. It was just me after that point. I did the only thing that made sense to me … I left."

The horror and sadness that swirled around Agnes was suffocating her. She didn't know if she should speak, and she wasn't even sure what would come out of her mouth if she did open it. They would merely be words. They would not change anything. The clock could not be reversed. This could not be fixed.

Agnes put her hand on Janie's leg and looked up at her friend, her eyes begging forgiveness for what she could not do. Helplessness tore at Agnes's core. It was a feeling she was becoming intimate with.

"This is only the second time I have spoken of this since my mum and Patrick died. I have tried desperately to leave it behind, but Elizabeth opened the door again."

"I am so sorry, Janie. I cannot imagine the pain you have endured."

Janie wiped a tear from Agnes's cheek.

"Yes, we are all faced with challenges and we endure. Please do not feel bad for me. I also have more than my fair share of blessings. It would not be right to be anything but grateful."

"That is my queue to leave," Agnes announced as Tom walked in the door.

"Please don't leave on my account. I was just checking in on Janie and Elizabeth."

The sparkle in Tom's eyes mollified the protectiveness that had erupted in Agnes. He was a good man and he dearly loved his wife. There was no doubt to Agnes that Janie was in good hands.

"I think my goddaughter is hungry, and like you, I cannot help where that is concerned. Please give her a kiss for me."

"Thank you for bringing your sister's things for Elizabeth. Please thank her. I'm not sure when I will get a chance to."

Janie's eyes implored Agnes to not feel anguish for her, and Agnes knew Janie well enough to know she would want her to forget. She would want to move on, and Agnes dwelling on her misery would only force the memories to stay in the present. They needed to be banished to the past where they belonged.

As Agnes walked home, she was mixed in emotion. The joy of being godmother to that magnificent child was tempered by the sorrow she felt over her mother's misfortune. An eddy of grief left her shaken, and the anger she had felt toward her husband that morning was forgotten.

Chapter 13

"We are only into November, and I am already sick of winter," Agnes complained.

"Well, my darling, I hate to make it worse by pointing out that winter is not yet upon us."

Agnes grunted and finished her last bite of scrambled eggs before clearing the table.

"We have had superb weather. There hasn't been a single day below freezing until just earlier this week. How can you be tired of it already? Two days of cold and you have had enough. Perhaps we should move to Mexico," Art teased.

"If you could find work and were so inclined, I would be at the train station before you could blink. Palm trees, soothing tropical breezes … what a splendid dream. We may have only had a few days of cold, but those few days have brought half a foot of snow already."

"Speaking of finding work," Art said, changing the subject, "I have something I wish to discuss with you."

Agnes turned to face her husband, her quizzical look compounding his nervousness.

"Pete McNally has more work than he can handle, and he is looking to hire an additional painter or two. I don't have experience at it, but I could learn."

"I don't understand. What about Pa and the shop?"

"I am grateful to Sam for my job. It saved me when I came back and couldn't get anything else. But your brothers will want to work with their father one day. Then what will I do? I don't want to be left with nothing. And besides, I don't want to be a deliveryman all my life. I need to learn a trade. Then perhaps one day I can build my own business. I did promise you a castle, remember?" Art tried to make light of the change, hoping Agnes would see it as nothing more than the opportunity that Art did.

Agnes was stunned. Art's job was safe and secure and sufficient, and there had never been any need for his thoughts to drift anywhere beyond that. She was convinced good rarely came from change. In fact, she was sure of it.

"I would like for us to have our own home before long, especially when the children come. I don't want to be reliant upon or indebted to your parents."

Agnes was unsure if her uneasiness was more influenced by the thought of change or Art's mention of children. Both caused her significant consternation, but only one was outside her control.

"You will always have a job with Pa. He would never toss you into the street. You have to know that." Agnes's tone was turning emotional, almost pleading, and he was as surprised by it as he was unprepared.

"Darling, my income will not suffer. Pete tells me he has more work than he knows what to do with."

"For now. What about tomorrow? Six months from now?"

"There will be work. New buildings, old buildings … there will always be a need for painting."

"And what about the effort? It is hard work. You said yourself Pete has rheumatism in his hands. And what if you decide it is not for you? Your job with Pa will be gone. Then what?" Agnes was becoming agitated, so Art decided it was time to change the subject.

"How is our goddaughter doing?" Art asked.

"Do not change the subject, Art. I will not have it." Agnes's stubbornness had always been endearing to Art, but at this moment it was starting to make him angry. "I fail to see why you want to do this. Why change what is not broken?"

Art continued to be silent, not wanting to aggravate the situation further, but his silence only inflamed his wife.

"Have you no answer for me? Is it the end of the discussion because you have decided so?"

"No, it is not the end of the discussion," Art offered. "I am merely waiting for you to calm down."

Agnes's eyes narrowed in anger, the whites disappearing into a raging fury. She raised her finger and pointed it at her husband.

"Calm down? How is this for calm?" Agnes walked through the door, slamming it behind her. In her anger, she had neglected to recognize that she remained in her slippers and that her jacket continued to reside on its hook. She walked down the stairs, holding tightly to the railing, admitting to herself the silliness of her protest. But she could not reverse course.

"Agnes, come back!" Art yelled. "It is freezing. You are being ridiculous. You'll catch your death of cold."

Agnes did not turn back. She knew she was being ridiculous, but she didn't need her husband to tell her so. Turning back would be tantamount to admitting rash judgement, and she would rather get frostbite than admit any such regret.

Sarah opened the door to her shivering daughter.

"What on earth? Agnes, where is your coat? And your shoes?!"

Agnes stared blankly at her mother, unsure of what to say. She was ashamed for losing her temper, but she felt entirely justified in her anger.

"Why are men so short-sighted and pig-headed?"

Sarah laughed. She knew her daughter to be opinionated, and she was sure what was to come would not involve any mincing of words.

"Come sit. I'll make us some tea."

Sarah led her daughter to the kitchen and put the kettle on the stove.

"Tell me what has you in such a tizzy today."

"Art just informed me that he would like to learn a trade. He has a perfectly good job with Pa. It makes no sense."

"Does he? Does he have one in mind?" Sarah asked, intrigued.

"Does it matter? He wants to join Pete McNally's company and become a painter. He tells me that my brothers will work for Pa at some point, and he will be without a position. He wants to acquire a skill so that he no longer feels beholden to Pa for his livelihood. He also seems to consider his job an unrespectable one. He says he doesn't want to be a deliveryman all his life. And he wants us to get our own house. Isn't that the most preposterous thing you have ever heard?"

Agnes waited for her mother to voice her agreement, but Sarah did not oblige.

"Please, don't tell me you agree with him. Aren't you supposed to be on my side?" Agnes was hurt by the lack of instant validation, and she suddenly felt isolated and alone.

"I will always support you, but that does not mean I will always agree with you." Sarah gave her daughter the same look she gave her as a child when she felt the need to show her the error of her ways. It annoyed Agnes then, and it annoyed her yet still.

"Art wants to make his own way and that is entirely understandable. Sam will always provide a position for Art, but that is clearly not enough for him. He wants more for himself, more for his family. That is to be commended, not criticized. My darling girl, you must not let your fear of change hinder your good judgement. You must support the man you love, as he would do no less for you."

"I am not afraid of change. I just see no reason for it."

Sarah could see that she and her daughter had reached an impasse and continuing would only cause Agnes to become more agitated. She had always been a stubborn girl, and she would need to come to terms with this on her own.

Agnes felt deflated. She felt the one person who should have been on her side disagreed with her wholeheartedly.

"Here, have a peanut butter cookie." Sarah placed the plate of cookies in front of her daughter and poured her some tea. "How is Elizabeth doing? Time flies by so quickly. It is hard to believe she is two months already."

Agnes could offer her mother no more than a short nod. Sarah sighed quietly and let it go. She could no more criticize her daughter for her obstinacy than her own mother could for hers. Sarah knew her daughter would get there eventually, but it would not be an easy or straight line. Maturity is a lifelong journey. It is like a stone turning about in a stream; the jagged edges of one's perceptions smoothen over time, but they must be left to tumble.

Agnes's face contorted slightly as a mild wave of nausea flowed from her belly.

"They can't be that bad," Sarah teased.

"No, I think I am just coming down with something. I started to feel a bit off when I was eating breakfast this morning. I'll be fine."

"You can wear my coat to walk back home. My boots are too small for your feet so it would appear you are stuck with your slippers." Sarah shook her head, dismayed by her daughter's lapses into puerility. "If you are feeling unwell, I certainly hope this won't make matters worse."

Agnes spent the day cleaning and cooking a Shepherd's Pie. The smell of the sautéing lamb wasn't as inviting as it usually was, but Agnes was too caught up in her own thoughts to notice. She did, however, notice how tired she felt, and she decided to lie on the chesterfield for a rest. She didn't want to be ill for Janie's. She was looking forward to spending the evening with her friend and goddaughter.

Agnes awoke on the chesterfield as her husband kneeled before her with a bouquet of flowers in hand.

"Your prince begs forgiveness for upsetting his beautiful bride. He is truly sorry." Art bowed his head and extended the flowers, remaining that way until Agnes accepted them from him.

Agnes looked at him in earnest, serious and focused, but offered no clear indication of mood. Art was unsure which way the pendulum would swing.

"These are lovely. Thank you," she said as she stood up. "I'll put them in some water."

Art didn't speak. It was Agnes who needed to carry that conversation. She would not be told and Art was well aware of that fact.

"It smells delicious in here. Is dinner with Tom and Janie still on before cards?"

Agnes turned to face her husband. Her gaze remained focused and intense until she revealed her dimples with a conciliatory smile.

"Yes, we are still going. I couldn't pass up an evening with that darling baby." Agnes was at least conversing, but she still held back, embarrassed by her behaviour and unwilling to admit it.

"Tom will be driving tonight so I will be at his mercy. I can't imagine we'll be too late. We'll be at the Stockyards. Morty is hosting, but his wife's family is staying with them right now."

"You can do it. I won't object."

Art looked sideways at his wife for her out-of-place comment. She had already given her blessing for the evening. She could only be referring to their earlier conversation.

"To the painting?" he asked cautiously.

"Yes, to the painting. However, my agreement comes with a condition."

Art remained silent, awaiting whatever Agnes required in trade.

"You will allow me to do your job instead, until you decide this will be a long-term venture."

Art shook his head in disbelief and then howled in laughter, assuming her demand was in jest. Agnes remained stony, and Art realized he needed to backtrack.

"Darling, you yourself said that a married woman should not work."

Agnes stumbled on that point, knowing full well he was right.

"I may have said that, but the circumstances have changed."

"How so?"

The mounting pressure worked its way through her body, leaving her feeling as though she were on trial.

"Changing jobs is fraught with risk. You cannot deny that. It would only be for a few months until you are settled and sure. That way you could return to Pa if you wanted, and we wouldn't be leaving him in the lurch in the meantime. And besides, it is not like I have anything to do during the day. I am bored silly."

Art let Agnes's demand soak in, taking great pains not to appear to jump to judgement too quickly.

"My dear, if you wish to get a job, why not look to the phone company or a department store? This is a man's job." Art wasn't trying to be offensive, but it didn't matter. His words made her stand up in defence, like a rearing bull.

"I'll have you know, Mr. Craig, I did that job long before you came along. I'll have none of your male versus female prejudice. You won't win that argument."

Art knew she was right. He realized that he would have to tuck his male pride into his pocket and acquiesce on this point if he was going to win the more important battle.

Art held out his hand in conciliation and Agnes shook it. There. It was settled. Art loosened his grip and pulled his wife toward him, embracing her with relief as much as love. He was happy they were settled. Rifts between them were rare, but when they occurred they were never less than dramatic.

"We must get going. Mary and Percy will be waiting for us."

Agnes and Art gathered up the food for Tom and Janie's.

The air was crisp, and their frozen breath was a reminder that fall was fading fast. But even with the briskness, it was a beautiful evening.

"Hello, you two. How are we both doing?" Agnes asked, her smirk causing Percy to laugh out loud.

"Mighty fine, Agnes. Mighty fine."

Baby Elizabeth was asleep in the bassinette when they arrived. Agnes and Mary rushed to her side and cooed at her sleeping form like love-struck teenagers.

"How is my goddaughter sleeping at night? She certainly looks as though she is not starving," Agnes noted proudly.

"Yes, she is a chubby little thing. She eats all the time. Delores said that is why she is sleeping so well. She has been only waking once during the night. This morning she slept until half-past four, which gives me hope that she'll soon be sleeping right through."

"I hear you gentlemen are going to the Stockyards Hotel this evening. Wasn't it raided yet again last month? I read they confiscated barrels of liquor. John said Alex McCurdy has been gunning for him, coming into the restaurant with his crew and making all sorts of accusations. Nothing is ever found, of course, but it is really disruptive and upsetting to his customers." Mary was well aware of John's frustration with the morality squad. He spoke of it constantly.

"The St. Boniface police generally don't get involved in Temperance Law violations or any of the morality laws for that matter. That's the jurisdiction of the Provincial Police. Too many cooks in the kitchen, so to speak. They raided the hotel last month and got their fines; they should be good for a while. We only care about real crimes," Tom said sardonically.

Half a year had passed since the St. Boniface police force had been put on notice, and the memories of the fear that ensued had all but vanished. Anger and frustration over the morality laws were all that remained.

Tom, Art, and Percy arrived at the hotel at half-past eight. They went to the restaurant where John and the others were waiting.

"Sorry for the locale, but I thought it would be better than my mother-in-law," he said snidely.

Morty did the accounting for the hotel. He had gotten the owner out of a pinch or two, and he was quick to help Morty out. The men had a table tucked into a darkened corner of the restaurant, which was full that evening. The Stockyards was by no means The Fort Garry. There were no elegantly dressed couples enjoying fine dining over polite conversation.

This was decidedly more saloon, closer to cowboy than king.

"Morty, how much hooch did they get during the raid?" John asked. "I'm sure Alex was quite pleased with himself."

"Three large barrels. They cleaned the hotel out," Morty said. "But the gin mill has been busy since," he snickered as he placed a jug on the table. "And it's the real McCoy. No coffin varnish for us."

The table erupted in laughter as the men grabbed their mugs and began banging them on the table. This was Percy's first experience with "card night" and he was astonished and speechless, though perhaps not to the extent that Art was his first time. Art's initiation had been decidedly more ambush in nature, and despite the lack of coughing and spewing at Percy's, Art was still entertained by his brother's shock.

"Let's get this game going, boys. No sense holding onto money that won't be yours by the end of the evening," Tom taunted.

The restaurant was loud and lively, and the activity at the card table didn't stand out as out of place. The alcohol had been drained during the last raid, but somehow that misfortune had been remedied. Jugs began appearing on more than a few of the tables, and the volume in the room continued to rise.

It was about quarter to one when the last pot was won, and still the restaurant was showing no signs of clearing out.

"We'd better get out the padding for our knees. I think we'll be on them a bit tomorrow. I know Margaret'll be fit to be tied," John said. "Looks like the only guy who won't have to worry about it is the guy who stole all our money."

"Stole? I won fair and square."

"Percy, it was beginner's luck. Nothing more," Pete joked.

The room suddenly got quiet, and the men turned to find two morality officers standing in the middle of the room. Tom and John had their backs to them. They recognized them immediately and turned back around right away. The men worked for Alex McCurdy and were never far from him.

Tom and John turned back quickly, but not before Dineen's and John's eyes met. Dineen's icy stare sent shivers through John's spine, but it was his look of recognition, his smug grin, that sent John into a silent panic. They remained still, terrified of the consequences should they be inextricably linked with whatever McCurdy's men were able to prove. Tom's career would be over, and McCurdy wouldn't stop until John's restaurant was shut down for good.

"Well, well, well, what do we have here?" Officer Dineen said, sure he had just stumbled onto a smoking gun.

The restaurant was full, but the two officers had singled out their table to start. They were in no rush. They knew they had hit the jackpot. Another officer stood guard at the door; nobody was going anywhere.

Dineen noticed the cards sitting on the table and a single nickel that Percy had missed. "Gambling without a permit in a place of business … now we take that seriously, don't we, Officer Miller?"

Morty followed Dineen's eyes to the nickel. "No illegal gambling going on here, officer. We were using this nickel for coin tosses, nothing more."

Both Tom and John were beginning to perspire. John wanted desperately to wipe his brow, but he was terrified to move.

"And what do we have in those glasses? Water, I suppose?"

As Dineen took a step forward, a shot exploded, sending the impact of the discharge reverberating through the hotel. It was followed by another and then another. Instinctively Tom jumped up and turned toward the sound. Dineen had already done the same and was running with the other officers back through the door.

Tom did a quick scan of the table, and the only thing that stood out was Art's empty seat. In the commotion, no one had noticed that he had dropped to the floor. He lay on his belly with his hands cupped over the back of his head, protecting it from the artillery fire.

Screams pierced the air, coming from every direction, and the sound of footsteps on the wooden floor planks echoed overhead. Tables toppled and glass smashed. It was mad chaos.

Tom ran through the door and toward the direction of the gunfire, leaving the others on their own in the restaurant. Driven by fear, they grabbed their coats and ran toward the kitchen door.

"Private Craig. Vacate! Vacate! That is an order!" Percy yelled as he stood over his brother. Percy could not wait for Art to snap out of it.

In the commotion that ensued, the men ran in whichever direction suited them. As Art and Percy cleared the parking lot, two men were shouting obscenities at a third as they ran toward a car. Once inside they skidded on the densely packed snow and abruptly sped away.

"All clear!" Percy yelled. Art stopped running. "Art, it is me, Percy," he said softly, almost in a whisper.

Art turned around. His body was trembling, his stare vacant. He looked lost. Percy was terrified of the emotional effect this would have on his brother. It couldn't possibly end well.

They cleared the icy parking lot, skirting mounds of snow and ice as they ran. They continued up Marion, crossing the Seine River before they stopped, out of breath. When they looked back, the road behind them was clear of cars and pedestrians. Twenty minutes later they were at Art's.

Chapter 14

Agnes awoke to Art's sleeping silhouette, his deep and methodic breathing filling the room. She was well aware of the late hour at which he arrived; she had awoken at one and he had yet come to bed. She decided to let him sleep.

She placed a few sausages into a frying pan and scrambled some eggs. As she began to set the table, she was startled to see Percy on the chesterfield.

Percy sat up, rubbing his eyes to clear them of the cloudiness that obscured them.

"Percy, you frightened me. What in the devil are you doing here?" Agnes said, bemused by his presence. "Of course, I am always happy to see you, but it is not expected at half-past six."

Agnes began to put the pieces together and realized that something was not right. Her intuition was crying out, and she could not rest until she knew why.

"What is the matter? Why did you not go home last night?"

Percy stood up, ran his fingers through his hair, and attempted to smooth the wrinkles from his trousers with his hands. His mind raced with the words he could use to explain, and none of them led to a happy ending.

"Agnes, sit down. I'll explain."

"I will not sit down, thank you. Anything that you would suggest I listen to sitting down would no doubt be better listened to whilst I am standing up. Now, please tell me."

Percy cleared his throat. "As you know, we were at the Stockyards Hotel last evening."

Agnes was staring at Percy with a look of "and?..." on her face. She was never one for small talk, always preferring to get directly to the point.

"We were there later than we planned. We were getting ready to leave and then...."

Agnes's patience was wearing thin. She began to pace, as if willing Percy to speed up. Agnes had forgotten about the sausages on the stove, and the sudden smell of cooking pork offered a reminder. She turned the heat off and moved the pan to the back burner.

"I'm going to get right to the point. There is no other way to say it. There was a shooting at the hotel as we were about to leave. I can assure you we are all fine. I really don't know any more. Art and I ran out of the hotel as soon as we heard the shots. We didn't see what happened."

"Shooting? You must have been mistaken. I'm sure it was something else you heard. This is Norwood, not the O.K. Corral," Agnes said, somewhat dismissively.

"It was clearly gunshots. I am well acquainted with the sound." Percy was tired and had little patience for Agnes's opinions.

"Of course you are. I'm sorry. I'm just shocked. You all made it out? Nobody was hurt?"

"Tom ran toward the shots. We didn't see him later. He...."

Agnes cut Percy off before he could speak any further.

"He ran toward the shots? Why would he do that? Why would he put himself in harm's way? He has a wife and child at home. Stupid, stupid man." Agnes was pacing again, unable to think straight.

"That is his job, Agnes. Leaving wasn't an option. He swore to uphold an oath to protect, and that is what he did."

Agnes knew he was right, but it wasn't any easier to accept. She could only see Janie in her mind and hear the sound of her trembling voice as she spoke of the horror of what had happened to her. Janie had had enough tragedy in her life, and Agnes couldn't bear the thought of her being faced with any more.

And what of Agnes's sleeping husband? Agnes's concern shifted like a crashing wave. She looked toward the bedroom door and then back at Percy, her eyes open wide to the sadness in her heart.

"We should have had this discussion before now. I hoped the situation would improve, but it seems quite locked into place."

Percy felt as though he was about to deliver a death sentence.

"Overseas, Art's job was to stand watch at night. It was his sole responsibility to ensure the men in his group woke up in the morning when they were lying in wait, and when they weren't he was at the front of the line. Night after night he stood guard, watching for the enemy, preparing for attack. If he fell asleep, it could have been catastrophic; lives were at stake, including his own. He was based in the thick of it. His experience was far worse than mine. It really was. This is why he has difficulty sleeping at night. His body may have returned, but his mind, it seems, is still there."

Agnes was overwhelmed. She closed her eyes, yet the tears still escaped. Art was tormented and it devastated her. With one brief thought, she gasped.

"What of last night? What will it do to him? How was he?" Agnes was fearful of the answer.

"As you would suspect, I suppose. Sudden loud sounds bring him back to the front. Last night was no different than the lake. That is not correct;

it was different, actually. It was real gunfire. It was the closest he has come to war since he came back."

"What can I do? I have to help him. He can't live like this for the rest of his life." Agnes was desperate. It felt as though time was her enemy, and he was accelerating into the darkness.

"He didn't go to sleep until just after four. We talked until then. If Sam can spare him, he should sleep."

"Today is as good as any, I suppose."

"As good as any for what?" Percy asked.

"Nothing. I'm just talking to myself. Pa will make do for the day. Art can sleep. That will be the best thing for him. There is no sense letting this breakfast go to waste. Sit down. You'll eat, and then I will drive you home before Pa takes the truck to the shop."

Percy sat in silence as Agnes cooked. He too was exhausted, having only had a few hours' sleep. He had survived on less before, and he would make it through that day as well.

The smell of the cooking sausages brought on a wave of nausea that Agnes could no longer ignore. She did the calendar math in her head and could only come to one conclusion, and on that particular day that one conclusion brought her no joy.

"Aren't you going to eat?" Percy asked as Agnes sat down.

"No, I don't have much of an appetite. I'll eat later."

"How are things between you and my sister these days?" Agnes asked bluntly. The change of subject made Percy laugh.

"Agnes, I can always rely on you to forego niceties. You have a particular knack for it." Percy took another bite before continuing. "I doubt I need tell you anything. Isn't sharing what sisters do?"

"Yes, but she can only tell me what she knows, now can't she?" Agnes said slyly.

Percy let out a full belly laugh. "You have me there. I care for your sister very much. There, is that what you wanted to hear?" His perfunctory response drew her ire.

"Care for her deeply? Am I your pastor? You can do better than that, surely."

Percy continued to laugh. Agnes was always able to add sarcastic wit, however unintentional it was, to every conversation. He loved that about her.

"Do you love her?"

"You surely get right to the point, don't you?"

"You aren't going to escape this. I won't let you leave until you give me a straight up answer." Agnes was hell-bent on getting the truth from him.

Percy knew he was in a corner, and the only escape was an answer.

His only question was whether or not it should be a truthful one.

"You are exasperating, Agnes. I don't know how my brother puts up with you," Percy said tongue-in-cheek.

"Exasperating? You say that like it is a bad thing," Agnes said with a grin.

"OK. I surrender. Yes, I am in love with your sister. That is not news as I told her that myself last week."

Agnes was content, satisfied with the response and with herself.

Agnes retrieved the keys from the main house, dodging questions about the evening prior. They would know soon enough.

"I thought I heard your voice. Is everything all right?" Percy was the last person Mary expected to see that early in the morning.

Percy looked at Agnes, his eyes searching for permission to speak. They hadn't talked about reactions and repercussions, and he was trying to decide what, if anything, he should say.

"I woke up to this lump on my chesterfield this morning. It seems the boys were up a bit later than they should have been, chatting into the night like schoolgirls. Pa, if it is all right, I would like to drive Percy home before you take the truck to the shop. I'm going to let Art sleep a bit longer." Sam didn't ask why Art wasn't driving and Agnes didn't explain.

"Of course," Sam replied.

Agnes accomplished the day's deliveries herself under the guise of illness. As weak an explanation as it was, there was a dimension of truth to it. Tomorrow was another day, and she would worry about tomorrow then.

Agnes arrived home at half-past four. She was drained, her day spent mired in movement. Motion had been her ally, leaving her mind untethered and unquestioning.

Art was not home. His note was scribbled over Agnes's. *Agnes, I have gone to meet with Pete. I will be home shortly. Your loving husband.*

Agnes felt a weight lift from her. Her expectations for her return home had leaned toward the apprehensive, and she found herself revived. Art was out and about and moving forward. The fear she had felt for the change that lay before him was dissolving. It wasn't going to be merely a change; she saw it as a new beginning.

As she crumpled the note, the door opened. Art hesitated before he entered. He was on a ledge and he knew it. One wrong step and a loose stone could send him tumbling.

Agnes didn't wait for Art to settle. She ran to him and threw her arms around his neck, burying her face against him. Art exhaled the weight of the world and breathed in his wife, devouring her and kissing her with a ravenous appetite. Art carried Agnes to the bedroom, closing the door on all but the two of them.

Agnes fell asleep in the shadow of bliss. All felt right, the past suppressed under a tidal wave of passion, the future still safely beyond the bedroom door.

Art admired his wife as she lay next to him. He smiled to himself as he studied the curve of her cheekbone, the contour of her chin, her long and slender neck. She was a stunning woman, there was no doubt in his mind, but it was her spirit that had enchanted him so. It was indomitable and irrepressible, and it devastated him when she was troubled. And she had been lately, and he knew he was the cause.

There was a knock at the door, and Art slipped out of bed to keep from waking his sleeping wife. He quickly dressed and closed the bedroom door behind him.

"Tom! This is a surprise. Come in." Art stepped aside to let Tom in.

"You look like you just woke up. Did I disturb you?"

No, I was already awake. Agnes is still sleeping, though."

Tom grinned. "Ah, one of those naps. Those are the best kind," he said as he patted Art's shoulder.

"Can I get you a coffee? Tea?" Art asked.

"Thanks, but I can't stay. I just wanted to let you know the latest news. You must be curious."

"Curious … yes. I assumed I would read about it in the paper tomorrow. It must be really interesting if you came here to tell me yourself. Glad to see you are no worse for wear."

"McCurdy is dead. Died this morning. Uttley is bad. Doesn't look like he'll make it. Dineen was shot too. He could go either way."

"Pardon me. Did you say McCurdy was dead?" Art questioned, assuming he had misheard. He wasn't even aware that McCurdy had been there. Although, as he thought about it, it made sense that if his men were there he would have been as well.

"They had planned another raid at the hotel last night. I had no idea it was happening, clearly. Unfortunate timing on our part, I guess." Tom was trying to speak like a friend and not an officer, but it proved challenging for him. "McCurdy and Uttley were inspecting the upper floor when Dineen and the other two came into the restaurant. The gunman was in one of the rooms. McCurdy and his men were unarmed and they were taken by surprise. The gunman and another man escaped. They forced the owner of the hotel to drive them off."

Art thought back to the previous night, to the three men, the shouting, the speeding car. He had witnessed the getaway.

"I believe Percy and I saw them drive off."

"It is a good thing you didn't both find yourselves between them and their escape. They wouldn't have thought twice about shooting you."

"What about you?" Art asked. "There is no denying now that you were there. What will this do to you?"

Tom exhaled and shrugged his shoulders. "Not really sure. Time will tell. We weren't caught breaking any of their ridiculous laws so it will hopefully end there. And I'm thinking they probably have more to worry about than us right now. McCurdy just died. That won't sit too well."

But Tom couldn't help but worry because of the scrutiny that the department had faced in the past. He could easily be made into an example.

The bedroom door opened and Agnes walked out.

"I thought I heard your voice. How are you? I hear you all had quite an adventure last night." Agnes didn't let on how relieved she was to see him unharmed.

"Hello, Agnes. Yes, it was quite the evening. Sorry, I don't mean to run off, but I must get home. Art, I warn you, you may need to give a statement at some point if McCurdy's men bring up the card game. I certainly won't be bringing it up unsolicited. They didn't see me in the restaurant, and they haven't yet asked why I was there. The assumption was made that I was nearby when the shots were fired. I won't volunteer what they don't ask of me directly. And if they do ask, I will tell them you all left through the kitchen when the shots were fired and heard and saw nothing. That's the truth, but it may not be enough to satisfy them."

Within a few days, the Stockyards Hotel incident was common knowledge, not only in and around Norwood and St. Boniface but across the country. Fortunately, the activities of the restaurant that night remained in the restaurant, leaving reputations free of the sully the uninvited association would have brought. McCurdy's officers and the hotel owner provided the necessary details to determine the murderer's identity, and all efforts were funnelled into apprehending him.

There was little conversation around town that did not include mention of McCurdy. On Sunday, the pastor summoned prayers from the congregation for McCurdy's family, and a collection was undertaken to help them pay for funeral expenses. Even those who did not agree with McCurdy's politics and views on morality were hard-pressed to feel anything other than stunned and saddened at the death of one of their own. They also prayed for Uttley and Dineen, both of whom still remained in hospital.

"We cannot let the unfathomable actions of a single wayward soul dampen our spirit. Evil will attempt to bring us down, but we will not let it. This is a challenge that we can and will rise up against. We are strong. We are unified in our faith in God and our unshakable belief in God's grace. We do not always understand God's will, but we are ever steadfast in the knowledge that it is as it should be." The words of the pastor were what the congregation needed, a soothing remedy for their battered and weakened spirits.

Agnes, Mary, and Margaret were all in agreement that their mother and Sam need not know of the location of the card game that night. It would only raise questions and concerns, and there was already ample worry to fill their minds.

"It looks like they have a pretty good idea of who McCurdy's killer is. They believe he was also responsible for a bank robbery in Winkler last month. He sounds like a man with a dark soul. Men like that don't change. Let's hope he is caught before he can hurt anyone else—and far away from here." Sam spoke of the incident, his voice filled with repugnance for the man and his actions. Sam was a forgiving man, but he knew forgiveness only helped those who had a mind to change.

"The paper said that McCurdy had reason to believe there was alcohol on the premises again. He sent his men in to inspect the lower level while he assessed the rooms. The shooter was supposedly found in a state of undress with a hotel chambermaid. He gave them privacy to dress and that decency cost him his life."

Other than Sam, the men had remained quiet. But John could remain quiet no longer.

"Yes, I agree it was decent that he didn't place them in handcuffs while they remained in a state of impropriety, but it is the very definition of impropriety that precipitated this incident to begin with. What is impropriety and who decides it is so? Certainly not the average man. It should be between man and God, not the Manitoba Provincial Police. Who decides it is improper to drink alcohol or cavort with the chambermaid?"

Margaret placed her hand on her husband's arm to attempt to calm him down. It wasn't that she didn't agree with him; she simply didn't want to see him further agitated, especially considering what they were about to reveal.

"Margaret and I have something we would like to share with you all," John said.

The revelation piqued everyone's interest and lead to misplaced assumptions and speculations.

"Margaret, the girls, and I are moving to Vancouver."

The women's faces dropped, but none more than Sarah's. The eagerness for another child was blasted from the room.

"Moving? Vancouver? Why?" Sarah asked in disbelief.

"We have had a persistent offer on the restaurant for a year or so, and it has become too good to pass up. We are going to start over there."

"But why?" That still didn't answer Sarah's question. She couldn't fathom what would have effected such a decision.

"McCurdy and his men have made it very difficult to do business in this town. McCurdy is gone, God rest his soul, but his men will now have something to prove. It wasn't good for us before and it will only be worse now. As for British Columbia, aside from the better climate and the sea, the repudiation of Prohibition is in the works there. That can only be good for business."

"When?" Sarah could still not form a full sentence for her shock had gotten the best of her.

"The paperwork will be completed in a month's time, and we will leave immediately after that."

Mary and Agnes too were saddened at the thought of them leaving, but for them it had the makings of a fantastic adventure and that overruled the loss.

John seemed genuinely happy, but Agnes could see a hint of sadness in Margaret's eyes. Silence fell upon the room and the air became thick.

"Art and I too have something to share." All eyes shifted from Margaret and John to Agnes and Art.

"Art has decided to join Pete McNally's company and learn the painting trade. And I will be managing the shop's deliveries for a few months, until Art gets his bearings. It will give me something useful to do. Art can only eat so many casseroles," Agnes joked.

Sarah and Sam were not surprised. The others, and most ostensibly Percy, were. Agnes could see the look of concern on Percy's face as he studied his brother, and she could read his mind; he was fearful of the uncertainty that such a dramatic change would have on Art. Agnes understood Percy's concern and deep down she felt it as well, but she instead buried it.

"This has been quite the day for news. Congratulations are in order," Mary said as she hugged her sisters and brothers-in-law.

Sarah could endure the separation of her daughter, but the thought of her two granddaughters being fifteen hundred miles away was more than she could bear. She would miss seeing them grow up, their energy, their mischievous grins. There would be no more hugs, no more kisses, and no more grandmotherly advice. But it was not her decision to make.

Chapter 15

Tuesday brought news of James Uttley's death. He had managed to live five more days. Before he died, he gave a detailed accounting of what had happened in room number eight that night, and the police now had a good idea of whom they were looking for. The pursued was now the killer of two men, not one, and a reward of $2,500 was announced for his capture—dead or alive. Dineen was still alive and expected to stay so.

"It is a good thing you are painting indoors. It is only supposed to get to minus eighteen today."

"Even if I could tolerate the cold, the paint could not."

"You didn't sleep well last night." Agnes refrained from saying "again."

Art was well aware of his restless night, and he had finally come to the realization that his issue would not resolve itself. He was tired and growing increasingly so, and his ability to function properly was becoming impaired.

"Sorry if I kept you up. It is simply the transition. I will get the rhythm of it. I'll be sleeping like a baby before the week is out," he said with a smile. Agnes smiled back, hoping all hope that he was right.

"Well, I must be off, my love. I must catch the streetcar in ten minutes time or I will be late."

Art gathered what he needed, dressed for the frigid weather, and was off. As he closed the door behind him, Agnes ran to the toilet and retched. It had taken incredible focus and resolve to maintain her composure as she sat with Art, and once he was gone there was no need to restrain herself any longer. She rested in front of the toilet, on her knees, her hands grasping the cold porcelain. She would endure. She knew she must.

The day had been an exceptionally busy one for the shop. There were more deliveries than usual, and Agnes was kept out later than she normally would be. But despite the late hour, Art was not yet there. He had arrived home at four the day prior, and it was his understanding that this was to be the schedule. Earlier start and earlier finish. Agnes was curious as to why he was not home, but she was not yet worried.

Twenty minutes after she arrived, Art walked through the door. He was cheerful, and he embraced his wife as he always did.

"How was your day?" Agnes asked as she took Art's coat.

"Quite good, actually. I think I might have a knack for painting. I'm enjoying the preciseness of it all. How was your day?"

"Busy. With the cold weather, nobody seems to want to go out. It was deliveries all day. Pa said the shop was quite quiet. Was there a delay at work? You were later than yesterday."

Art looked down at his feet as he answered. "Ah … no delay. Just a small errand to run. What's for dinner? I am famished." He changed the subject abruptly, but she didn't press for more. She didn't have the energy.

"Pa's roasted chicken. I'm too tired to cook." Agnes looked apologetically at her husband and his guilt choked him.

"Come, sit down," he said, leading his wife to the chesterfield.

Agnes sat down as she was told, and then Art took her feet in his hands and swung her legs around so that they rested on his lap.

"Lay that beautiful head of yours down and relax. We are in no rush to eat."

Art began to massage Agnes's feet, gently pressing his thumb into the ball of her foot as he rubbed all the stress away. As his hands moved to the back of her calf, her quiet, contented murmur grew louder, more emphatic. Art looked at his wife, her eyes closed and her face relaxed and blissful, and it fully occurred to him how much she much she must love him, how much she endured for him. She deserved so much better, and he was determined to give it all to her.

Soon her humming turned to a soft snore. Art gently lifted her feet off his lap and slipped out from under them. Agnes had bought all that was needed for dinner, and he placed the food on the table. He arranged two settings and then lit the candles, turning off the kitchen light before he walked over to his sleeping wife.

He bent down and kissed her cheek and then her forehead. He kissed her gently over and over, covering her face until she opened her eyes. She strained to adjust her vision to the dark and to the closeness of her husband's face. It only took a moment before she saw him clearly and she smiled.

"How long was I sleeping?" she asked.

"Not as long as you deserve, but long enough for me to get dinner ready."

Agnes sat up and saw the candlelit table and gasped.

"How thoughtful you are, Mr. Craig. First, your magical hands and now this. You are spoiling me."

"I have not yet begun," he said as he winked.

Art pulled out Agnes's seat and pushed her in. There was nothing for her to do but relax. Her nausea had abated as the day wore on, and it was a welcome relief that she did not have to mask the discomfort. Instead she devoured her dinner as though she hadn't eaten all day, which was closer to the truth than it was not. Art was contented as he watched his wife.

"The last time I saw you eat like that, you were expecting," he said with a hint of glimmer in his eyes.

Agnes choked on her mouthful and coughed to clear her airway.

"Are you all right?" Art asked, concerned.

"My bite went down the wrong way. I'm fine. I was busy today and skipped lunch. I guess I am hungrier than I realized."

Agnes had not yet had a doctor confirm her pregnancy, but her altered cycle and ample nausea had all but confirmed it for her. The pain of her previous losses was still sharp in her mind, and she would not allow herself to get caught up in a whirlwind of anticipation only to become disappointed again ... and heaven forbid, disappoint her husband. She could not bear that look on his face again, and she vowed she would never be the cause of it.

As the evening wound down, Agnes prepared for bed and the usual affections that greeted her. Art was never as sleepy as she was, and his bedtime disposition was usually more amorous than her own. Despite wanting nothing more than to go to sleep, she always indulged her husband. But on this night, he seemed more sedate than usual. He kissed his wife, said his good nights, and rolled over toward sleep.

In the morning, Agnes awoke with an altered sense of herself. It was the first solid night of sleep she had had in ages. Art's usual insomnia had not kept her awake, and she knew she had either slept too soundly to notice or he too had slept.

Agnes rolled over to find the bed beside her empty. As she fought to gain her senses, she could hear the sound of running water. Art was never out of bed before she was. Never. But as astonishing as that was to her, it was the cheerful whistling that was most astonishing. It wouldn't have seemed out of place at any other time, but it most definitely did at the crack of dawn.

"Good morning, my darling wife," Art said as he kissed her. "'Tis a fine morning. How did you sleep?"

Agnes didn't respond. She couldn't form the words. But Art didn't seem to notice. He was lost in his good cheer.

"Are you not sitting down to breakfast?" Art asked as Agnes continued to mill around the kitchen.

"I must have overindulged at dinner. I have no appetite." The lie was only a partial lie. It was true she had no appetite, but not for any reason that occurred to Art.

"You'll not guess where we are working today," Art prodded.

Agnes was focused on her nausea and did not hear him.

"Agnes, darling, are you all right? You seem preoccupied."

"Perfectly fine. What were you saying?"

"We are painting the dining room at The Fort Garry. If you have a break in your deliveries, perhaps you could come and we could visit 'our' room again," he said with a grin. "That might be fun."

"You think of nothing else, do you?"

He laughed. "Perhaps if I was married to someone less desirable, other thoughts could occupy my mind, but, alas, your allure proves too strong for me to resist and I am drawn to you like a moth to a flame."

Agnes rolled her eyes at his shameless and self-serving compliment. It was no surprise to her that men thought with their loins as well as their brains, but it was always a surprise just how unbalanced it truly was.

"I am going to stop in and visit with Janie at the end of the day. I might be a few minutes late."

"Give that goddaughter of ours a kiss for me."

Agnes was more than happy to. "I will."

Art left and Agnes sat down on the chesterfield as she tried to regain her equilibrium. She was overcome by the constancy of the debility, the exhaustion, the discomfort. It felt far worse than her previous experiences, and she was sure it would lead to no good.

Agnes endured the day yet again, relishing the passing of time and looking forward to the end of the day. The feeling of unwell did diminish as the day progressed, but it never left entirely.

"Look Elizabeth, Aunty Agnes is here." Janie passed over her daughter as Agnes held out her hands.

Agnes buried her face in Elizabeth's neck, inhaling until her lungs could hold no more. Her smell was sublime.

"She is getting so big."

"I don't notice it as much because I see her every day, but she is growing out of her clothes quickly so I know she must be."

Agnes lay Elizabeth down on the chesterfield and stroked her head. Her hair was as soft as silk under Agnes's hand. As Agnes continued to lavish Elizabeth with affection, the sweet child smiled up at her.

"Did you see that? She smiled at me!" Agnes was awestruck.

"She has been doing that for a few weeks, but it has only been a few days since they started to look like real smiles, you know, the happy kind. When she looks at me with that gummy grin, I just melt. I think she knows she has me under her spell," Janie said with a laugh.

"I haven't seen you since it happened. How is Tom? Have there been any repercussions at work?"

Janie shook her head. "No, none at all. The Provincial Police have actually recommended a commendation for Tom's support after the shooting. They say his actions helped save Dineen's life. I don't want to question our good fortune; it could have turned out much differently, and I shudder to think how differently."

Agnes looked at Janie with admiration. She was not sure she could dismiss it so easily. *She hadn't* dismissed it so easily. Her worry had devoured her. It still devoured her. It devoured her at every turn.

"Are you feeling all right? You look a bit off today," Janie wondered.

Agnes wanted desperately to confide in Janie, but she could not. She would not.

"Perfectly fine. Just had a busy day. Many deliveries." Agnes gave Janie no reason to think otherwise.

"I love Elizabeth with all my heart, but I do miss the freedom to come and go as I please. At times I envy that in you."

Agnes was free to take Janie's words any which way she chose to. Her brain was tired and she chose to give them no thought; it was just easier that way.

"I learned something troubling today."

Janie waited for Agnes to acknowledge. Agnes looked up from the baby and locked eyes with her. Janie's face twisted slightly and Agnes stiffened.

"I heard from my cousin in Saskatoon this morning. She knows the sister of the man who killed my father...."

"Jasper Flincher," Agnes added coldly. She too would never forget that name.

"Yes, that's his name. His sister knows I live in Winnipeg now and wanted to warn my cousin that Jasper has recently moved here. Jasper and his sister are estranged. I don't know where he is exactly. But here, somewhere. What if I run into him, Agnes? I think I would fall apart."

Agnes could see the fear in Janie's eyes, but she did not feel it. She only felt anger. Intense anger.

"If it is true, I do not think you should be worried. He is probably in Winnipeg and not this side of the river. Winnipeg is a big city, and I doubt you would travel in the same circles as he would anyways. And even if you did come face to face, he could do nothing to you. He can't hurt you anymore. I would hazard he would be more threatened by you than you by him."

Janie let that sink in and then she grinned. "You are very wise, Agnes, and you are right."

"Do not give him any power over you. He doesn't deserve your worry. He is a reprobate of the lowest kind. Even if he doesn't live out his remaining days mired in guilt for what he has done, he will face his judgement before God in the end. I know that warms *my* heart," Agnes affirmed.

Janie smiled back before nodding in agreement.

"You have to look no further than this perfect child. Every breath, every step of your life, whether they have been within your power or not, has brought you to this moment. You cannot live with regret or fear or sadness. You can only cherish what you have."

Janie's eyes began to well up as she nodded again. Agnes's words hit their intended mark, and the guilt and the blame that Janie had long held onto began to loosen.

"I have my husband and my child and I am grateful to God for them both, but I am as grateful to God for you."

It was Agnes's turn to tear up. Oh, how adept she was at dishing out advice, yet so unable to live by her own words. She was a hypocrite and she knew it.

Chapter 16

"Margaret, I will miss you so. How can you leave us?" Agnes was distraught at the thought of her sister moving so far away.

Margaret embraced her sister tightly and Agnes winced. Her chest burned with the pressure.

"What is the matter? Why did you flinch?" Margaret asked, worried.

Margaret tried to remain emotionless, but it proved futile. There was too much going on and she couldn't hide it from her sister.

"Nothing is the matter. I am simply sad to see you go."

"That is hogwash and you know it. Don't treat me like a fool." Margaret knew she had little time, and she was not about to spend it in a circular argument.

Agnes's thoughts raced in her head. She could choose to be stubborn and let her sister leave in a state, or she could tell her the truth and let her leave contented. Agnes could see Margaret didn't want to go, and she wouldn't be responsible for making the sadness of her departure worse.

Agnes looked around to ensure there was no one within earshot.

"Please keep this to yourself. I cannot bear the thought of disappointing my husband or Mum again. I am expecting."

Margaret looked at Agnes to make sure she heard her properly. Agnes's intense gaze was confirmation enough. Margaret knew as well as anybody the pain in failed pregnancy, and she was not about to turn the revelation into a spectacle. She simply embraced her sister as gently as she could and whispered her good wishes in her sister's ear.

"Your secret is safe with me."

"Thank you, Margaret. I have not told anyone but you."

Margaret felt bad for her sister's compulsion for temperance, but she understood it. She also knew the reality of the situation would reveal itself before long. Few secrets could be held onto forever.

"Your secret will go with me to Vancouver. Nobody will hear it from my lips. I promise."

Agnes was still in disbelief that they were leaving. Vancouver was a long way away ... fourteen hundred miles and three provinces. It might as well have been back to England for the distance it would be.

"Perhaps you will come and visit," Margaret hoped.

"Perhaps. It is a long way to go for a visit." Agnes knew that meant the likelihood of seeing her sister in the foreseeable future was slim. Agnes was sad for it, but she would not let her sadness add to her sister's; it was clear that Margaret didn't want to leave.

As Margaret went to talk to Sarah, Percy seized the opportunity he had been waiting for and made his way over to Agnes.

"I'm honoured. You broke away from Mary to come talk to me. It must be important," she teased.

Agnes could tell from the look on Percy's face that it wasn't time for humour.

"It has been a few weeks. How is the new career going? How is Art faring?" Percy's tone was probing, not the usual congenial chitchat.

Agnes turned and looked at her brother-in-law and wondered if he knew something that she did not. His expression convinced her otherwise and she relaxed again.

"Quite good, actually. I was worried about the transition. His sleep had been so sporadic. And his reactions ... well, you have seen his reactions. He seems to be enjoying the work, and he is sleeping better than he has since we have been married."

Agnes could see the disbelief in his eyes. Agnes did not demur; she simply continued to smile, and then she changed the subject.

"How is my sister? I do not see much of her these days."

"Is that blame or congratulations? I cannot tell." Percy laughed. "Your sister is well, as am I. *We* are well. Are you satisfied?"

Before Agnes could respond, Mary joined them.

"Were your ears burning?" Agnes asked her sister. "Percy was just telling me how good you are." Mary blushed and Agnes walked away smugly.

"What's new with my brother?" Art asked the next morning at breakfast. "I haven't seen hide nor hair of him for weeks. You and he seemed quite engaged in conversation yesterday. What subject was so engaging?"

"I said that same thing to him about Mary. They seem to be seeing quite a lot of each other so I assume things are progressing nicely. He is always so secretive. Must be the allure." Agnes managed to answer his question without really answering his question.

"I still cannot believe that Margaret and John are leaving today. I wish they would have waited to see how things played out. If things are changing in British Columbia, I can't imagine they will stay the same here. That is a long way to go, and to take my nieces."

Art was disappointed to see them leave as well, but he was less optimistic than Agnes that things would change.

"Where are you today?" Agnes asked.

"We are at the new Legislative Building for the better part of a month. It is an impressive building. They do tours for the public. You might like to see it sometime."

"It seems the buildings keep getting bigger and grander. I don't know how they can continue to outdo each other."

"Off I go or else I'll be late. 'Til we meet again tonight," he said as he planted a long and lingering kiss on her mouth.

Agnes's pregnancy nausea was not abating, and if anything, was growing more severe. But she was growing accustomed to managing it in full view. After she ate a piece of plain toast, she left for the day. Sam was waiting for her at the house.

"Good morning," Sam said in his usual cheerful manner.

"Good morning, Pa. Ready to go?"

"Joanna's husband stopped by this morning. She is ill and won't be able to work. Today is our light delivery day. Could you work the counter when you are done? It would be a big help. I have a truckload coming from the abattoir today and won't be able to manage the front."

"Of course. I'll stay as long as you need me."

"That's my girl."

The truth was Agnes couldn't say no to Sam for anything. He had always been there for her, and she would be there for him no matter what.

The sky was clear and the air entirely frigid that morning. The temperature had hovered just below freezing for the opening of December but then dropped dramatically. It was now inching its way downward toward the darkest of winter.

Snowploughed streets and shovelled walks continued on as far as the eye could see. Agnes enjoyed the beauty of the snow, the stretches of pure white, untouched, and it made the cold almost bearable. Almost, but not nearly enough. Today wasn't as cold as it could be, as cold as it would still get, but it was still painfully so. Agnes's fingers burned with the numbness, and she found relief from the car's bonnet, which gave off enough heat to warm her hands through her gloves.

Mrs. Donnelly had been kind enough to wrap up two fresh baked muffins for Agnes. They were still warm, and Agnes removed her gloves and wrapped her hands around them. As she pulled the covering, the smell wafted up to her nose and she turned her head and tightened her lips. She wrapped the muffins back up tightly and placed them on the seat beside her.

Agnes finished her deliveries by noon and made her way back to the shop. Sam was in the back processing what had just been received from the abattoir, and he looked relieved to see Agnes.

"Good, you are back. It has been challenging managing both."

The bell on the front door chimed as a customer entered and Sam did not hold back his relief.

Agnes walked out to the front and greeted the customer.

"Mrs. Anderson, how are you today?"

"Just fine. Thank you. What do you recommend today, Agnes?"

Mrs. Anderson had been a customer for many years. She always came at precisely the same time on Mondays and Wednesdays each week. Many of Sam's customers were like that.

"Sam is preparing the beef and veal as we speak. The chicken and pork are fresh and look quite good. We have some delicious pork loin roasts, if that is of interest."

"That sounds wonderful. I haven't cooked Mr. Anderson a pork loin roast in a long while. I'm certain he would fancy it. And one chicken as well. A bit on the larger side, if you could. My daughter and the grandchildren are coming for dinner tomorrow."

"How nice. How is Caroline?"

Agnes and Caroline were the same age. "Very well. She is expecting again. This will be her third. And you? Any plans for little ones?"

Agnes didn't respond to the question directly. She only offered her congratulations in response. She packaged up Mrs. Anderson's purchase and promptly moved on to the next customer.

"What can I do for you today, Mrs. McGregor?"

"Hello, Agnes. I overheard you tell Mrs. Anderson that the beef was not quite ready. How long will it be?"

"Please tell me what you need. I'll see if Sam can prepare something for you right now."

"No need. I don't want to rush him. I'll take some chicken today if I can have a sirloin roast delivered tomorrow. I don't need it until then so that will be perfectly fine."

"Absolutely. I can bring it over first thing. Is there anything else you need?"

Sam's customers were loyal. They appreciated his level of service as much as the quality of his meats. So many vendors were beginning to charge for their delivery service, or worse, cancel it altogether. But not Sam. He had always put his customer's satisfaction above his pocketbook.

At the end of the day, Agnes locked up the shop. Sam finished his last cut and removed his apron, which was completely soaked red.

"Your mother will have my head for this apron."

Agnes laughed. "I imagine she will."

Agnes's exhaustion had the best of her by day's end and she could barely make it up the stairs to her front door. Art was already inside, and to Agnes's surprise had the table set for dinner.

Agnes's heart sank at the sight. She wanted only to crawl into bed and go to sleep.

"I'm sorry. I have not prepared dinner. Sam needed me at the shop, and I have not had time to prepare anything. All I can make you is a sandwich."

Art looked sorrowfully at his weakened wife. He felt entirely responsible for her state.

"Not to worry, my love. Dinner is taken care of."

Agnes was taken aback. "Did you cook?"

Art laughed. "No, I wouldn't do that to you. Sam called your mother and told her you were working later than usual. She took pity on us and brought us some beef stew."

"Oh, thank you, Mum," Agnes said toward the door.

"Here, sit down." Art said as he pulled out a chair. "I will warm the stew. You can tell me about your day."

"Joanna was ill today so I helped Sam with the customers after the deliveries were done. Nothing too fantastic, just steady busy."

Art placed the pot on the table and spooned the stew onto Agnes's plate. Agnes was even too tired to say thank you. It wasn't the usual "I've had a difficult day" tired, but an "I've been drained of every ounce of energy I have and there is nothing left" tired. Her limbs felt as heavy as tree trunks, and her shoulders felt as though they carried the weight of the world.

Agnes picked at her food and did not notice Art studying her.

"What is wrong? You are not yourself. And please do not tell me you are tired because you had a busy day. You have had busier, and I have never seen you so lacking in energy. Are you feeling unwell? You look as though life has been drained from you."

Agnes was ashamed she was holding back from her husband, but she felt justified in her actions. As she thought of what to say, she felt a mild flutter in her belly, and the look on her face gave her away.

"What is it? What are you not telling me?" Agnes could feel Art's concern, but she was still not ready to reveal the truth. So much could still go wrong.

"I am just tired. I know that is a boring answer, but it is the truth."

"Then bed it is for you right after dinner. You need your rest. And you need to tell Sam that you are finished at the shop. Painting is going well and I will stick at it. We don't need you to work. I can provide for us."

Agnes shook her head. "You agreed to a few months. It has been barely one. Let's discuss it again after Christmas. We'll see how we are getting on then."

Art agreed, but only did so because he told himself he would force the issue if he felt it was necessary. It had been a trying month—the shooting,

Margaret leaving, the effort of back to work. He was hopeful a few good nights' sleep would be just what she needed.

Agnes lay down after dinner and did not wake until the morning. She did not move; she did not stir. She relinquished control of her body and mind, and nothing but time would bring her back from the deep and nourishing sleep she succumbed to.

"You are looking refreshed. How are you feeling?" Art asked.

"Much better. I don't recall ever being that tired. It crept up on me. How did you sleep?" Agnes couldn't remember the last time Art's restlessness kept her awake.

"Like a baby, just like you." Agnes cringed at the irony of the comment.

The morning was as cold as the day prior, and Agnes's lungs burned as she breathed in the frosty air. There were only a handful of deliveries to make and with Joanna back at work, there was no need for Agnes to stay beyond. Thinking of her chesterfield and a book was all that would get her through the morning.

There was no relief from the cold. The cab of the truck was open to the elements, and it seemed whichever direction she was driving a steady wind would blow across her and envelope her in a whirl of wintry air. But there was one saving grace and it was a welcome one ... the cold air also helped numb the nausea.

"Agnes, please come in for a cup of coffee. You look like you need a good thaw."

"Thank you, Mrs. Brown, but I must keep on schedule. I truly appreciate your offer."

Mrs. Brown looked sympathetically at Agnes as she stood all bundled up, barely room to breathe for the scarf and hat that sheltered her face. One more delivery and Agnes would be done.

Agnes knocked on Mrs. McGregor's door, but there was no answer. Agnes continued to knock until she felt sure there was nobody home. Agnes had suggested she would be there first thing in the morning, and she hoped she hadn't left Mrs. McGregor waiting. Sam would have to try later in the day.

As Agnes approached the yard gate, Mrs. McGregor's front door opened. Agnes turned to see a man standing there. He looked as though he had just woken up.

"I'm terribly sorry if I disturbed you," Agnes said apologetically. "Is Mrs. McGregor home?"

"She had an error to run."

"I have her meat delivery. Can you accept it for her?" Agnes didn't recognize the man. It wasn't her husband.

"Sure," he said as he held out his hands.

"Please sign your name here, beside Mrs. McGregor's name," Agnes said as she held out her board.

The warm air emanating from the house felt good on Agnes's face, and she found herself wishing she was at home.

The man passed the board back. "Thank you, Mr...." Agnes said as she looked at the board. "Flincher," she said, the name barely escaping from her mouth. The name said "J. Flincher."

"Are you all right?" he asked.

Agnes was momentarily paralyzed. *Could the J. be Jasper?* She wondered if this could be the man whom Janie spoke of, the man responsible for such heinous acts against Janie and her father.

"I ... I'm fine." Agnes took the board back and walked down the steps. She stumbled on the bottom one but caught herself before she fell.

"Are you sure you are all right?" he asked again.

"Yes, thank you." Agnes scurried back to the truck, her heart in her throat.

Is this the man? Agnes felt ill, and not the persistent ill that had plagued her but a dreading, foreboding ill that wholly incapacitated her. Thoughts raced through her mind. How would she find out if this was the man? Should she tell Janie? So many questions and she had no answers.

Agnes regained her composure and began the short drive back to the shop. But she could not turn off the thoughts that continued to race through her mind and her diverted attention proved calamitous.

The delivery truck veered off to the side of the road and squarely hit a car which had been parked against the curb. The impact sent Agnes's head hard into the steering wheel, and the blow rendered her unconscious.

The sound of the impact brought people into the street. Steam billowed from the seams in the truck's bonnet, which had buckled like an accordion. A passerby lifted Agnes off the steering wheel and gently leaned her back against the seat. She had a gash across her forehead that was red with blood.

"Miss, are you all right? Miss?" The man gently shook Agnes's shoulder.

Agnes opened her eyes and looked at the man blankly. Slowly the fogginess began to fade, and she came to the realization that she had been in an accident. She began to panic. The kind stranger kept his hand on her shoulder in an attempt to calm her down, but it was futile.

The pain in her forehead was numbed by the cold air, but she could feel the warm blood oozing from the wound. She raised her gloved hand to her forehead and then brought it in front of her face. It was wet with blood, but that was not what had her worried. *The baby. What have I done?*

Through the steam, Agnes could see Sam running toward her. A witness had gone to the shop, which was only a block away, to retrieve him.

"Agnes, my God, are you all right? What happened?" Sam was clearly distraught.

"I'm fine. Just a little bump on the forehead. Nothing to worry about," she said with a half-laugh as she tried to lessen Sam's concern.

"I think it is more than a little bump. We need to get you to the hospital."

Sam's words were no sooner past his lips when an ambulance pulled up beside the truck. Sam stepped aside to let the attendant take a look at Agnes.

"She needs to go to the hospital," Sam said.

Sam waited patiently as the attendant looked Agnes over, checking her gash and her pupils.

"She does need to be addressed by a doctor. Her gash needs stitches and she may have a concussion."

"I do not need an ambulance." Agnes felt silly with all the fuss. "It is only a few blocks. Pa, you can drive me."

"Agnes, you will go in the ambulance. I will not hear another word about it." It was rare for Sam to raise his voice and it took Agnes by surprise. "I'll get the car and will bring your mother to the hospital."

The driver and attendant helped Agnes into the back of the ambulance as Agnes's cheeks burned with embarrassment. As she lay on the stretcher, her hand rested on her belly. She would never forgive herself, she thought, and then the tears started to flow.

Chapter 17

Agnes attempted to sit up when her mother entered the room, but she was promptly scolded by the doctor.

"Doctor, how is she?" Sarah asked.

"We have sewn up the gash in her forehead and she has a slight concussion. Most of the damage appears to have come out in the large bump on her forehead, which is good. When there is no bump, it is worrisome; it generally means more internal damage, a more significant concussion. She will be no worse for wear within a day or so. Perhaps a lingering headache ... certainly no lasting damage. It appears there was no abdominal impact so the baby should not be affected."

Sarah's mouth opened widely. She couldn't possibly have heard what she thought she heard.

"I'm sorry, did you say baby?" she asked, stupefied.

Agnes had braced herself for the onslaught, and it appeared it was about to begin.

"Yes, I believe your daughter's pregnancy should not be affected. She will need rest, but beyond that I anticipate no additional course of treatment."

The doctor excused himself, leaving Sarah and Sam alone with Agnes. Sarah's eyes descended upon her daughter. They silently questioned her, begging for an answer, but Sarah only saw sadness and fear in her daughter.

"A baby? Why didn't you tell us?" Sarah said as she embraced her daughter.

Agnes didn't answer her mother, but it didn't matter. Sarah knew. She also knew she would have done the same thing, given the circumstance, so she couldn't condemn her daughter for keeping it from her.

"Does Art know?"

Agnes continued her silence, her hard façade now cracked under the weight of her secret. It was no longer reticence. Her silence was now born of shame.

"Oh, dear," was all Sarah could say.

"Where is Art today? I will go get him and bring him to you," Sam said.

"No, no, he cannot leave work early. He has not been there long enough to have earned that right. He will be back home in two hours. You can tell him I am here then."

Sam didn't agree, but he chose not to argue. He didn't want to add to the anxiety that was already plaguing her. He wasn't so sure Art would be able to manage the same restraint. And he felt whichever reaction Art found himself in the middle of, he would be entirely justified in it.

"How far along are you?" Sarah asked. She was concerned for her daughter.

"I'm not sure exactly. About ten weeks I think." Agnes spoke with a diffidence that bespoke her shame.

"My goodness. That is such a long time to keep it to yourself." Sarah said, trying hard not to judge. "How are you feeling? How have you been feeling?"

Sarah's question appeared to brighten Agnes. The guilt she felt for keeping such a secret was overshadowed by the relief she felt for it being made known.

"I have had horrendous nausea. It has mostly been in the morning, but some days it goes on right into the night. And I have been very tired. I didn't imagine it was possible to be so tired."

"These are all good signs. The more profound the sickness, the healthier the baby. That is how I was with you. I was dreadfully ill for the first few months, and you came into this world with the strongest of constitutions. I would hazard a guess that you are going to be giving me another granddaughter."

Her mother's presence and words of reassurance began to transform her dread, dread for what she had felt would be the inevitable outcome, into a glimmer of excitement and joy. The baby she carried appeared to be progressing as it should and maybe, just maybe, she would have the child she longed for.

"Your brothers will be arriving home from school shortly so I must go. Sam will bring Art here as soon as he gets home."

"Thank you, Mum."

"Pa, I am so sorry about the truck. What will you do for deliveries? I caused this mess, and I will have to try and fix it. Perhaps I can just walk them. Your customers really aren't spread that far."

Sam laughed. "I have insurance for just such calamities. If the truck can be repaired, the garage will provide one on loan. If it cannot, then the insurance company will provide a replacement. As for what will happen in the meantime, it will all work itself out. We will have to file an accident report with the police for the insurance. They will want to know what happened."

Sam's words forced Agnes back to the accident and her encounter with Mr. Flincher. It was the sole reason for her distraction behind the wheel. How was she going to explain that? She was not yet sure she would.

"I understand. I will speak with them whenever they need me to."

Sarah and Sam kissed their daughter and departed for home. Sarah felt uneasy leaving her, but she knew Art would join her soon, and that was a meeting that was best left to the two of them.

Agnes lay on the bed, staring at the same dotted ceiling she stared at when the doctor told her she had lost her baby. The excitement of this child was growing, but it was still tempered by the dread of loss. Until the child was born, she knew she could not fully release herself of the burden of worry.

Agnes's head pounded like a drum. The doctor had given her something for the pain, but it had little effect. She ran her fingers over the gauze, tracing the tape at its edge. How she wished she could reverse the day. How she wished she could have gone to Mrs. McGregor's in the morning. The knowledge she was now burdened with was a heavy weight, and she didn't know how best to deal with it. If this was the man, he was only living two streets over from Janie. If she told Janie, Janie would be devastated, but if she didn't and Janie came upon him unexpectedly, it would be far worse. The only positive outcome was that Janie knew nothing and good fortune kept Jasper Flincher away.

The door opened and Art walked in. He looked harried and distraught, as though he had run the entire distance to the hospital.

"What happened? Are you all right?" Art desperately looked for answers.

"I am fine. A couple of stitches and just a bit of a headache. Silly me. I must have hit a slippery patch. I ran into a parked car. It looks worse than it is. I assure you there is more damage to the truck than there is to me."

Art embraced his wife tightly, and Agnes moaned as the drumbeat in her head crescendoed. Art pulled back abruptly, concerned there was more that Agnes was not telling him.

"You don't seem fine to me. Perhaps I should find a doctor."

"No, I'm fine, Art, really. Just a headache. The doctor said that I can leave in a few hours. I have a mild concussion, but the doctor said he is happy with my condition. No need for worry."

"No need for worry? How do I not worry? My wife is lying on a hospital bed after being in an accident. That qualifies me to worry." He believed his wife was fine, but the shock of it all still left him on edge.

Agnes knew she would have to tell Art about the baby before the doctor did. She had faced her mother's reaction, and now she had to face her husband's. The doctor could come in at any moment, and Art would inevitably ask questions. She knew she must do it now.

"I do have news, tremendous news." Agnes forced a smile.

Art looked at his wife inquisitively. He recognized that smile. Generally no good came from it.

"We are expecting a baby," she said. She waited for his response before she continued. She didn't have to wait long.

"A baby? Really?" She was relieved to see his excitement. He wore it all over his face. "Did the doctor just tell you? How far along are you?"

A lump formed in Agnes's throat and she couldn't swallow. She knew what was to come and there was no way around it.

"Yes, the doctor just confirmed. I am about ten weeks now."

"Ten weeks? Shouldn't you have known before now? That seems like such a long time." Art was bewildered.

Agnes knew the questions wouldn't stop and she couldn't lie.

"Yes, I knew."

"What do you mean you knew?" This made no sense to Art.

"I suspected, but it wasn't confirmed until now."

"Suspected? If you suspected, why didn't you go to the doctor? Why didn't you tell me? After ten weeks, I would imagine your suspicions would be more than just suspicions." Art's thoughts turned to the accident and dread engulfed him. "The accident. Is the baby all right?"

"The doctor doesn't anticipate any issues, aside from my history. There was no impact anywhere other than my head."

Art looked slightly relieved. "You still didn't answer my question. Why did you not visit a doctor?"

Agnes hesitated answering because she had no doubt what his reaction would be.

"Because of the last two times. I didn't want to see you get excited only to have to disappoint you again. I couldn't bear your disappointment again."

"Last *two* times?"

Agnes realized what she had said and didn't want to have more to explain.

"I meant the last time."

Art's cheeks reddened as he squinted his eyes. He focused on his wife as she lay in the bed and all he could see was deceit. His blood boiled.

"Do I not deserve to share in my wife's pain as well as her joy? Is that not my right? I am your husband and you promised me that. Omission or deceit, Agnes, they are one and the same!"

Agnes's tears had no effect on Art for he was blinded by his anger. He was astonished that she could have kept this from him. But time brought clarity, and as his thoughts began to settle, so did his anger. He was going to be a father and that was a thrilling prospect for him. While he didn't understand her actions, he conceded that they were done out of love.

Agnes's tears became acrid to him. His words had caused them, and he felt such shame for directing them at her after all she had been through.

"I'm sorry, my darling. I truly am. Those were vile words, and I wish I could take them back. Please forgive me."

Agnes's expression begged forgiveness. The words had stung, but she knew they were little less than she deserved. She had tried to spare him pain, and she only succeeded in causing a fuss and hurting him more in the end.

"Sam will have to find someone else for deliveries. I will not have you running around all over town in your condition, especially after today."

Agnes knew this was a fight that she could not win, nor did she have any desire to try. Her condition made the effort horribly difficult, and she felt tremendous relief now that she no longer had to hide it.

"Of course. I don't know that I have the energy to continue. I know women work throughout pregnancy, but...."

Art interrupted her. "But you don't have to. I can support our family. Is that what happened? Did your fatigue cause the accident?"

Agnes thought she had dealt with all the questions that could be asked of her, but Art was still not satisfied.

"The roads are icy. I'm amazed there haven't been more accidents."

Art seemed to accept her statement, which Agnes knew was only that; it was not an answer. The real answer was the first in a line of dominoes.

The first night at home was a sleepless one for Agnes. Her head continued to pound like the timpani in a marching band. It would not let up no matter which position she found herself in and no matter how calm she tried to keep herself. She had rid herself of the worry of the pregnancy, but had not been successful doing so with J. Flincher.

Within a few days, the headache subsided, as had the lump on her forehead. Art had been nothing but attentive, and her mother had not left her side while Art remained at work during the day. It had been round the clock care and Agnes was beginning to go batty. She longed for solitude and she had none.

"Mum, you must have some sewing to do. I will be fine. It has been a week now and I have not turned to dust. I can manage on my own, really." Agnes was not just letting her mother go; she was begging her to go.

Sarah could see the look in Agnes's eyes and she understood. Agnes had been very diplomatic and Sarah smiled at her own mulishness. She knew she would not have lasted a single day with her own mother on her every move.

"I'm going to walk to the shop. I haven't cooked in a week and the cold will do me good."

Sarah couldn't protest. She knew God's will was absolute and keeping her daughter locked up could not change it.

The weather over the last week remained very cold and there had been no new snow—it was almost too cold to snow. The sidewalk remained hard packed from what had fallen more than a week prior, and it squeaked under Agnes's boots as she walked. Agnes was so relieved to be out that she paid no attention to the bite.

As the bell chimed, Sam walked out from the back of the shop. Joanna was on a break and Sam was manning the counter himself.

"Agnes, what are you doing here? Does your mother know?" Sam knew how persistent his wife could be, and he was doubtful she would have let her go.

"Yes, she knows I am here." Agnes laughed. She knew full well what Sam was thinking. "Mum has taken good care of me, but it was time that I let her get back to her life. I shudder to think she was neglecting you and the boys at my expense."

Sam smirked. "How diplomatic. I can't imagine she let you go without a fight."

"Her fight or mine?" Agnes teased.

"Two peas in a pod. That much is certain," Sam quipped.

The bell chimed as the door to the shop opened. Agnes turned to see Mrs. McGregor enter. The sight of her made Agnes gasp. Agnes had thought heavily about the mysterious Mr. Flincher in the first days after the accident, but she contrived in her mind that it couldn't possibly be the same man and she let that worry go. It now faced her square on, and she had no choice but to learn the truth. If it was the same man, she would have to bear the burden of that knowledge.

"Agnes, how good to see you out and about. I was so sorry to hear about your accident."

Mrs. McGregor had never been anything other than cheerful and friendly, and Agnes could not imagine an association with someone so vile.

"Yes, the winter can be very hazardous for driving. Thankfully I am no worse for wear."

Sam put his arm around Agnes's shoulder and squeezed tightly.

"We are very grateful that it wasn't worse than it was. God was certainly watching out for our girl that day."

Agnes thought of her words carefully. "I'm sorry that I was unable to deliver your order first thing as promised. My day got turned around. Thankfully there was someone home to accept it when I arrived. I hope it was all right to leave it with him."

"Yes, that was quite fine. I had to step out for an errand. My husband's nephew is staying with us while he looks for work here in Winnipeg."

"What type of work is he looking for?" Sam asked. "I am in need of a delivery driver."

Agnes inhaled abruptly, causing her to cough and sputter as she tried to clear the saliva from her throat.

"Agnes, are you OK?"

"Yes, I'm fine," Agnes replied. "Just a tickle in my throat."

"He was a glassmaker, but I am sure he would be happy to take anything at this point. He has had some misfortune in his life and has moved around a fair bit since he left Saskatoon. I guess he hasn't yet found a place that appeals to him. My husband is hoping he stays here. He has always thought of Jasper as a son."

Agnes felt sick to her stomach. All colour drained from her face, leaving it ashen and pale, and she began to sway on her feet. Sam tightened his grip around her shoulders to steady her, fearful she would drop.

"Clearly you are not fine," he said as he guided her to a chair behind the counter.

Mrs. McGregor looked on horrified. "This is not a good time. I'll come back. I have to go to the market and get a few things."

"My apologies, Mrs. McGregor. Joanna will be off her break in a few minutes, and she will be more than happy to help you with your order. Thank you for your understanding. And please have your husband's nephew stop by. I would be happy to consider him for a delivery position if he is interested. And now I must be off to take this young lady home."

"That is very kind of you, Mr. Warman. I will do just that." A happy Mrs. McGregor left without her meat order, but she did not leave empty-handed.

After Joanna returned to the counter, Sam helped Agnes home. His worry was grossly misplaced and she knew she would suffer greatly for it, but she was unwilling to offer the explanation that would disburden her from the overprotectiveness that lay ahead.

Chapter 18

Agnes told her mother she was going to lie down. It was the only thing she could have said that would have kept her mother away. Sarah had chastised herself for letting Agnes walk to the shop. She was one daughter down, and it appeared her capacity to worry was now to be shared by the remaining two.

Agnes lay down on the chesterfield with her favourite book. She wanted desperately to keep moving, but she knew if her mother saw her she would be fretted over for all eternity. She tried to read, but she could not focus long enough to let the words play out. Jasper Flincher was on her mind, and there was nothing she could do to rid herself of his face.

As far as she could see, in every outcome she could conjure, there was no winning. If she told Sam about Jasper Flincher, she would be betraying Janie's confidence, which was an unconscionable offence, but she would be preventing that monster from trespassing upon their daily lives. If she kept Janie's confidence, she would be as much as welcoming him in and all but guaranteeing a disastrous encounter. Neither scenarios were good, but only the first one offered the possibility that Jasper could be kept away without Janie's knowledge. Agnes would swear on her own life that Sam would keep the secret to himself, and it was a risk she would have to take. Her own conscience would have to endure the beating for the sake of her friend.

Even though it was nobly decided, Agnes found the decision did nothing to ease her heavy heart. She continued to reason and justify in order to assuage her guilt, but relief eluded her. Then suddenly it occurred to her ... there *was* another answer.

Her cheeks flushed with spirit. And it was just in time, as the door opened and Art walked in. Agnes was overjoyed to see him, no longer worried about the ramifications of her physical weakness, and she threw herself at him.

"To what do I owe this welcome?" Art asked, surprised but elated."Nothing. Do I need more than love?" Agnes tried to look hurt, but she had never been good at pretending.

"I'll take love any day," Art said with a wink.

"Don't take your coat off. We are having dinner with Mum and Sam at my mother's insistence. Sam misinterpreted a moment of unsteadiness for near-death, and my mother is insisting I not cook this evening."

"Unsteadiness? Are you sure you are all right?" Art asked, concerned.

"Better than all right. Fantastic."

"Well, I can't argue with fantastic," Art said.

"I didn't get a chance to talk with you this morning. You were in a rush to get out. You seemed restless last night. Did you have another bad dream?"

"Nothing worse than usual," Art said. But that didn't make Agnes feel any better, as the *usual* was not very good.

"Do you want to talk about it?" Agnes asked.

"There is nothing to talk about, my love. It was just a misunderstanding with the wrong end of a paintbrush and the paintbrush won."

Agnes laughed. He could always make her laugh and she loved him for it. He had a wonderful way of taking the pointed edges off uncomfortable situations.

It was always chaos at her mum and Sam's house for dinner. The boys were not yet worn down, and it was difficult to get a word in edgewise, which that night suited Agnes. She wasn't in the mood to answer questions.

"Your colour has returned," Sam said. "I'm happy to see that. You had me worried."

"Pa, I love you, but you worry too much," Agnes chastised light-heartedly.

"You are my daughter. It is my right." No matter how much she shunned the worry, she couldn't help but melt when he said those words.

The nausea was beginning to abate, but the exhaustion was not. Agnes was ready for bed right after dinner.

"Thank you for dinner," Agnes said appreciatively. "You spoil us."

"Nonsense," Sarah returned. "It is my right. Just like it will be your right." Agnes gained strength from the sentiment. She had not allowed herself to think much about the future, but the prospect of motherhood was quite exciting.

"Mr. McGregor's nephew came in just before closing. Nice chap. He will fill the role nicely, I believe," Sam informed Agnes as she was putting her coat on.

The colour drained from Agnes's face, but this time she managed to blame her unsteadiness on her boots.

"Isn't that a bit premature, Pa? How can you make a decision so quickly? Maybe you should wait and see who else turns up." Agnes was beginning to panic. She hadn't expected the nightmare to progress so quickly.

"I'm in need of a deliveryman and he is in need of a job. Seems like a perfect match to me. As you know, John Hubbard is only helping me for another week while his father remains in hospital, and then he is planning to join the army. I'll need someone fully committed to the job after that."

Agnes knew she didn't have much time. She couldn't allow this horror to unfold before her eyes, not when she had the power to stop it.

Agnes held fast to the belief that God would always take care of His sheep, but she had come to realize it was not always in the way she imagined. It took a great deal of faith to weather the unexpected twists and turns of life, and while Agnes's faith had trembled on occasion, it had never fractured.

It was Agnes's turn for sleep to elude her. Her mind twisted and turned to the thoughts of Janie and Jasper Flincher. After an hour of listening to Art's snoring, she got out of bed and let the kitchen occupy her.

It was just after midnight. *A batch of cookies will do the trick*, she thought. One batch turned into two and two turned into three. It was four o'clock before Agnes realized the time. She slipped back into bed and was woken by Art a few hours later.

Art placed his hand on Agnes's belly and kissed her lightly on the cheek. She was locked in a deep sleep and did not move. There was nothing he needed from her that he could not get for himself that morning, and he wanted to let her sleep. The rest was exactly what she needed.

Art was careful not to disturb her, but he allowed himself the indulgence of watching her sleep for a few satisfying moments. He wondered what dreams were filling that pretty head of hers. Save for the fright that the accident gave him, he was perfectly content with his life. He couldn't imagine he could be more contented.

Agnes woke to an empty bed and no knowledge of the time; however, the light from the window told her it was much later than usual. As she sat up, she looked over at the clock ... ten o'clock. Agnes was in a state of disbelief.

> *My love,*
> *It looks as though you were quite busy last night. My taste buds thank you but my waistline does not. I hope you had a good sleep and whatever kept you awake earlier is no longer.*
> *Enjoy your visit with Janie.*
> *Your loving husband,*
> *Art*

Agnes intended to enjoy her visit, but above all she was focused in her purpose. The outcome was not guaranteed, she knew, but her determination was strong and her intent well-placed.

Janie wasn't expecting Agnes, and it came as a pleasant surprise to her. She hugged Agnes as though she had just come back from the brink of death.

"Agnes, finally. I have missed you so much," she said as she pulled her in and closed the door. "I would have come see you, but it has been too cold to take Elizabeth out. Tom has been working extra shifts because of illness, and I had no one to watch her. I have missed you so. How are you?" She reached out and gingerly touched the bandage in curiosity.

"Let me put this in the kitchen and then we'll talk."

Janie hadn't noticed the two bags of groceries and when she did, showed her disapproval to temper her mounting guilt.

"Agnes, you shouldn't. You spoil us with such extravagance. I should be taking care of you. You were the one in the accident."

Agnes flashed Janie her "don't be silly" look and Janie knew arguing would be futile.

"Thank you. You are a good friend. It has been difficult to get groceries this week and we are really low. You are a godsend. You really are." Janie began to empty the bags onto the counter.

"And now, I make you lunch," Agnes said. "Sit." Janie didn't argue.

After Agnes finished making sandwiches, they sat down to eat. It had been a week since they had seen each other, and Janie was curious as to why Agnes wasn't as chatty as she usually was.

"Is everything all right? You seem preoccupied," she asked.

Agnes had been staring off without realizing she had been doing so.

"Thank you for the card. It was very thoughtful. I wanted to visit sooner, but I too have been a prisoner in my own home. My mother has not let me out of her sight. She worries far too much."

"For a week? I though you just suffered a bump on your head. Was it worse than you let on?" Janie asked, her own worry showing.

Agnes suddenly realized that she hadn't told Janie about the baby. She had been so focused on the drama of the last week that it had completely slipped her mind.

"It wasn't just my head that she was worried about. She was also worried about my belly."

Janie's face contorted with worry. She thought the worst and dreaded what was to come.

"She was worried about the baby. But all is fine."

Janie's face erupted into a smile.

Janie waited for Agnes's confirmation, and then she launched herself at her friend as she erupted in excitement.

"Oh, Agnes, that is fantastic. How far along are you?"

"About eleven weeks now," she answered rather sheepishly. She knew the reaction she was going to get, and she knew she deserved it. She had chastised Janie for keeping secrets from her, and she had no legitimate excuse for doing the same.

To Agnes's amazement, Janie let it go. Janie was disappointed her friend hadn't confided in her, that she hadn't been able to share in her joy sooner, but she understood her reticence to announce it to the world. It had been a very intense and personal pain for her.

"I have been quite ill with nausea. My mother is convinced it is a girl."

"Your mother is a very wise woman. I would never bet against her, that's for certain," Janie said with a laugh. "A girl! Elizabeth will have a friend." Janie started to tear, and Agnes let herself get caught up in Janie's excitement.

Elizabeth began to coo, and Agnes jumped up before Janie could. She raced to the bedroom and scooped her goddaughter up in her arms. She missed the smell of her skin. When Agnes placed her on the change table, the baby looked up at her and offered a toothless grin and Agnes crumbled. It was almost too much to bear.

Elizabeth continued to smile and brought her hands together as if to clap. Agnes could barely pin up the nappie—her hands were shaking, her entire body trembling as she came under Elizabeth's spell.

Agnes carried Elizabeth out to her mother. At the sound of Janie's voice, Elizabeth began to cry. She was hungry, and she had had enough of entertaining her godmother.

"Do not fret. The tides will be turned before long," Janie said reassuringly. "Your child will cry for you."

Agnes allowed herself to believe it, and she prayed that she was not making a mistake by doing so.

"How is Tom?" Agnes asked.

"Good. Busy. There has been an abundance of illness among the officers. The time of year, I guess. He has worked many extra shifts. I haven't seen much of him in the last week, sadly. I miss my husband," Janie said with a frown.

Janie's mien turned decidedly darker. Agnes felt the change and attributed it to Tom's absence.

"My husband has been vexed by the notion that Jasper Flincher could be nearby. I too am bothered, but Tom's feelings are decidedly vengeful. I am worried. He has been quite angry. I am worried he is actually seeking him out. I take comfort in knowing how difficult it is to track someone down. I understand Jasper has moved around regularly. People like that don't leave much of a footprint."

The door opened and Tom walked in.

"Speak of the devil," Agnes said.

"I guess I should be flattered that the two most beautiful women in the world were talking about me."

Agnes laughed. "I see your ability to flatter knows no bounds, Mr. Martin. You are quite the charmer. Before you get yourself too comfortable, would you be so kind as to drive me home? I promised Art I wouldn't push myself too hard."

"Ah yes, the accident. You are looking well. I am assuming you are on the mend," Tom hoped.

Janie snickered. "Yes, she is on the mend, but that is not the only reason Art wants her to take care of herself."

Tom acknowledged the look that passed between Agnes and his wife, and he waited to be let in on the secret.

"Elizabeth is going to have a playmate," Janie revealed.

It took a moment for Tom to grasp the meaning of what his wife was saying, but when he did he showed his pleasure.

"That is fine news, mighty fine indeed. Art must be thrilled with the prospect of fatherhood. I highly recommend it," he said as he winked at his wife. "Happy to give you a ride home. Let's be on our way, then."

Agnes said her good-byes and confirmed that she would see them for church on Christmas Day and dinner at her mother's house afterwards.

"Wouldn't miss it for the world," Janie said.

Thankfully the engine was still warm and turned over quickly. It wasn't far to go and she would have been perfectly fine to walk, but comfort wasn't the reason for the request.

"That is very exciting news," Tom said again as he pulled out from the curb. "Janie will undoubtedly be thrilled to have someone to share it all with."

"I know where Jasper Flincher is," Agnes blurted out.

Tom pulled off to the side of the road. He turned and looked at Agnes and waited for the rest of the details to come.

"I was doing deliveries a week ago and delivered to Mrs. McGregor's house. She wasn't home, and the man who answered the door signed for the delivery. The name he wrote down was J. Flincher. I had no way of knowing if that was him or not, but I was so upset by what I saw that I got distracted. That is what caused my accident."

Tom's cheeks were beginning to redden, more so than just from the cold; his jaw was clenching in anger.

"I wanted to find out, but my mother wouldn't let me out of her sight after the accident. I couldn't do anything from home, and I couldn't tell anyone without betraying Janie's confidence. Yesterday I walked to my father's shop and Mrs. McGregor came in. She said her husband's nephew was staying with them while he was looking for work. She said he had been in the glassmaking business and had moved around a bit since he left Saskatoon. That was enough for me, but then she said his name was Jasper."

Tom looked straight ahead. Agnes could see the vein in his forehead pulsing. She didn't know what he was thinking, but she was becoming frightened. She was beginning to regret telling him, but she could see no other alternative.

Tom continued to stare through the windscreen, remaining silent and brooding. The silence was excruciating for Agnes. She did not know him well enough to predict what he would do, and she remained terrified of where her thoughts were taking her.

"I was hoping this would right itself, that he would just leave and neither of you would be the wiser, but that became an impossibility yesterday. My father told Mrs. McGregor he would be willing to speak with him about the deliveryman position that he has open. Mrs. McGregor was, of course, thrilled. Sam offered Jasper the position. He will start the day before Christmas Eve. We can't let that happen."

Tom still said nothing. He put the car into gear and continued to drive. Once parked at Agnes's house, he turned to her, offered his arms for an embrace of congratulations, and that was it.

"I'm sorry, Tom. I hope I did the right thing by telling you."

"Yes, you did. Thank you." Tom was too angry to pick up on what Agnes didn't say, which was neither subtle nor obscure.

Agnes said good-bye and watched Tom drive away. She worried about what he would do with the knowledge he now possessed. Whatever the outcome, she knew it was out of her hands. She only prayed she hadn't compounded the misery.

Chapter 19

It was a cold walk to the church on Christmas Day. The weather had been consistently frigid for the better part of a week. Sam and Sarah avoided the uncomfortable air and drove with the boys, while Percy drove Mary and Bill, and Art and Agnes walked. Art wanted to buy a car, but his main priority was a home of their own; a car became a luxury they could live without.

The group sat together, occupying two pews. Agnes noticed the McGregors walk up the aisle, and she desperately hoped that Tom had not seen them. Unfortunately her hopes were dashed. Tom was fixed on Mr. McGregor as they took their seats. Agnes hadn't spoken with Sam in a few days and assumed that Jasper had started his new position. Mr. and Mrs. McGregor were unaccompanied, their two children grown and moved away, so it appeared that Jasper had the good sense to avoid a house of worship on Christmas Day. It would have been an abomination of all that was Christmas if he had tainted the day of the Lord's birth with his vile presence.

Tom bore an expression of satisfaction and, while Agnes wanted nothing more than her friend's happiness, she knew it would be short-lived. Jasper was not sitting in the church that day, but he was not far away. He was still slithering through town, touching their lives when he had no business doing so.

Aside from the unfortunate thoughts of Jasper Flincher, it was a pleasant service. Elizabeth slept peacefully in her mother's arms while the minister spoke rather appropriately of the blessings of children. Art recognized their own divine blessings and gave his wife's hand a loving squeeze. In fact, they all took time to ponder how fortunate they were, for they were all happy and healthy and secure.

The house was full for Christmas dinner, yet it felt remarkably empty without Margaret, John, and the girls. The void left by their departure was deep, but baby Elizabeth's presence helped to temper the sense of loss. A baby could bring joy to a room like nothing else.

"Sam, I understand that you have filled your deliveryman position. How is that working out?" Tom asked.

Agnes quickly turned toward Tom, her face overcome with a look of horror. *What are you doing*? she wondered. Panic overcame her, but Tom was none the wiser for it. He was focused on Sam, awaiting his response.

"Not well, unfortunately. Strange situation, that one. Mr. McGregor's nephew was to start the day before yesterday and he didn't show up. I thought perhaps we had our signals crossed on a start date, but Mrs. McGregor came in that morning to apologize. She said he left abruptly, had taken his things, and without so much as a whisper as to where he might have gone. Something certainly sent him away in a hurry."

Tom bore a look of contentment, of smug satisfaction, and when his eyes met Agnes's he nodded to acknowledge her complicity. Together they had spared Janie much undeserved sorrow, and it was a secret that would bind them together for the rest of their lives. They both loved Janie, and now they proved to each other that love knew no bounds.

Agnes knew not what Tom had done to drive Jasper away, but she had no doubt that he was the cause. If Tom had wanted Agnes to know, he would have told her, but he had not. It was Tom's burden, and as Janie's husband, it was one he was prepared to carry alone.

"As is so often the case, misfortune for one is good fortune for another. Sadly, Mr. Hubbard's illness has taken a turn for the worse, and he isn't expected to survive. His son John has asked to stay on. He will need to support his family now, so the army is no longer an option for him."

"We received a letter from Margaret and John earlier this week," Sarah said excitedly, "and they are all doing well. They arrived safely and are settled into their new home. They tell us it is beside a lovely park, which the girls are already enjoying. It is much warmer there, and they have not had to hide from the cold the way we have. It sounds delightful to me." Sarah smiled, but she could not hide her sorrow.

"Did they mention if they had found a location?" Mary asked.

"Yes, they have found a grand one in a very busy area, and they are expecting to open for business in early January. It all sounds so exciting."

"I wish we could be there for the opening," Mary added. "I'm sad that it is so far away. It would take a good deal of planning to take such a long trip. Perhaps that would be a good destination for a honeymoon."

At first the comment went over everybody's head. They all nodded in agreement, thinking about the distance to travel, but then the word "honeymoon" registered.

"*Honeymoon*?" Agnes asked, dumfounded. "What are you talking about?"

Mary held out her hand to show the engagement ring that glowed on her ring finger.

Agnes grabbed Mary's hand and after staring at the ring in disbelief, she looked back and forth between her sister and Percy.

"When did this happen?" Agnes could barely get the words out.

"This is a day for the record books. It is not too often that my sister is at a loss for words," Mary teased.

The room erupted in laughter, but Agnes was still too shocked to let the jab sting.

"Percy tells me he asked Mum and Sam's permission a few weeks ago. He asked me this morning, right before church. I have been wearing the ring since and not a single person noticed," Mary said slyly.

Agnes jumped up and gave her sister a big hug. "I'm so happy for you both. This is such wonderful news."

"It's about time, Percy," Agnes chided before giving Percy a hearty hug.

"And Mum and Pa, you both knew for a couple of weeks? And you never said anything?" Agnes pretended she was hurt.

"It wasn't for us to tell," Sam pointed out. "But now you know, and I am sure you will more than make up for the two weeks of not being able to talk about it." Mary snickered and Agnes rolled her eyes at her in mock disdain.

"I'm the luckiest man in the world. I'm more proud of my son than any father has the right to be, and I will have the two best daughters-in-law in the world," Bill said proudly.

Bill wasn't one to waste words. He was unable to make small talk simply for the sake of filling the air, but when he spoke he spoke with purpose and conviction. It was a sentiment that made everyone in the room "aww," and the attention that came back to him made him blush with embarrassment. Mary, who had been sitting beside him, kissed him on the cheek and it was as though he had been kissed by an angel. He fought the emotion and changed the subject.

"Very exciting that we will be having a new baby in the family soon," Bill said as he winked at Agnes.

"I forbid either one of you to leave," Sarah said to Mary and Agnes as she wiped her eyes.

"Rest assured, Mum, we will never leave you," Mary promised.

Sarah not often revealed her feelings, but those who knew her well could see that her tough exterior, a toughness built from a lifetime of living, had softened over time. She had always found strength in her family, but they had also become her greatest weakness. She was unable to hide her worry or her sorrow.

Sarah had assembled a feast fit for a king's court. The table was covered with a festive, gold tablecloth and adorned with roast beef, turkey, and a rainbow of accompaniments and sweets. It was an English garden of texture and colour. And to those who had the good fortune to see it, it was a sight to behold.

"Mum, you have outdone yourself. This table is heavenly," Agnes said in awe.

They all stood in silence as they gathered around the table. The dancing flames atop the flickering candles were mesmerizing and brought waves of warm light to the room. It was more than the smells and colours that inspired the senses; the table bespoke a joy of the most unaffected kind.

"Let us take this time to thank God for the many blessings that He has granted us," Sam said as he bowed his head. "We are grateful for our family and our treasured friends. We ask God to be with us as we prepare for weddings and babies. We ask Him to watch over Margaret, John, and the girls as they embark on their new lives in Vancouver. And most of all, we thank God every day for guiding us in life and providing us with the strength and courage to weather life's storms, and the humility to accept life's gifts with grace and gratitude."

Chapter 20

Art rolled on his side and tucked up against his sleeping wife. He wrapped his arm around her side and rested his hand on her round belly. He ran his hand over every curve, tracing the arm that he felt protruding from within. His child was awake, moving beneath his hand, and he was as awestruck as the first time he felt movement. He was going to miss the experience of seeing his wife grow with the baby. It was truly miraculous.

"I'm sorry to wake you, darling, but I couldn't help myself," Art said as Agnes sat up. "Very soon that child will be in your arms and not your belly, and I won't be able to do that any longer."

Agnes loved Art's sentimentality. Most men paid little attention to their wives when they were pregnant, and not only did Art lavish her with love and affection, he also noted every change, every movement, with wonder.

"You may enjoy seeing my belly like this, but I have had more than enough of the aching back and sleepless nights. This child is as active as any who has ever been. I fear we are going to be run off our feet with it."

"I'll do the chasing if you do the feeding," Art bargained.

Agnes laughed. That sounded fair to her. In fact, even the mere thought of running around made her out of breath and her swollen feet throb. She didn't begrudge any of it, but she was certainly anxious to see it over so she could meet her child.

The rain was loud against the window. It had been pounding for two solid days, and the ground could no longer hide it. Puddles of rain water pooled on the roads and sidewalks, having nowhere else to go. Agnes didn't mind; she loved the rain and the sound it made. She found it incredibly soothing.

"I will leave for work, but as I have told you daily for the prior fortnight, you must promise me you will go next door to Mrs. Hammond to call the hotel to summon me home at the first sign."

"And as I have said every day of that same fortnight, 'yes, you have my promise.'"

Art kissed Agnes's belly and then her cheek and was on his way. Every morning he wondered if it was the day he would become a father. He wondered with nervous anticipation, full of hope for what could be but fearful for what would. He was aware of his own failings and shortcomings, and it made him curious as to what legacy he would be passing on. This child would be loved more than any other child in the world, but he feared love would not be enough. He only had himself to look to for that.

Agnes set to scrubbing the floors and washing the walls. She had to fill the time with something and walking outdoors was out of the question with the rain. She needed an activity or she knew she would go insane with the monotony of anticipation.

Halfway through the morning, she diverted her attention to cooking. She managed a few dozen cookies, a cake, and then turned to meat pies before she ran out of ingredients. As she rolled the crust for the meat pies, the first jab of pain began. Agnes ignored it as indigestion. A short while later, another pain forced her to bend as the sharpness intensified and shot further throughout her body. Agnes was still not ready to acknowledge the cause.

The rain pelted the living room window, obscuring the view of the yard. Few cars were on the street, and even fewer people were on the sidewalk. It was half-past two, Agnes noted, and Art would be home in a few hours. She was anxious to see him but more anxious by the thought of what remained to be completed before she did.

Another gripping pain wrapped her belly, and she finally acquiesced to the cause; and despite the implication, she resolved to finish her chores. There was much to do, and she could not rest until it was all done.

One by one, the wrinkles were ironed from Art's shirts while the pains went disregarded. They were increasing in severity, but Agnes's immersion in the tasks at hand helped to alleviate the anxiety that would have rendered anyone else impotent.

When the last of the shirts was hung, Agnes looked around the living room for means to occupy her remaining time. All seemed complete so she abandoned the living room for the bedroom, and there too she found nothing. She went speedily into the remaining bedroom, the room where the baby's things were stored. The newborn clothes and bassinette were Margaret's and had been passed along by Janie as they were no longer needed for Elizabeth.

Agnes removed the clothing from the bassinette and placed it in the bureau drawers, organizing by colour and type. As she placed the last item in the drawer, a deafening boom of thunder shook the window, startling Agnes and sending her stumbling backwards into the bureau. The pain of the impact was overshadowed by the pain of another contraction. Agnes moaned in agony; it was the strongest one yet.

"Agnes! Are you all right?" Art said as he slammed the front door behind him.

He ran toward the sound, tracking a stream of water behind him. Agnes was leaning against the bureau, grasping her belly. She looked at

Art, her eyes pleading, her face flushed in distress.

"Is the baby coming?" Art was disturbed by the state he found his wife in. He had been told it would be a slow process, being the first, but it seemed anything but.

Another pain gripped Agnes. They were coming quickly now and she knew it was almost time.

"Yes, it will be here soon. Please go get Delores and my mother."

Art and Agnes had moved a few months prior so they could be in their own home before the baby came, and they now found themselves wishing they still lived in her parents' carriage house.

Art ran the two blocks to Delores's through the pounding rain. Every inch of his body was drenched. After he knocked on Delores's door, he removed his hat to shake off the moisture.

Delores answered the door almost immediately. She had no need to ask the reason for the visit. There could only be one. She gathered her things and was out the door without delay.

Agnes could see the trail that Art had left and she was aghast. Her clean floor. She quickly grabbed the mop and bucket and began to soak up the water. The contractions were within seconds of each other now, and Agnes was having difficulty staying on her feet. All she wanted to do was lie down, but she resisted the urge. As she was putting the bucket back in the cupboard she felt a "pop." She had never experienced anything like it before, but the stream of warm liquid down the inside of her leg convinced her, her bag of waters had broken.

Another contraction overcame her. Agnes placed a towel inside her bloomers and wiped up the liquid from the floor. She removed the covers from the bed and placed multiple layers of towels down before piling pillows against the headboard.

There was nothing more Agnes could do so she removed her bloomers and the wet towel, placed them in a bag, and then positioned herself on the bed. The contractions were now on top of one another, with barely a moment between them. She felt an urge to push, but she tried desperately to hold back. The pain in her back was excruciating, and she adjusted herself onto her side to reduce the pressure.

She couldn't hold on any longer, and she knew the baby was there. She was going to have to do this herself, she thought. As quickly as the thought occurred to her, the front door opened.

"Agnes!" Art yelled.

"In the bed..." she said, trailing off as she bared down.

Delores removed her wet clothes and ran into the bedroom. Agnes was curled up, about to push, and Delores positioned herself at Agnes's feet, lifting Agnes's skirt up over her knees.

"The baby is crowning, Agnes. This won't take long. Just breathe deeply and try to remain calm."

Delores was telling Agnes to remain calm, but she had been calm all along. It was an entirely different experience now that she was the one giving birth. She felt she was in control and she was more than prepared. The only thing left to do was being done.

Art remained in the living room, pacing to manage his tension. Agnes screamed out in agony as the shoulder emerged, and he winced. The door behind him opened and he turned to find Sarah standing there.

"How is she?" Sarah asked hastily as she hung her coat in the closet and leaned the dripping umbrella against the wall.

There was no need to reply. A deep-throated moan was followed by the sweet sound of a baby's cry. Art looked at Sarah as tears welled in his eyes. He was overcome by the sound. Sarah smiled and embraced her son-in-law.

Art wanted desperately to go to his wife and Sarah could see that.

"Agnes is not quite done yet. She won't want you to see her before she is cleaned up. Sit. Relax. I will bring you your baby." Sarah rubbed Art's arm reassuringly. "She'll be just fine."

Sarah went to see her daughter and Art did as he was told, taking to the chesterfield to endure the agonizing wait until he could see his wife and baby. But as quickly as he sat, he stood back up and resumed the pacing. It was all he could do to soothe his anxiety and impatience.

Agnes was resting with her baby atop her chest when Sarah entered the room, the sight of which filled Sarah with endless joy. It had been a difficult road to get to this place, and she was so thankful to God for blessing her daughter with a child.

Agnes looked up at her mother as she walked in the room. She wore the look of bliss. She was intoxicated with the feelings that had engulfed her, sweeping over her like a tidal wave.

"Mum, come meet your granddaughter," Agnes said.

"A girl, oh my," Sarah said as her eyes began to glisten. "How wonderful." Sarah felt a part of her heart had been ripped away when Margaret left with the girls, and now she found some of it had been given back.

Delores wiped down the baby, cut the umbilical cord, and swaddled her snugly. She held the baby out to Sarah and Sarah took her, bringing her close to her and kissing her cheek.

"I'm sure this sweet baby would like to meet her father as well. Agnes will be done in here in a few moments, and then you can all come in for a visit."

Sarah left the room carrying her grandbaby. Art stood up as she approached him. At the sight of his child, his knees felt weak. Sarah stood before him and held her out. Art didn't take her immediately, fixating on her instead, trying to process what he was seeing, what he was feeling.

"Art, meet your daughter," Sarah directed lovingly.

Art looked up at Sarah. "Daughter?" he responded.

Sarah nodded while she held out his baby girl. Art finally took her, the realization that he was a father sweeping over him and consuming his very breath. He looked down at her and was overwhelmed by her innocence. She was as exquisite as anything he had ever seen, a perfect porcelain doll.

"She's beautiful," Sarah said. "You have a beautiful baby girl."

Art looked at her again, this time unable to hide his tears. He smiled through them, engulfed in the poignancy of those words. And with those words, the rest of the world disappeared.

"Art, would you like to see your wife?" Delores asked as she emerged from the bedroom.

Art passed his daughter back to Sarah and went to Agnes. She lay on the bed, framed in an aura of maternal rapture.

"How are you, my darling? You certainly are a sight to behold." Art bent over and kissed her.

"You are a fortunate girl," Sarah said. "It appears you had an easy time of it. Most are not nearly as fortunate."

"We arrived just in time. It is quite unusual for a first labour to go so quickly. When did you start to feel your first contractions?" Delores asked.

Agnes hesitated. She knew what was to come. "Just after breakfast."

"*Just after breakfast?!* Did they not progress regularly?"

"They did. I knew there was time and didn't want to have everyone waiting at my feet until the baby was ready."

Delores was annoyed that her advice was not heeded. "Agnes, this could have been disastrous. You should not have left it so long. What of complications, and while you were on your own? It is the midwife that determines if it is time."

Delores's scolding was duly noted, but it had little effect on Agnes. Nothing could bring her down from the cloud she was on. She held out her arms to take her baby back.

Delores managed her tasks diligently and efficiently, as the convention of birth rarely veered off course at this point. When she excused herself to leave, Agnes was glad for it. With the business side done, Agnes had no desire to share these long-awaited-for moments with anyone other than those she loved most, and she certainly wanted no fuss.

As the front door closed, Agnes placed the baby on the bed and swung her legs around to stand up.

"Darling, are you certain you are ready to get up? There is no shame in rest," Art said gently.

"There may be no shame in rest, but there is also no honour in indulgence."

She was not ill and had no desire to be treated as though she was. Women gave birth every day, and there was no need for unnecessary prudence.

Art disagreed but remained quiet. It was Agnes, and her mind was as firm as an oak.

After her mother returned home, Agnes felt the void left by her reassuring presence and began to fear her own inexperience. A child was not a floor to be cleaned, nor a meal to be cooked. It was not an absolute, more a river, ebbing and flowing, full of life and not always to be controlled. She feared her own expectations.

Agnes placed the baby in the bassinette and brought her into the kitchen. She slept peacefully while Agnes prepared for the visitors she knew would undoubtedly come that evening. The baby was so quiet, too quiet, and Agnes continued to peak and touch to assure herself she was merely sleeping. Agnes feared that constant fear would remain with her forever.

The knocks on the door began just past seven. Sam and Sarah arrived first, followed by Mary, Percy, and Bill.

"Pa, I'm so happy to see you," Agnes said as she rushed to hug him. "Would you like to meet your granddaughter?"

"More than anything," Sam responded.

Agnes reached into the bassinette and lifted out her sleeping daughter. She remained asleep, unaware of the attention being paid to her.

"This is Dorothy Agnes," Agnes said as he passed her to her grandfather.

"*Dorothy*. What a lovely name," Sarah said. "And Agnes after her mother. How wonderful."

Sam took Dorothy in his arms and softened at the touch of her. He had been through this twice prior with Margaret, but it never became tiresome. Sam adored children and they adored him in return.

Sam sat down on the chesterfield with Agnes while Dorothy was passed around the room. She remained asleep, having fed just before the guests arrived.

"Mrs. McGregor came into the shop yesterday and shared some disturbing news with me. Her nephew, the chap who was going to deliver for me, was killed."

"What do you mean 'killed'?" Agnes asked, astonished. "When? How?"

"She really didn't tell me any more than that, and I certainly didn't ask. Quite dreadful really. I feel bad for her husband. I remember Mrs. McGregor telling me he thought of him as a son."

Agnes's mind was racing. *Do Tom and Janie know? What will Janie think?* It would have to come as a relief that this man who had tormented her thoughts could no longer appear. Try as she might, Agnes knew she could not even come close to comprehending the constant strain that Janie had been under.

Dorothy began to fuss and Agnes reached for her. It was time to feed and she excused herself to the bedroom. As Dorothy latched on, Agnes kissed her daughter's head. It was incredibly soft, but it was her smell that overwhelmed Agnes. This precious little baby had beguiled and charmed her mother, heart and soul. She was in love and nothing could ever quell the rush.

"My darling, tomorrow is a work day for you, and you'll be worse for wear should you not get the rest you need. I'll be up with Dorothy, as is a mother's joy, but you must sleep."

Art wanted to tell his wife she was wrong, but he could not for she wasn't. He had a long day the next, completing a job that could not run late, and he had to be ready to work it fully and properly. He was becoming adept at the skill and business of painting, and he found he quite enjoyed it. For the first time in his life, he felt he had an occupation and not merely a job.

"You are quite right, darling, although it pains me greatly to agree with you. I wish I could sit with you all night and beam at this wondrous child of ours. You have done well, my love. She is perfect, as are you."

Agnes smiled at Art's sentiments. He had always had a way with words, and he never ceased to make her feel as though she were the most cherished wife in the world. In her eyes, she was.

The dead of night had never seemed so dark to Agnes; every sound and every thought was amplified in the silence. Dorothy's hungry cries and suckling chirps were all that filled the empty air. Even Art's snores were stifled beyond the closed door

In the quiet and beyond her daughter, she had only her own thoughts to occupy her. She didn't know what to think of Jasper Flincher's death. She would undoubtedly have thoughts soon enough, as she and Art were set to have dinner with Tom and Janie in two nights' time. She could not let Sam's news go without learning more. It would eat at her until she had the full story.

Agnes did not want to disturb Art with her comings and goings. Dorothy was placed in the bassinette against the chesterfield, and Agnes lay there as she tried to regain some strength between feedings. It was neither peaceful nor comfortable, but she was so weary the discomfort was barely acknowledged.

As Agnes dozed between conscious and unconscious, she was awakened from her sleep. She was not able to immediately process the disturbance, and she turned to Dorothy, who was sleeping soundly in her bassinette. Agnes, believing it to have been a dream, began to relax again. But it repeated itself. The moaning and thrashing that had become so agonizingly familiar filled the room. It was distinct, if slightly muffled, filtering through the closed door.

Agnes leapt up from the chesterfield and went to the bedroom door, opening it gently despite her instinct to rush in without pause. Art was caught in another fiendish dream, the clarity and intensity of which was cheating him of the peace that was rightfully his. Agnes had not witnessed this distress in a while, and it unnerved her so.

Agnes could only watch, terrified of what could happen should she awaken him. This particular episode was a strong one, and it was as though she were witnessing him dying for the pain it caused her.

As he thrashed about, beads of sweat were beginning to form on Art's forehead. She rushed to the cabinet to get a cloth, and in her haste the neatly stacked pile toppled over. She stopped herself from tidying it, and instead ran warm water on the one that she held in her hand. By the time she returned to the bedroom, Art was undisturbed once again.

She gently dabbed the moistened cloth on his forehead, careful not to wake him, and kissed him tenderly on the lips. She so loved this man, and the suffering these demons were causing him hurt her deeply. She wanted desperately to help, to make it go away, but she was beginning to believe it never would. What pained her most was that it didn't matter if the anxiety was born of happiness or something darker; the result was undoubtedly the same. *If a perfect and longed-for baby can bring about such a reaction, then what hope is there?*

As she wiped a tear from her cheek, that perfect and longed-for baby began to cry. Agnes went to her to offer the comfort that she needed. The sound of her cries made the world stop for Agnes.

Dorothy settled, and Agnes lay back on the chesterfield to try to get some rest before the baby fussed again. As she closed her eyes, they began to burn. It was half-past four, and she had barely had an hour's sleep. Try as she might, sleep eluded her. Something was nagging at her, and as quickly as she strained to find the cause it came to her.

Agnes went to the open cabinet and removed the linens, which she had left lying haphazardly on the shelf. She folded them neatly and placed them back where they had been sitting. Beside them Art's shaving tray was in a state of disarray as well. She removed it to straighten the brush and razor, which had been lying on the shelf. A small bottle behind it caught her eye.

It was distinctive—a pharmaceutical bottle. Pills shifted inside it as Agnes lifted it in the light to take a closer look. The label was smudged, as though it had been wet at one time, but Agnes could clearly make out the name "Adalin" and the word "sleep."

Agnes was taken aback. It certainly explained why Art had been sleeping better, but for the life of her she could not fathom why he would keep it from her. The easy answer was that he didn't want to worry her, but that held little comfort for Agnes.

Agnes placed the razor and shaving brush in the position they had been found. She wasn't sure she would confront Art. If he had kept this from her to spare her worry, then she certainly didn't want to add to his by confessing her own knowledge of it.

Chapter 21

Art did his best to remain quiet, but it was of no use. Agnes was awakened by his movements, however deliberate and slight they were.

"I did not mean to wake you, my love. You must have been up most of the night ... and all while I slept soundly. I feel terrible about that," Art said.

"Nonsense," Agnes replied as she rubbed her eyes. "You will work hard all day, and I will be sitting on my behind doing nothing more strenuous than feeding Dorothy. Your sleep is well earned."

Art bent down and kissed his wife and daughter. He was a fortunate man and he knew it. His only wish was that Agnes would allow him to do more for her, to pamper her as he chose to, if only occasionally. But she would have no part of. She shunned indulgence, especially her own.

Agnes prepared Art's breakfast as Dorothy continued to sleep. Agnes was tired but was determined to persevere. She was only at the beginning, and admitting to it would serve no purpose other than to make her feel worse.

"I have never experienced a newborn this completely. I had not realized they slept so much," Art said, dumbfounded.

"Considering they generally cry when they are not sleeping, it might not be a bad thing," Agnes said with a laugh.

Art peered into the bassinette between bites of his breakfast. The look of pride on his face filled Agnes with immense joy. Perhaps it was the exhaustion, but Agnes felt complete. It was just the three of them, together as a family doing something the two of them had done every morning before.

A clinking at the window caught their attention, and they both turned to see the cause of the sound. Perched on the sill was a Song Sparrow. His rust brown colour was not particularly striking, but his sound more than brightened his allure. He peered in as he tapped at the window with his beak. His delicate song filtered into the room, and it was as though he wanted to be a part of it.

"Music with breakfast," Art replied cheerily.

"How did you sleep last night, darling?" Agnes asked. "I hope we didn't keep you awake."

"Better than you did, I'm certain." That didn't answer Agnes's question, nor did it give her any relief, but she chose to leave it. If there was a time, this wasn't it. She was far too tired to enter into such a serious conversation.

After Art left for work, Agnes tidied up, fed Dorothy, and then lay down on the chesterfield. She hadn't intended to sleep. She awoke three hours later, horrified by the sound of Dorothy's cries. She had no idea how long Dorothy had been crying; her face was red, but there were yet to be tears so it was not possible to tell. Her little tongue was wagging in her mouth, and the pitch of her cry pierced Agnes's ears with painful acuity.

Agnes tried to gain her bearings as Dorothy nursed, but they were slow in coming. The sun streamed in through the living room window and offered some of the energy that she craved, and eventually her thoughts sharpened.

It had only been one day, but Agnes was already feeling claustrophobic and in need of open air. Perhaps it was the long, dark night she had endured. Regardless, it was hot and sunny and perfect for walking, and she decided it was just what she needed.

She had watched so many mothers pushing their prams around town, and that she was finally doing it herself was surreal.

The pram's cover gave ample shade to Dorothy, but Agnes still kept a constant eye on her. As the pram bounced between sections of sidewalk, she worried about the jostling that Dorothy was enduring. She also worried about the heat. She hadn't realized it was so hot. But Dorothy slept peacefully through it all and remained entirely unaffected by all that worried her mother.

As Agnes turned the corner onto Janie's street, Janie appeared. Elizabeth sat up tall in her pushchair, and Agnes could not believe how big she was getting.

"Elizabeth, my sweet girl. Look at you." Elizabeth bounced in her seat at the sight of Agnes, and her enthusiasm was rewarded with a kiss.

Before Agnes could say hello, Janie was at the pram. She was agog at the baby who lay within.

"She is lovely, Agnes. I was so pleased when your mum stopped by last evening with the news. We were just coming to see you."

"And we to you," Agnes said with a laugh.

"How is it that you are out and about after a day, and I was in my dressing gown for three weeks before I felt presentable to the world? I have always known you to be more formidable than me, and now there is no denying it."

Agnes knew that Janie meant it as a compliment, but it didn't really feel that way. She had long been teased by her sisters that strength of will wasn't always a virtue, and she worked hard to soften herself; but at times she resigned herself to the fact that she was what she was.

"It is such a marvelous day. Let's go to the park and sit. My yard is so drab this year; I haven't had the time to tend to the garden. The park is full of flowers and so very beautiful."

"Splendid idea, Janie." Agnes said.

They weren't far from it, a few blocks. It was Agnes's childhood park, and it held many fond memories for her. She could see Uncle Bertie's house from the bench that she sat on. In fact, she believed it to be the bench that Sam proposed to her mother on.

"I am so very happy for you, Agnes. Our two girls will be the best of friends," Janie said.

Agnes raised her head and let the warmth and light of the sunshine soak in. It felt wonderful. And the smell of the flowers was extraordinary, as though she were smelling them for the first time. It was a perfect summer day.

"I cannot believe how big Elizabeth is getting."

"Prepare yourself. They do grow quickly. And once the time is gone, you cannot get it back so enjoy each moment. Dorothy will be one before you know it."

"Sage advice to be sure. I'm sure every mother has said the same thing. I have the benefit of many more experienced than myself surrounding me. I doubt I would be allowed to forget anything so important," Agnes said, placating Janie. It was entirely unintentional. Every new mother felt they would do things differently, better. Agnes was no different.

Janie looked at Agnes and cleared her throat, as though she had something important to say. She hesitated, which drew Agnes's curiosity all the more.

"It appears that Elizabeth will have a sibling before the year is out."

Agnes was taken aback. She did not expect those words to come from Janie's mouth.

"That is tremendous, Janie. Tom must be so happy."

Agnes hugged Janie and reaffirmed her congratulations. Agnes could not even comprehend a second only one day after giving birth. She would get there, but she doubted it would be as soon.

"I do have more news," Janie said. "Jasper Flincher is dead."

Agnes was stunned into silence. She didn't know how to respond. She wasn't sure if she should tell Janie she knew, but she quickly decided that she should feign ignorance.

"Dead? How?"

"My cousin first told me. She said that Jasper had been killed in

Winnipeg. I told Tom, and he admitted he already knew. Apparently Jasper died around last November. His body was found a few weeks later without any identification so they didn't know who it was at first. A body of a man believed to have been murdered during a robbery was found in the stockyards, and it was months before it was identified as Jasper."

"Tom knew?" Agnes was astounded.

"Tom has long wanted to become a detective, and he asked if he could follow the investigation when the body was found. It is so astonishing to me that it ended up being Jasper."

Agnes believed there was no such a thing as coincidences. This all seemed so odd to her, and she couldn't make sense of it.

"A few months after the body was found, a man was arrested for robbery. He was found with identification on him that didn't belong to him. Some of the identification was for Jasper Flincher. Supposedly he denied it to police but admitted it in prison. He died whilst in prison and he never went to trial. Jasper was a horrible man, Agnes, but I wouldn't wish a death like that on anyone. He still had family who loved him. I know what that feels like."

Agnes was still trying to comprehend what Janie had said. The words were churning in her brain. She understood the outcome but not how the pieces fit together.

"I feel a sense of relief that I no longer have to worry about him or even think about him, but this world is becoming more sinister, Agnes. Look at what happened at the Stockyards Hotel. Then this. Are we to not feel safe?"

Agnes paused. She agreed that the world had its fair share of darkness, but she didn't agree it was getting worse.

"It is difficult to not feel that the world is evil and getting more so, but it is really no worse than it has ever been. We have just been faced with our fair share of it, and it leaves its mark. But those marks make us who we are, and we are better for it. God doesn't give us what we cannot handle. And for those people like your father and Jasper Flincher, they stand before God and face judgement. Your father loved you and tried to protect you. When he realized he failed in that, he tried to right the wrong. You may think evil triumphed, but it did not. Your father showed you how much he loved you and he was rewarded with heaven. Be sad for yourself that you lost him too soon; that is all right. But be happy for your father, not sad. As for Jasper Flincher, that is between God and Jasper."

Janie laughed through her tears.

"You are right, as always. How did you ever become so wise?" Janie wondered aloud.

"It is not wisdom, Janie. It is faith. I believe all is as it is meant to be. I truly do. Let God guide you and He will never fail you. And we shouldn't question each step because we cannot always see where we are being led. We must not just look at our feet. We must look at the journey they are on."

Elizabeth caught sight of a bird on a neighbouring bench and it made her laugh. She was mesmerized by it, and as it flew off she followed it with her pointed finger, as though it were the most amazing thing she had ever seen.

"The innocence of a child..." Agnes mused. "Why is it that we become so filled with life that we forget to live? To truly see the wonder and beauty in something you have to see it through a child's eyes. They are not yet encumbered by hardships and fear and worry."

"This is all new for her. Innocence or not, if Elizabeth saw the same bird over and over again, it might lose its appeal. I think the true challenge in appreciating the beauty in something is seeing it as though you are seeing it for the first time. That is a rare gift indeed."

Agnes agreed. She hadn't thought of it like that before, and she reveled in it. She knew that when something stirred her soul, she was seeing something in it that she hadn't seen before. Today, the park was alive with colour, the rain bringing a kiss of moisture that brought the flowers to life. They weren't merely surviving; they were thriving, the palette of their petals a Monet canvas. They were reaching for the sun, drinking in its warmth, just as Agnes had been, and it was a spiritual energy, a connectedness that only the beauty of nature could provide.

Agnes didn't want to get up from the bench, but she knew she must. Art would be home soon and Dorothy would want to feed. Even with a cover, Agnes was too self-conscious to tend to her daughter in public. It was time to go home.

"I must be getting back. Dorothy will wake soon."

"Of course. You must be tired. You will have many sleepless nights, and you must take care of yourself or else you will be no good to her. I learned that myself," Janie said, happy to offer whatever advice she could.

"Will you come for dinner tomorrow?" Agnes asked.

"Absolutely not," Janie replied swiftly, much to Agnes's surprise and dismay. "You will come to our house. I think you forget that you just had a baby, and it is your time to put your feet up."

The change in Janie's tone was amusing to Agnes, and she couldn't help but laugh. And she was tired, too tired to argue, so she gratefully accepted Janie's offer. It had been weeks since they had been together as couples, and she looked forward to it.

Agnes stopped at a small patch of lavender at the edge of the park. It grew wild, partly hidden in a bush. A Monarch butterfly rested on a stem, and the contrast of yellow and purple was magnificent. She reached in to pull a stem out, but its woody stalk proved too thick to break and she unwittingly stripped it of its flowers. The scent of lavender on her hand made her bound and determined to try again, and she continued until a bounty of stems filled her hand.

Fatigue was no match for the joy she felt. In fact, it made everything brighter and more vibrant, as the cloud of excess thought was stripped away, leaving her mind free to be in the moment. It had only been a day, yet she couldn't remember her life before.

Agnes was feeding Dorothy when Art arrived home from work. He was in awe of his wife. It was astonishing to him that a woman's body could nourish a baby the way it did, and seeing them together made him more in love with her than ever.

"How are my two favourite girls?" he asked.

"Wonderful. We went for a walk to the park with Janie and Elizabeth. It was nice to get out of the house."

"It smells like you brought the park home."

"I couldn't help myself. You know how much I love lavender, and it was there, growing in the bushes."

Art kissed his girls, and then Agnes placed Dorothy back in her bassinette. She was soon asleep again, content to shut the world out while she adapted to her new life.

When Agnes stood up, Art embraced his wife. She let go of her strength and rested herself against him, relying on him to hold her. It wasn't just a night of baby that had her so fatigued, but weeks of it—discomfort, anticipation, and worry.

"Come, my love. Sit with me. You look drained."

Art took Agnes's hand and led her to the chesterfield. He put his arm around her shoulder and rested her head against his chest. She hadn't realized how stiff she was until she started to relax. Art's arms were the one place she allowed herself to let go, and it was as though her mind and body were disconnected. It was a contrast so absolute that she could feel herself separating.

Ensconced in his arms, Agnes began to drift off. Art reached into his pocket and placed a box on Agnes's lap. The movement brought her back, and she sat up at the sight of the box.

"What is this? Art, what did you do?" Agnes said, beginning to admonish him, even ahead of seeing the contents.

"Nothing that you don't deserve," he said, winking.

Art kissed Agnes's forehead and gave her leg a squeeze. Agnes opened the tiny box and could see a delicate silver chain and a dainty "D" resting against the satin lining.

"Oh Art, it is beautiful," Agnes said as she pulled it from the box.

"Here, let me put it on you."

Art clasped the necklace around Agnes's neck while she held out the charm, admiring it. It was neither Christmas nor her birthday, but she knew she couldn't scold him for indulging her so lavishly. It was such a deeply personal and thoughtful gift.

"You are the most thoughtful husband. Thank you."

Agnes settled back into his arms and enjoyed the intimacy for as long as her nature would allow.

"You must be famished. You work so hard."

Agnes got up from the chesterfield and looked into the bassinette. Dorothy was still asleep. Agnes looked from her sleeping babe to her pendant and smiled again.

"Thank you. I really do love this. I will treasure it always."

Agnes blew Art a kiss and then bounced into the kitchen.

Art remained in the living room and watched his sleeping daughter. He reached down and picked her up, cradling her in his arms. Art's feelings toward her were far less sentimental than Agnes's, but affecting all the same. He too felt love, but his was less emotional and more protective. When he looked at Dorothy, he saw responsibility. Sam had told him a father's role was simple in the beginning—"it is a mother's job to nurture and a father's job to keep the roof on." That is how nature intended. Nature may have had its rules and conventions, but Art could not help but be in awe of this tiny creature. She was perfect in his eyes.

That night was no different than the previous night, but Dorothy seemed keen to remain awake for longer periods in between feedings, and Agnes spent the time rocking her gently as she walked about the room. Agnes felt claustrophobic in the darkness and found herself wishing for daylight. She enjoyed solitude, but solitude in the dead of night was very isolating, very lonely.

Daylight did bring relief. As the darkest of the night began to retreat, the utter blackness gradually dissolved, lightening the stark nothingness that had lain beyond the windows. Even before the sun appeared on the horizon, the birds began to sing their songs. They announced the rising sun with music worthy of a stage. Agnes had never paid the dawn the attention it deserved; and as much as she didn't fancy the dead of night, she acknowledged the transformation would not be as spectacular were it not for the darkness that it overcame.

When Art appeared from the bedroom, breakfast was on the table. Agnes seemed weary to Art, despite her working hard to appear sunny.

"Darling, you will not disturb me if you sleep in our bed. You cannot continue to remain out here all night every night. Promise me you will rest in bed today. You will not be any good to Dorothy if you cannot stay awake. The park will be there tomorrow."

"We are having dinner with Tom and Janie tonight. I would like to go over in the afternoon. Would you be a dear and walk over on your own after you wash up?"

"Splendid. I haven't seen Tom and Janie in a long while. A good game of cards is definitely in order."

Agnes arrived at Janie's just shy of four. It was another hot and sunny day, and Dorothy was well hidden in the shade of the pram cover. She juggled her daughter in one hand and a chocolate cake in the other, held a bag of biscuits up with her teeth, and tapped at the door with her foot.

"Goodness, Agnes. Here, let me help," Janie said as she set Elizabeth down. Elizabeth, who had been walking for the better part of a month already, tootled off toward her toys.

Janie took the bag and cake and stepped aside to let Agnes in.

"Agnes, what are we going to do with you? You didn't need to bring anything over. And a cake? You will never rest, will you?"

"I am perfectly content, Janie. I had a lie-down this afternoon as the cake was cooling. As you can see, I am not asleep on my feet."

Janie rolled her eyes, knowing full well that Agnes would never admit to any sort of weakness. Janie, on the other hand, was more than happy to share her woes openly.

"This child has me running off my feet. Ever since she started walking, she will not sit still. When I move to retrieve her, she runs in the other direction. I swear she is trying to wear me out."

Agnes laughed. "I doubt she is as mischievous as that. She is simply enjoying her newfound skill. It must be wondrous to be able to move when you haven't been able to like that before. She has a new view of the world, one far different than she did when she was crawling. "

"You laugh, Agnes. Just wait. It will happen to you, and then you can tell me how much fun it is to worry about every sharp corner."

When Janie put it like that, it provided a perspective that Agnes could relate to well and it was no longer as amusing as it had just been.

"Put Dorothy on the chesterfield and come with me into the kitchen while I make tea. I'll bring Elizabeth in with us so she doesn't decide that Dorothy is one of her toys."

Janie put Elizabeth in her highchair and placed a teething biscuit on the tray. She had a mouthful of teeth already, and she made easy work of the snack.

"You shouldn't have gone to the trouble of making the cake, but I am quite glad you did," Janie said appreciatively. "Your chocolate cake is beyond compare. It is my favourite dessert in this world. And, try as I might, mine will never come close to yours."

"You are too kind, Janie. Mine is not really mine. It is my mother's recipe and hers before her."

"It is still your hands and skill that pull it together. I have no such skill."

Agnes was not going to continue to reassure Janie as it would be disingenuous. She knew what Janie was saying was true. She had a few things that she did well, but cooking was never Janie's forte.

Shortly into their cup of tea, Tom arrived home. Elizabeth ran to her father with her arms outstretched and nothing in this world could have welcomed him home any better. One could not be unmoved by such a tender display of affection.

"Agnes, I hear congratulations are in order," he said as he greeted Agnes with a kiss. "Let me see this baby who Janie has been going on and on about.

"She is beautiful, just like her mother," Tom complimented as Agnes blushed. "I'd say she is the second most beautiful baby in the world."

Agnes laughed. "We could dispute that point, but since there is no arguing that they are the *two* most beautiful babies in the world, we can be content to agree on that."

"Fair enough," Tom said.

Elizabeth began to fuss, and Janie took her into the bedroom to feed.

"I'll leave you two to debate the beauty of our children. I'll be back shortly."

Agnes was left alone with Tom while Dorothy remained asleep. The room suddenly became awkward for Agnes as she began to recall the fate of Jasper Flincher. Agnes could not let it go. Opportunities such as this did not often present themselves.

"Janie tells me that Jasper Flincher is dead."

Tom was not surprised that Janie had told Agnes, but he wasn't expecting her to say so quite so abruptly.

"Yes, the coincidence was uncanny."

"Yes, coincidences generally are, by their very nature, uncanny."

Agnes's tone changed and Tom could sense her silent questioning.

"Bad things come to bad people, Agnes. You need not worry for him. His day is done," Tom said rather casually.

Agnes was awestruck. This wasn't the Tom she knew. His tone was flat, his intent almost didactic. It was not what he had said or how he said it that had her so vexed; it was what he wasn't saying. She did not weep for the man who had caused so much sorrow—he was nothing to her—but her sense told her there was more.

"They certainly do, but deserved isn't always justified. We may wish our own judgement, but when we move beyond mere thought we step into God's dominion, and nothing good can come from that."

Tom narrowed his focus on Agnes. He couldn't read her either, and for him too it was what Agnes was not saying that had him distressed.

"Agnes, I cannot feel bad for such a man. I am a police officer, and it is my duty to ensure that those who treat the law with contempt are punished for it."

"That is true, but whatever his past, was he not a victim in the end as well?"

"The law is not perfect, Agnes, just as we are not. If it were, Jasper Flincher would have never been in the position he found himself in when he died. But he did become a victim, as did the person who killed him. That is fate."

Chapter 22

"What could have possessed you to choose November to get married, Mary? It is five degrees, and there is a foot of snow on the ground already," Agnes pointed out. "One should be in a garden, not in front of a fireplace trying to stay warm."

"Yes, you keep telling me. I like the snow. It doesn't bother me in the least. I think it is quite pretty."

"Yes, it is pretty, and I would welcome it were it not for the cold. My body was not made for winter."

"Percy could not get time away from work until now, and he wanted to take a honeymoon right away. There was no grand design to give you frostbite," Mary said light-heartedly.

"And you still have no idea where you are going?"

"None whatsoever. Percy insisted on making it a surprise for me. All I know is that I was to be ready to go tomorrow morning."

"Tomorrow morning ... after you spend your first night in your new home. You are a very fortunate girl," Sarah said to her daughter.

"Yes, I am. I didn't think it possible to be this happy. Percy is wonderful."

Sarah was comforted by the immense joy in Mary's voice. She would dearly miss the companionship of her daughter; she was the last of her girls to leave and only the boys would remain. Their new home was in Winnipeg, not far—only across the bridge—but it felt so much farther for Sarah.

Agnes continued arranging Mary's hair as Dorothy lay on the floor. Dorothy played with a red bird toy that hung over her head. She was mesmerized as it swung back and forth, and she reached up to it and batted it with her hand.

"Were you nervous?" Mary asked her sister.

"Nervous for marriage? Not really? Nervous that Art would be glad afterwards that he made the right decision, yes. It is a difficult thing to admit, but I did worry that I might not be the best wife. You try hard and wonder if it is ever enough."

Agnes's walls were thick and her doors rarely opened. It was a rare moment indeed and Mary knew it.

"I worry about the same. Mum is such a good mum and Sam loves her so. Will I be able to be as good? Could anyone?"

"Mary, of course you will. You are such a good person, better than I am," Agnes said with a laugh. "I know I have my faults, but you, you are goodness. You are kind, you are loving, and you are accepting. I only wish I had half your goodness."

Agnes kissed her sister on the top of her head. Her words, and the sincerity with which they were delivered, were manna to Mary. She knew her sister loved her, but that love was often delivered under the guise of sarcasm and playful banter. Rarely did it come so heartfelt and pure.

"There, I would say you are now worthy of my brother-in-law," Agnes said jokingly. "You are radiant, Mary."

Mary looked at her hair in the mirror, and her opinion was apparent. Agnes had done a brilliant job and she felt like a princess. All that remained was the dress.

Mary's dress was crafted by her mother, as was Agnes's before hers, and like Agnes's it was simple yet elegant. When Mary put it on, she transformed into a lady, graceful and sophisticated.

The wedding was attended only by immediate family and a few friends. There were twenty-two in total, and it was exactly how Mary and Percy wanted it.

Sarah and Sam transformed their living room into a painting. There were few real flowers, as the time of year proved it a challenge, but the lack was more than made up for with flowers of ribbon and lace. The room came alive with colour, not bright and vivid summer colour, but muted tones befitting a November garden.

The ceremony was touching and intimate. Percy could not have been a prouder groom nor his bride more exquisite. It had been slow coming, but they showed that the strongest and most enduring bonds are born of patience and not simply love. Percy may have taken time to overcome his shyness, but once he freed himself from the bonds of fear he moved heaven and earth to prove his love.

"As best man, it is my honour to toast the happy couple. Mary, you have gone from being my sister-in-law to being my … sister-in-law," Art said with a dramatic pause. The room erupted in laughter, much to Art's pleasure. "You are doubly family and I couldn't be happier. Two Berries and two Craigs. If that doesn't spell trouble, I don't know what does." The laughter continued as did the happiness that emanated from the room.

"In all seriousness and sincerity, Agnes and I are over the moon for you both. We want to wish you a happy life together filled with incredible joy, prosperity, and longevity. I would love to toast you both with champagne, but we would need to go to British Columbia to do that. Alas, John and Margaret will have to do that for us. Let us raise our glasses to Percy and Mary. Many blessings to you both."

"Hear, hear," was said by all. The sound of clanking glasses filled the room, and there was not an unsmiling face to be found.

Percy stood up. "I would like to thank you all for being here. It means so much to Mary and me to share this day with the people we love the most. We are only sorry that Margaret and my brother and sister are not here with us. However, their absence will be remedied in three days' time when my lovely bride and I arrive in Vancouver for a visit.

Mary jumped up and threw her arms around her new husband, and the room erupted in clapping and whistling. This time around, Sarah was not shocked by the hooting and hollering, and she was even beginning to relax her long-held beliefs of the sanctity of propriety. Appropriate or not, she was pleased to see her daughter so incredibly happy.

During the reception, there was no shortage of people to occupy Dorothy, and Art and Agnes savoured the time they had to themselves. It was the first time since Dorothy's birth that they had had an opportunity to relax and have fun, and they took full advantage.

Percy grabbed Agnes's hand and pulled her onto the dance floor when a slow song began. "We haven't had a chance to talk. How are you?"

"You are asking me? This is your wedding day. I should be asking you."

"I couldn't be happier."

"I found some sleeping pills in the cupboard," Agnes blurted out, surprising Percy. She surprised herself as well.

"You found them?"

"What do you mean? You knew?" Agnes pulled back and looked at Percy. She was appalled and went on the defensive. "How is it that you knew and I didn't?"

"They are only mild, Agnes. They are nothing to worry about. The doctor suggested them to help him fall asleep. He told me that he only needs them every once in a while. He didn't want to worry you. You have enough with the baby."

While Agnes felt a pang of jealousy that Art had confided in his brother and not her, she understood why he had done so. She was relieved that he had seen a doctor, which was all she had wanted in the first place. There was most likely some embarrassment for him, and she didn't want to bring attention to it. There seemed no good reason. He had been doing so much better.

Percy returned Agnes to her seat where Art was engaged in a conversation with the bride.

"Do you realize that our children will be double first cousins?" Agnes pointed out, clearly thrilled by the prospect. "They will be almost as close as siblings. How exciting for them."

Mary giggled and turned a shade of red.

"And Vancouver! Percy, you sly dog. I am quite envious," Art said. "Are you going for the family or the alcohol?" he teased.

Percy laughed. "It will be nice to have a pint or two. I won't deny that."

"The good people of British Columbia finally saw the error of their ways. Margaret and John's restaurant is flourishing since they repealed Prohibition in June, and I doubt the province is going to be cast into hell as a result," Art said sharply.

"Well, maybe we will just have to stay put in Vancouver. How would that be, Mary?"

"Stay in Vancouver? Our mother would be on the first train out to bring you both back. You can just forget that silly notion." Agnes was teasing, but at the same time not really. Sarah let one daughter slip through her fingers, and she wasn't about to do it again if she could help it.

The Craigs had a deep history in Vancouver, and the prospect of them returning was not an absurd one. Art and Percy lived there as children and only moved back to Winnipeg a few years before the war. Two siblings were alive and remained there; their mother and two other siblings were buried there.

Bill was left to care for his five children, the youngest not yet five when his wife died of tuberculosis. Within three months of her heartbreaking death, his son Cecil, then twelve, became caught in a waterwheel and died. His shirt became ensnared and he drowned. The oldest, Edith, a girl of only fourteen, had been tasked with caring for her ailing mother, and shortly after the mother's death she too became ill. She suffered in a weakened state for four years before she perished. Art was fifteen at the time and well-remembered the traumatic loss and sadness that filled the house. Bill was a strong man, having endured the death of his own mother at a young age, but the loss of his wife, Annie, left him broken.

"Time to break up this private party," Tom said as he and Janie approached the foursome.

"Percy was making us envious with all this talk of Vancouver. It is certainly much warmer there than here. I think I may hide in their trunk," Agnes mused aloud.

"Yes, colour me green as well. Sounds like a swell time," Tom said. "Say, did you read the paper yesterday? Looks like the bloke who killed McCurdy was killed in Chicago. Same for the bloke who ran from the hotel with him. Police said they were shot in in self-defence, but the word is it might have been a gang killing. I guess if you walk into fire, you will get burned. Fate always catches up."

They were glad to hear the men posed no further threat, but Tom's talk of fate reminded Agnes of Flincher's death and she was quick to change the subject.

"All that dancing has made me hungry. Art, darling, please be a dear and get me a plate while I check on Dorothy. Mum has been so good, but she must need a break."

Chapter 23

1932

Mary and Percy joined Art and Agnes at their home for dinner. It had been a month or so since they had been together, and the children were quite happy to be in each other's company again. Their energy and exuberance knew no bounds. It was a deafening pitch of screams and squeals.

"This is not a playground! This is our home. Please behave or we will have to separate you." Agnes was becoming exasperated. "Dorothy and Donny, I am quite serious."

"They are not solely to blame. My three are just as rambunctious. It is the turn in the weather that has them so unmanageable. They have to get rid of that energy somewhere, and when it cannot be outside it must be in. Last week they were playing in the sunshine, enjoying the blessed warmth, and suddenly a week later it is minus thirteen. How it can swing forty degrees within a few days is beyond me."

"We live in the land of extremes. There is no denying that."

Agnes finished setting the children's table and then called them to sit. There was no misbehaving at the dinner table. They knew better. Their hides had been tanned enough to have learned what was acceptable and what was not.

"How was Vancouver, Percy? Did you get to see Margaret and John?"

"I did. The office isn't that far from their restaurant. They took pity on me and fed me often. I was a very happy man."

"I am quite envious. You have been there twice since they moved and I have yet to visit. The girls are now teenagers, and if it weren't for photographs, I would not know them. I cannot wait for our trip this summer. I have heard Vancouver is lovely in June," Agnes said.

"How was the business part of the trip? Why were you out there again?" Art asked.

Mary and Percy's eyes locked and they engaged each other in a silent conversation, the tone of which had Agnes incredibly curious.

"What? Don't hold back. What are you not telling us?" Agnes pushed.

Percy nodded to give Mary the permission to speak.

"Percy has been offered a new job with Marshall-Wells in Vancouver, and he has accepted." She remained quiet as she awaited her sister's reaction. There was none. "The house is already under offer, and we will be moving in a few weeks' time."

The silence at the table was thunderous. Agnes's expression turned to astonishment once she realized that Mary was not joking.

"You can't be serious? You cannot leave us here. You will be out there with Margaret, and we will be left behind." Agnes tried frantically to come up with persuasive reasons, as though she had the power to sway them, but the shock had rendered her speechless. It was a state wholly unfamiliar to her. "Dorothy will be devastated. No, no, you can't leave."

Dorothy had overheard the conversation and began to cry. Her heartbroken sobs drew tears from her cousins Margaret and Norma. Dorothy was more a sister than a cousin to them, and her sadness reduced their excitement for their adventure to a rush of loss.

Agnes did not hear her daughter. Dorothy's weeping was silenced by the voices in Agnes's head. Agnes continued to fight for the words that would make Mary renounce her disheartening revelation, but they did not come. In one short turn, the happy gathering had turned heavy-hearted. It felt as though Agnes's world was crumbling. She could no longer look at her sister and dropped her head in despair. Mary knew their plans would not be well received, but she had not anticipated such a strong reaction.

Art rubbed his wife's shoulder in consolation, but it had the opposite effect from the one he intended. One by one, the tears began to fall on her plate as her sadness mounted. She loved her life. The lives she and Art shared with Mary and Percy meant the world to her, and it was about to vanish. The pain was unbearable.

Mary was overcome by Agnes's grief. Agnes rarely let herself go in front of others.

"Come with us," Mary blurted. It was not something that she had thought of as a possibility until that very moment.

Agnes looked up at her sister, her eyes red and wet with tears.

"Come with you? That's not possible," Agnes responded.

Art pondered the thought and then began to nod.

"Why is it not? In fact, I think it might be a splendid idea," Art said. "We have been talking about having me go out on my own. Winnipeg is in steady decline. It is now nothing but a shadow of its former self. We must face it. Businesses are shutting down faster than they are starting up, and there is so much unemployment. Families can't feed themselves and social services can't keep up. It is food before anything else, especially for something as unnecessary as a coat of paint. I am only working half the time I am able because the work is simply not there. Vancouver has to be better."

"Vancouver has been hit hard by the depressed economy, but not as hard as Winnipeg, at least not for my company. It is the reason we are going," Percy added to the justification.

It didn't take Agnes long before she came to the only conclusion that she could.

"We cannot because it would kill Mum. It would be the death of her and you know it," Agnes said as she turned back toward Mary. "Mum is closer to seventy than not, and she is not as strong as she used to be."

The others could not disagree, but they did differ on how it should affect them.

"Yes, Mum is getting older, but even so she would not deny us our futures and our happiness. She would expect us to live as we want and not in a world of obligation to her. That would kill her far sooner. Look at what she did herself. She brought us over from England for a better life. She will understand. And besides, she has three sons still here, two of whom still live at home. Marriage and babies will not be far off for them. Mum will have her fill."

Agnes allowed herself to ponder the possibility. She found herself caught up in the dream, and her hesitation was seen as an open door.

"Other than your parents and your brothers, what reason do we have to stay? You have said over and over how much you dislike the cold winters. It is March and yet it is still twenty-five below. I would bet the tulips are already pushing up soil in Vancouver. There it rarely gets below freezing. And the ocean and the mountains ... there is nothing like it." Art's enthusiasm was catching and Agnes felt herself drawn into it.

Agnes looked around the table. All eyes were upon her. Mary and Percy sat eager for a response. The children now sat silent at their tables, fearful to show their hope. The room held its breath for Agnes to speak.

"This is mad. It truly is. But, yes, let's do it." Agnes covered her mouth, stunned by the words that had just come from it. She was not known to speak without thought or give in to flights of fancy. She was neither impetuous nor spontaneous, and for the moment she shut her mind off from thinking about the ramifications of the decision.

"Yes, let's do it," she repeated, as if to convince herself.

Art stood up and lifted his wife off the chair. He embraced her tightly and spun her around, and Percy and Mary began to cheer.

"Dorothy, Donny, would you like to move to Vancouver with your cousins?" he asked.

They both came running to their parents, and Art scooped them up, one in each arm. Art had long missed Vancouver. He left a part of himself there and he looked forward to returning. He was born in Winnipeg, but since the war it had not felt like home.

Art bent down, picked up his wine glass, and raised it high. "This calls for a toast. To new beginnings," he said.

"To new beginnings," the others repeated.

In the blink of an eye, the direction of their lives had changed. All that had come before was tied up nicely and tucked away. They would leave it all behind and begin again, a fresh start with the greatest of hopes. Agnes remembered coming to Canada as a young child. It had been both frightening and exhilarating. The memories in her mind's eye had faded, but the sensitivity to the emotions remained strong. Life there had been filled with sadness and suffering, but her life in Canada had been wonderful. Agnes believed that change rarely brought good, but she believed such monumental change to be the exception. Her own life was proof of that.

"Tying up loose ends for us should not be difficult. We have no house to sell; we only need give a month's notice to our landlord," Art said.

"Where will we stay when we get there? It will take time to find a house. And what of our furnishings? Do we take them? We can't possibly sort all this out so quickly." Agnes was beginning to panic as her mind attempted to sort through the tasks that began to list out in her mind.

"I'm sure we can stay with John and Margaret until we find a home. We can figure out the rest in the next few days. Don't fret. Everything will work out perfectly. I have no doubt."

Art's optimism helped ease Agnes's worry. She had never been comfortable with unmapped plans. As long as there was a task to complete, it was well prepared for.

"John and Margaret would be thrilled for you to stay with them. They have plenty of room. They know we are coming, but you, you will be such a wonderful surprise." Mary was overjoyed at the thought that they would all be reunited. "John has an agent friend who is gathering a list of suitable homes for us. He can do the same for you."

Agnes continued to grow more comfortable with the prospect of moving, but Mary's reassurances did nothing to ease the burden of their mother's suffering. It would undoubtedly come and it would most definitely torment Agnes. They decided they would tell her after church on Sunday. Agnes had two days to think how best to deliver the news and two days to imagine it over and over. She worked herself into a frenzy as she lay in bed that night, going over every possible scenario, imagining every possible response. None of them ended with a smile. Her mother's voice echoed in her mind, her look of desolation imploring her to change her mind.

Neither could fall asleep. Both wrestled with doubt.

"Are you having second thoughts?" Agnes asked.

"No, no second thoughts. I could not live with myself if this did not turn out well. I have long wanted to be a self-made man, and I jumped at the chance before I was sure of your feelings. It was selfish of me and I feel bad for it."

Agnes could hear the guilt in Art's voice. She turned on her side to face him and draped her arm over his chest.

"That is not selfish. What is good for you is good for us. It is your effort that keeps us clothed and fed."

"I want us to own our own house like Percy and Mary do. I want a home that is really ours. I cannot do that on a painter's wage alone, but if I employ others I can eventually manage the business and step back from the physical work. I enjoy painting, but I am getting to be an old man," he said with a laugh. "There are too many doing the same work here, and with such a short season there isn't room for another company. I imagine Vancouver is growing."

Agnes ran her fingers over Art's greying temples. She loved how his salt and pepper hair made him look distinguished.

"If you are an old man, then I guess I find old men attractive," she said as she ran her fingers from his temples to his chest.

Art laughed and turned toward his wife.

"You are quite the vixen, aren't you?"

Art gently pushed Agnes onto her back. Her kisses were soft and they made him weak. It wasn't long before he surrendered to the pleasure and fell back into his place.

Agnes soon fell asleep. Art was not as fortunate. He was tired, body and mind, and despite the release it was not enough. He slipped out of bed and took a pill from the cabinet. Agnes had been relieved when he finally explained himself. Art had assured her he only needed them occasionally, which was the truth, but she was unaware that what she had found in the cabinet that night was no longer strong enough and the weakness had since been remedied.

The pills numbed Art's senses and took him to a place of nothingness. Sleep came without pause, and despite the hope the dream did as well. The foxhole, the guns, the smoke, the smells. He could not see through the cloud of battle. All he could do was keep moving and hope and pray he was moving toward safety. But as the fog cleared, it was clear he had not. The enemy stood before him, the end of the rifle inches from his face. He stood there frozen, the sounds of battle loud in his ears. He always woke as the rifle was firing.

This time Agnes remained asleep as Art sat up, wet with perspiration. He was still numb from the pill, and his mind eventually found sleep again, but not before he poured himself a shot of gin.

Art woke up in a good mood, and it was quite clear to Agnes that he had not changed his mind.

"We are finishing up a job today, and I will tell Pete that I am leaving."

"You have been with him ten years now. It is hard to believe."

"It is. And I am ready to move on. This will be good for us. I will make a better life for us, I promise. We will have a new car, not one that is in constant need of repairs. And we will own our own house. I won't stop until we do."

"I have no doubt. And I love you for it," she said warmly. "We are going to Janie's today. We had planned on having lunch there and then going to the market. We need a few things."

"Grand. 'Til dinner then." Art kissed his wife and slipped out the door.

Agnes spent the morning taking an inventory of what they would take with them—only what was absolutely necessary and only what would cost more to replace than move. They were not spendthrifts, and there was little she could see herself parting with. It would be so wasteful to leave things behind, only to have to purchase them again.

Just before noon, Agnes bundled the children up from head to toe. It was Arctic outside and the icy wind made it feel even colder. It wasn't far to Janie's, only a few blocks, so she knew the discomfort wouldn't be long-lasting. And as Agnes thought about the cold, it occurred to her that she would never have to endure another Winnipeg winter. Every year she complained about the winters, and every year she dreamed about living somewhere warmer. But as she stood faced with the prospect, she felt an impending sense of loss. Winnipeg was all she could remember, and on many levels it saddened her.

Janie ushered them into the warm house, and they were accosted by an army of children before they could even remove their coats. Dorothy and Donny were greeted by the twins—Sammy and Tommy—Elizabeth, and little Peter.

Dorothy escaped the crowd and ran off with Elizabeth to her room. Donny found himself caught in the usual tug-of-war between the twins.

"Come, sit. Lunch will be ready in a few minutes."

"It smells incredibly good in here. I hope you didn't go to too much trouble," Agnes questioned.

"As much trouble as someone who can't cook can go to," Janie said light-heartedly. "I just made a pot of soup. It has everything in it but the kid's boots."

"We'll save the boots for dessert, then," Agnes teased.

"How was dinner with Mary and Percy last night? Did Percy have a good trip? It must be exciting to travel. I would dearly love to go to Vancouver one day."

Agnes swallowed hard. She was going to tell Janie, but couldn't bring herself to do it, not right then. Agnes wasn't one to procrastinate, but she knew Janie would be devastated and she wanted to hold off hurting her as long as she could.

As Janie got up to set the table, Elizabeth came running into the room.

"Mummy, Dorothy is moving to Vancouver. Can we move too?"

Agnes coughed hard as her throat turned as dry as a prairie breeze. It hadn't occurred to her to tell the children not to say a word and she reprimanded herself for such a foolish oversight.

"Vancouver? You must be mistaken, dear," Janie said as she continued to set the table.

"Children," Janie called. "It is time for lunch."

"No, Mummy, it isn't a mistake. Dorothy told me they are moving to Vancouver."

Janie turned to Agnes, who was looking apologetically at her. She could see there must be some truth to this, and she waited for answers.

"What does Lizzie mean?"

"She is speaking the truth, Janie. It was decided yesterday that we are to move to Vancouver. Percy is being transferred with his job and we are to go as well."

Janie pulled out a chair and sat down.

"Let me see if I understand this ... both you and Mary are leaving? You are both going? My two dearest friends."

Janie looked lost. Like Agnes had before her, Janie looked for some recognition of misunderstanding. Janie shifted her focus to the table and stared blankly, dispiritedly, as though she had been told something from which there was no possible recovery.

Lizzie had been eager to share the news, and her mother's drastic change in expression made her realize it wasn't news to be cherished. In a flash, Lizzie too realized what it meant.

The boys came running into the dining room like a herd of wild elephants. The usual admonishment they would have faced was nowhere to be heard, and the thick air stopped them in their tracks. The room was filled with searching eyes, eyes looking for the cause of such tension. Peter was too young to notice, and he entered the room with only one thought on his mind.

"I am hungry. Can we eat?"

"Janie, I am sorry. I expected to tell you after lunch and not have it blurted out like that."

Dorothy caught her mother's tone and felt immediate remorse for having caused it. She had not imagined the source of her excitement could ever have been taken in such a way.

"Art has decided to venture out on his own, and he believes there will be better opportunity in Vancouver. As you know, he has lived there. As well he has a sister and brother there. And of course Margaret and John are there."

Janie was hurting, and she didn't want the children to see it. She put on a brave face and continued to support her friend the best that she could.

"Well, that all sounds very exciting."

Janie's words were of no relief to Agnes, who could see they were not sincere. Few words were spoken during lunch, and Agnes was impatient for the children to return to their play so she could speak without reserve.

"This was all quite unexpected. I was in your position only last night. When Mary told me of their move, I was knocked sideways. I could not imagine her not being here. Asking us to go with them was a spur of the moment thing, and now I say the same to you in the spur of the moment. Why not? Tom could easily get a job with the police department there. You have no other family here. We are your family," Agnes pleaded.

"I cherish the thought, but we cannot. Tom was promoted not that long ago, and he would be loath to start again. I needn't ask him. I know the answer."

Janie would always support her husband above all else, and she would do it without complaint, but in this instance her loyalty was marred by her own desire.

"We are only a train ride away. You can visit often," Agnes said enthusiastically.

Agnes too was sad, but she had a new life to look forward to. It was always worse for those left behind, for they were faced with nothing but loss.

"That is exciting about Art venturing out on his own. He has wanted to do that for some time. It is all too easy to get comfortable, and then one day you realize that your life has passed you by."

"That is so true. Look at Tom. He fixed his circumstance. He is a detective now. He has wanted that since he became a police officer. I think that Percy's success has caused Art to doubt himself. He is proud of his brother, but I believe he feels he has let himself down. He needs to do this for his pride and sense of purpose."

"I can understand that, but it doesn't make me like it any better," Janie said through a stiff smile.

Chapter 24

Sarah and the children had been attending the same church since they had first arrived in Norwood. In the twenty-eight years since, Sarah and Sam had been married there, and their children and grandchildren had been christened within its hallowed walls.

As they sat down on the same pews that they had sat on week after week, Agnes looked at the fixtures as though she were seeing them for the first time. The church was suffused with the blues, reds, and yellows of Christ's robe in a glorious rainbow that radiated the noonday sun through the stained glass. Perhaps it was simply the perfect circumstances, but she did not recall seeing such beauty within it before. It was as though heaven had opened up. Agnes felt an incredible peace and she felt God was speaking to her, reassuring her all was as it was supposed to be.

Agnes had been sure to tell the children not to say a word to their grandparents about the move. Telling her mother was going to be difficult, and she didn't want an abrupt slip of the tongue to be the starting point.

As they parked the car in front of the house, Art squeezed Agnes's hand. He did not say a word, but he needn't. His eyes spoke of love and support and faith in their decision. It gave Agnes the strength she needed to face her mother.

Agnes's chocolate cake sat on the table, alongside Mary's fried chicken and Sarah's salads and cured ham.

"My favourite part of the week," Sam enthused. "I'm a lucky man to have a wife and daughters who can cook so well."

Sam sat in his chair. It was deep and oversized and had wide arms perfect for sitting grandchildren. It had been his father's before him, and it *was* Sam as much as anything that existed in that house. Agnes sat on the arm as a child, telling Sam's father all about her week. He had welcomed Sarah's children as his own grandchildren, and they embraced their "poppa" from the beginning. They were treated no differently than the children Sarah and Sam had together, and Agnes remembered Sam's parents with incredible fondness and love.

As had been the case beyond their memory, one by one Sam's grandchildren sat on the arm of his well-worn chair. They often argued about order, but in the end they all cherished their time with their grandpa. He was interested in hearing all about their lives, their week in school, their hopes and wishes, and they were more than eager to tell him. They loved him with all their hearts, and they would miss him beyond sadness—they just didn't know it yet. They were young and were consumed with the excitement that lay before them. But they would one day.

As the last grandchild had his time with Sam, Mary spoke up.

"Mum, Pa, we have something to share with you."

Sarah looked at Sam, wondering what it could be. Babies were always the first thought.

Mary had her parent's full attention, and she clasped her sweaty hands as she prepared to break the news.

"Percy has been given a marvelous promotion at work."

Sarah and Sam both turned toward Percy, and Sam stood to offer Percy his congratulations.

"Please. There is more."

Mary's voice was starting to quiver. She had not thought she would be nervous, but she found herself being incredibly so. She was tormented with the thought of disappointing them. Her worry was now for Sam as much as it was for her mother. She knew what she would be taking from them, and it grieved her like nothing had before.

"Percy's new job is in Vancouver. We leave in a few weeks."

The room fell silent. Sam sat back down and remained still. He continued to look at Mary as he absorbed the information, her discomfort rising with his unwavering gaze.

Before either Sarah or Sam could speak, Agnes wanted to get her part out. If there was to be shock and sadness, it might as well occur all at once.

"We will be going as well. Art will be starting his own painting company."

Sam turned toward Agnes as a gasp escaped from Sarah's rattly chest.

"You are both going?" Sarah asked her daughters.

Mary and Agnes looked at each other and then nodded as they turned back toward their mother.

"Yes, Mum. We are."

Neither Mary nor Agnes knew what else to say. There really wasn't anything that could make the situation any easier to accept.

"Well," was all Sam could muster.

"That sounds like a wonderful opportunity for you all. Percy, Art, I am happy for you both. You must certainly follow the path that opportunity leads you down," Sarah said through a smile that neither Mary nor Agnes could determine was genuine or not. "And I am so pleased that you will both be reunited with your sister. How I miss her and John and the girls."

Mary and Agnes were dumbfounded. This was clearly not the reaction they had expected.

Sarah's cough had turned deeper, and she strained to clear her chest.

"Mum, are you all right? Have you been to see a doctor? Your cough is not going away. It seems to be getting worse," Agnes said, worried.

"I am fine. It is just the time of year. It will be over soon enough."

Sam had yet to say anything and Agnes's attention turned to him.

"Pa, what are you thinking?"

Sam didn't answer at first. It was clear he was swallowing hard and trying to stay whole. Agnes was taken aback; she had expected the opposite from each of them.

Dorothy sat down on the arm of Sam's chair and put her head on his shoulder.

"Grandpa, please don't be sad. I'll stay with you." Dorothy wasn't thinking about what she was saying. She was only trying to stop the heart of someone she loved from breaking.

Sam blinked hard and kissed Dorothy's head.

"Your grandpa will miss you. He'll miss all of you. Now if you'll excuse me, I need to visit the gentlemen's room."

Sam walked out of the room and Agnes's heart broke. He looked as though the colour in his world had been turned off. He looked shattered.

Sarah barked as she tried once again to clear her chest. She did not appear shattered. She did not appear destroyed. It was as if there was something else on her mind.

"Mum, please take care of yourself. Coughs can turn before you know it. You should see a doctor."

Sarah nodded to appease the concerns.

"And your father will be fine. He just needs time to absorb the news. You know how much he loves his grandchildren."

Agnes questioned what they had decided and wondered if the decision should be undone. *How can we cause such heartache?* she wondered. *It would be selfish and cruel.* The question confronted her conscience with full force.

Sarah could see her daughter's consternation and, despite her own, she sought to remedy it.

"Agnes, do not fret. This is an exciting time for all of you. Cherish it. However, you must understand that a father loves his daughters like no others. You were his before I was. He has loved you as his own from that first day on the train."

Agnes always knew her mother to be practical and sensible in all that she did, a woman who rose to the task and always put others first. But Agnes wondered if it was that her mother placed others first or that she simply never thought of herself at all. Sarah had shown no sadness at their disclosure; she had only expressed her wishes for their happiness and good fortune.

"I understand, Mum…" Agnes said, pausing as Sam returned.

"Moving is probably a prudent thing to do. Our own business has declined heavily. People just aren't buying meat the way they used to. They can't afford to. Half the abattoirs in town have closed their doors. The drought hasn't helped either. Farmers cannot afford to feed their livestock. Vancouver should be better for you."

Percy sat up. He had not said a word since Mary had spoken up. He had never been one to get caught in the thick of things, and this was no exception.

"The company has acquired a few warehouses in the Vancouver area in the last couple of years, and I will be a district manager, just making sure things run smoothly. Business is down there as well, but the decline has not been as steep as here."

"That sounds like a fine promotion. Congratulations. Your father must be proud."

"He is. Thank you, Sam. He is coming with us to Vancouver. With the two of us and our families gone, there is nothing left for him here."

Percy realized how insensitive that sounded and he kicked himself for it, but Sam was a gentleman and he hid the wound well.

"And you, Art, you are going to take the world by storm. There is nothing like working for yourself. It is not easy, but there is reward in independence."

"I agree. I have wanted to do this for some time. I certainly won't rest until I have made a success of it," Art said assuredly.

"I have no doubt you will," Sam said.

Like her mother, Agnes would not show her feelings to her husband. Art tried to comfort her for the sadness he knew lay beneath the surface, but she wanted no part of it.

"The worst of it is over. We have told our dearest friends and my parents. It can only get better from here," Agnes said as they started the drive home.

The days that followed were filled with whatever was needed to prepare one's life to start anew. Vehicles were sold, notices of all sorts were given, schools were notified, belongings were packed, and tickets were purchased. Slowly the ties that bound were severed. Some ties were easy and some not quite so.

"How are the preparations going?" Sarah asked. As much as Agnes loved her mother, she had avoided this "last" visit, pushing it off as long as she could.

"I think we are ready."

"Come, sit," Sarah said as she patted the chesterfield beside her.

Sarah had aged profoundly, and Agnes could not remember if it had been gradual or an abrupt change following the news. Either way, it was the first time that Agnes had noticed and it saddened her tremendously. Her mother no longer appeared the vibrant woman she remembered. She was now firmly in the twilight of her life. It was a wretched send-off and Agnes felt an undeniable foreboding.

"Mum, have you yet seen a doctor?" Agnes asked, concerned by her mother's apathy for her own well-being.

"Yes. There is no need to worry."

There was a layer behind Sarah's smile, but Agnes knew it would be pointless to question. She would not get the truth no matter how hard she pressed.

Agnes sat as she was directed. She had sat on that same chesterfield too many times to fathom and yet, much like with every other aspect of her life in Winnipeg, it now seemed new. She wondered how altered and obscured her world was because of her pedantic character. She recognized it as a flaw, but she could not help herself.

"I have something for you girls," Sarah said.

Sarah's cough crackled like thunder and she winced at the pain, but she didn't miss a beat. She excused herself and returned with an open box.

"What do you have there, Mum?" Agnes asked.

"I have something that I want to share with each of you girls. I'll give Mary's to her myself."

Sarah reached into the box and pulled out a necklace. "This is the necklace that Eleanor gave me."

Sarah opened it up and showed the tiny picture to Agnes. It was grainy, but one of the women was unmistakable ... it was her mother. Agnes didn't recognize the other woman, but she knew her to be the woman she had referred to as Aunt Eleanor.

"You were so young when Eleanor died. You might not remember her," Sarah said with sadness in her voice. "She was my dearest friend in the world and I still miss her today. Margaret was very close to her. She loved her like a mother, and this necklace will be precious to her. I want her to have it."

Agnes remembered her, practically speaking, but she was unsure how much of it was fed to her through the years versus what she had actually retained in her mind. Regardless of her memory, her thoughts of Eleanor were incredibly warm ones.

Sarah reached in again and pulled out a smaller wooden box. Agnes gasped.

"Mum, what are you doing?" Agnes didn't have to ask. She knew and it terrified her.

Sarah put the box on her lap and held it in her hands for a moment before she gently slid the lid back. She reached in and pulled out the dried rose.

"I have not held this rose in twenty-eight years, not since I married Sam. I loved your father dearly, but I never wanted to disrespect Sam or have him question my love for him. As much as this rose is precious to me, it is only so because it came from your father. *Your* father. It belongs to you now more than it does to me."

"I don't know what to say, Mum. Thank you. I will treasure this always."

Sarah reached into the wooden box and pulled out a piece of paper.

"No, Mum," Agnes said as she began to tear up. "You can't part with this." Agnes was feeling desperate. These were her mother's most prized possessions, and she was just giving them away. Agnes was certain there was more to this cough than her mother was letting on.

"This has meant as much to you as it has to me. When you were a little girl, you would read it and pretend you had written it. You are my soul, my child, and I wrote this for you as much as I wrote it for me."

Life is but a journey, and one that I take with pride. God shall guide me.

Life is full of challenges, all of which I accept with purpose. My heart is pure and my head held high.

Life is difficult, but it only makes me stronger. God protects me. Nothing can break me.

Life is painful, but its lessons teach us to feel. And I feel from the depths of my soul.

I am Sarah. I am strong. I am proud.

Sarah had written this as a girl, after her own father had died. It had given her comfort and strength through all that life had placed before her, and Agnes had taken the words to heart as well. It was a bond that they shared and it was unbreakable.

Agnes inhaled deeply, as if it were her last breath. Love and heartache danced in the abyss of her soul, and she could not break free. The child she had been and the woman who she was began to grieve a loss so strong and so deep that it could not be imagined. She began to mourn the death of someone not yet dead and a piece of her broke off, crumbling onto a mountain of memories preserved for the dusk of her own life.

"My old bones are rattling about in this big, empty house. I only have two children left at home, and it seems a good time to sell."

There would be nine less at Sunday brunch, and it would be a matter of practicality. So much was going to change and no one could pretend otherwise.

"This home has served us well and I will dearly miss it," Agnes said with a heavy heart.

"It has served us well. But memories stay with us. They are not left behind. We will not be worse for it."

Agnes could only smile at her mother's sentiment. She was forever the faithful pragmatist, unwavering in her constancy.

There were but a few days left ahead of their journey and so much yet to do.

Chapter 25

It was a typical March day in Winnipeg, overcast and biting cold. Now all that remained between them and the train station were final good-byes and a myriad of chiselled, icy roads.

The houses had been emptied of their belongings that morning and taken by truck to a rail car. All that they maintained in their possession was what was needed to get them to Vancouver—tickets, clothing, and food. The rest would meet them at the other end of their journey.

As Art, Agnes, and the children walked out of their home of ten years, there were no feelings of regret. To Art and Agnes, it had never really felt like home, never more than temporary, and the prospect of owning their own home one day more than made up for any sadness of leaving what had been comfortable and familiar.

The car had been sold, and the final trip to Union Station was by streetcar. As they crossed the street that Agnes had lived on most of her life, she felt a tightening in her chest that made her gasp for air. Art carried suitcases in each hand, and it tormented him that he could not comfort his wife.

"I wonder what Grandma and Grandpa are doing right now," Dorothy asked.

Children only thought of the moment and Agnes could think of nothing but the future. Her daughter's words were salt in the wound. Agnes soothed her soul by telling herself that they would return to visit, but she knew that reality was less certain. As she looked up the street one last time, she asked for God to protect her parents and she prayed for their health. There was nothing else she could do.

They travelled over the Red and Assiniboine Rivers, both of which had not yet begun their spring thaw. The running water moved below the frozen surface, out of sight. In areas where it had broken, it had buckled upwards, creating mountains of ice. It was a stunning testament to the power of nature.

A streetcar carried them along their route that day, but the city was experiencing a striking transformation. The city's streetcars were being replaced by motor buses, one by one, and streets that had never known public transportation now carried passengers. The downturn in the economy seemed to be having no effect on the city's progress.

As they approached Union Station on the right, Agnes caught sight of The Fort Garry on the opposite side. She thought of their wedding night and grew nostalgic for the memories.

"One of the best nights of my life," Art said sweetly as he caught Agnes looking at the hotel.

Union Station, while grand in structure, was quite bleak in appearance. The station's monotone, white limestone façade lacked any sort of imagination, save for the arched glass doorway and canopy. Even so it was quite dull against the cloudy sky. But the enthusiasm for what lay beyond the exterior more than made up for its lack of physical beauty.

Inside the doors, Agnes looked for her sister. To her amazement, she saw her parents, her brothers, and Tom and Janie and the kids. They were all there, waiting to say their good-byes.

"We couldn't let you leave without one final hug," Sam said to Agnes.

Agnes rushed into Sam's arms. Suddenly she felt she didn't have the strength to leave. Sam could feel her weakness.

"This is where God is leading you and you must go with grace and courage. You are blessed and He will keep you safe along the way."

"Thank you, Pa. I love you with all my heart," she said as she buried her face in his cheek.

Agnes looked to her mother next; she was standing back. She bore neither a look of sadness nor of disquietude. She looked remarkably at ease.

"Mum, I will miss you terribly. Please promise you will visit very soon."

"Agnes, my dear, I will see you in my thoughts every day. We will never be apart."

Her mother's words gave her no comfort. They sounded so final. All Agnes could do was hope for the best.

Janie's embrace said more than words could. Janie wasn't an extrovert and friends were not easy to come by for her. She was guarded in her emotions and gave only of herself to those she trusted with her heart. Agnes and Art would be leaving a gaping hole in their lives that would not easily be filled.

"Tom, please take care of my Janie or else you will have to deal with me."

Tom was a stoic man, rarely reduced to displays of emotion, and even he was teetering on the edge.

Their impending departure was announced, and a collective panicked gasp surrounded the group. They turned to each other for comfort, for a parting look that would hold them steadfast in their memories.

"We must be going," Art said to Agnes and the children.

"Yes, we need to take our seats," Percy confirmed.

After a final wave and a blown kiss, they found themselves on the train. There were no lingering waves and tearful good-byes through the window, as their seats were on the side of the train opposite the platform. As the train pulled away from the station, Agnes rushed to find a vacant window, but there were none. She could only sit and look out at St. Boniface in the distance.

The locomotive hissed as the steam began to build from within. The brakes screeched as they were released, and the train whistled as it pulled out of the station. It chuffed along as it began to build steam, sending plumes of steam and smoke up to the sky.

Within minutes they passed over the Assiniboine River and under the Norwood Bridge. Agnes was not seeing anything she hadn't seen thousands of times before, but this time it was different; this time she wasn't going home to Norwood. She felt lost, without a home, and she longed to turn back. Her heart raced and she caught her breath, but she persevered.

Dorothy and Donny were captivated by the passing landscape and paid no attention to the mood of their mother. Their cousins were equally engrossed in seeing Winnipeg pass into the distance. It was difficult for Agnes, but once beyond what was familiar, what lay before them eased her sorrow. If only it had done the same for Art. Agnes had been too engrossed in her own misery to notice her husband's mood darken. Art had become concerned, not for what was being left behind but for the train ride itself, and he did his best to hide it from his wife.

Donny and Dorothy joined their cousins in the berth beside, swapping places with Mary and Percy. Their first lunch consisted of a generous supply of baked goods—muffins, fruit breads, and sweet rolls. There was a kitchen on the sleeper car, but Agnes and Mary decided it made no sense to pack cooking utensils for the day and a half journey.

The afternoon light illuminated the fields of snow that unfolded endlessly toward the horizon. Small and large prairie towns broke the monotony of the alabaster landscape, offering their landmark grain elevators to the freight trains that passed through. It was a quick stop in Regina, and then the train was again on its way.

The children filled their time with reading and games, while the adults played cards. It was a rare, carefree time when there was no work to be done and no guilt over not being able to find any.

"I hope it will not be long before we find a suitable home," Agnes said. "I don't want the children to feel unsettled."

The truth of the matter was it had nothing to do with the children. Disorganization, however short term, was poisonous to Agnes. She could not take it, even in small doses.

"We will have homes to look at soon after we arrive. I am confident it will be days, not weeks," Art said.

That seemed to ease Agnes's mind somewhat. But there was so much to do, so much that was nagging at her, that until it was all complete she would not be able to relax.

"Agnes, do not worry. All will be well. This is an adventure, and we will have a grand new life before we know it."

As they arrived in Moose Jaw, they prepared to disembark. It was a longer stay, and they decided to eat a warm meal at the restaurant in the railway station.

The station was much smaller than Winnipeg's but was more interesting in design, with its six-storey stone clock tower rising high above the other buildings. There didn't seem much to the typical, prairie town, especially in the dark, but it was quaint and inviting.

Darkness had set before they had arrived in Moose Jaw, and the blackened sky obscured the prairie horizon. It wasn't long before exhaustion and boredom lured them. Within minutes of their heads hitting their berths, they were all asleep, save for Art. The whirring of the wheels on the rails lulled the others to sleep, but for Art it only carried him to war. Time had yet to heal old wounds; it had only hidden them from view, waiting for the spark that would release them. It would take two pills that night before Art would succumb to the motion of the train.

In the morning, the curtains were pulled back, revealing unkempt passengers. The mattresses and bedding were stowed in the upper berth, and the benches were pulled back to reveal the seats that they would occupy until it was time to sleep again. Agnes did not remember much of her life at age eight, but she recalled vividly the contrasting experience upon embarking in Québec City. The train then had a skeleton interior— hard wooden benches and no padding whatsoever to soften the journey—and they had only two blankets and two pillows to be shared by seven. It had been tremendously uncomfortable. These padded and upholstered seats were luxurious by comparison.

Like the colony cars of old, there were two toilet rooms, one at either end of the car. The men also enjoyed the use of a washroom, as well as a chesterfield upon which they could sit and enjoy a cigarette and the company of other men. The women enjoyed no such social area, only a comparable dressing room with washbasin. Percy and Mary could have afforded to travel in the first-class sleeper, especially considering their move was being paid for by Percy's company, but they chose not to so that the family could stay together.

There was enough to keep the children engaged so there was generally none of the misbehaving that usually accompanied boredom. They continued to fill their time watching the passing landscape, playing games, and speaking incessantly about what they hoped for their new lives.

The rolling foothills introduced the passengers to Calgary, which was nothing more than another short stop on the journey, but it was a city and was a welcome break from the endless snow-covered fields.

"Darling, are you unwell?" Agnes asked Art. "You look pale and you have hardly spoken two words since we woke up."

Art offered a half-smile. "I am fine. Perhaps a bit of motion sickness."

Percy knew otherwise, and he worked to keep his brother's mind engaged and off the rolling train. Unfortunately, there was nowhere to run or hide in such a confined space, and one could only bide one's time until it was over.

Calgary was a sprawling city, not unlike Winnipeg; however, what lay beyond Calgary was quite unlike anything they had seen before. In the distance, the snow-capped Rocky Mountains stretched toward the sky, each peak higher than the last. It was incomprehensible to someone seeing them for the first time; they were otherworldly, almost mystifying.

As Calgary passed into the distance, the rhythmic rolling of the foothills became more pronounced and the landscape began to offer more than the unbroken flatness of the prairie, which, up to that moment, Agnes had never seen as dull and unimaginative. But nothing could compare to the feast her eyes were devouring.

The tracks meandered through the foothills toward the Rockies, ascending gradually and following alongside the swiftly moving Bow River. Unlike the Red or Assiniboine, the Bow seemed angry, foaming and frothing as its waters hugged icy curves and rushed down the precipitous slopes.

The snow-covered grasslands gave way to the dense forests that lay in gorges and lowlands at the base of the mountains. Swiftly moving torrents of icy water fell victim to gravity, falling beyond the edge of steep precipices. They seemed to defy the laws of nature, falling slowly at first, almost still, as if attempting to reverse their fate, and then thundering down to the rivers below.

The mountains seemed full of life, each wanting to tell the stories of their creation to those willing to listen. Three peaks stood side by side, each with their own beauty and scars, but each connected inextricably at their foundation. They held each other up, but they reached toward the sky independently. They bore the name "Three Sisters" and like Agnes and hers, they were strong and passionate.

With Banff at their backs, the train continued to rise to new heights. The locomotive laboured to carry the weight of the cars higher and deeper into the heart of *God's country*. "The Continental Divide" was as impressive as it sounded, slicing the continent from north to south, from the Bering Strait to the Straits of Magellan. It is over this great divide that nature rules, directing a seemingly endless supply of water either westward to the Pacific, or north or east to the Arctic or the Atlantic.

"Mum, Dad, come look," Dorothy directed, excitedly.

The children were enjoying the scenery up-close, with binoculars that their grandfather had given them as a parting gift. Dorothy spotted a lone mountain goat perched high on a sliver of a rock.

"I think it is stuck. How on earth did it get there?"

Binoculars weren't needed to see the animal in the distance. They watched in awe as it moved delicately from rock to rock, rocks not wide enough to hold a human foot. Yet, somehow this miraculous creature could move effortlessly through its unrelenting domain.

"I'm speechless. This is beyond anything I could have imagined," Agnes said. "It is truly spectacular, isn't it, darling?"

Art was looking out the window beside him and did not hear Agnes.

"Art?"

Agnes's voice turned on a light, and he shifted to look at her.

"Are you enjoying the scenery?"

"I am. It is magnificent," he said dully.

Art was not as enthusiastic as the others, and Agnes believed it was simply the motion. But Art found the passing scenery hypnotic; if he looked straight on, it would go by in a blur and take his mind off the whir of the wheels on the track.

The Kicking Horse Pass, with scarcely enough level ground to put two feet side by side, let alone a long and winding track, traversed the Great Divide. It was rocky and rugged, a harshness whose beauty was so spectacular that it could not help but open up your soul. It was a grand cathedral, and Agnes was altered by its majesty.

Passing from Alberta into British Columbia, the train began a rapid and pronounced descent. After they passed frozen Wapta Lake, they entered the first of two spiral tunnels.

"A brochure at the Banff Station said that prior to the building of these tunnels, trains had to descend up or down in a straight fashion. It was quite treacherous and accidents were commonplace," Percy stated. "It is fantastic to me how they can bore holes in mountains to let trains pass through."

As they entered the first tunnel, the car darkened. The train hugged the three quarter loop before it emerged into the sunshine and doubled back toward the second tunnel. The children chattered enthusiastically through the dramatic curve, while the adults remained quietly captivated. Agnes looked to Art and his demeanour remained constant. She felt bad for the ill he was feeling and worried the curves of the tunnels would make it worse.

The second tunnel was not as long as the first, but it was as sharp and remained as dark at its core. Within it the smoke from the locomotive could not dissipate, and the smell began to fill the car. As they emerged from the tunnel, Art startled his wife as he jumped up abruptly and dashed toward the toilet. Agnes stood to follow, but Percy put her hand on her shoulder to keep her in place.

"I'll go. I don't think you would care to see the men's toilet," Percy said as he tried to calm Agnes.

Percy got up and walked the length of the car. The door to the toilet was closed and he knocked.

"Art, are you all right?"

Inside, Art was frantically reaching for his pills, but in his haste his hand could not seem to find its way inside his pocket. He was in a frenzy, like an eddy in a rushing river, the water spinning, pulling him down. The darkness of the tunnels and the pungent smell of smoke were overpowering, and he passed the point that he could manage it on his own. He was on a ledge, and he needed to be pulled from its edge.

As he worked to get the lid off the bottle, the train began to slow—they were approaching their next stop. The sudden deceleration forced him sideways, and as he fought to regain his position the bottle tumbled from his hand and onto the floor. The lidless bottle rid itself of its contents. In a panic, Art dropped to his knees. He blew the dust off one and placed it in his mouth. The pill's effect was immediate, not for the medicinal qualities, which had not yet enjoyed the benefit of time, but for the anticipated relief.

"Art, are you all right?" Percy asked again, this time his voice rising in pitch.

"Yes," Art said tentatively. "I'm fine. Go back to your seat."

Art picked up the pills and continued to relax as he did. But as he picked up the last one, an overwhelming wave of grief swept over him. *What have I been reduced to? What has become of me?* He felt incredibly ashamed.

Art opened the door to find his brother standing there. Percy said nothing. He simply looked at his brother and attempted to gauge his mood.

"I am fine. A bit of motion sickness. I just needed to move."

Percy wasn't buying it. He understood his brother's triggers. He had been there and he knew. He had worried about the train ride, but had hoped all would be fine. Percy had not been living in denial; it had been a reasonable hope. Everything, save for the train, was different, but those differences weren't enough to free him. Anticipation and excitement weren't enough. His family wasn't enough.

Art slapped his brother on the shoulder and then walked back to his seat, leaving Percy standing there. Since he was there, Percy decided to use the toilet. As he was fastening his trousers, he noticed a pill on the floor. He bent down and picked it up. He looked at it and recognized the logotype stamped on it. He put the pill in his pocket and returned to his seat.

"Thank you, Percy," Agnes said. "I think the tunnels did Art in."

There was truth in what she was saying but not for the reason she believed. Art looked at his brother briefly, but his eye contact was fleeting.

As they continued westward toward Vancouver, they descended into the Kicking Horse Canyon. There was no questioning whether it was a canyon or valley. The sheer mountain walls rose vertically from its lowest point, where the Kicking Horse River, whose raging currents exploded in a thunderous roar, had eroded the land for eons with its impressive strength.

"Mum, Dad, look … another tunnel," Dorothy said as she looked beyond the curve into the distance.

Art was asleep in his chair and did not hear his daughter, which to Agnes and Percy was a very good thing. They were approaching the longest tunnel in Canada, the longest straight-line tunnel in the world, five blackened miles in length and running directly under the summit of Mount Macdonald.

As they emerged into daylight at the other end, Art remained asleep, the effect of the pill still felt. Within a short time of emerging from the tunnel, the train made a brief stop at Glacier Station for a quick view of the Illecillewaet Glacier. It was a gently sloping sheet of solid ice with a dense forest of conifers, trees hardy enough to survive in such a desolate environment, framing the glacier at its base. It was as though a wave of water had rushed over the rocky plain and frozen in a singular moment in time.

The train continued through spectacular vistas, each as awe inspiring as the last. It was almost too much to take in at once, too much for the senses to absorb and process. After a short stop in Revelstoke for a hot meal, the train passed through Craigellachie as the sun began to set. It was there that the last spike was driven into the Canadian Pacific Railway forty-seven years prior. The building of that great railway was a monumental effort by any standard, connecting the east and west coasts of the second largest country in the world, certainly the greatest country to those who lived there. It was no small feat, to be sure.

It was the last night of their wondrous journey, and from beyond the setting sun to the beginning of the Fraser Valley—the very approach to Vancouver—the sky would remain covered under a veil of darkness. But it didn't matter. The excitement of the journey was replaced by the excitement of the arrival.

The train continued to roll toward Vancouver, the whir of the wheels having gone unnoticed for a while. There was no longer a feeling of newness, only of longing for the trip to end.

"Wake up, it is morning. We will be there soon," Margaret blurted enthusiastically from the top berth.

"Margaret, shoosh. Quiet yourself. There are others sleeping," Mary said in a harsh, whispered tone to her daughter.

Margaret and Norma began to giggle and Dorothy joined in from her own berth. The sun was not yet up over the horizon, but it was beginning to lighten the pre-dawn sky at their backs.

Soon the train was abustle with activity. Agnes and Mary both remembered pulling into the Winnipeg Station on that early morning in 1904. They couldn't contain their own excitement, as much as their mother tried to calm them. Now they both looked to their own children and smiled as they thought of the circle that they had travelled.

"Mary, life certainly has a sense of humour," Agnes mused.

Mary laughed. "It does at that."

"Just when we believe we are unique, God proves us wrong."

As they ate their last meal on the train, they kept their focus directed on what lay outside the train. For Percy and Art, it was a homecoming. Their father had come the week prior, and now their closest family would all be there. For Agnes, Mary, and the children, it was new and exciting.

After the spectacular Rockies, the mountains of the British Columbia Lower Mainland seemed somewhat dull by comparison. Less than two days prior, they had left Winnipeg and Agnes, Mary, and the children's view of the world had changed completely. A field of wheat had been spectacular, and now snow-capped peaks that defied imagination had become their new normal.

As the train passed through the remaining towns on their final approach, water was never far from sight. Rivers and lakes were carved into the land at every turn.

"It looks as though you could fit a half dozen Red Rivers into that one right there," Mary said, astonished.

"That's the Fraser River. At its widest point, I dare say you could. It runs right out to the sea. In fact, it is quite a bit longer than Britain from end to end," Percy added. "You will see there is no shortage of water in Vancouver. The sea will be at our doorstep."

Agnes and Mary had travelled across the Atlantic as young children, so they could well grasp vast. But it was the endless supply of mountains, lakes, and rivers so perfectly etched into the raw and wholly unaffected terrain that had them mesmerized. It was beautiful and dramatic and overpowering.

They had been warned of the clouds and dampness, of the excessive rain that would fall for days and weeks and months on end. Upon seeing the lushness of the greenery, it was clear the rain served a purpose. However, on this day, there were no clouds and no rain; rather, the sky was striking in its depth of blue. As far as the eye could see, there were fields of green. It was a verdant oasis.

"Margaret said she and John would meet us at the station. I hope I gave them the right times. What if they aren't there?" Agnes was starting to worry.

"Agnes, they will be there. And if by some strange happenstance they aren't, I know where to find them. It is a short taxi or streetcar ride away." Percy was reassuring, but not enough to smooth out the ruffles from the multiple details that could go awry.

Art put his arm around his wife as the train came to a stop. He kissed her cheek and assured her all would be well. The children had no such fears.

The train began to decelerate as it pulled into the Waterfront Station. Behind the building, nothing sat between the Burrard Inlet and the track that brought them to Vancouver. The sound of squawking gulls and the smell of the salt air filled the car before the doors even opened. It was as though they had stepped out of their lives and into another.

They gathered their belongings and made their way to the door. As they stepped onto the platform, the sounds and smells became even more striking. The children dallied along, focused on everything but the direction that they were supposed to go, and they required some gentle nudging from their parents.

Inside the red bricked and columned building, Agnes's immediate worry quickly dissolved. Agnes and Mary spotted their sister within moments of each other and ran toward her like adolescent schoolgirls. In the ten years that Margaret had been gone, they had only seen her a few times. They hadn't realized how much they missed her until they saw her standing there.

"Sorry, John, we are happy to see you as well," Agnes said, laughing through her tears.

"I learned long ago to not come between my wife and something that she wants."

"Amen to that," Art said as he held out his hand to shake John's.

It was the happiest of reunions. Nothing could sabotage their joy, not even the hole created by the family left behind. That pain would be felt, but not that day.

Chapter 26

Margaret and John's home was a modest but pleasant white clapboard house, not unlike their house back in Winnipeg. It had a quaint front porch, which was completely sheltered by an enormous hemlock tree.

"It feels like a different world here," Agnes said to her sister.

"It is a different world. Did you notice the flowers? And no snow anywhere to be found. I certainly don't miss the Winnipeg winters. And I am sure you won't either," Margaret said.

"Percy, Tom will be coming by in a few hours to show you some houses. Hopefully you find what you are looking for without too much trouble."

"That is much appreciated, John. It is good of you to help us out."

"My pleasure. We're pleased as can be to have you here."

"Art and Agnes, we may have found you a home as well. It is only a few blocks from the restaurant. One of our customers owns a few houses in the area and one of his tenants has moved. Left a few days ago. He said he would hold it until tomorrow. You can take a look if you want; it would save you some effort."

"That sounds splendid." Agnes exhaled some pent-up stress. She was overwhelmed and her sister could see it.

"It is only the first days that are like this. There is much to do and you can't escape it, but it *will* get done. And we are here to help. Now, I won't be going into the restaurant today so the children can all stay with me while you work away at your lists."

"Thank you, Margaret. I don't want us to be too much trouble."

"I see you haven't changed at all," Margaret teased.

Agnes was not fazed by Margaret's teasing. In fact, it hadn't even registered in her consciousness. She was too focused on the myriad of tasks and details that were swirling around in her brain. As soon as she would settle on what needed to be done, she would think of something else.

With Mary and Percy off to look at houses, Art and Agnes walked to their prospective house. It was south on Commercial Drive, just under a mile. The Drive, as it was known, was active and vibrant. Shop after shop after restaurant lined the street. There were no large department stores or warehouses. They were all charming and uniquely individual, but sadly store after store boasted signs of sales, selling off wares at "never before seen" prices. The crash, it seems, had hit businesses there as disastrously as it had back home. The Winnipeg papers said it was a global disaster, which one could believe after reading story after story of loss and destitution from around the world—but global was now before them.

Halfway to their destination, they passed The Saucy Q, a cheeky name that always made Agnes chuckle. In the ten years that it had been operating, it had developed a heady reputation, which was saying something since it was an area known for its restaurants. The Drive was heavily flavoured Italian, but it was laced with immigrants of all types.

The Saucy Q was not large, but then neither were any of the restaurants or stores that surrounded it. It was comfortably casual, which was part of its allure. Sheer red curtains covered the front window through which red and white checkered tablecloths could be seen draping the tables. The food was second to none and they put on no airs. Airs were put on a few miles farther west.

They continued their walk down Commercial. They turned at East Sixth and stopped at the sixth house. It was similar in size and shape to their house back home, but its yard was overgrown with large bushes which kept the sunshine locked out. Agnes's heart sank. Their last home was cheery and bright, directly facing the afternoon sun, and it had a lush lawn in the front with plenty of flowers that bloomed all spring and summer. This house faced south, but it would be shaded by the towering trees that lined the street. It seemed there would be no escaping the darkness; large bushes and trees were more the rule than the exception in Vancouver.

Agnes sighed louder than she had intended.

"My darling, let us look inside, and if you do not like it we will look at others. I promise you this is only temporary. When the business is set, you will have your castle." Art felt he was the cause of his wife's disappointment and it upset him.

Agnes pulled her shoulders back and took a deep breath.

"It looks lovely," she said.

There was nothing remarkable about the house. It was no better and no worse than their last. It was functional and, pride and indulgence aside, Agnes knew it would suffice; the yard could be worked on. They settled matters with the landlord and at the end of the exchange had let the house for a year. Agnes was deeply relieved to be settled on a home. They could begin moving their things in the following day when their furnishings arrived. But the following day was a long way off yet; the house needed to be scrubbed from top to bottom first.

Walking up Commercial provided an entirely different prospect than walking down it. The snow-capped peaks loomed in the distance, no subtle contrast to the busy street afoot. There was an element of illusion for Agnes, a sleight of hand that had altered her reality. It didn't feel real yet.

Together they paid attention to every footstep and every blink. They wanted to absorb all that they could of their new neighbourhood.

"Look, darling, the Grandview Theatre. We'll have to go one evening after we are settled. It has been far too long since we have gone out, just the two of us."

Art was right; it had been too long and they were due for a night out.

"Well?" Margaret asked as they arrived. "And it looks like you did some shopping."

"Yes, cleaning supplies," Agnes said. "I will head back over there after a bit."

"Does that mean you took it?"

"Yes," Art said as he dangled the keys. "It is ours for the year at least."

"Marvelous. You can tick one thing off your list then. Let's have some lunch before you go back. We'll have dinner at the restaurant tonight."

The children had been playing at the park across the street. Betty and Eileen had left Winnipeg before any of the other children were born, but you would never know the girls hadn't all been best friends all along.

"Dorothy and Donny, would you like to come to the new house with me? I need to do some cleaning while your father goes to the bank."

They were eager to see their new home and rushed to say yes.

"Betty and Eileen will have to go back to school tomorrow. Do you wish to get Dorothy and Donny enrolled then?"

"No, I think I will wait until Monday. There is no sense starting them off on a Friday. And tomorrow our furnishings will arrive at the house and they will want to help with their rooms."

The reality was Agnes would not stop until the entire house was settled, everything in its proper place. First things first, even if that meant not registering the children for school for a few days.

As soon as Agnes revealed the house, Donny was gone, his boyish enthusiasm unleashed. His first order of business was to explore the bushes in front. He emerged from one of the larger ones with bits of cedar branches entwined in his hair. He'd found a new playground and it was a bittersweet consolation for Agnes, who had only thought of removing them all, one by one.

"Donny, look at you! We have only been here one minute and you are filthy already."

Agnes's anger was interrupted by the thundering sound of a freight train. The clanking on the track and the high shrill of the blowing whistle was so immediate it was as though it was rolling up the street. The train could be heard from their house in Norwood, but there it was more distant. Agnes's consternation was met by Donny's unadulterated enthusiasm. It was as if they were opposite sides of the same coin; their reactions could not have been more different.

Inside, Dorothy and Donny chose their bedrooms, and to Agnes's relief they did not argue about it. Donny chose the room in the front because that was the direction of the train track, and Dorothy chose the room at the back for the same reason. As Agnes and Dorothy worked away at the sweeping and scrubbing, Donny could be heard running from room to room, his footsteps echoing through the empty house. It was a sound that grated on Agnes's last nerve, but she chose to let it go. *What else is a young boy to do in an empty house?* she thought.

With the afternoon behind them, Agnes and the children made their way back to Margaret's. Art had telephoned to make arrangements to have the delivery truck come at nine the next morning, and he had arranged with the bank to move the account. They were getting settled, much to Agnes's relief.

"Tell us about your new house, Mary," Margaret said excitedly.

"It is not far from here. Just a half mile away, right next to Woodland Park. We still have to go through the legal and banking formalities. If all goes well, we should have it in a few weeks. Until then the hotel will be our home."

The directions meant nothing to Art and Agnes, but Margaret and John knew the area well and were enthusiastic about the selected location. Art and Agnes also didn't have to worry about legal and banking formalities, since theirs was only a rental. Theirs was a different set of circumstances entirely, and they tried to wear them well.

"Starting a new business is so exciting, Art. Tell us about your plans," Mary coaxed.

"I am fortunate to have a brother in the hardware business. Percy tells me many large builders and carpenters have accounts with Marshall-Wells, and he is going to use his connections to make introductions. Once I know whom I can call on, I will ensure they know I am the best painter around. Hopefully, before long I will have more business than I can manage myself and I can start to hire."

"Brilliant plan," John said. "And I have your first job lined up for you already. As you can see, the restaurant needs a good coat of paint. I'm sure many of the shops along The Drive are in need of the same. It won't be long until you are humming along."

Agnes was proud of Art for his dreams and aspirations, but the thought of an unsteady paycheque was quite worrisome. She knew that she was capable of working if need be, but she also knew Art would have no part of that. There was no halfway; they were in fully.

True to promise, the truck arrived just shy of nine. The contents were emptied and placed roughly in the room for which they were intended. They had rid themselves of old clothes, toys, and books, keeping only items that couldn't be replaced or would need to be replaced if disposed of. Agnes placed the linens on the beds and transferred clothing from boxes to bureaus and closets. Once the bedrooms and living room were sorted, Agnes went to work on the kitchen.

"Mum, I'm hungry," Donny moaned.

Agnes had been so busy organizing that it had completely escaped her attention that they were well into the afternoon and she had not fed her children.

"Of course you are. It looks like it is a good time to go to the market for some groceries. Shoes and coats, both of you."

Agnes retrieved the grocery list that she had prepared the day before, and they walked off toward the market. They passed a toy store, and Donny stopped to gaze longingly in the window. It was a train set he had his sights set on, but he didn't ask. He wouldn't do that. But he wanted it all the same.

"Do you see something you like?" his mother asked, teasingly.

Donny wouldn't have asked, but when prompted he couldn't help but oblige.

"I'm a bit keen on that train is all. I was just looking, Mum," he said before continuing to walk on.

Agnes remained at the store's window.

"I do believe that train set would fit nicely in your room. We'll have to talk with your father about it. How does that sound?"

Donny knew that when his mother said that, it usually meant he got what he wanted. She was the one who usually said no. Yes was more often than not his father's response. He gave his mother a big hug and bounced off down the road.

"Now, what do you want, Dorothy? You both deserve something special for your new rooms."

"There is nothing that I need, Mum. Thank you."

"My sweet girl, I didn't ask you if you *needed* anything. I asked you if you *wanted* anything."

Agnes loved her daughter with all her heart, and she worried that she was too mature for her own good. Dorothy rarely allowed herself to have fun, to just be a child. She was too anxious to be motherly, and Agnes was determined to make sure she was true to her age.

Groceries were purchased from the market, as was meat from the butcher. All would be delivered promptly, with the exception of treats that Agnes bought for the walk home. The last few days had been eventful and the children had handled them superbly. Agnes was very proud and she wanted to spoil them a bit.

Art had beaten them home. When they arrived, he was already in the living room, standing behind a new addition to the family.

"Art, what on earth?" Agnes asked with a laugh. Agnes had wanted to do something special for the children, but the thought of a pet had never crossed her mind.

"Daddy, you bought us birds," Dorothy gushed as she ran toward them.

Art was beaming. It was entirely the reaction he had hoped for. He had planned on the purchase even before they left Winnipeg. He thought the children would enjoy them as much as he would, and it appeared he was right.

"They are budgies. You'll have to name them. How about you each name one?"

One was predominantly blue, sky blue to be exact. It had a white face and black and white feathers. The other was a very bright green with a vibrant yellow face and black and yellow feathers.

"I want to name the blue one Bluey," Donny said proudly.

Dorothy laughed. "Bluey? That's rather silly. Why don't we just name the other one Greeny, then?"

"Yes. Those are grand names," Donny said.

"If you couldn't tell, I was just joking," Dorothy said as sarcastically as she could.

"Well, you can name the green one whatever you want, but the blue one is Bluey from this point forward. Dad said I could choose."

Dorothy huffed and put her hands on her hips.

"Mine is Queenie, and she will rule their kingdom."

It was Donny's turn to laugh, and Dorothy clearly did not appreciate it.

"All right, enough, you two," Art said gently.

"I would like to hang a few pictures, and I need you to tell me where you would like them," Art requested of his wife.

Together they went to their bedroom. It was a tiny house, and the bedrooms were just behind a wall that separated them from the living room. Art put his arms around Agnes's waist, twirled her around, and pulled her tightly against him. He kissed her passionately and she struggled to break free.

"Art, the children could come in here."

"They have seen us kiss before."

"Yes, but not in the bedroom."

"Well, if that is the problem...." Art took his wife's hand and led her back into the hallway, embracing her again and locking his lips on hers in a kiss so passionate she felt it in her toes.

"You are rather frisky today," Agnes whispered with a laugh.

"You needn't look further than yourself for the cause, my love, my sweet, beautiful darling." Art took Agnes's hand and began to plant kisses up her arm, even amid her fit of giggles.

Art continued to hold his wife's hand, but his expression blanked, his smile dropping to a level of seriousness that caught Agnes off guard.

"I'm dreadfully sorry that I am doing this to you, that I am making you start over again. You have been nothing but patient and supportive. I do not deserve you." Art was contrite, his apology heartfelt.

"Nonsense. We are in this together and together we will remain."

Art looked into their barren bedroom and winced. He wanted so much for his wife. He wanted all that he had promised her and more. Agnes could see how much it was troubling him and it broke her heart. For Agnes there were no unfulfilled promises. He had already given her the world.

"I do not need trinkets to fulfill me. It is what I hold in my heart that matters. I need nothing else."

Art kissed his wife again, but this time the passion was replaced by tenderness.

"We'd better get back out there before we are faced with two birds on the loose." Art spoke only half in jest; he knew his son too well.

"Donny, I understand there is something in the toy store that you had your eye on."

With his father's words, Donny allowed himself to get excited.

"All right, I take that as a yes. Let's go then."

Dorothy and Donny were far from spoiled. They were given very little, and what they received was given with tremendous consideration. Money was not abundant, and it had become less so over the last few years as the economic depression took a firmer grip. Back home, over half the families had been on assistance, but Art had managed to keep his family above that line. Easy it was not, and he hoped his prospects would be better in Vancouver.

As Art and Donny got closer to the storefront, Donny ran off ahead. With both hands firmly planted on the window and his nose pressed up against the glass, he looked in. The train—an engine, four cars, and a caboose – sat on top of three red blocks. It was not the biggest train, nor the grandest, but it was the one that Donny wanted.

Donny walked home, holding tight to his present. He clutched it to his chest, making sure it could not be taken from him.

"Look, Mum, just the one I wanted, and it's not even my birthday."

Agnes couldn't help but smile. *These moments make the struggles worthwhile*, she thought.

"Dorothy, did you think I would forget about you?" Art asked.

Dorothy looked at her father, lost as to what he could possibly have bought her. He reached into the inside of his coat and pulled out a baseball glove and ball. To most girls, this would have seemed like the most ridiculous gift in the world, but not to Dorothy. She jumped up and wrapped her arms tightly around his chest.

"I know how much you like to play baseball. And I dare say, you can throw better than most boys. There is a bit of room in the backyard, and there is a field I noticed up the street. Your old glove is too small for you. You can just give it to Donny."

"Thank you, Dad. I really love it." Dorothy ran her fingers over its laced seams and lifted the glove to her face so she could inhale the rawness of the leather. It was unmistakable.

Agnes was pleased to see her daughter passionate about something, and she winked at her husband for thinking of it.

Chapter 27

They had yet to experience the rain that they had heard so much about, but on the second day in their new home they woke to a thick layer of cloud and a dense fog that had rolled in from the harbour.

A knock at the door was answered by Agnes—it was Margaret.

"This is a pleasant surprise. What brings you by so early?"

"I know your phone service hasn't been connected yet. John wanted me to pass a message to Art that tomorrow would be a good day to start at the restaurant. I know Sunday is the Lord's Day, but we must do it when the restaurant is closed."

"Of course. I know that Art is eager to get started. He purchased his supplies yesterday so he will be ready to start. Can you stay for a cup of tea? I have something for you. I forgot to give it to you when we first arrived."

"Yes, please. That fog has brought a nasty chill."

As they sat down to their tea, Agnes handed Margaret a small box.

"What is this?" Margaret asked.

"Open it."

Margaret removed the lid from the box and looked at the old necklace and then at Agnes, curious.

"Open the heart," Agnes directed.

Margaret did as she was told, working her fingernail in the narrow seam and gently pulling it apart. Inside she saw a picture of her mother with another woman. She didn't recognize the other woman at first—it had been too many years—but she knew who she was. Margaret took a deep breath. Eleanor had been another mother to her, and the memories of her death were deeply etched in her mind.

"Why is Mum giving this to me now? This is all she has left of Eleanor."

"Mom gave me her box and the rose Dad gave her."

Margaret didn't have to wait for the "why." There could only be one reason she was doing this, and it was a reason she didn't want to contemplate. Margaret had been gone for so long that her mother no longer flooded her mind at every turn, but the necklace stirred some maternal longing and she suddenly became a girl desperately in need of her mother. Margaret knew her mother would die one day. Everyone did. However, it now seemed more than just an "everyone dies sometime" assertion; it had become painfully personal.

"How was Mum?" Margaret asked hesitantly.

"She had a bad cough that she has been holding onto for months. She claims she saw a doctor, but I can't say for certain. I could tell it hurt, but you know Mum—she wouldn't say ouch if a car ran over her."

Margaret laughed. This had always been the case and clearly nothing had changed.

"Mum, Donny and I are going to go outside to throw the baseball."

"Please put your coats on. Your Aunt Margaret says the fog is thick, and you'll catch your death if you don't."

They had seen the fog, and it was part of the allure that was drawing them outside. When rising temperatures baked the remaining Winnipeg snow, a shroud of fog would hang heavy in the crisp spring air, but it was nothing like this. This was as thick as soup and as cold as the sea. One could barely see their feet, and it was about as exciting as anything that Donny had ever seen.

"Yes, Mum." They both put on their heavy coats as they were told.

"Come give your Aunt Margaret a kiss. I must be leaving soon."

Dorothy and Donny gave their aunt a kiss and then went into the backyard. There wasn't much space behind the house, just some open area between the house and the garage and a picket fence that enclosed the yard between the neighbouring houses. It wasn't large by any stretch, but the kids didn't seem to be bothered.

Art had gone out to get more supplies, and Agnes continued to finish the pie filling that she had started before Margaret arrived. Agnes could see the children perfectly through the window above the kitchen sink. That day "perfectly" was relative. She could see into the backyard perfectly but could not see any detail, as the fog remained thick. In fact, it appeared to be growing thicker. The sounds of children at play and the occasional moving shadow in the mist was all that Agnes had to know the children were safely ensconced in the yard.

As Agnes closed the oven doors on her pies, a loud crash filled the kitchen. Agnes screeched and sprang away from the sound like a coiled spring. A perfect circle of a hole now marred the window, and the ball that caused it continued to bounce on the floor until it came to a dead stop.

"Donald Arthur Craig!" Agnes screamed, even before she had a chance to confirm the identity of the thrower. She knew Dorothy would have been much too careful to have been the perpetrator of such a mishap. The second day in their new house ... *Art will be furious*, she feared.

"Wait until your father gets home!"

Agnes was livid. She could not breathe for her anger. They couldn't afford to fix a window when there were so many other things to buy.

"Mum!" Dorothy yelled from the fog.

Agnes didn't answer.

"Mum!"

"What?!" Agnes continued to seethe as she looked at the broken glass in the sink.

"Donny ran away."

The words sank in quickly and her anger turned to worry. *Donny ran away.*

"Go after him, Dorothy."

Agnes began to pick up the glass as Dorothy ran off after her brother. There wasn't much glass, the circumference of a baseball's worth, but the hole it left might as well have been much larger. It would still have to be replaced.

The front door opened while Agnes continued to clean the shards that covered the counter and sink.

"Dorothy? Donny?"

There was no response and when Agnes looked up, she saw Art standing behind her in the kitchen. He was looking at the hole in the window and was trying hard to contain his anger.

He saw the ball on the floor and didn't need an explanation. It was abundantly clear.

"Donny ran off and Dorothy chased after him. It was an accident. The fog was so thick and he couldn't see. Please do not be angry."

Agnes was trying to minimize Art's anger, despite her own.

Dorothy ran down the alley. When she reached Grandview, she could see Donny disappear through the thick fog into the trees beside the Woodland Bridge and she followed in pursuit. Through the trees, it was a steep drop down an embankment of nearly twenty feet.

"Donny! Wait!" Agnes screamed, but Donny continued to run.

Loose rocks shifted under Dorothy's feet as she shuffled and slid down the hill. It was a miracle she maintained her footing. It was inhospitable terrain, and she was by no means being careful.

Donny turned and watched his sister descend the hill. The soupy fog, heavy with moisture, sank into the Cut. He stood in the gully alongside the track as he waited for her to reach him. Dorothy could see he was upset; his face was tear-stained, and his little body heaved to regain his breath.

"It was an accident, Dorothy. I didn't mean it. Really, I didn't." Donny was pleading with his sister as if she could reverse what had happened.

"I know, Donny. Come home. Mum and Dad aren't mad."

"You're lying. I heard Mum. Dad will give me the strap. I know it."

Donny was inconsolable. Dorothy held out her hand to coax her brother toward her, but he wouldn't move. He just stared at her as his tears continued to fall. Dorothy figured she would just stand there and let him calm down, and then she would talk him into coming home. But Donny turned and began to walk down the middle of the track, so Dorothy followed along from the gully.

"Donny, you shouldn't be walking on the track. If you are worried about Dad getting angry, then you should stop. He will surely give you the strap if he finds out."

It wasn't enough to dissuade Donny. He continued to walk and Dorothy continued to follow. Suddenly, the sound of a train could be heard in the distance. Dorothy began to panic. She looked behind them, but could not yet see it. Its whistle blew, each successive blast louder than the last.

"Donny, this isn't funny. Come here now!" Dorothy yelled.

The train continued to roll toward them, the ground vibrating with intensity beneath Dorothy's feet as it did. The train was no more than fifty feet away when the sound of screeching brakes filled the air. The conductor set off the whistle and let it continuously blow. The train was slowing, but not nearly fast enough.

Dorothy ran toward her brother, who stood there, entranced. He was hypnotized by the moving train, paralyzed of his senses. She reached out for his hand, but she only managed grab his sleeve. She tugged on it to pull him off the track, but he lost his footing and stumbled sideways. Dorothy was on her knees pulling her brother toward her when the train rolled by. In an instant, he was free, and the force with which she pulled brought Donny on top of her. Donny didn't move; he just lay there. Dorothy slid herself out from underneath him. As she sat up, her hair was blown back by the force of the train and she winced at the sound.

The train continued to slow. It hadn't come to a stop yet and wouldn't for a few minutes. She knew it was stopping for them, and she was terrified they would get in trouble.

"Donny, get up. We need to go," Dorothy said, panicking.

Donny didn't move. Dorothy stood up and had started to brush the dust and stones from her coat when she saw it. Donny's shoe was under the moving train. It came into view, flashing in and out as the wheels passed in front of it. Dorothy screamed when she looked at her brother's leg. It had been severed just below the knee. From that point, Dorothy's thoughts were not her own, her actions not born of conscious thought.

Donny lay still on the ground. Dorothy pulled at his coat to sit him up. He looked up at her, eyes wide, unblinking and silent.

"You'll be all right, Donny. I'll get you home."

Dorothy squatted, grabbed her brother's hands, and quickly turned so that he was against her back. She stood and moved as quickly as she could toward the hill, her brother dangling behind her. She took one step up the hill and realized it was too steep to carry him like that so she laid him on his back and dragged him instead. She tried to avoid the rocks and step on roots so that she wouldn't slip and lose her brother, but she was walking up backwards and could only see what was before her and in her periphery. After five agonizing minutes, she reached the top of the hill. She picked her brother up as she had done before, holding him against her back, and ran toward home as fast as her young and tired legs could carry her. He was limp, his legs dangling loosely, which made him difficult to hold onto.

Agnes knew Donny would be scared to come home, fearful of the consequences he faced. She had time to calm down and her anger had settled, now no more than a ripple in a pond. Art was not so composed. His fears, his uncertainty, his exhaustion, they all came crashing through that hole in the window, and Agnes knew she had to calm him down before the children came home.

Art was pacing in the living room, the wooden heels of his shoes echoing loudly on the planked floor. He was not himself. He was consumed by his emotions and they held him trapped. Agnes was frightened.

"Art, darling, please calm down. It is only a window. It can easily be replaced. I'll walk over to the restaurant right now and ask John for a recommendation." Agnes walked toward the closet to retrieve her coat when she heard a noise at the front door.

Agnes opened the door and saw Dorothy standing in the doorway. Dorothy pushed by her, still holding Donny. Dorothy laid her brother down on the floor, his head hitting it with a thud.

"Dorothy, what on earth?" Agnes asked.

Dorothy was out of breath and tried to speak, but the words wouldn't come; instead the tears did.

Instantly the trail of blood that followed them from the door was noticed by their mother. Agnes followed it to Donny's leg and her face turned white.

Agnes let out the wail of a wounded animal. She dropped to her knees, panic stricken. Donny remained still, his eyes closed.

Dorothy took a deep breath and screeched. "Donny was hit by the train! I told him to move. I did. But he wouldn't!" Dorothy yelled, pointing at Donny's leg.

"Donny, Donny," Agnes said as she shook her son. "Dorothy, go to the neighbour's and have them call an ambulance. NOW!"

Dorothy ran to the door. The door slammed behind her like a gun shot. Artillery fire began to go off in Art's head. Bang, bang, bang. It was so close.

The force of the door sent the birds into a panic. They squawked and flapped their wings, attempting to escape the danger. Feathers flew through the cage in a rainbow of colour.

Agnes caressed her son's head and kissed his warm cheek, but her affections were interrupted. Art fell on top of his wounded son, shielding him from further attack. Agnes was pushed off balance—Art could see nothing but his son and the battlefield.

Pungent smoke filled the air and Art wiped at his eyes.

"Down! That is an order!" he yelled as he pushed Agnes to the ground.

Agnes lay there, horrified.

"Art, what are you doing?!" She begged for an answer as she tugged at him.

Art sat up and turned toward Donny's wound. He ripped off his shirt and tied it tightly around the jaggedly torn pant leg. Another blast sounded and Art fell back on top of him.

"Medics, where are the damn medics?!"

Dorothy burst back through the door. With her was the neighbour, whom they had not yet met.

"The ambulance will be here soon. It wasn't easy. These are bad times. So many have shut down. The operator had trouble reaching one," he said as the sound of the siren came within earshot. He looked on stunned, as though the realization of what Dorothy had told him being true had altered him somehow.

Within moments two ambulance attendants were in the front door.

Agnes stood to greet them.

"It is my son. His leg is hurt. It was a train," she said, coherent but barely.

"Sir, please step back."

Art did not move.

"Sir, please step back!"

"He can't hear you," Agnes said. She didn't know what else to say, how to describe her husband's state. This wasn't about him. It was about Donny, and there wasn't time to worry about how it looked.

The pool of blood under Donny's leg was more than enough to convince the medic that immediate attention was required. He tackled Art off Donny in the same way that Art had done to Agnes. As Art rebounded to resume his position, the other attendant, a man much larger in stature, held him back.

"We need to get this boy to the hospital immediately. He has lost a tremendous amount of blood and he will go into shock."

Agnes could only nod.

"We do not have a car. Can we go with you?" she asked.

"We can fit two," he responded as he lifted Donny onto the stretcher.

Agnes looked at Dorothy and tried to determine what she should do. She couldn't leave her home alone, but then she couldn't leave Art in this state either. She proceeded the only way she thought she could.

"Dorothy, go to the restaurant and get your Uncle John. Have him bring you to the hospital."

As the attendants were putting Donny on a stretcher, Agnes had to get through to her husband. He just stood by, lost and fearful. Agnes was not sure where his mind was—was he there with her or off in some faraway place?

"Art," she said calmly, not wanting to attract attention in front of the others. He continued to look at Donny on the stretcher, his face blank of expression. "Art! We need to go to the hospital with Donny."

Agnes finally slapped Art's face, and he raised his hand in defence, but Agnes wasn't frightened. She was prepared to do whatever she needed to, even if it meant she was putting herself in harm's way. Art quickly realized what he had done.

"My darling, I am sorry. I would never raise my hand to you." He was as lost as Agnes had ever seen him, but she couldn't think of tending to him now. Donny needed her.

The drivers wheeled Donny out to the waiting ambulance and secured the stretcher in the back.

"One of you can sit in the back, and the other can sit up front with Joe."

Art was in no position to make decisions so Agnes knew she had no choice but to take over.

"Art, you need to sit up front with the driver so we know where we are going. I will sit in the back with Donny."

After a moment, Art nodded his agreement. Agnes guided Art to the front seat, and then she took her place in the back. Donny's eyes remained closed, but he had begun to whimper and Agnes called to him.

"Donny, it is Mummy. I am right here, sweetheart," Agnes said as she squeezed his arm through the blanket that covered him.

Donny opened his eyes ever so slightly.

"Mummy, please don't tell Dad," Donny quietly pleaded as tears fell down the sides of his face.

Donny appeared so tiny and helpless as he lay on the stretcher, and it was more than Agnes could bear that she was unable to lift him up in her arms and rock him and comfort him.

"My darling boy," was all Agnes could say.

◊

Dorothy ran into the restaurant. She was out of breath, her chest heaving and wheezing through her dirty coat, her lower legs and shoes covered in blood. It was lunch but the restaurant was quiet. The few patrons there turned to see the commotion. They could not believe the sight before them. The waitress recognized Dorothy and ran to her. She bent down and looked into Dorothy's crying eyes.

"You are John and Margaret's niece, yes? What happened to you? What is wrong?" she asked as she looked her over.

Dorothy pushed past the woman and ran to the kitchen. The sound of a pot hitting the floor soon filled the restaurant. Margaret froze at the sight of her niece standing before her. She knew something was dreadfully wrong, and her mind raced with every conceivable thought.

◊

The ambulance moved quickly through traffic. The drive to the hospital was not a long one. They arrived inside of seven minutes, but it felt like an eternity to Agnes.

The ambulance came to a stop and the back doors opened. The attendant unhooked the side latches of the stretcher and jumped down from the back of the vehicle. Together the attendants pulled the stretcher out and rushed it toward the emergency room doors. Art had circled the vehicle and arrived at Agnes's side, and they followed the stretcher through the large double doors.

A doctor and nurse rushed to Donny's side.

"Five- to seven-year-old boy. His leg was severed by a train just below the knee. He's had extensive blood loss and his blood pressure is dropping. He remains unstable." The attendant continued to rattle off medical details that all blurred together in Agnes's ears.

The stretcher never stopped moving. The attendants spoke as they rushed toward an observation room. Agnes and Art followed the stretcher through the swinging doors but were ushered back as quickly as they entered.

"I'm sorry, but you can't be in here," the nurse said harshly.

"He is just a boy. He needs us with him," Agnes pleaded.

"That is my son. I won't leave him," Art demanded as he began to push his way back in.

"If you do not leave, I will have you forcibly removed," she said as she stared him down. She was not a small woman, and something in her eyes caused Art to stand down.

"Wait in the waiting room. We will update you as quickly as we can. I have a son as well," she said, her tone turning softer.

Agnes quietly sobbed. He was her son. Her Donny. Her sweet boy. *This can't be happening*, she thought.

Art put his face in his hands. It stopped him from seeing what was happening but didn't stop the sound of his wife's anguish.

Art put his arm around Agnes and led her to the waiting room. Eyes descended upon the grief-stricken pair. The room was full, no empty seats. Children were crying and their parents were trying to quieten them.

Agnes's face was puffy and red from her salty tears. She looked around the room, searching for comfort, but she found none. Crying children were the last thing she wanted to hear. She was numb, dead inside.

◊

"Dorothy, what is wrong?!" Margaret demanded.

"Mum and Dad have gone to the hospital with Donny," she said, not wanting to say the dreadful words.

"The hospital? Why? What is wrong? Good grief, what happened, Dorothy?" Panic set in for Margaret as well. She knew this could be no insignificant thing.

"Please take me to the hospital. Mum wanted you and Uncle John to come."

Dorothy continued to cry. She believed it was her fault. She couldn't help but think so. Donny fell because she pulled at him. *He would have moved on his own. Wouldn't he?* Those thoughts began to torment her.

John came into the kitchen. He had been emptying the garbage out back and he stopped in his tracks, as though he hit an invisible wall.

"John, we have to go to the hospital. Agnes and Art have taken Donny there."

"Donny was hit by a train." Dorothy finally got the words out.

"Good God. Is he alive?" John asked in shock.

"Of course he is alive," Margaret said as though it was the most ridiculous question she had ever heard. The truth was, she didn't know.

Dorothy began to weep again. "It is all my fault," she said sadly.

"Hush, child. How could it possibly be your fault?"

"Amelia," Margaret called. "Amelia, I need you to manage as best you can. We have an emergency. We are mostly through the busy time. Turn away if you have to. Please have Jack clean this mess up."

Margaret stepped out of the puddle of sauce that surrounded her. Her legs and shoes were splattered like Dorothy's and didn't appear dissimilar.

The sun had finally broken the fog that had held heavy in the sky, warming the air and drying the dew from the windscreen. Not a word was spoken; Dorothy remained quiet as a mouse in the back seat. She relived the accident over and over again, wondering what she could have done differently, and praying to God that her brother would be all right.

Chapter 28

Art and Agnes sat in the waiting room awaiting word from the doctor when Margaret and John arrived. Agnes had not thought of her daughter once, and the realization consumed her with guilt.

"Mum!" Dorothy rushed into her mother's arms.

Agnes embraced her daughter. Her heart ached for it yet she felt only half-fulfilled by it.

"Agnes," Margaret said as she pushed her way through the crowd to her sister.

"We haven't heard from the doctors since we arrived. They are operating at present, and we have been told we should hear inside the hour."

Margaret embraced her sister and then sat down with her on chairs that had just become empty. Art was nowhere to be seen.

"Dorothy is a good girl. She came straightaway as you told her to. But she feels as though this is her fault. You need to tell her it isn't."

"Her fault? My gosh, no. Not in any way. It is my fault entirely. It is I that yelled at Donny when he broke the window. If I had not done so, he wouldn't have run off and none of this would have happened."

"You cannot blame yourself either for something that happened solely by chance. Dorothy told me what happened. It was an accident, pure and simple. It is nobody's fault."

"Where is Art?"

"Trying to get an update. He can't sit still."

Art returned to the waiting room more agitated than when he left. He acknowledged John and Margaret but didn't engage them in conversation. He continued to pace and fidget, his hands uncomfortable in whatever position they found themselves in.

Dorothy walked up to her father and wrapped her arms around him. He was stiff and unaffected by the embrace. She was not deterred.

"Dad, would you like to come sit with me?" she asked, hopeful his acceptance would show forgiveness. There was no acceptance, and the grip of guilt tightened around her.

"Dorothy, come here," Agnes said. "Do not blame yourself. If you hadn't been there with him, it would have been far worse. You saved him. You didn't hurt him. The doctors are taking good care of your brother. Do not worry."

Agnes provided the embrace that Art could not. Dorothy consumed it, but it didn't ease her shame.

"Mr. and Mrs. Craig?" a doctor called from the door that led to Donny.

Art had not been far from the door, and Agnes ran to meet him. The doctor appeared blank of expression and unemotional, and Agnes could not read him. She began to worry.

"Mr. and Mrs. Craig, your son's leg was severed cleanly but...." The doctor stopped as Agnes covered her face. "Mrs. Craig, would you like to sit down?" Agnes shook her head. She couldn't speak. "There was significant foreign matter in the wound and damage to the skin. We have cleaned it and closed it up. He has lost a substantial amount of blood and he is not yet stable. His biggest risk is shock, and if he survives, infection also. All we can do is wait at this point and hope he stabilizes over the next few hours."

"No, no, no, NO, NO!" Art began to shout. "This will not do. No, it won't," he continued to yell.

Agnes cowered as Art began to flail his arms wildly. There was no opportunity to express her own feelings, and they got pushed down to the others that she held so skillfully inside.

"No, I won't have it. You are not telling the truth. Why are you lying to us? Do you want to take my son from me? Is that it? Get your own son. He is mine. Do you understand me? You cannot take him."

Art began to mumble incoherently. Agnes put her hand on Art's shoulder to calm him down, and he shook it loose and stepped away from her.

"Mr. Craig, please calm down. I understand you are distressed, but you are no good to your son like this," the doctor said.

"Calm down? I'll calm down when you give me my son back."

For the doctor, there was little doubt that Art's irrational behaviour was not merely that of a distressed father. He had seen it before, and Agnes's disheartened expression only confirmed his diagnosis.

The doctor called to the nurse for assistance. Within moments two orderlies flanked the doctor. Their presence only made Art stand taller. They dwarfed him in size and strength, but it didn't seem to concern Art.

Fear mounted in Agnes, and she knew she had to calm him, to contain him before his behaviour escalated and there was no going back. From the other side of the room, Margaret and John watched the interaction and John rushed to their side.

"Art, please! Come sit down," Agnes pleaded. "The doctor is just doing his job. He is taking care of our boy, and he'll have him as good as new. We just need to trust in that."

Agnes moved to stand in front of Art; she forced eye contact and that seemed to calm him down.

Art walked away.

"Mrs. Craig, your husband is highly agitated. I can give him something to calm him down."

"Thank you. Seeing his son like this has opened old wounds. He saw horrible things in the war and they still haunt him, I am afraid. It has been fourteen years, and it is as though it were yesterday."

The doctor understood all too well. "Yes, 'shell shock.' Has he seen a psychiatrist about his condition?"

Agnes had never thought of his behaviour as a "condition," and the formality of such a distinction thrust another arrow in her heart.

"I will give him whatever you recommend," Agnes said, her tone seeping with heartache.

"Very well. The nurse will return with an anti-anxiety pill. Please wait here."

As the doctor had promised, a nurse quickly returned with water and a tablet.

"Art, here, please take this. The doctor suggested it would help relax you."

Art recognized the pill and took it without pause. Agnes had feared he would resist, but there was no hesitancy. It came as a relief that he might be pacified from the tiny pill, and it didn't take long before he began to settle.

"Agnes, I need to get back to the girls and John needs to get to the restaurant. Please call us there if anything changes. How about we take Dorothy with us?"

"Yes, thank you. That would be good."

Agnes was overwhelmed and Margaret could see it. Margaret wrapped her arms around her sister, holding her tightly until she felt Agnes knew she was not alone. Agnes needed her sister. She needed that deep and unbreakable love that they had always shared. She needed it more than she ever had.

As Margaret pulled away, Agnes blinked hard to keep her moistened eyes from tearing. Margaret saw her sister as such an emotional contradiction; she was the most loving, kind person she knew, yet when it came time for her to receive, her walls were impenetrable. It was something she had never understood.

Art and Agnes were left on their own. People in the waiting room came and went and yet Art and Agnes remained. Agnes was waiting to see her son. The doctor told her he would let her know when she could. It had been a few hours since he had come out, and Agnes was getting anxious. *What could be so bad that we can't see him? Our baby is in there all by himself.*

Agnes lowered her head and began to pray. She asked God to watch over Donny and protect him, to heal him, and to bring him back to them. Agnes was so incredibly lost and felt more alone than she ever had in her life. She wished her mother was there, but she knew her mother could not make it better. Agnes was not so naïve to think that anybody other than God could fix this horrible mess.

Mary and Percy arrived just past dinner time. Mary brought sandwiches and juice, but neither Agnes nor Art were hungry. It took Agnes a few moments to realize that the kids weren't with them.

"They are with Margaret. They are having dinner at the restaurant. Margaret will take them back to the house after. They'll enjoy it better than the hotel. They are tired of it already. I guess the novelty has worn off," Mary said with a laugh.

Mary curbed her smile quickly when her sister didn't react. Agnes looked so lost and it broke Mary's heart. Mary tried to understand her sister's devastation, the incomprehensible agony she must be enduring, but she couldn't. She was not living the nightmare as a mother; she was living it as a sister and aunt. Mary felt guilty for thanking God that her own children were safe. *How can I thank God for such a thing? Wouldn't a good sister wish she could trade places?*

A doctor appeared shortly after Mary and Percy arrived. It was a different doctor this time, and Mary and Percy stayed back while Agnes and Art went to speak with him. This one was younger. He looked barely old enough to drive, Agnes thought, let alone be a doctor.

"Mr. and Mrs. Craig, would you like to see your son?"

Agnes's legs buckled at the thought. She longed to see Donny. It had felt like an eternity.

"Please come with me," the doctor said.

He led them through the double doors and down a long hallway. As they approached a second set of double doors, he led them into an empty room. Now they were out of earshot of a waiting room full of people.

"I would like to provide you with an update on your son before you see him. There are a few things you need to understand first."

Art began to fidget again. The doctor seemed prepared for his nervousness this time.

"Mr. Craig, Dr. Simmonds has suggested another dose of Luminal. Can I get you one?"

Art didn't worry about what Agnes would think. He was past that. He nodded his answer. As the doctor left the room to retrieve the medication, Agnes asked him how he was. It concerned her deeply that the doctor felt that he needed medication to calm his nerves. But before Agnes could ask Art about it, the doctor returned with the pill.

"Mr. and Mrs. Craig, you need to understand how dire your son's condition is. He is gravely ill and his prognosis is not good. He has not regained consciousness and will not be aware that you are in the room. We have given him a transfusion, but due to the amount of time his body was without sufficient blood, there may have been damage to his organs. Blood is needed to carry oxygen throughout the body, and if there is not enough, the body cannot survive."

On some level, both Art and Agnes knew what the doctor said was true, but they refused to accept it and the doctor could see that. He continued to emphasize the severity, but to no avail. Agnes and Art only wanted to see their son, and anything else was only a barrier and an unnecessary delay.

They were taken to a room with four beds, all of which were occupied. Donny lay still, his eyes closed. He seemed so small and helpless in such a large bed. Agnes wanted to pick him up and take him home. *He doesn't belong here. He should be home with his family and his toys.* Agnes couldn't hold back the tears.

"Oh, Donny, my darling boy. It's good you are sleeping. You need your rest. When you wake, you will be as good as new. You just had a tiny accident. Nothing for you to worry about."

Agnes teetered on her feet as the room began to spin. Art reached for his wife, but his laboured reflexes were too slow to prevent her fall. She slipped through his fingers and bounced off the corner of the bed railing, landing hard on her side on the floor.

"Good God, Agnes, are you all right?" he asked as he reached down to help her up. "What happened?"

Agnes was dazed and disoriented.

"I'll be all right," she said.

"Let me get a nurse," he said as he looked around for a uniform. "You fainted."

"No, no, I'm fine. I just got a little dizzy."

Art didn't have to call a nurse; one had witnessed the fall. An older nurse, dressed head to toe in starched white, appeared at Agnes's side.

"Mrs. Craig, you fainted. You haven't had anything to eat or drink in many hours, have you? Your blood sugar is surely low. Here, take this sugar pill. It will help elevate your blood sugar, and will have you feeling better in no time."

The nurse held her hand out but Agnes did not take the pill.

"Agnes, it will make you feel better. Take the pill." Agnes hesitated but finally took it.

It wasn't simply the lack of food that had weakened Agnes. It was a multitude of things, not the least of which was the horrible sanitary smell of the room. It had always produced the same nauseating effect, but never to fainting. As a young girl back in England, Margaret had been gravely ill, and the smell of the hospital room had remained with Agnes. She never got over the association. She had always despised hospitals.

"Have a sit down on the chair, dear. You should rest," the nurse suggested.

Agnes did as she was told and sat in the chair alongside the head of Donny's bed. When Agnes's strength and vision returned, she turned toward her son. His eyes remained closed and he appeared ghostly pale. Agnes couldn't get over how pale he was. She leaned over and kissed his cheek. It was only tepid, not as warm as it should be, and she pulled back.

"Art, he is so cold. I think he needs more blankets. Please get a nurse." Agnes didn't want to leave him, not even for a moment.

Art did as he was asked. The nurse took his temperature under his arm, listened to his breathing, and checked his pulse.

"Mr. and Mrs. Craig, his temperature is what we would expect given the circumstances. His shallow breathing is more of a concern. We will continue to monitor it."

Agnes felt helpless and wanted something to be done, to see some improvement and nothing was happening. It was agonizing.

"Nurse, my sister and my husband's brother are in the waiting room. Can they come in and see our son?"

"Yes, but only for a few minutes."

"Art, would you go get them? They'll want to see Donny."

Art nodded and walked toward the door and the waiting nurse.

"Nurse, can I please have a word with you?" Art made certain he was out of earshot from Agnes before he spoke. "My doctor in Winnipeg provided me with a prescription for Luminal before I left. I have a short supply at home but will need a prescription refilled. Can I see a doctor about doing that?"

"I believe you will need to be examined before a prescription can be given. I'll ask Dr. Simmonds what needs to be done."

Art walked the long walk back to the waiting room. The crowd had thinned out a bit, but it was still quite busy. He wasn't sure if Mary and Percy would still be there, but they were.

"Would you like to see Donny? He is not awake, but I know it would be nice for Agnes to have you there, Mary."

"Of course. Yes, we would."

The sun had not yet set, but Vancouver had been thrust into darkness by a thick blanket of cloud that choked the city of its precious light. Rain pelted the windows, and sheets of water cascaded down Heather Street in a raging river.

As they approached the door to Donny's room, they could see Agnes in the hallway. She had her head in her hands. Art ran toward her. The door to Donny's room was still open, but a curtain now surrounded Donny's bed.

"What is it? What happened?" Art asked, frantic.

Agnes was beginning to hyperventilate, and Mary rubbed her back to calm her down.

"Agnes, slow down. Take deep breaths."

The sound of Mary's voice helped her gain some calm, but Art, who could only imagine the worst, began to lose what little calm he had.

"My boy, my boy." She began to sob. "He was breathing so quietly. I was listening for it. But it got so quiet and I couldn't hear it anymore. I called the nurse and she told me to leave. The doctor came in and they closed the curtain. I don't know what is happening."

Art looked into the room and could only see the doctor's and nurse's feet beneath the curtain. Mary continued to comfort her sister while Percy went to his brother.

"This is agonizing, Percy. I can't lose my boy," Art said, his voice cracking.

Percy put his arm on his brother's shoulder. The thought of Art losing his son was a terrible enough thought on its own, but Percy worried for his brother's stability. He was not strong, and that level of devastation would likely be insurmountable.

Agnes put her head on Mary's shoulder and continued to weep silently. Mary didn't speak; she simply provided her sister the shoulder that she needed ... but it wasn't for long. Agnes snapped her head up and drew a deep breath. She bumped into her husband and sent him off balance as she rushed toward the door. As she approached the bed, the nurse pulled back the curtain enough so that she could walk out. She saw Agnes approach and she stopped her.

"Mrs. Craig, the doctor needs to speak with you."

"Please step out of my way. I need to see my son."

Agnes was panicking. She knew something was terribly wrong. She felt it in her heart and every fibre of her being was disintegrating into nothingness.

"I SAID, PLEASE STEP OUT OF MY WAY!"

The nurse knew better than to come between a distressed mother and her child, so she stepped to the side. Agnes pulled the curtain back to find the doctor writing on a board. She moved around him to get to Donny and she knew. The doctor didn't have to say a word. Donny's precious little face, the one that she had smothered with kisses, was lifeless. He no longer looked like her child. He was a shadow of her baby boy and she cried out. She was mortally wounded and nothing could heal her—not time, not God, not her daughter, and not her husband. As she fell onto the bed, Art rushed to her side. Agnes wailed as she lay over her dead son. Art tried to pull her back, but she resisted. Art turned to the doctor.

"I am sorry, Mr. Craig. We did all we could. Your son was not able to survive the trauma of the accident. The blood loss was far too great, and by the time we were able to give him more blood the damage was done. He went into shock and wasn't able to recover. I am terribly sorry. You can have some time with him."

The words played over in Art's head. "We did all we could." "I am terribly sorry."

Art turned to Mary and Percy who were standing by, horrified. They had just arrived in Vancouver. This was not possible. They had just seen Donny the day before. He couldn't be dead.

Percy walked up to his brother and put his hand on his arm. Art pulled back, not wanting to acknowledge the gesture. Acknowledging it meant acknowledging Donny was dead. Percy feared Art's unravelling.

Mary went to comfort her sister. She stood behind Agnes and felt lost as to what to do. She wanted her to have the time to grieve, to have these remaining moments with her son, but she didn't want her to feel alone. Mary looked down at her nephew and buckled at the sight of him. Her despair was as deep as it was dark. This beloved child, this gift from God, had been taken from them and it made no sense. How could God give something so precious only to take it away so soon?

Agnes sat up and looked at Donny. His eyes were closed and he appeared to be sleeping peacefully, but he no longer looked like Donny, the mischievous boy with the smile that could light a room. Agnes could hear his laugh, the cackle that she teased sounded like a bird. But there would be no more of it. And as much as she would lay down her life to hear it one more time, it was never to be again.

"Donny, my sweet boy, go into God's arms. He is waiting for you. Dad and I will be right here whenever you need us. You just have to call out to us. Do not be afraid. Heaven is glorious; I promise you." Agnes swallowed hard and took a deep breath as she choked on her words. The tears poured from her like the rain from the clouds.

Mary rubbed her sister's back as she said her good-byes. Mary tried to stay strong for her sister, but she could not hold back her own tears.

"Donny, I hope you can hear Mummy. I love you with all my heart, my darling boy, and one day I will see you again in heaven. Until then, I will see you whenever I look up into the sky. You will be forever in my heart."

Agnes rested her head back down on her son. Mary gave her a moment and then put her hand on Agnes's back.

"Let's give Art some time with Donny too."

Percy stood by his brother's side as he took one final look at his son.

"I'm sorry, my son. I failed you." Art buried his face in his hands, and a lifetime of raw emotion poured from him. It was as though he had never cried before, all the tears escaping in a single rolling wave. "That damn baseball." He could barely get the words out. His voice cracked with each one.

Mary and Percy remained by their siblings, offering the support that they could, all the while their own hearts were breaking.

"Agnes, it is time we got you home," Mary said. "The doctors will need to tend to Donny."

Agnes looked up at her sister and paused through her tears. She knew what Mary meant. They were going to take him away, and she would never see him again. Agnes looked back at her son, and as she wiped her eyes and took a deep breath, the deepest breath of her life, she said good-bye to her baby boy. She kissed his forehead and turned and walked toward the door and didn't look back. She kept walking until she was back in the waiting room, standing amongst those whose loved ones were still alive. She was envious of them, but mostly she was sad and angry.

Chapter 29

Two days after Donny died, it was still raining. It hadn't stopped. The ground was saturated, yet somehow it continued to take all that the sky would give it. Art and Agnes awoke to the second worst day of their lives. They were burying their baby that day, and the rain didn't matter. No amount of sunshine could lessen the pain; no amount of sunshine could bring Donny back.

Agnes's body ached. There had been no sleep, no solace. With every thought, she had aged immeasurably as she strained to understand why this had happened, but there was no *why* to understand. How could there be a *why* for something that could never make sense?

Agnes pulled herself out of bed and went to the kitchen to make a cup of tea, hoping that would offer some comfort. Her mother had always made her a cup of tea and a piece of buttery toast when she was feeling blue. It had always helped before, but that day she was beyond blue.

Dorothy was in the kitchen, dressed, and working hard to keep busy.

"Dorothy," Agnes said, surprised. "You're up."

Dorothy gave her mum a kiss on the cheek and pulled out a chair for her.

"I made you tea and toast, Mum."

Agnes looked at her daughter and smiled. It was not her "why" but it was her "what now?" It was exactly what she needed to get her through the day.

Agnes embraced Dorothy with as much love as she felt the day she was born. She had been a God-send then, and she was even more of one that day.

"Thank you. This was very thoughtful of you." Agnes was proud of her girl.

"Is Dad coming to eat?"

Agnes wanted to answer, but she couldn't. Art had been in a haze since Donny had died and he was barely functioning. Agnes had tried to get through to him, tried to offer her love and support, but he wasn't ready for it, and Agnes wasn't going to push him.

"He'll be out soon. He is just resting."

Dorothy was only ten, but she was not so naïve that she didn't understand that *resting* was a loaded word. For the most part, her father was a happy man, and she did not doubt he loved her. But there had been times, dark periods, where he had retreated away from them and

Dorothy had difficulty discerning his lethargy from apathy. She feared what Donny's death would do to him, and she promised herself she would do nothing to make his world any darker.

"Your Uncle Percy and Aunt Mary will be here shortly to take us to the cemetery." There was no strain in Agnes's voice—she had pushed her feelings down so far that she was numb to them.

Dorothy loved her brother, and she knew she would miss him terribly, but she now had a job to do and she couldn't fail at it. Her world had changed and there was no pretending otherwise.

The knock at the door came earlier than expected. Dorothy opened the door to the rain. Mary and Percy stood in the doorway dressed in black. They were sombre in spirit, appearing as ghosts in the heavy mist. Dorothy stepped aside to let them in. Bluey and Queenie began to squawk at the wind that blew through the living room. It was the liveliest the house had been in a few days.

"Are you ready for the day?" Mary asked. "I know you can be a brave girl for your mum and dad."

"Yes, Aunty Mary," Dorothy replied dutifully.

"Where are your parents?"

"Mum was getting a cup of tea and I don't think Dad has dressed yet."

"Speak of the devil," Percy said as Art appeared.

"Yes, the very devil himself," Art quipped flatly.

The air was thick with sadness and guilt. Very little was said and even less was acknowledged. There had never been any lack of skill at stifling feelings; it was a skill well developed over time, over a lifetime of practice.

Mary went looking for her sister. The door to the washroom was closed and she knocked on it.

"Agnes, we're here."

"I'll be out in a moment."

Agnes sat on the side of the tub holding onto her mother's box. That box had always been magical to her. It held the love between her mother and father, and it was all that was left of him. It had been made by his own hands, and it had survived a journey across the Atlantic and travelled by train from one end of Canada to the other. Agnes slid the lid back and peeked inside. It was the first time she had done so since she had arrived in Vancouver. She placed the box on her lap and pulled the rose out. She held it up to her cheek and closed her eyes. She tried to picture her father in her mind, but she couldn't. She was looking for comfort and what she found felt hollow. A part of it was missing.

"Papa, please watch over our boy. He is with you and James and Elizabeth now. Please keep him safe and tell him I love him."

Agnes took a deep breath to stop the tears from coming. She gathered herself and joined the others.

"It is raining still. We'll need to remember our umbrellas."

Mary turned toward her sister's voice and offered an embrace. Agnes accepted what she could of it.

The drive to Mountain View Cemetery was not a long one. Dorothy sat between her parents in the back seat. Dorothy knew better than to say anything, so she sat quietly, listening to the sound of the wipers on the windscreen and watching as they whisked the pelting rain away. They worked hard, she thought. But as hard as they worked, as effective as they were at what they were doing, the results of their efforts were only temporary—they couldn't stop the rain from falling.

They entered the cemetery through a break in a thick hedgerow that ran the length of it along Thirty-third Avenue. The cemetery was a mass expanse that reached to the north and the south beyond Thirty-third. Donny was to be buried in a new tract in the north end. To the south, the "Old Cemetery" is where Art and Percy's mother, brother, and sister rested.

Mountain View was aptly named. As they turned southward into the cemetery, the North Shore Mountains sprang up from the skyline. They were shrouded in mist and cloud, which made their majesty all the more profound that day.

The car continued on the roadway north. They drove past grave after grave, and it felt as though they were going to reach the mountains that lay before them. At the southern boundary, they turned westward and a small gathering could be seen a few hundred yards in. Umbrellas sheltered the sea of black that flanked the open plot. They were the last to arrive, and the waiting mourners watched with sadness as the car approached.

Art opened his umbrella and then helped Agnes out of the car. It was a large enough umbrella to shelter the three of them, and together they walked toward the casket. Dorothy caught her cousins' glances but turned away quickly. It wasn't just their eyes that made her uncomfortable; she knew all eyes were upon them and she didn't like it.

The minister greeted them as they approached. He shook Art's hand and offered his condolences. Dorothy thought he looked incredibly old and he frightened her.

Art, Agnes, and Dorothy took their place at the front of the gathering, and then the minister began the service. Agnes didn't have the strength to look at the other mourners. She could barely take care of herself, let alone offer strength to anyone else.

"We are called together to mourn the death of Donald Arthur Craig, a tremendous young boy whom God has called home."

The sound of Donny's name made Agnes's knees weak. She began to sway, and Art tightened his grip around her waist.

"But we cannot mourn his death without celebrating his life. It was not a long life ... but then time is an interesting thing. Sometimes time seems to stand still and sometimes it races by. For those who were blessed to know Donny, time passed quickly when in his presence. He was a curious lad who had a love for exploring and discovery. Everything he saw was exciting to him. He was exuberant, a boy who saw the wonder in the world, a boy who brought wonder to those around him. Perhaps that is what God brought to us through Donny—that we should stop and appreciate the sound of the raindrops in a puddle, the feeling of mud between our toes, and even how much it hurts when our heart is broken. Perhaps God is teaching us how to feel, how to love, and how to appreciate all that He has given us and all that He has to offer us. It is difficult for us to understand why God chose to bring Donny home, but we have to trust in Him, trust in the fact that we are all on our own path toward Him."

It appeared many took his words to heart. Before he spoke, they hadn't truly heard the rain or seen it; it had been more a nuisance than anything. They hadn't see it as nourishing. They hadn't see it as beautiful. They thought of Donny, and the rain now gave them great comfort.

Dorothy didn't need to hear the minister talk about rain. She had always loved the rain—its sounds and its smells—and at the moment, she could think of nothing but the casket. She tried desperately to picture her brother lying in it, but she could only see an empty, vacant space. She could not mourn his death because it still didn't seem real to her. It felt as though he were there, in the crowd, and she looked around at his eye level, hoping to see him, but she didn't.

Agnes stepped away from the umbrella and looked up at the sky. The rain fell on her face, washing away her tears. She felt Donny. She heard him. He was there with her, and she knew he would always be.

At the cemetery, friends of Margaret and John's came out to support them in their loss, but at the restaurant it was just family. There was no pretending, no false strength needed ... but it was given just the same.

"How are you?" Margaret asked her sister.

"Right as rain," Agnes answered. "What does not destroy us makes us stronger, isn't that right?" Agnes forced her words through her clenched jaw.

Margaret let it go. She wasn't going to be the one to push her sister. Agnes would work through this on her own. She was more worried about Art. Everyone was. He wasn't as strong as his wife.

"Bill, how are you doing?" Agnes asked.

Bill had been staying with Art's brother, Nelson. He would be moving in with Mary and Percy once they were in their new house.

"I'm sorry, Agnes. I lost my boy, Cecil, when he was just twelve. I know how much it hurts. His death was just as senseless. Sometimes God makes no sense. All we can do is take it. We have no choice. You have a good husband. He will help you through this."

Bill's words weren't uplifting, but they were comforting. He undoubtedly knew what it felt like to lose a child. And Bill's sorrow had been even greater, if it was even possible to compare; he lost his son only months after losing his wife. Bill was right—Agnes had her husband to help her through this. He was there to support her and comfort her, and he would help her stay strong.

Agnes looked around the restaurant for Art but did not see him. She looked in the kitchen and out back. He was nowhere to be found. It was still raining, and Agnes didn't think he would have gone far.

"Percy, have you seen Art?"

Percy looked surprised. "What do you mean? Where is he?"

"If I knew where he was, I wouldn't be looking for him," she said slightly annoyed. Then she caught herself. "I am sorry. I didn't mean to snap at you. I have looked everywhere. I haven't seen him since we arrived."

Dorothy was within earshot and spoke up. "Dad said he was going for a walk."

"It is raining. Did he say where?"

"No."

Agnes had a horrible thought.

"He wouldn't go there. Not today. It would be too much."

"Did I do something wrong?" Dorothy asked, frightened.

Agnes did her best to keep the tension from her voice. She was worried. Art was the kindest, most loving husband and father, but he was not without his struggles. And since the accident there had been no peace, no rest, and there was a vacancy that she had never seen before.

"No, Dorothy. You did nothing wrong," Agnes said as she kissed her daughter on the head

"I'll go," Percy said. "Stay here with Dorothy."

Percy didn't have to ask. He knew where Art had gone.

Percy parked his car behind the house. As he got out of the car, he noticed the broken window. Other things had occupied them since the accident, and they had yet to have it fixed. It was roughly patched with plastic sheeting and tape, and one could easily have wondered if the house was even occupied.

Percy didn't attempt to check the house; he knew Art wouldn't be there. Dorothy had described the opening in the trees beside the bridge. As Percy approached the gap, the train sounded. It was not far off and he froze. Suddenly, certainty fought doubt.

Percy rushed through the gap in the trees. The ground was saturated. With every step, his feet plunged farther into the mud. It was only a short distance until the level ground gave way to a steep incline to the track. As Percy stepped beyond the trees, he could see down to the Grandview Cut. The engine had just passed where he stood, and it sent another shrill whistle up into the air. With Percy's momentum, the loose ground under his feet gave way, sending him sliding down the embankment. Halfway down his foot caught on a root and he stopped abruptly, falling backwards and landing on his backside. He was not shaken from the fall; his attention was solely focused on finding his brother. As Percy sat on the hill, his overcoat encased in mud, he scanned the Cut. He looked beyond the Woodland Bridge and then turned and looked toward Commercial. Nothing. There was no sign of Art.

The train continued to pass, the rolling of the wheels on the track sending vibrations through the ground. *Where could he be?* Percy was sure he would be there. He didn't know where else to look. He was at a loss.

The end of the train approached, and Percy continued to search his mind for his brother's whereabouts. Percy stood and swiped at the mud on the back of his coat. His hands were paralyzed, the cold, wet earth numbing them to the bones. His warm breath held heavy in the cold, misty air.

And then he saw him. As the train passed, Art appeared. He stood there, unaware of the eyes that were upon him, his own eyes fixated on the track. The blood had been washed away by the heavy rain, but the red paint on the rail marked the spot. Other than the markings, there were no other indications a life had been lost, nothing to show that his world had been drastically altered.

The rain held constant and it did not discriminate. It soaked Art as it soaked the trees, and like the trees there was no recognition of it. Percy didn't announce his intrusion. He let Art continue to search for whatever it was he needed to find peace.

Art reached down and picked up a fragment of shoelace. He held it in his hands and closed his eyes. Whatever he saw in his mind filled him with such agony that he could not keep it in. He looked up to the sky, and with every ounce of strength he could find lashed out at God.

"How could you do this? My boy. How could you take him from me?"

Art dropped his head. He sobbed, his shoulders rising and falling with every anguished breath.

Art raised his head again, his sorrow turning to anger.

"WHY didn't you take ME?!"

A murder of crows startled and flew up from a nearby tree, crying their harsh caw as they escaped into the open sky.

Percy stood and descended the remainder of the hill. Art had yet to notice him and Percy didn't call out to him. Percy crossed the narrow gully, which brimmed with the rainwater that had washed down the hill. Art remained still, his every thought fighting for a release from the swirling tornado in his mind. There was no sense, no peace. Every memory played out in detail, tormenting his soul with exacting precision.

The thoughts in Art's head were louder than the sound of Percy's footsteps on the stones. Percy stopped when he was a few yards away. He didn't want to startle his brother.

"Art."

Art didn't respond.

"Art," he said a little louder.

Art looked at his brother; he was dazed and confused and disoriented. Percy was out of context, and Art struggled to bring him back in.

"Art, it is time to go home. Agnes wants you home."

"Percy, why are you here? Agnes, where's Agnes?" The thought of his wife brought Art up a level.

"Agnes is at the restaurant. She should be heading home any minute. She'll want you there."

Percy's words worked their way through Art's mind. He stepped outside his emotions, which had controlled him to that point, and he realized that he shouldn't be where he was at that time.

"Yes," Art said. He put the piece of shoelace in his pocket and crossed the track toward Percy.

Meanwhile, Agnes did her best to keep herself composed as Percy searched for her husband.

"Thank you for closing the restaurant today," Agnes said to John.

"It is I who should thank you. You saved me from losing money today. It seems we have been doing quite a lot of that lately. It is not a good time, but what can you do? Every business is hurting it seems, every business except Percy's, that is," John said with a laugh. "I guess people can't do without hardware. I don't know how long we will be able to keep our doors open."

"I didn't realize it was that bad. I'm sorry."

"Please don't be sorry. There are others who are so much worse off than we are. We'll weather this storm. It can't continue forever. We'll look to happier days."

Agnes couldn't imagine anyone worse off than she was at the moment. She forced a smile. "Yes, happier days."

Chapter 30

The sun filtered through the sheer curtains that covered the bedroom window. As Agnes awoke, she could hear the familiar pattern of Art's sleeping breathing. She looked over to the clock—it was ten past seven. Agnes sat up and rubbed her eyes. It was nice to see sunshine. Outside of their first day, they had been shrouded in darkness and the sun was a welcome sight.

Agnes could hear the birds chirping in their cage. She loved the sound; it was like springtime in a park. *How could one not be happy with such a cheerful sound?* But as quickly as she thought of Bluey, she thought of Donny—Bluey would always be Donny's. She could see Donny's enthusiasm in her mind, his childish excitement at seeing the birds for the first time.

Banging in the kitchen redirected Agnes. *Dorothy must be awake*, she thought. She got up and dressed, leaving Art in bed. The smell of apples and cinnamon filled the air. It was a comforting smell that reminded Agnes of her mother.

Today was Dorothy's first day of school, and it was one of mixed emotions. She no longer had a sibling to walk with her. Her cousins would attend the same school, but they were coming from the opposite direction. She would be alone, just her.

"Dorothy, it smells terrific in here. What have you been baking? I smell cinnamon."

"Muffins. I thought they would be good in my lunch."

With so much going on, Agnes had neglected to think of Dorothy's first day. She should have been up before her daughter to make her breakfast, to talk her through her nervousness, her excitement. She should have helped her pick out her clothes and do her hair. And there was little food in the house; not much could be pulled together other than the muffins that Dorothy had made. Agnes could only promise herself that the following day would be a better one.

"Ah, yes, your first day. It is very exciting. Are you ready?"

Agnes was trying hard to stay positive for Dorothy's sake. The pain of Donny's absence was suffocating, but she couldn't let Dorothy see it. Dorothy deserved a good first day. She deserved to have a happy mother.

"Yes. It will be fun to go to a new school with Margaret and Norma."

"We are meeting your Aunt Mary and cousins at the school at half-past eight. We'll get you all enrolled together. Do make sure you meet new children too. I know you love your cousins, but it would be good to make new friends as well."

Dorothy nodded, but she knew she didn't need any other friends. There were no better friends than Margaret and Norma. The three girls were one and the same, none without the other. And Dorothy looked as much like them as they looked like each other, and it only made their bond more magical.

"Do you have your school bag ready? We need to leave in a blink."

"Yes, Mum. Is Dad going to say good-bye?"

Agnes could see the sadness in Dorothy's eyes. She longed for her father's affection, but he remained unable to give any of himself.

"Your father is sleeping. He didn't sleep well last night. You'll see him after school."

"Please give him a kiss for me. Tell him I made him some muffins. I made a big one especially for him."

"Of course I will." Agnes hurt for her daughter. "He loves you very much, Dorothy."

Dorothy smiled at her mother, but her eyes betrayed her heart. It was as though Dorothy knew they were only words, truthful words, but words based on a shifted foundation, and they no longer carried much weight.

It was a short ten-minute walk to Dorothy's new school, and it was taken on the grandest of mornings. The haze that had accompanied the previous few mornings stayed away, but the dew was still thick on the grass, and it glistened under the rising sun.

Dorothy was mature beyond her years. She did not need her mother to hold her hand or reassure her. She had her cousins to hold her up when she needed support, and they never failed her.

"Dottie!" Margaret screamed as she rushed toward her. It was as though she hadn't seen her for months, but it had only been a day. Dorothy lit up and held out her arms to embrace her cousin. The two collided in a frenzy of excitement.

"Oh, to be young and silly," Mary teased.

School enrollment was simple, but it wasn't without its challenges. For Agnes to answer that Dorothy was an only child was a crushing blow to an already fragile state of mind. Mary squeezed her sister's hand for comfort, but it wasn't enough. Agnes remained strong until she was safe in her home, and then she collapsed in grief. There was nothing she could do to hold back the pain. But it didn't matter; there was no one she needed to hold it back for. She was alone.

"Mum," Dorothy called. "Mum, are you here?"

"Back here, darling," Agnes answered from the bedroom.

Agnes had spent the day on house and home. She had neglected them and she felt bad for it, but she knew that life didn't stop, even for mourning.

"How was school?" Agnes asked eagerly, hoping for some cheer.

"Good. I like my teacher. She is from Winnipeg too. I'm not in Margaret or Norma's classes, but I get to see them at lunch time. I'm excited about that."

"I'm so happy that you settled in so nicely. I have a surprise for you."

"Really?" Dorothy's eyes lit up.

Agnes opened her top drawer and took out a book and handed it to her daughter.

"A journal. So you can write all about your new life here, all the new friends you will meet and all the new places you will visit. My Aunt Jane gave me one when I first moved to Winnipeg. I thought you might like one as well."

Dorothy took the journal and stared at it as though it were a crown of jewels. It was covered in red satin with a gold leaf design—and it had a lock. Dorothy couldn't believe it had a lock. She had seen journals in the stores and had admired them, but she never believed she would have one.

"The clerk said it was unlocked and the lock was inside the cover. I thought you should be the one to check."

Dorothy gently pushed the small button on the side of the lock and it popped open. It was the most incredible sound that Dorothy had ever heard. She was so overcome with emotion that she could only giggle, and the young, girlish sound warmed Agnes's heart.

Dorothy wrapped her arms around her mother's neck and kissed her cheek.

"Thank you, Mum. I love it. It is the best present ever." Dorothy was caught up in the excitement, enjoying the extravagant pleasure, until the reality of the situation brought her plummeting down. "We cannot afford this. I don't need it."

Dorothy was a good girl, a kind-hearted and practical girl. Agnes let her pride for having such a daughter get in the way of what being such a girl meant for Dorothy. Others noticed; Mary saw a girl who worried too much, a girl who took too much of the weight of the world on and didn't allow herself to be a child. There was never any giving in to whims or fancies, never any reckless abandon, never any *what were you thinking?* She was ever obedient and responsible.

"That is not for you to worry about, my dear."

Agnes didn't share that it had been purchased with grocery money. It was a willing sacrifice and Agnes would make do. She had learned to stretch food. Cooking well with little was a skill she honed from her mother and older sister. Agnes was not one to give into whims or extravagances herself, but she wanted this for her daughter, and she was sure Art would be working regularly straightaway.

"Why don't you start your journal off with your first day at school, and then you can come help me make dinner?"

As Agnes began to peel potatoes, the front door opened. She wiped her hands off on her apron and went to greet her husband. She took his coat and offered him a kiss.

"How was your day?" she asked, hopeful and fearful at the same time.

"I went to Percy's office. I will do an advertisement in their customer newsletter. John still wants me to paint the restaurant on Sunday, although I'm not sure why. His business is quite slow. I can't imagine he is profitable these days."

"Come, let's get you comfortable in your chair. I'll bring you a drink."

Art sat in his favourite chair. He put his feet up on the foot stool and reached for the newspaper. Agnes returned with a gin martini, just the way he liked it—stirred with an olive. She bent down and gave him another kiss.

"Relax, my darling. I will call you when dinner is ready."

"You are too good to me. I don't know what I would do without you." And he meant it. He truly didn't know.

Agnes finished preparing the stew. It was mostly filled with carrots and potatoes, more so than meat, but it was tasty as always. She quickly realized that Dorothy had not come in to help with her usual chore of setting the table. At first she was annoyed, but then she remembered the journal and knew she couldn't fault her for her excitement. Agnes took the bowls to the table herself and stopped in surprise. Dorothy was not in her room with her journal, but rather cuddled up to her father in his chair, her face tucked under his chin, both of them asleep, both of them content. Dorothy had been starved of her father, and she desperately needed this closeness with him.

"Wake up, sleepy-heads. It is dinner time. Wake up or I will have to eat it all myself."

Slowly they woke, both rubbing their eyes before they sat up. Art acknowledged his time with his daughter with a wink and Dorothy grinned; she was under his spell. Agnes could have watched them all night, but dinner was ready and she couldn't have her family eat cold stew.

"How would you like to go to Stanley Park on Sunday with your cousins? Your Uncle Percy and Aunt Mary are going and I thought you might like to join them. There is a zoo there. They have all sorts of interesting animals. I will be at the restaurant on Sunday, but you can go with your mother."

Dorothy's attention was piqued. "Stanley Park?" She had not heard the name mentioned before, but she liked the sound of a zoo. And her cousins would be there.

"Stanley Park is the largest park you have ever seen. Probably the largest park you will ever see in your lifetime. It is right down beside the water. Your Grandpa used to take your Uncle Percy and me there when we were children. We loved to go."

"Really?! That sounds grand." Dorothy couldn't hide her excitement. "I wish you could come, though. It isn't fair that you have to work. It won't be nearly as much fun without you." Dorothy's face dropped into a pout.

"We will have plenty of opportunities to go together. Don't you worry about that. There are lots of exciting places to explore in Vancouver. I very much enjoyed living here as a boy. You will enjoy it as well. You live in the best city in the world. Just wait and see."

Dorothy was sad her father couldn't come, but her excitement for the adventure took her mind off it. She knew it was going to be the best day, and she would have plenty to write about in her journal afterwards.

"You have outdone yourself on dinner tonight, darling. This is your best stew yet. And I could eat that entire loaf of bread. We are very fortunate, aren't we, Pumpkin?" he said.

"Yes, I have the best family in the world," Dorothy said without realizing the impact of her words.

As they sat at the table, Donny's empty place had been noticed but not outwardly acknowledged. Now, Dorothy's well-intentioned words drew attention to the empty space, as though a bright light were shining directly on it. There was no denying it.

Dorothy dropped her head when she realized what she had said. However unintentional, she felt terrible. She was hurting too, but the thought of hurting her parents was more than she could bear. She wanted to run to her room and bury herself in her bed, but she wasn't given that opportunity.

"I think it is time for dessert. Dorothy, why don't you remove the dishes from the table and bring it in? It is on the counter."

Dorothy did as she was told and cleared the table. The activity occupied her mind, shifting her feelings away from guilt, which was her mother's intent. Agnes could see the heaviness on Art's face, and she could offer him no such diversion. All she could do was squeeze his hand.

"Excuse me a moment, darling."

"Look what Mum made, Dad," Dorothy said as Art returned to the table. "Apple crumble, your favourite."

"She sure did. Aren't we a lucky pair?"

"No, Dad, it's not pear. It's apple."

Art laughed. "You seem to have inherited your mother's wit. Very clever."

Dorothy basked in the attention from her father, something she had been craving, but the contentedness she felt was gone within minutes. As dessert disappeared, so did her father. Vacancy transformed him from the father she longed for to a man she didn't recognize. Right before her eyes, he became a stranger to her.

Dorothy's confusion turned to sadness. She couldn't understand how a person could change so. *If he truly loved me, he wouldn't change. He would stay for me. Am I not good enough?* Agnes could see the transformation in Dorothy as plainly as she could see it in her husband. Agnes too felt helpless. She felt she had lost all control in her life. She had lost the ability to mother and to be a wife, to comfort and to heal. God had altered her direction with no explanation, no apology.

Agnes did the only thing she could; she tended to her family before it could unravel any further.

Chapter 31

Agnes woke long before dawn. The house was silent and dark. She quietly got out of bed, wrapped herself in her dressing gown, and went to the kitchen. It was too early to see what type of day would greet them, but Agnes didn't need light to hear the wind as it bellowed in the yard. It lashed at the plastic on the window, angry that it could not break through.

Agnes turned the light on to the empty room. It seemed emptier than usual. Perhaps it had just been the early morning hour. Time aside, it felt terribly lonely, and she found her mother in her thoughts. It had only been a week, but it felt like it had been a lifetime. Her mother was there, large as life in Agnes's mind, but she loomed as a memory and her distant presence could not offer any comfort. What had been unyielding was beginning to dissolve before her eyes.

By the time Dorothy awoke, Agnes had baked bread and made biscuits. Breakfast and lunches were assembled, and Dorothy left for school before her father was out of bed. Agnes let Art sleep, using the time to scrub every surface in the kitchen. What was scrubbed once was scrubbed twice. Agnes's fingers were raw and blistered by the time she allowed herself to be finished, but she paid them no attention.

It was half-past eight by the time Art woke up. Agnes had already been awake for four hours when Art entered the kitchen.

"Good morning, darling. How did you sleep?" she asked before giving him a kiss.

"Good. I hadn't realized it was so late. You should have woken me."

"Come, I have some biscuits and coffee waiting for you."

Art picked at his breakfast. He hadn't much of an appetite.

Agnes removed his plate and refilled his coffee cup. "What are your plans for the day?"

Art hadn't thought of the answer himself.

"I think I'll solicit the businesses on Hastings to see if there are any opportunities."

"That's a good idea. Can I help? I can make enquiries as well. We can cover twice the ground."

Art dismissed Agnes's offer without much thought. Agnes was hurt, but Art didn't notice.

"I'm sure you have plenty to do here at the house."

Art finished his coffee, packed up, and left. Agnes was left alone again in an empty house.

Bluey and Queenie chirped happily throughout the day and provided some company to Agnes as she cleaned the remainder of the house. At half-past three, Dorothy arrived home and went straight to her journal. Art arrived home minutes later.

Agnes took his coat and welcomed him home with a kiss.

"How was your day? Any luck?" she asked, hopeful.

Art sighed, his disappointment showing through as plainly as the excitement Dorothy felt at seeing her father.

"Not yet. I'll keep trying." It hadn't even been a week, but Art was beginning to worry.

"Dad," Dorothy said as she rushed into his arms. "Can we train Bluey and Queenie?"

Art had promised the children that he would train the birds with them, but he found himself hesitating; he could not look at Bluey without thinking of Donny.

"Please, Dad."

Art looked at the longing on his daughter's face and couldn't refuse her.

"Keep talking to them the way you have been. They have to get comfortable with your voice."

"Hello, Queenie and Bluey. How are you today?" Dorothy felt silly talking so childishly in front of her parents. She spent all her time trying to be mature and if it wasn't for her father doing the same thing, she wasn't sure she could do it.

"Pretty birds you both are. It is a nice day for a treat, isn't it?" Art added.

After placing a chair in front of the cage, Art slowly opened its door and positioned his hand near the bottom of it. The birds began to squawk and flutter their wings, but the cage prevented them from moving back farther. Art persisted patiently, leaving his hand remaining on the bottom of the cage. Within minutes the birds calmed down.

"There you have it. Such nice birds," he said calmly.

They were soothed by the sound of his voice.

"It is your turn, Dorothy," he said as he pulled his hand slowly out of the cage.

Excitedly, Dorothy did exactly what her father had done. She slowly put her hand in the cage and rested it on the bottom. She spoke soothingly to the birds until they both came down from the top of the cage and rested on their perch. Art broke off a tiny piece of millet spray and handed it to Dorothy. She took it in her hand and placed it back in the cage. Her hands shook with nervous excitement and she giggled. She moved her hand slowly toward Bluey, who was the closest to her. Bluey hopped to the back of the cage, gripping his claws on the metal rungs and walked up as high as he could go. Queenie remained where she stood. Before Dorothy could react, Art reassured her.

"It will take time. They need to learn to feel safe and trust that you will be consistent with them. Try Queenie."

Dorothy slowly moved her hand toward Queenie, who remained in place until the very last moment, when she joined Bluey at the top of the cage.

"Not to worry, Pumpkin. You made great progress today. A few more tries, and you will have them eating right out of your hand. We'll try again tomorrow."

That seemed to satisfy Dorothy's doubt. Art hoisted her up off her chair and swung her around as she shrieked in delight before placing her back on the ground. He hadn't done that in years. She was getting too big. As much as she wanted to grow up, she loved her father's attention.

The remaining few days of the week came and went without divergence. They maintained a consistency that was neither good nor bad; they were just as they were.

Saturday night Dorothy went to bed praying for sunshine. She could hardly contain her excitement for Sunday's trip to the park. If it was ruined by bad weather, she felt she would never recover. As it turned out, Sunday brought with it a stunningly beautiful day.

Dorothy bounced out of bed as she looked out her window at the clear blue sky. She wasn't going to let anything spoil the day. The last week had been mired in darkness; it was the saddest time of her young life, and she longed to forget, just for a day.

Agnes was in the kitchen, and to Dorothy's joy, so was her father.

"Good morning, young lady. Are you looking forward to your day?"

Art's mood seemed more vibrant to his daughter than it had as of late. Dorothy found herself hopeful the clouds were parting and their lives were being returned to them. *Perhaps God is listening to my prayers,* she thought.

Agnes had woken early to prepare for the picnic—tarts, cookies, and baked rolls. As usual, Margaret was bringing the meat. Sadly, based on the lack of business at the restaurant, they were merely saving it from waste.

"I wish you could come, Dad. We will miss you."

"I will be thinking about you all day, Pumpkin, and will hold my breath until you can tell me all about how much fun you had."

After Art left for the restaurant, there was still an hour before Margaret would arrive to take them to the park. Dorothy decided to use the time on the birds. She was determined to get the birds to eat from her hand that day. She had spent time with them every day that week and little by little, they became less timid. She could feel it … *today is the day*.

"Hello Bluey and Queenie. It is a good day to go to the park, don't you think? I certainly do." She laughed aloud at how silly it was to be talking to birds that could not understand her.

She placed her hand slowly in the cage, and the birds continued about their business unaffected. She placed some millet spray between her fingers and moved it toward Bluey to start. Like every time before, he hopped to the side of the cage and climbed his way to the top.

"I thought you were a budgie, Bluey, and not a chicken."

Agnes chuckled to herself from the kitchen. Her daughter did have a quick wit and it made her laugh. She reminded her of her sister, Mary, when she was young.

"All right, Queenie, it is all yours. You are a brave bird, aren't you?"

Dorothy moved her fingers toward Queenie and Queenie didn't move. Queenie began to peck at the millet and continued doing so quite contentedly until Dorothy pulled her hand away. Dorothy was elated. The next step was to get her to eat from her hand and not just from the spray. Dorothy rubbed some of the millet off the spray and put it in the palm of her hand. Bluey remained at the top of the cage, but as Dorothy put her hand back in the cage he climbed his way back down to his perch. Not to be outdone by Queenie, he shuffled from the edge of the perch so that he was wing to wing with his cage mate.

Dorothy was fascinated by the behaviour. The transition of timid to tame was mesmerizing.

Queenie didn't make any attempt to visit Dorothy's hand. She had gorged herself on the spray and had no interest in eating anymore. It was Bluey's turn, and he continued to shuffle over, pushing Queenie along the perch. Bluey leaned forward to get a better view, and Dorothy moved her hand slowly toward the bright blue bird. Bluey quickly pulled himself upright again, but Dorothy didn't move. She wasn't taking no for an answer. Bluey leaned forward again and this time took a nip at Dorothy's finger. It didn't hurt and Dorothy remained still. Dorothy wasn't about to let a bird rile her that easily. Bluey was testing her, and she must have passed because Bluey stepped off the perch and onto Dorothy's hand before he started to peck at the seeds. His tiny feet tickled her, and it took all the concentration she could muster to not laugh and pull her hand back. She persisted and Bluey rewarded her with his trust.

Margaret arrived with Betty and Eileen shortly after eleven. John was working at the restaurant with Art, and Margaret was to be chauffeur. Dorothy had been waiting at the front window for the car to pull up.

"Mum, Aunty Margaret is here! Mum!"

Dorothy couldn't hold back her enthusiasm. As she rushed from the front window, the curtains and rod that they hung from almost went with her.

"Dorothy, dear heavens. Slow down. I know you are looking forward to the outing, but you must calm yourself or you will start to whistle like a boiling kettle."

Dorothy tried to slow herself as she knew she must, but the knock at the door came and she got lost in her frenzy.

Agnes rolled her eyes at her daughter's exuberance. *Oh, to be young again*, Agnes thought. She was half-filled with disapproval, half with envy.

"I hope you are ready for a fun day."

"I sure am, Aunty Margaret." Dorothy held her hands clasped together in an effort to calm herself, but she could not contain her enthusiasm.

Agnes laughed. "I don't think she has thought of much else all week."

"Very good. It should be a brilliant day. We have planned to meet Percy and Mary at the zoo. That's the first order of business."

Dorothy liked the sound of that. Dorothy's cousins were in the back seat, and she took a seat beside Eileen. They were twins but not identical. Dorothy didn't think they looked all that much alike. They were five years older, but it might as well have been twenty to Dorothy. They seemed so grown-up. And Dorothy didn't know them well, which only accentuated the gap. Despite the newness of them, Dorothy instantly loved them. They were family, and it was something she could not get enough of.

The snow-capped peaks of the North Shore Mountains drew closer as they drove northward on Commercial Drive. For Dorothy it was like looking at a children's picture book. It was beyond imagination, too wondrous to be real.

They turned westward on Hastings Street toward Vancouver's downtown core. The farther west they drove, the denser the cityscape became. The buildings became wider and taller, and Dorothy tried to imagine how busy the streets would be on any other day. It was the Lord's Day and businesses were closed. Save for the homeless that milled around, it was quite quiet. Winnipeg didn't have a widespread homeless problem, probably because it was too cold in the winter to survive on the streets. Those with bleak prospects, those who had nothing left to lose, made their way westward as they looked to improve their circumstances, continuing until they hit the "end of the line." They were drawn to Vancouver seeking opportunity, and when they didn't find it they stayed for the mild climate. Being homeless was enough of an affront, but being homeless and exposed where no places of refuge existed, not the slightest relief from the bitter and biting cold, was simply more than most could handle. Dorothy could hear her aunt talking to her mother about the plight of the poor in the city, and the direness of their misfortune was not lost on her.

They meandered their way toward Georgia Street and something in the distance caught Agnes's attention.

"Margaret, what is that building?" she asked of the massive skeleton of a structure, only partially completed.

"The Hotel Vancouver. It has been as you see it now for a few years already. Money is a scarce commodity these days, even for those who dare to build something as grand as that hotel."

Even in its unfinished state, it did appear it would be grand. The point of the roof was certainly the tallest that they could see.

"After all that work, it would be a shame if they couldn't finish it," Agnes said.

"Indeed."

As they turned westward, the city began to open up. In the blink of an eye, the urban maze ended and the land was allowed to breathe again. Homes and trees dotted the road along Georgia Street all the way to the gateway to Stanley Park. As they approached the park, they could see where all the traffic had gone. People weren't at home; it appeared the entire population of Vancouver was at the park. The road, which had become flanked by water on both sides, was a sea of cars and streetcars. It was traffic unlike anything they had ever seen.

"I have never seen so many cars," Dorothy said in amazement.

"Welcome to Stanley Park on a sunny Sunday," Margaret said. "It seems everyone else in the city had the same idea as we did," she laughed. "This may take a while."

Dorothy didn't mind. She was floating on a cloud, soaking in everything that she could lay her eyes on.

"Aunty Margaret, is that the ocean or a lake?" Dorothy asked, flummoxed that there could be water on both sides of a road that was not a bridge.

"You are actually looking at both. Over there on the left is Lost Lagoon. It used to be connected to the sea, and the water used to rise and fall every day with the tide. It was blocked off from the sea and turned into a lake. Its water isn't salty anymore and it stays as you see it, which is as the ducks and geese like it. We'll come back another day and feed them. It's quite a lot of fun. Over on the right is Coal Harbour. It opens up as you get around Stanley Park. Stanley Park is almost an island. There is just a wee bit of land connecting it to the rest of Vancouver. We'll come out of the park on the other side later."

Dorothy was spellbound. Her mind was filled with new, and she found she could hardly remember Winnipeg. She certainly didn't ever want to go back.

The traffic moved at a snail's pace as they entered the park, but it soon picked up. As they rounded Coal Harbour, they now faced where they had come from, offering them an entirely different perspective—small marine buildings and the boats they housed gave way to enormous docks and the immense steamships that sat anchored against them.

In the shelter of the harbour, rower's cries could be heard echoing off the water as their long, sleek boats sliced through the glassy mirk. Dorothy put her head through the open window and inhaled the salty air. The sun's rays were intense and luminous through her closed eyes, and its radiance warmed her face. In short order, they were parked and not far from the others. All that separated them was a quick walk up a tree-lined path.

The trees were the largest Agnes and Dorothy had ever seen. And it wasn't just the sheer size of them that was so amazing. It was the number of them. Little space separated them, their branching canopies reaching out toward the others and blocking out the sun.

Dorothy had never heard the likes of it before, the birds so noisy they almost deafened. They crossed a stone bridge and Dorothy was the first to spot them.

"Margaret, Norma," she called as she ran toward them.

It had only been two days since she had seen them, but it felt like it had been an eternity.

"Dottie!" Margaret responded gleefully.

The girls hugged and bounced with girlish excitement. Agnes and the elder Margaret greeted Mary and Percy, happy that they had found each other. The twins joined up with the other kids and led them toward the cages. The first one housed two black bears. They were the largest animals that Dorothy had ever seen. They didn't pay the visitors much attention, preferring to pace back and forth in their cage, perhaps to stave off the boredom of captivity. Dorothy was thrilled to see them, but seeing them out of their natural habitat saddened her. They were prisoners of their circumstance and they could do nothing to change it. She knew she would be entirely unhappy if she were so confined.

The black bears were the largest animals Dorothy had ever seen until she laid her eyes on what inhabited the next cage. Trotsky, a Brown Siberian bear, was standing on his hind legs. He appeared as tall as a tree. Dorothy had heard of the fierceness of these animals, but Trotsky seemed more meek and mild than fierce. In fact, she thought he appeared quite docile and amiable, almost human, as he sat himself down on his hind haunches. He was poised for the treats that he knew would come, and much to Dorothy's delight, the children obliged and began to throw peanuts at the massive bear. As tall as Trotsky was standing, he was as wide sitting. His girth was beyond compare, his lap the size of an automobile. One by one, Trotsky would catch the peanuts and eat them straightaway or he would pick them off his ample belly if he was unable to catch them. Either way, Trotsky received them with gratitude, most undoubtedly grinning with appreciation. The other two Brown Siberians didn't seem quite so outgoing. They were uninterested in putting on a show for treats, rather resting lazily at the back of the cage, content to keep to themselves.

The monkeys were Dorothy's favourites. They swung from their ropes and hung precariously from the trees. They didn't sit still except to groom each other. Dorothy loved their playfulness. It was as though they had no cares, living only to play.

"Mum, they are fantastic, aren't they?" Dorothy said enthusiastically.

Agnes was pleased her daughter was enjoying herself. She needed a break from the stresses at home. For Agnes, living in the moment was proving more difficult. Donny had been such a curious lad, and she constantly had to keep him close or risk having him run off somewhere. At the park, she found herself looking for him at every turn, and at every turn she realized he was gone; it was as though it had happened all over again. The pain was unbearable, and she didn't think she would ever get through it.

The otter, whose name was Friday, was a lively little creature. His swimming was haphazard but appeared so by design. He spun around as he torpedoed through the water. There was nothing uniform or consistent about his movements; they were almost frenetic, but in a fun sort of way.

"Mum, Donny would like the otter. He likes to swim as well."

Mary held her breath at Dorothy's comment, fearing it would send her sister off an emotional cliff, but Agnes remained strong for her daughter's sake.

"Yes, darling, he certainly would."

Dorothy didn't realize what she had said. If she had, she would have been horrified. She was having the time of her life while her worries remained in safe keeping beyond the boundary of the park. There they awaited her for the end of the day.

Mary could see the mask that her sister wore and she worried. Agnes had always been constant and unwavering in her emotions, but she had never faced anything of this magnitude. She was holding in her grief, not sharing it with those who wanted to help, and Mary feared the consequences.

While Dorothy liked the monkeys, Agnes was drawn to the ponds.

They were filled with swans, both black and white. Agnes loved birds and these were spectacular in their grace and elegance. They were flawless, both perfectly white and perfectly black, a complete and striking contrast to each other. They made no sounds; they just swam along contentedly, comfortable being swans. The ducks, on the other hand, were much livelier. They were well used to people and were not shy in their expectation of treats. They waddled through the crowds quacking loudly, looking for whatever people would give them.

"Children, come here," Margaret directed.

She pulled a loaf of bread out of her handbag and handed a generous piece to each child.

"Make sure the pieces are quite small. They can choke on the bread if they are too large."

Dorothy took her bread, and after watching other children in the crowd feed the ducks, took a tiny piece and threw it in front of her. A mallard male, with its glossy green head, picked up the bread with its beak as another male charged for it. Dorothy threw another piece, and the same duck was able to get it before any other approached. Before long it was walking toward her anticipating the next offering. Dorothy stepped backwards as the duck followed her. It was great fun.

"Mum, would you like to try?" Dorothy asked through her laughter.

"I'm enjoying watching you." And indeed she was. She found it cathartic to watch her daughter feed the ducks.

Down another path, they went toward the gardens. The rose garden, which was just beginning to bloom, was awash with a rainbow of colours. Beyond the Pavilion, a rock garden, a maze of intricately designed, rock-lined pathways, extended over a mile. They were dotted with fantastically sculptured shrubs, arbours, and flowerbeds.

Agnes loved to garden and she missed hers in Winnipeg. She was in awe of the grandeur of these gardens, the undeniable genius that went into creating such works of art. It was shocking to her that such beauty existed, and she had never seen anything remotely comparable. She knew she would never look at a garden the same again.

"Who is hungry?" Percy asked. "I know I am."

It was a question he needn't ask. The children all responded enthusiastically, as he knew undoubtedly they would.

"Percy, we will meet at Ceperley Park, near Second Beach."

Percy agreed. Stanley Park Drive circumnavigated the immense park, and the point to which they were destined was the opposite end of the park, close to the spot where they would exit at the end of the day.

Margaret continued to drive eastward on Stanley Park Drive. The easternmost tip of the park, known as Brockton Point, was the first unobstructed view of North Vancouver and the majestic North Shore Mountains from within the park. It was marked by a small lighthouse, which was built to protect boats from running aground. The multitude of boats that day had nothing to fear from the calm seas and pristine sky. The few wispy, white clouds posed no threat as they drifted lazily over the rugged peaks toward the sea.

From Brockton Point to Prospect Point, the point closest to North Vancouver, the road directly faced the mountains. The park road hugged the waterline, and for much of this portion of the park there were no trees to block the view between the water and the road. They drove at water level with the mountains at their fingertips. It was hard to imagine such grandeur could exist anywhere, let alone in the city in which they now lived. Dorothy's mind and heart were racing; Agnes's mind and heart were sadly elsewhere.

As they approached Prospect Point, the road snaked inward through dense forest toward the centre of the park. Sunlight all but disappeared, but rays of opalescent light managed to find their way in, illuminating the ancient moss and ferns and adding a touch of magic. The trees closer to the water's edge were slighter, less sheltering, and the park's canopy opened up again, revealing the sky; but the sea remained hidden.

"There it is, up in the distance. The hollow tree. You'll both like this," Margaret said as she pointed ahead.

"Hollow tree?" Dorothy asked, fascinated by the notion.

Sure enough, the car approached a small loop in the road. A tall stump, as tall as many of the living trees around it, but whose girth was larger than any tree that they had ever laid their eyes upon, perhaps sixty feet around, stood on display. It was long dead, stripped of life, no branches or leaves to be seen. From the direction of their approach, a large crack revealed a hollowness, but it was what was seen from another angle that gave the ghostly tree its name.

Margaret turned off the road and parked on the loop alongside half a dozen other cars. There was a crowd gathered in front of the tree as people waited their turn for a chance to stand inside it. As soon as the car came to a stop, Dorothy jumped out and ran to the tree. It was as though the tree had been fissured by giant hands, now revealing a perfect opening, the base of which was wide enough to fit a car. Dorothy waited patiently for her turn and tugged at her mother to join her.

"Dorothy, you don't need me to join you," Agnes said dismissively.

Dorothy looked disappointed, but it wasn't enough to sway her mother.

"But I *want* you to come with me. Please, Mum. It will be fun."

Dorothy didn't break eye contact with her mother and eventually wore her down. Margaret and her girls joined Agnes and Dorothy in the cavernous hollow of the beloved tree. As they looked upward toward the sky, a funnel of light shone down on them. It felt hallowed, as though God was shining a light just on them. Agnes closed her eyes and let the light permeate her eye lids. She felt her son. With every part of her, she felt him. She could see him. She could hear him laughing. Electricity flowed through her body, and a peaceful calm washed over her. Agnes wiped the tear away before anyone could see it.

"See, Mum, aren't you glad you came in? Have you ever seen anything like it? That was fantastic," Dorothy gushed.

"Yes, it was quite something."

"All right, just another minute until picnic time," Margaret announced.

Dorothy was ravenous so lunch couldn't come too soon.

Chapter 32

Dorothy was eager to share her day with her father. She had enjoyed herself so entirely that she had forgotten about her triumph feeding Bluey.

The drive back from the park dragged on. It was five o'clock, and Dorothy was worn and only wanted to get home. After saying her good-byes to her Aunt Margaret and the girls, Dorothy ran for the door. Much to her delight, it was not locked. As soon as she set foot inside, she saw her father.

"Dad! Dad! It was so much fun. I can't wait to tell you all about it."

Dorothy stopped in front of her father's chair. He smiled but his eyes told a different story. He put down his drink and continued to clutch Donny's train in his other hand, squeezing it tightly.

Dorothy knew her father was sad and she knew why. She missed Donny too. She felt so helpless knowing that she couldn't make his pain go away. It destroyed her that she wasn't enough to fill the void, that he didn't love her enough to be happy with just her.

"Dorothy, why don't you go write about your day in your journal? I'll call you when dinner is ready."

Dorothy knew her mother's suggestion was more a demand, and she thought better than to protest.

When Dorothy was called for dinner, she wasn't expecting to see the table set for two. She searched the kitchen for another setting, but there was none.

"Mum, aren't you eating?" Dorothy asked, perplexed.

"Yes, I am eating with you. Your father is not feeling well and has gone to bed."

Her mother's tone and eyes directed Dorothy not to press the issue further. Dorothy did as was expected; she remained quiet, ever the good girl. During dinner Agnes lingered deep in thought, and Dorothy did nothing to break the silence. When she had finished her meal, Dorothy removed her plate from the table and tidied the kitchen spotlessly. All the while, Agnes toyed with her food, never taking her eyes off it. Dorothy kissed her mother on her cheek and quietly went to her room.

Agnes slipped into bed when all was quiet in the house and Dorothy was well asleep. Art's snores filled the room, and Agnes could not rest her brain for the sound echoed in her mind. Agnes rolled over and tucked herself under Art's arm. There she felt safe; there she felt loved.

Art was awake at the crack of dawn, which was unusual for him. Agnes had already been awake a short while and was in the kitchen making a pot of coffee.

"Good morning, darling," he said, surprising his wife.

"You startled me," she gasped. "I didn't hear you."

"I am sorry for my early departure last evening. It had been a long day. I was dreadfully tired."

"No need to apologize. I am pleased you had a good sleep." He looked well rested to Agnes. "Dorothy missed you last evening. She had wanted to tell you about her day."

Art searched his mind for clarity, and he found the painful and shameful truth. He had neglected his daughter and guilt reached in and tore at him. Agnes could see his disappointment, and she hoped it would be enough to waken him. If not for her, then for their daughter.

Agnes made Art some toast and poured him a cup of coffee.

"You must be hungry. You missed dinner last night."

"Not entirely. John fed me well at the restaurant."

"How did that go? Did you finish?"

"Yes. I was painting it the same colour, so I didn't have to do as many coats."

Art took a sip of his coffee and furled his brow.

"Darling, this coffee tastes different. It isn't as strong as usual. Is it a new kind?"

"No, it is the same. Perhaps your taste buds are still asleep," she said teasingly. The truth was she had saved the grains from the previous day and had only freshened them up with a sprinkling of new. She was trying to conserve where she could because she was becoming more fearful of their finances.

"Pumpkin," Art said as Dorothy came into view.

Dorothy lit up at her father's cheerful welcoming.

"I hear you had a fantastic day yesterday. I can't wait to hear about it. Do tell."

Dorothy was so excited, she wasn't sure where to start. "I will, but I have something better. Watch this."

Dorothy walked to the bird cage. She opened the door slowly and spoke softly and reassuringly. After removing some seed from a millet spray and setting it in her palm, she placed her hand in the cage. Neither Bluey nor Queenie jumped away.

"Such good birds you are," Dorothy said sweetly. "It is a good time for your breakfast. Why don't you come and enjoy a treat?"

Within seconds they both hopped off their perch and onto Dorothy's palm. They began to peck away at the seeds as Dorothy stretched her head around to ensure her father was watching. He was.

"Pumpkin, that is terrific," he said proudly. "Let's wait until they are done feeding, and then I have something for you to try."

Dorothy was keen to find out what her father had in store. She waited patiently as they pecked at the seed. And as luck would have it, they didn't stop until the last seed was gone; then they stepped back onto their perch.

"All right, close your hand and stick out your finger. Try to slowly and gently nudge it up to the side of their leg. Be very gentle. Eventually they will learn to step onto your finger, even when there is no food to entice them."

Dorothy was eager to try. She did as her father told her to, sticking her index finger out and nudging it against Queenie. Immediately Queenie stepped onto Dorothy's finger. Dorothy was so thrilled she could hardly contain herself.

"Dad, now what?"

"Slowly pull your hand out of the cage. Let's see if Queenie is good with that."

Dorothy began to pull her hand out of the cage, and as her hand approached the door Queenie jumped back onto her perch. Dorothy was disappointed.

"That is outstanding for your first try. Don't give up just yet. Let's try Bluey. He's seems more agreeable, don't you think?"

Dorothy couldn't disagree. She put her hand back in the cage and extended her finger, moving it toward Bluey. To her delight, Bluey stepped right onto it. Dorothy pulled her hand back toward the cage door and Bluey didn't move. She hesitated at the door, not wanting to frighten the bird, and then pulled her hand straight through. Her hand remained free from the cage with Bluey balanced atop her finger, unflinching and content. Eventually, Dorothy put her hand back in the cage and Bluey returned to the perch.

"Well, there you have it, Pumpkin. Just brilliant!"

Art was pleased, as was his daughter, but Dorothy's overwhelming joy came not from her own accomplishment, but from the praise her father had bestowed upon her. That is what fulfilled her.

Dorothy's world was brighter that morning and she left for school a very happy girl.

"What are you doing today?" Agnes asked, hopeful. She was beginning to worry about their position. They did not have an extraordinary amount of savings when they left Winnipeg, and with train tickets, the new painting supplies, rent on the house, and a funeral, what they had left was dissipating rapidly; in fact, it was all but depleted.

"One of the shops was interested in a touch-up. We just need to discuss particulars, and I should be able to start tomorrow or Tuesday. I'll spend the remainder of the day making enquiries."

"That's wonderful," Agnes said, trying to sound enthusiastic about the opportunity. She was still worried. He couldn't make a go of it moving from one small job here and there to another. It wasn't viable, not in any way. "Perhaps, it wouldn't hurt to talk to other painting companies to see if they need any help."

Art looked at his wife, who was trying desperately to appear encouraging and positive. Agnes could tell immediately her suggestion was not well received. It was clear to her it was not an option.

"It has only been a few weeks, my love. You will be looking at a successful business owner soon, I promise you."

The truth was Art could never imagine himself working for someone again. He had crossed that chasm, and his pride was too fragile to cross back over. He believed he was trying, and perhaps he was on some level, but his heart wasn't in it. It wasn't in anything at the moment. He tried to deny it, but he knew it.

Agnes smiled, offering him as much reassurance as she could. She would support him no matter what. *That's what you do for those you love.*

Agnes spent the morning writing a letter to her parents. She hadn't written since the funeral. She had relied upon her sisters to keep them apprised. Writing to them about Donny's death made her feel like a child again, a child who had been caught misbehaving. Agnes was ashamed. She had not done what she was supposed to. She had failed to care for her child and he died. It was irreversible, unpardonable. Agnes missed him terribly. She could hear him at every step. She was devastated, but her feelings of guilt governed her heart.

Agnes wiped her eyes as she finished the last of her letter. She sealed the envelope and addressed it. It sat heavily in her hand, as though the weight of the world filled it.

"I'm sorry, my boy. I truly am," she said as she closed her eyes.

It was a day not unlike the day before. The sky was blue, save for a few wispy clouds, but the air was crisper as a sea wind blew in from the west. Agnes buttoned her coat up to the top and pulled her hat down hard on her head to prevent it from flying away. As she stood on the street, her letter now in the hands of the post office, she struggled with what to do next. The thought of going home and milling around in that empty house was an unbearable prospect, one that she couldn't bring herself to do. There was no desire to shop, and no money for it even if there had been. Agnes was at a loss.

She looked up and down the street. She felt like a woman without a home, alone with nowhere to go. She felt lost, adrift, without purpose.

She found herself walking toward the restaurant. She walked around to the back alley. It wasn't quite lunch yet and the front door was still locked. John and Margaret's car was parked in its usual spot so she knew at least one of them was there, yet she held back.

Margaret's back was to the door as she stirred a pot on the stove. The sweet, smoky smell of her maple sauce filled the air. It filled Agnes's soul as much as it did her nose. It was a comforting smell. It reminded her of home. At that second, Agnes found herself needing her mum and Sam.

Agnes stood at the door, waiting to understand why she came. She thought of turning around. She wasn't in the mood to talk and Margaret would want to talk. She'd want to know how she was getting on and Agnes really didn't know.

John walked into the kitchen and took Agnes's opportunity to leave away from her.

"Agnes, this is unexpected," John said.

Margaret turned to find her sister standing there.

"It surely is. What brings you by?"

"I was dropping off a letter for Mum, and I thought I would stop by and thank you again for such a lovely day yesterday. Dorothy couldn't keep her eyes open. She practically fell asleep in her dinner."

Margaret laughed. "I am pleased she enjoyed herself so. I hope you did as well."

"I did. It was delightful."

"Well, since you are here, you might as well stay for lunch. Or do you have other plans?"

Agnes found herself thinking that was the silliest question. *What could I possibly have to do?* She had no quick response so all she could do was accept Margaret's invitation.

"It will be like old times. Put an apron on and help me glaze these chickens for dinner. The sauce is ready."

It *was* like old times. Agnes used to go to their restaurant back home when she was bored and had nothing to fill her time. That was before Dorothy was born, but not much had changed. Margaret and John still prepared the same food in the same way. John would always say, "Tradition is the greatest currency. Without it we are poor."

Agnes enjoyed basting the chickens. It didn't require any thought. The repetition, she found, was relaxing. John had learned the art of wood-fired cooking from his pork farmer father and Sam from his own butcher father. Together they shared what they knew, honed their skills, and made it a true family tradition. Business had been robust until the crash. Then, it was all the average family could do to put any food on the table, let alone spend the money for the luxury of having someone else cook for them.

John opened the doors for lunch at noon. Business had been slow, but some days more money went out than came in. That day was one of them. Not a single customer came in, and there sat a kitchen full of food. Agnes felt terrible for her sister and John. They had worked so hard, and to see their misfortune was disheartening. Sadly, their misfortune was connected to other misfortune, linked inextricably in a tangled web, and it seemed no amount of hard work or wishful thinking could improve matters.

All was not woe. Percy was doing well. His company was surviving, growing even. They were advantaging themselves by painting a picture of prosperity, not gloom, and it appeared to be working. Those who had money to spend could spend it however they wanted, and they were led toward the rainbows. Advertising became entertainment, whisking consumers away to a happier and more prosperous life. But what worked for big did not work for small and businesses such as John and Margaret's were forced to survive on hope.

"I think it is about time we turn over the lunch pail, at least for now. I don't think we have any other options. We are in business to make money, not lose it, and that is all we seem to be doing these days. We can ignore the fact, but it will lead us right into bankruptcy."

John sounded defeated. This had been their life's work, and it was not turning out as planned. It seemed little those days was.

"Let's not turn this into a total waste. Let's take this good food ... no, *great* food," he said, trying to inject some humour, "to the church and see who we might help today. While circumstances are challenging, we still have no right to be anything but grateful."

Agnes tried to look at the positive, but she found it difficult to agree with John's sentiment.

What hadn't been prepared for the dinner menu was packed up. Margaret offered some to Agnes, but she initially declined.

"Good grief, Agnes, don't be so stubborn," Margaret said. "It is not an act of charity. I recognize that you don't need it. This is your daughter's favourite, and I am entitled to spoil my niece where I can. End of discussion."

Being the older sister afforded a certain superiority, much in the way it did to Agnes with Mary. Margaret knew things had not been easy for her sister on so many fronts. Art had worked very little and, from what John said, his prospects were looking dim.

The car was packed with food and the three of them left for the church. First United was John and Margaret's church and would become

Agnes's that Sunday as well, so she was glad to go.

"We've attended since we arrived in Vancouver. We're looking forward to the three of you joining us this week. Percy, Mary, and the kids will be coming as well," Margaret announced.

"I am hopeful God will forgive us for working yesterday on the Lord's Day rather than attending church. Sunday is the only day we can paint," John said guiltily.

"We did attend church, an outdoor one. Stanley Park was as close to heaven as I have ever seen," Agnes offered.

Agnes was shocked to see the line at the church. One after another men stood, looking misfortuned and downtrodden.

"Our church offers meals to those in need a few days a week. We have given food from the restaurant over the last couple of years when we have been able. I'd rather it go to a hungry mouth than the wastebin. Sadly, every day it seems the lines get longer."

Agnes was dismayed that there could be so many without meals to eat. The most basic of life's needs and these people couldn't even provide that for themselves. Agnes wondered how many of them had families.

John answered Agnes's silent question. "Sadly, it pales in comparison to how many there are across the city. This is just one church offering comfort to the destitute. There are a half dozen others across this part of the city alone. Vancouver has been hard hit by the crash, but it has been hardest for the men who have come in search of work. For most of these men, there are no families here, which is fortunate in one way. If you want to see just how bad it truly is, you needn't look farther than the shantytown in the False Creek flats. There are shacks upon shacks made of God-knows-what offering shelter to men who have nowhere else to go. Last I heard, the city was forcing them out. It is very sad. These are people with no other options."

The food was gratefully received by the church kitchen staff. It was clear to Agnes that they knew John and Margaret well.

"Your gift could not come at a better time. Bless you both. We have all but run out of food, yet the line still rounds the end of the block. There is no greater sadness than having to turn the hungry away with an empty stomach."

"We are pleased that we can help, Michael. You are doing great work here, and I am sure that each and every person who has stood in that line is grateful for it."

"You are too kind, John. We are only doing the work God leads us to do."

"Michael, this is my sister Agnes. She has just moved here from Winnipeg. She will be attending church this Sunday with her husband and children … *um* … child." Margaret caught herself, but it was too late. She was horrified like never before. It was an unforgivable error that no amount of wishing could erase.

Margaret looked at her sister, her eyes begging forgiveness, but Agnes did not look at her. Agnes had reached out and shook the hand that Michael had extended.

"We are so pleased that your family will be joining ours. We have an outstanding congregation here, as I am sure Margaret and John have told you. If there is anything we can ever do for you, please don't hesitate to ask. We are always here for our parishioners," he said warmly.

"Thank you. We look forward to it."

"What a nice man," Agnes said as they got back into the car. No mention was made of the slip.

"John, would you be so kind as to take me to Dorothy's school? I think I might walk her home today."

Agnes thanked Margaret and John for lunch and for the dinner that she took with her. It had been a difficult day, but she was almost through it.

Agnes watched her daughter exit the school. She was beaming as she said good-bye to her cousins.

"Dorothy," Agnes called.

Dorothy looked toward the sound of her name and saw her mother. Her smile became even broader and she ran to her.

"Mum, what are you doing here?" Dorothy asked, surprised.

"I spent the afternoon at the restaurant, and I thought I would come and walk my girl home."

Dorothy couldn't hide her happiness. She looped her arm through her mother's, and together they walked the short distance to their house. Dorothy didn't speak. She simply rested her head on her mother's arm as she walked. She couldn't get close enough to her.

The front door to the house was unlocked. As Dorothy stepped inside, she saw her father in his chair. She didn't have to look farther than the drink in his hand to know how the evening would be. As she stood on her mountain top, a little bit more of the girl in her broke off and crumbled away.

Chapter 33

The May sun was just below the horizon, its light diffusing hues of amber into the hazy dawn sky. From the bedroom window, the sun was obstructed from Agnes's view, but its progress was not. It rose swiftly and effortlessly, changing the palette of Agnes's canvas moment by moment. The house remained quiet, Art's soft snores giving the only indication that she was not alone. Even the birds were quiet.

In a few short hours, her parents would arrive. So much had happened in the two months since she had seen them. She had missed them terribly, but with each passing day her heart became numb to the distance. It had become numb to many things. What she saw, what she felt, it was as though she had been draped in a veil. She could still see, but nothing was as bright as it had been, and she bore this burden, quietly, on her own.

Agnes dressed and went to the kitchen. There was much to prepare. Sam had insisted on staying with them; he needed to make sure all was well with his own eyes. Agnes had always been the strongest of the three girls, but he sensed a change. It was nothing overt, nothing dramatic, just a hint in the words she used. But it was there, gnawing at him, whispering to him in the back of his mind and it wouldn't go away.

It was Saturday so there was no school. Even if it hadn't been Saturday, Agnes wouldn't have made Dorothy go. She knew Dorothy couldn't bear to wait any longer to see her grandma and grandpa. Dorothy had even picked flowers for her room. Her room was too small for the two of them so Sam would have to sleep in Donny's room, which was as it had been that first day.

The smell of baking bread woke Dorothy up. She jumped out of bed and ran to the kitchen while still in her night clothes.

"It's Saturday! Grandpa is coming!" She loved her grandma, but it was Sam who had her heart.

"Good grief, Dorothy, calm yourself," Agnes said, trying to be serious, but she couldn't. She was happy to see her daughter in such good spirits. "Why don't you get dressed and I will make you some toast?"

"What time is Aunty Margaret coming to get us?"

"Eight o'clock."

"Is Dad coming?"

"No, he has a job today. He'll be gone before we get back."

Agnes wished he could be with them, but it was more important he work when he had the opportunity. The jobs had been inconsistent at best, and he was earning just enough to pay the rent. There was barely enough for food and certainly not enough for anything else. The phone had been removed, and the thought of a car was a distant dream. Yet still Agnes continued to be hopeful that their circumstances would improve.

Agnes left Art a note wishing him a good day and telling him she loved him. Margaret arrived about eight, and then they were on their way to the station.

Dorothy could hardly stand still as she waited for the announcement that the train had arrived. It was beyond what human patience was built to endure, especially the patience of a ten year old.

Eventually the arrival was announced, and Dorothy ran to the door and waited to catch the first glimpse of her grandparents. She stood there holding her breath, waiting. The train emptied and the line dwindled, and still they did not emerge. Dorothy looked back at her mum, frightened that they had missed their train, but Agnes was not yet worried. She had expected them to come out last, and last they did.

They were moving slower than Agnes remembered. It had only been a few months, but her mum had aged. Sam had one arm looped around Sarah's back and his other hand was holding hers out front. Even to those who didn't know them, it was clear that he loved her dearly.

As they reached the entrance, Sam held the door while he helped his wife over the lip of the landing. Nothing around him—not the location, not even his children—was more important than his wife was then and there. His sole focus was helping her. And even as his granddaughter opened the door and ran toward them, he didn't loosen his grip on his beloved wife.

Dorothy was so anxious to see her grandparents that she didn't notice her grandmother's frailty. Dorothy's excitement and the happy memories she held transformed her grandmother into what she wanted to see, what she wanted her to be.

"Grandpa, Grandma!" Dorothy gushed.

"Dottie, darling," Sam said as he embraced his granddaughter with his free arm.

"Grandma," Dorothy said as she kissed her.

Dorothy held the door for her grandparents to enter the station while Sam smiled appreciatively. Margaret and Agnes waited a few steps beyond. Agnes held her breath as she saw her mother. For the first time, she appeared real, no longer this indestructible foundation that could never crack. The shadow of death was a cruel monster; it had stolen her son and now it was stealing her mother.

"Mum, Pa, we have missed you so much." Agnes kissed her parents, each on the cheek.

"Sorry I am so slow, my dear. I'm feeling a bit weary from the trip. It is a beautiful one, but a long one to be sure." Sam had resisted the idea of her taking such a long journey, but she would not listen to him. She needed to see her daughters.

"No need to apologize, Mum. I could barely walk after sitting on that train for two days."

Sarah appreciated her daughter's thoughtfulness and understanding.

"How I have missed you all. You are always in my thoughts."

"Yes, we certainly have missed you. Your mother talks of little else," Sam said with a laugh. "Now we need to get your mother into a comfortable chair and put a cup of tea in her hand."

"Of course," Margaret said, ready to serve. "I'll get the car and bring it around to the front door. I'll meet you there."

"Very good. Thank you, Margaret," Sam said appreciatively.

Agnes stood behind her parents as they walked through the station. Dorothy was less off-put by her grandmother's declining health than Agnes was. Grandmothers were expected to get old, mothers were not. Acknowledging your mother's immortality meant acknowledging your own.

The first stop was Mary and Percy's.

"You have a lovely home, Mary."

"Thank you, Mum. We are quite comfortable here."

"Where is Art?" Sam asked.

"He is working today. He'll join us at the restaurant for dinner tonight," Agnes said.

After generations of sweeping feelings and emotions under the rug, it was learned to not to ask questions to which the answer might not be favourable. Sam was keenly interested in how Art was making out with the new business, but he dared not ask, at least not in front of others. He had never understood the need for such guardedness, and to treat imperfection with such shame was absurd to Sam. Families were supposed to share the good *and* the bad.

After an early lunch, Margaret drove Agnes, Dorothy, and her parents to Agnes's home.

"I will be back at six to drive you to the restaurant for dinner."

"That sounds wonderful, Margaret. I'm looking forward to seeing it. I have formed pictures in my mind over the last ten years, but I am sure they are nothing compared to the real thing."

Art and Agnes's house was different than Percy and Mary's in every respect. Art and Agnes's was quite small, as was their yard. With the exception of an additional two tiny bedrooms, it was no larger than the carriage house they lived in when they were first married. You could fit two of Art and Agnes's homes in Percy and Mary's, and Percy and Mary's wasn't really that large compared to some of the other homes around the park.

Sarah took to Dorothy's room for a rest when they arrived. The trip had taken a toll on her, and she didn't have the energy to remain awake with the others.

"Dorothy, thank you for these flowers. They are so colourful. It was very thoughtful of you to think of me."

"You're welcome, Grandma. I hope you have a good rest." Dorothy kissed Sarah and then closed the door.

Dorothy interrupted a deep conversation when she came back to the living room, and she sensed she was not welcome in it.

"Dottie, I hear you are quite the bird trainer. You will have to show me," Sam said, skillfully segueing from his discussion with Agnes.

Dorothy brightened and walked excitedly to the birdcage. She took a piece of millet spray and placed it in her hand before going through her routine.

"I am very impressed, my dear. That is no easy feat."

Dorothy beamed. Like her father's praise, her grandfather's was equally as potent to her.

Dorothy walked over to Sam and placed her finger on his shoulder. She turned her finger slightly to nudge Bluey off it. When Dorothy pulled her hand back and Bluey stood freely on Sam's shoulder, he couldn't help but laugh. As he turned his head toward the bird, Bluey sidestepped his way over to Sam's neck and nuzzled himself in. Sam was thrilled, in awe that such a small creature could make him feel so alive.

"One more thing," Dorothy said.

Dorothy put Bluey back on her finger and moved the bird toward Sam's face.

"Pucker up, Grandpa."

Dorothy moved Bluey in until he was almost touching Sam's lips.

"Bluey, give Grandpa a kiss. Grandpa would like a kiss."

Bluey did what was asked of him and put his beak to Sam's lips. Dorothy pulled Bluey back and placed him in his cage.

"What a good boy you are," Dorothy praised. She took another piece of the millet spray and placed it on the bottom of the cage. "Here's a treat for you."

"Well, I must say that is a first for me," he said with a hearty laugh. "I am quite certain I have never been kissed by a bird before."

"Agnes, let's take a walk. You can show me your neighbourhood. Dorothy, you'll be all right here with your grandma, won't you?"

"Yes, Grandpa. I'll write in my journal while Grandma is sleeping."

It was a hot May day. The sun was high in the southern sky, and it beat down on them with a fierceness usually devoted to the rarest of summer days. Often the mountains and sea were great protectors—the sea a soother, cooling the breezes swept across it, and the mountains a provider of shelter—but that day there was no breeze and the rays of the sun shone down unimpeded.

"Janie said to say hello. She misses you."

Agnes sighed. She missed Janie too. She longed for the intimacy of that friendship. She had never realized how much she had depended on it until she no longer had it.

"Please tell Janie I miss her too. I am hoping they will come for a visit."

"They have been coming to the house after church. We are quite enjoying their company. Tom is a pleasant chap."

"I didn't know," Agnes said sadly. She felt so out of touch with her life, as though she was only an observer.

"I'm sure she wrote all about it in the letter." Sam patted his breast pocket. "I'll give it to you at the house."

"Vancouver looks like a grand city, Agnes. Are you happy here?"

"Vancouver is lovely. You will quite enjoy Stanley Park."

Sam exhaled with determination. He was not bound by the same rules as the women of the family. He was not afraid to ask the questions that should not be asked.

At the end of their street, where Woodland and Grandview met, they stopped and sat on a park bench. It faced the bridge that crossed the train track. It was directly beside the path that Donny had taken to escape the punishment that had awaited him. But Agnes was unaware of it. She had never been told exactly where it happened and she had never asked.

"I can see that Vancouver is lovely, but that is not what I asked. *Are you happy here*?" Sam spoke slowly and deliberately, making his intent clear.

"What is happy?" Agnes wondered, revealing more of herself with that one question than she ever had before.

Agnes had turned Sam's question around and he didn't know how to respond. For a brief moment, he sat in silence and then reached out and took Agnes's hand in his. He turned to look at her and broached the subject that had not yet been spoken.

"I'm sorry about Donny. Losing a child ... well, there are no words. You have the support of a family that loves you very much, and we are here for you."

Agnes said nothing and Sam remained quiet. He hoped Agnes would speak, that she would say something that would reveal her feelings, but she didn't. Instead she cupped her other hand over her face as her shoulders began to heave and fall. Suddenly Agnes became again the little girl whom Sam had fallen in love with so many years ago, the headstrong and intense girl who had captured his heart. His heart was breaking for her. Like her mother, she fought herself, fighting so hard to appear strong when she was falling apart on the inside. *Why? For what reason?* There were too many generations of those moments in time, their scars closing the door to the heart just a bit further, their sorrow passing down. It was always gradual, but in the end you could see it as plain as day; but by then it was too late.

"It is my fault," Agnes said without raising her head. She couldn't look at Sam.

Sam took Agnes's chin and turned it toward him. He held it until she looked him in the eye.

"You cannot blame yourself. You did not cause this. Whether you believe in God's will or in the randomness of creation, you did not cause this. It was Donny's time. Our children do not belong to us and we do not belong to each other, so we must cherish each other while we can. Donny was blessed to be chosen, and you prepared him well for that journey. You were a good mother to him. And Donny is just as surrounded by love now as he was when he was here. Don't forget that. He is with the multitude of others who have passed before him, including your father." Sam needed to believe this as well. He had lost his first wife and his child during childbirth. That pain was very real to him.

Agnes listened to Sam. She believed him with her head, but her heart was still resisting. It was still hurting.

"How is Mum doing? She looks frightening frail. Please be honest. She would never tell us herself. She wouldn't want us to worry."

The irony, the inward blindness of her statement, was not lost on Sam.

"I don't believe in pretending. What is not real should not be portrayed as such, however earnestly it seeks to spare feelings." Sam said. He hoped Agnes was listening.

His voice lowered. "She is not long for the world, I am afraid. I know it, and you can clearly see it for yourself. I believe she endured the strain of the journey to see you and your sisters one last time. It isn't in her nature to move on without completing what is before her."

Sam wasn't going to push his daughter, not on the first day of their visit. They would be there almost a week, and he was hopeful she would open up to him. He sensed there was more going on than just Donny's death, and his only wish was to help, to offer comfort where he could.

Sam and Agnes reflected in silence, neither uncomfortable with it.

A shadow emerged from the trees alongside the bridge. It seemed odd and out of place to Agnes, and she continued to look for it to quell her curiosity. It was less than a hundred feet, but passing cars had obscured her view and she couldn't make it out straightaway. It was like a ghost, one minute there and one minute not.

"We should be getting back. You mother will be waking soon."

Agnes stood to follow Sam's lead, but her attention was on the shadow. As Agnes looked back one last time, the shadow suddenly had a face ... it was Art's.

"Let's turn here and go the alley way," Agnes suggested as she tried to hide her surprise.

Sam didn't question. Agnes didn't want Art to know she had seen him. She could only think of one reason why Art would emerge from the bushes, and she didn't want to trespass on his privacy. And besides, she was confident he would tell her.

Art took longer to arrive than Agnes thought he should. He had only been a few steps behind them. Art did arrive after a few minutes, dressed in his rainbow-splattered coveralls. At first Agnes thought nothing of it; those were the clothes he worked in. But then it occurred to her he hadn't been wearing them when he emerged from the trees.

"Dad," Dorothy squealed as she ran to the door.

"Pumpkin," Art responded as he picked her up and gave her a kiss.

"Sam, Sarah," Art said, acknowledging them warmly. "How good to see you. How was your trip?"

Art shook Sam's hand, and after removing his coveralls he greeted Sarah with an embrace.

"How was your day, darling?" Agnes asked. "You look tired. You are working too hard. Come sit."

"The day was good," Art said through his groggy smile.

"How is business coming along?" Sam wondered.

Agnes interrupted before Art could answer. It was a subject she tried to avoid.

"Pa, can I get you a martini? I know you like your gin martinis as well."

Sam looked at his watch. "I think it is a jolly good idea. It's past five in Winnipeg."

Agnes laughed at his cheekiness.

"Mum, what can I get you? Would you like a glass of sherry?"

"If your father is, then just a wee smidgen for me, please." Sarah raised her hand, holding her thumb and forefinger an inch and a half apart. The spread had increased over time, and Agnes enjoyed chalking it up to aging eyes.

"That's my girl," Sam said with a wink.

Sarah had always referred to Sam as "your father" with her children. She needn't; they felt that way on their own. But it was important to her. It was her way of honouring him. Her first husband, Thomas, had been gone for over thirty years, and memories of her life with him had long faded. England was a distant memory, as were the struggles and the sorrow. She was pleased with her life, content in her heart, and grateful for all of God's blessings. Thomas was her first love, the father of four of her living children, and he would always be in her heart, but Sam was her soul. He was her light and her joy and had been her best friend and companion for half her life. He was part of the fabric of her being and even death would not change that.

Margaret arrived to drive everyone to the restaurant, but Art and Agnes decided it was a good evening for a walk. It had been far too long since they had spent any time alone and they both needed it terribly, even if only for fifteen minutes.

They held hands as they walked, the first few minutes in silence. Agnes was enjoying holding her husband's hand. She felt like she did when they were first married, that excitement, that electricity at the slightest touch. She craved it, and when she had it she relished it.

"You never told me how your day was."

"Good. This job should keep me busy all week."

Art had been out of the house much of the time trying to find work. The jobs were few and far between and Agnes quietly worried, but she never spoke of her concerns. Despite her unwavering support, Art could see the strain on his wife's face and he assured her all was fine; she could only take him on his word.

As they approached the restaurant from the alley, Art tightened his grip on his wife's hand and pulled her behind a bush.

"What are you...?" Agnes could barely get the words out before Art kissed his wife as passionately as he ever had. Agnes's knees were weak as he wrapped his arms around her waist. He pulled back and looked her in the eye, his gaze long and deep. He was looking for himself, not for her. He needed her strength—he needed it to keep going. But by doing so, he revealed himself to her. His sadness could not hide. It was there in his eyes, reaching up from his soul.

Agnes kissed her husband back softly. It wasn't passion he needed, but tenderness. He needed forgiving and unconditional love to help him piece together the fragments of his being. Agnes would never give up on him. She loved him as though there was nothing else she could do, as though it were the only thing she was made to do.

As they stepped out of the bush, Art pulled a piece of greenery out of his wife's hair, and they both started laughing.

"You are impetuous, Mr. Craig," she said teasingly.

"You imply I didn't think about doing that. Perhaps I had been planning to pull you into a bush all day. Besides, what man wouldn't give in to impulses with a wife like you?" His playfulness was endearing to Agnes.

It was a Saturday night, and in good times the restaurant would have been brimming. It wasn't so that evening. The previous Saturdays saw but a few tables occupied and many a night went by where no one came in. Margaret and John decided to close the restaurant to the public that night, placing a sign on the door that explained a family gathering. Sadly, it went unnoticed.

Art and Agnes entered through the back door as the sumptuous smell of cedar plank filled the air.

"Cedar planked salmon. It smells divine," Agnes enthused.

It was quite lively in the restaurant. Art and Percy's father and their brother and sister and their families had also joined them.

"John, you made my favourite," Agnes said to her brother-in-law. "I can smell it."

"I threw a few of the cedar planks in the fire to tempt your nose."

"My nose doesn't need tempting, but I will enjoy it all the same," Agnes laughed.

"I caught the salmon myself this morning. Went out on a friend's fishing boat. They were practically jumping in. One was two feet," he said as he held his hands apart.

Agnes found it a relief to know that little money had been spent on dinner. They had all contributed to the side dishes and desserts, and the meat had been provided by the sea. So, short of lost business, John and Margaret weren't terribly out of pocket.

"Hello, Bill. How are you doing today?" Agnes kissed her father-in-law on the cheek. "How do you like living with Mary and Percy?"

"I get to walk in the park every day. I quite like it. I am grateful to them for letting an old man live with them."

"You are far from old, Bill. You are as young and vibrant as the day I met you," Agnes said with a wink.

"You lie, but I will forgive you for that." He returned the wink. "It is such a blessing to have my entire family here with me. I am only sorry that you don't have your mum and Sam here with you for much longer."

"Yes, they are only here a week and we will cherish every bit of it. Pa has to get back to the store. My brothers are managing it right now, but he doesn't like to be gone for too long. I keep telling him to retire, but he says his father worked until the end and he plans to as well."

"You can't fault a man for wanting to work hard. Those who find themselves idle when they are able are mischief in the making."

"That is very true, Bill," Agnes agreed.

Bill was close to seventy and had worked hard all his life. He was beginning to slow down, but his mind was still as sharp as a razor. His opinions were strong and he could debate with the best of them.

Sarah sat for most of the evening, the strain of the journey having taken its toll. Sarah's raspy cough persisted, rattling deep in her chest. The pain caused her to wince beyond what she could hide, but she didn't complain. Her family brought her such joy. Sam sat with her, his hand in hers until she reassured him she was fine and shooed him away. She didn't want him to worry and he didn't want her to be sick. Sadly, neither of them received their wish.

"Mum, can I get you anything?" Agnes wondered.

"No, my dear. I am content. Thank you," she said before looking toward the corner of the restaurant. "But it appears Art and Percy are engaged in quite a serious conversation."

Agnes looked in the same direction. Art appeared angry with Percy's tone, and his words and his reaction frightened her. She moved to stand, but Sarah placed her hand on her daughter's leg.

"Agnes, you know I love Art as a son," she said tenderly, "but he is heavy with burden. I can see it, and I know you can too. Take care with him. I am worried for you both."

Agnes was taken aback. She had tried desperately to hold her family together, to keep private matters private. Agnes looked back in her husband's direction. The conversation ended abruptly and Art walked away, leaving Percy standing there frustrated and angry. Art refilled his glass and didn't take a breath until it was empty.

"Mum, I can't keep you to myself. Mary wants to spend some time with you as well. I'll go get her."

Agnes walked over to her sister, who had been witness as well. Mary furrowed her brow as her sister approached her, confident things were going to end badly.

"What is going on, Mary? And don't tell me nothing."

"I don't know. I'm sure it is nothing. Just a brotherly disagreement." Mary truly did not know.

"A brotherly disagreement? About what? What would they have to disagree about? It looked like more than that." Agnes was going to get to the bottom of it with or without her sister's help. "You can go sit with Mum now."

Mary was being dismissed and she didn't argue. She knew her sister to be fiercely determined and getting on the wrong side of that tenacity was never a good thing.

Art poured himself another drink and met his wife as she was coming toward him. It was clear to him she was upset.

"Are you having a nice time?" he asked. "You have been busy. I have hardly had two words with you all evening."

"Is everything all right? It looked as though you and Percy were having a disagreement."

"Disagreement? No. Just a difference of opinion. Nothing for you to worry that beautiful head of yours about." He leaned in and kissed Agnes.

Art could see she wasn't convinced.

"We're copacetic, really, darling. Thick as thieves."

Agnes couldn't tell if Art was being honest or if it was the gin talking. She decided it was best to let it go. She looped her arm around her husband's and didn't leave his side for the remainder of the evening.

Chapter 34

Agnes rushed to get the last of the lunch dishes cleaned before the car arrived to pick them up. It was only half-past eleven; they had eaten early to be ready when the knock came. Dorothy was bouncing around like a bunny as she waited for her cousins to arrive. Even Agnes found herself looking forward to the outing.

"Mum, Pa, thank you so much for doing this for us today. It will be wonderful to have everyone together in one car."

All but John and Percy would be going. Neither could get away from work. Art had decided at the last minute, after much coaxing from his daughter, that his work could wait a day.

The driver arrived shortly after everyone else did. Sam had arranged for the car and driver for the twelve of them for the tour. Margaret and John had lived in Vancouver for ten years and had never been to the Capilano Suspension Bridge. It would be an adventure for all of them.

"Does anyone need to use the biffy before we leave? Children?" Mary asked, to which she received a room full of shaking heads.

The car was an open air tour car with four rows that seated three across. It listed its destinations on the side—Stanley Park, English Bay, and Capilano Canyon. Today was the canyon.

"That's quite the car. Let's hope it doesn't rain," Sam teased.

He was talking about rain in jest, but it would certainly put a damper on the outing if the sky chose to be mean-spirited. Save for hats, everyone was exposed to the elements; there was no cover to pull up. The first few days of Sam and Sarah's visit had been filled with dazzling sunshine, and then the temperamental side of Vancouver brought darkened skies and a flood of rain to the city. So far that day, no rain had fallen from the cloudy sky, and the damp ground was beginning to dry out.

There was not a bad seat to be found, and the only arguing was amongst the children who fought for a spot on the outside. Once everyone was settled, they started the short journey to the harbour and the ferry dock. The wind began to whip up as they moved northward toward the water.

"Batten down the hatches," the driver quipped. "She's blowing a wee bit today."

Hands were placed firmly on hats as the wind endeavoured to abscond with them. As they passed by the tall buildings, they could look up to their towering tops, unencumbered, the usual car roofs no longer blocking their view. They hadn't even arrived at the ferry docks, and they were already well into an adventure.

When they drove down the docks, the wooden planks clickety-clacked with the weight of the car. They rode alongside a long line of automobiles that were waiting to board the next available ferry, but this group needn't wait.

"This is why you take a tour," the driver said proudly. "I have a license to bypass the line. That line will take all afternoon and we'll be on the ferry in ten minutes." And true to his word, they were.

All traffic from Vancouver to North Vancouver had become restricted to ferry crossings. The only bridge to bring the shores together, the Second Narrows Bridge, had been damaged many times from direct strikes from harbour traffic, but the previous year's collision had been enough to close the bridge completely. There remained no other way to cross the Burrard Inlet to the North Shore. Three sides were surrounded by water, and the only side that wasn't was blocked by mountains a mile high in some places

Their ferry was a two level vessel, the lower deck for cars and the upper for viewing. Nobody in the car had experienced anything like it before, and the anticipation was continuing to escalate.

The tour car sat waiting at the front of a short line as the ferry backed up to the dock. There were only two other tour cars behind it. As it approached, the ferry slowed to the point where there was no wake, only water swirling placidly around the motor.

Upon signal, the driver drove the car over the ramp and onto the boat. Save for Art, who had been on such a boat as a child, there was not a single stomach that wasn't aflutter as the car rolled from land to water. The car came to a stop at the end of the deck, against a low, divided barrier which the water was visible through. It left those experiencing it for the first time feeling vulnerable. Many in the group had come over to Canada from England some thirty years prior, but there was no comparison between the large steamship and the ferry.

After he had parked the car, the driver encouraged his customers to enjoy the upper deck. The children were out of the car and on the stairs before the adults had even moved.

Sarah insisted she could handle the steep and narrow metal stairs on her own. "It must be this refreshing sea air," she boasted. "I am feeling like I have a second wind today."

Sam was happy his wife was feeling so spry, but he was anxious about a fall. One wrong step would be all it would take, so he walked behind her to break her fall should she could slip. But Sarah, with her hand firmly gripped on the railing, made it up the steps to the upper deck on her own.

Sam breathed a sigh of relief, as did her three girls, when her foot hit that top step, and despite the searing pain in her fingers as they held her steady, she was pleased she did it on her own.

"That's my girl," Sam said proudly.

The stairs emptied into a covered vestibule, part of which led to an open front deck and part to a covered deck in the back. The children were already at the bow, their view of the journey ahead completely unobstructed.

Art and Agnes joined their daughter at the railing. Dorothy's grin was etched on her face, her joy as bright as the sun that poked through the clouds.

The warm summer wind gusted across the cool water, whipping the clouds into a frenzy. Agnes raised her face to the sun and soaked in its warmth. She tightened the grip of her arm through Art's and kissed him on the cheek. She too was happy he had joined them.

Ahead, the North Shore Mountains rose sharply from the water, as though they were held up by some mystical force. The base of the mountains had been marred by man, but the glory of nature remained the way God had intended it the closer it was to the heavens.

To the west, the tree-lined shores of Stanley Park provided the last bastion of protection in the harbour before opening up into the Strait of Georgia. Directly to the east, the Canadian National Steamship Terminal housed a massive steamship which dwarfed their tiny ferry and blocked the inner harbour from view.

"Your mum came over from England with Grandma and your aunts and uncles on a ship just like that when I was a young girl," Agnes said to her daughter. "I was younger than you are."

Dorothy had heard the story many times, but she had never seen a steamship up close and was mesmerized by its grandness.

"Mum, there is a bench there if you would like to sit down," Mary pointed out.

"Thank you, but I would like to stand with my grandchildren," she said with a hearty smile.

As the whistle blew, the ferry began to move away from the dock. The children were exhilarated and feasted their eyes on everything they could. It was all new to them, and their youthful enthusiasm was a tonic for their grandparents.

The seagulls squawked loudly, circling the ferry overhead.

"You need to keep one eye up in the sky so you don't end up getting more than you bargained for from the gulls. They have a beastly sense of humour," Art warned.

It was not a long trip across the harbour, only fifteen minutes, but it was enough time to appreciate the majesty of nature.

"It is hard to fathom such beauty," Agnes said as she looked out across the water.

"You are quite mistaken. It is easy. I see it every day," Art countered.

He reached out and took his wife's hand and spun her around as though the deck were a dance floor. He reached out for her waist and dipped her backwards, planting a long and lingering kiss as he did. Her face turned many shades of red as she realized that most eyes on the open deck were upon them. Art only had eyes for his wife and he paid them no mind.

"What better a ballroom than this?" he asked as he looked beyond the decks in every direction.

Dorothy looked back at her parents and giggled. It gave her such joy and comfort to see them happy together. For that brief time, she had no worries. She was surrounded by everything important to her. Her narrow vision of her world had been rebalanced and it was good.

When the whistle blew, it was time to return to the lower deck and the car. As they took their seats, the ferry locked into place, jarring them a tad. The children were about ready to burst.

The gate to the front of the ferry was removed by a dock worker, and the driver drove off the ferry and onto the ramp. As they cleared the station, they could look back and see Vancouver on the other side of the harbour. It was surreal; their entire point of view had turned on its head.

It was a steady climb up Capilano Road to the Capilano Suspension Bridge, and soon the city was behind them. The tallest of trees lined the road, and as they looked upward they suddenly felt so small. It was like a dream, their senses bursting with colour and contrast.

It was a short walk from the car to the entrance. As the driver organized the tickets, Sam and Art organized the group. They had been told of the bridge's awe, but it wasn't until they saw the sign that the magnitude of it became real—*The World Famous Swinging Bridge*.

Once through the gate, the bridge came into view, as did the enormous canyon that dropped down directly. Butterflies began to flutter in Agnes's stomach as she looked upon the void.

"If anyone is scared of heights, don't look down," the driver warned. "There is plenty to see on the paths and trails, and you will more than enjoy yourself even still."

"Scared? We're not scared!" Mary and Percy's son said, rather offended at the suggestion.

"That's a brave lad," the driver replied. "Very good. Go enjoy yourself. I will meet you here in ninety minutes."

The children started to run but were promptly scolded by the adults.

"This is no place to be running. Stay here with us or you can go and sit with the driver."

The children grunted in unison, venting their frustration as children do. Restraint was proving challenging, their curiosities getting the best of them.

As they reached the bridge, the children hurried onto it, only looking back to ensure it was all right to do so. They were about to traverse a bridge that was four hundred and fifty feet in length and two hundred and thirty feet above the rushing Capilano River and rocky canyon floor.

Until then, Agnes had never thought about heights. She had never been in a situation where she had been high enough to feel insecure, but she learned straightaway that heights were not her friend. She told herself not to look down, but she found the draw too strong. Her eyes veered to the bottom of the canyon and she could feel herself falling, tumbling down toward it. If her body had not been frozen in fear, she would have turned and run back.

Sam and Sarah brought up the rear of the group, moving at Sarah's pace. The bridge was eight planks wide, and Sam was able to stand alongside her to hold her steady.

The wind continued to whistle, gusting through the canyon while it raced the raging river below. Its force added to the sway, and the children playfully accentuated their steps to effect as much movement as possible. For them, there was no fear. For Agnes, the bridge felt untethered, ready to drop at any moment.

"Agnes, are you all right?" Sam asked as she came to a stop.

Agnes did not reply. She continued to look straight ahead, her head unmoving.

Art heard Sam's question and turned back to face his wife. He could see the phobic fear on her face as he walked back toward her, the bridge swaying left and right with each step that he took.

"Darling, give me your hand. You are perfectly safe on this bridge, and I am here with you."

Agnes didn't reach for his hand so he took hers. The contact wasn't enough to shake her from her state. She was trembling uncontrollably.

"Agnes, darling, look into my eyes."

Agnes remained paralyzed with fear. Art moved so that he was directly in front of her, his eyes looking into hers. As he squeezed her hand, her eyes shifted toward his. He started to walk slowly backwards, never breaking eye contact, and she moved with him. As Agnes walked off the bridge and onto solid ground, she embraced her husband tightly.

Sarah and Sam stopped to make certain that Agnes was all right. The others were so focused on the scenery that they hadn't noticed anything amiss.

"What happened back there?" Art asked, concerned. "I have never seen you like that."

"I don't know," Agnes responded, still somewhat dazed. "I looked down and that was the end of it. I couldn't move."

Sam felt responsible for Agnes's state.

"I'm sorry. I wouldn't have suggested this outing if I had known it would make you feel so uncomfortable."

"Pa, please don't be sorry. It is not your fault. Even I didn't know I didn't like heights," she said with a nervous laugh.

Sam looked back at the bridge and worried about the walk back. He rubbed Agnes's shoulder and gave her a fatherly smile before walking ahead to greet the others.

"Are you sure you are well enough to continue or would you just like to sit on the bench?"

Agnes was embarrassed by the attention. "Art, I am fine. We should catch up to the others. They will wonder what happened to us."

Art held tightly to his wife, protective of the fragility she wore. It was a role he played infrequently, not because he was unwilling, but because the attentiveness was not welcome. Dependability had become deceptive for Agnes. It had become weakened by his capriciousness, and the cost of surrendering herself had become too high.

Agnes regained her bearings quickly. She felt silly for losing control. It wasn't something that happened often and, each time it did, she swore she wouldn't let it happen again. As they approached the bridge to head back, Art stopped her.

"Let me take your hand, darling, and close your eyes if you need to. I will guide you."

Agnes took his hand, not because she needed to but because she wanted to. She needed the intimacy, and at the moment the allure of it was stronger than her insecurity.

As they walked onto the bridge, Art looked at his wife. Her eyes weren't closed; they were wide open and looking straight ahead. She knew what she had to do and she was focused and unwavering. She was not going to give in to weakness nor was she going to bring more attention upon herself.

"That's my girl," Sam mouthed as he winked at Agnes.

Those three words from Sam carried her down that mountain.

Art remained by her side, and Agnes allowed him to dote on her, never pushing him away, never saying she didn't need him.

At home they all reminisced about the day and the excitement of the adventure. Dorothy took to her journal the instant she arrived. She was eager to fill the pages before the memories began to fade.

"Agnes, take a walk with me. It looks like the perfect evening to enjoy the setting sun.

By then Dorothy and Sarah were well into a discussion on politics. Art was asleep in his chair and wouldn't miss them either.

Sam and Agnes set out up the street, walking toward the setting sun and their favourite bench. The sky was aglow with burnt orange fire as it dropped toward the sea in the western sky.

"Isn't it breathtaking?" Agnes gushed. I can't imagine anything more beautiful."

"I remember the sunsets on the ship coming over from England ... well, at least the few days it wasn't storming," he said with a laugh. "You probably don't remember now, but it was incredibly stormy. However, when the clouds parted, the sun set against the horizon and you could almost hear the sizzle when the sun hit the water. The ship was in the middle of the ocean, nothing else as far as the eye could see. It felt as though the sun was disappearing forever, but then the stars came out and you were floating in space. The memory has stayed with me all these years. Last night's sunset from English Bay reminded me of that voyage. The sunsets on the ship were certainly pleasing, but they weren't the best part of that journey."

Agnes laughed. "Yes, that is when we met you. I was only eight, but I still remember meeting you on the train. I can't imagine our lives if you hadn't been in that next berth. I thank God every day that you were."

Sam stopped and turned toward Agnes, embracing her with all the love he felt and then some.

"It is I who has been blessed. When I lost my first wife and child, I was only a young man, and I thought that was all God had planned for me. I had made peace with that. But then I met your mother and her charming children. It took a while to catch her ... I would have tried for the rest of my life. After I met her, I could never have loved another."

They sat down on the bench, and Agnes placed her head on her father's shoulder. She felt secure, a whisper of childhood memories.

"I can't bear the thought of you both leaving. I have missed you so much. My heart is breaking right now."

Agnes tried to hold in her emotion, but she was failing. With Sam she didn't have to be strong. She had felt that way about her husband once.

Sam was worried about Agnes. He was worried for the burden she was bearing. She believed she was hiding it well, but those who loved her could see it. Beneath it all, she was fragile. They loved Art, but he was crumbling and his wife and daughter were suffering for it.

Sam reached into his breast pocket and pulled out an envelope. He handed it to Agnes.

"What is this?"

"Open it."

Agnes opened the envelope to see bills, many bills.

"What's this?" she asked, bewildered.

"I want you to have this. You and your brothers and sisters will share equally in what we have when your mother and I are gone, and I would like for you to have some of it now."

"No, I can't take this. This is yours, and you and Mum are still very much here. This is not mine," Agnes said adamantly. She handed the envelope back to Sam.

Sam gently pushed her hand back. "Take this for Dorothy. You don't have to spend it, but you will have it if you ever need it. If it makes you feel better, don't spend it until I have moved on to the next life. I will rest easier knowing you have it. Please do it for me."

Agnes could see the pleading in Sam's eyes, and she couldn't refuse him his request. "I won't spend it," she said adamantly.

Sam could see her stubbornness was softening, just a bit.

"This is our secret. Just yours and mine. Nobody has to know but us." Sam kissed Agnes on the forehead to seal the promise.

As they stood up to leave, the sound of a train filled the air. Agnes paused as she stood up. The clanking sound of the wheels on the track got louder, and the shrill of the whistle filled their ears as it approached. The same thought filled both of their minds.

Agnes woke at half-past four. It was only a few hours until she would be saying good-bye to her parents, and the thought left her unable to sleep. She was not of the mind to clean or cook, and the only thing that sounded remotely comforting was a hot shower. Agnes turned up the temperature on the tepid water until she could feel a sting on her skin. Steam enveloped her and she breathed it in deeply. She enjoyed the sting; she needed to feel something besides the pain in her heart.

The steam swirled in the room and coated the mirror. She wiped it down with her towel, but the steam was relentless. Her skin was tinged red as she patted it dry, the heat drawing beads of perspiration and dampening her again just as quickly. She opened the door a crack and a gush of cold air filled the room.

Agnes rinsed her hair with a mixture of vinegar and water to bring out the softness and shine and then towelled it as dry as she could. Curly hair was a gift passed from mother to daughter and not much effort was required to make it look presentable. Agnes remembered Janie's routine and felt blessed for her curls. It took Janie hours to get her finger waves just right. It was either finger waves or pulled back in some fashion.

There was little else those challenged with straight hair could do.

Agnes put her dressing gown on and tidied the washroom. She opened the door to find her mother standing there.

"Did you need to use the toilet?" Agnes asked, surprised to see her standing there.

"I was having difficulty sleeping. My arthritis is acting up. I thought I would get up and make a cup of tea. What are you doing up? And bathed already?"

"I was having trouble sleeping as well. I'll get dressed and make us some tea." Agnes hadn't spent much time with just her mum since they arrived, and they both saw their mutual insomnia as providential.

They spoke quietly as they sat at the kitchen table. Dorothy was asleep on the chesterfield just a few feet away from them. It had been her bed for the week.

Sarah took a sip of her tea to wash down her aspirin. It provided some relief to the searing pain in the joints of her fingers.

"Is your arthritis worse, Mum?

"Everything gets worse as you get older, dear. Just you wait," Sarah said with a laugh. "All those years with a needle and thread caught up with me. Eleanor used to tell me to use the sewing machine, and even William sent one over here after we arrived, but I was too set in my ways. I guess I have always been old fashioned. I wish now I hadn't been so headstrong."

"Well, nobody could sew clothing like you did. None of my friends wanted homemade clothes. For them store bought was always more exciting. But not me. I loved everything you made me," Agnes said proudly.

"What a sweet girl," Sarah said with a glint in her eye.

Agnes looked down at her teacup as she swirled the tea in it. There was so much that she could say, but she couldn't form the words. They were there on her tongue, but they wouldn't leave her mouth.

"You have been a good daughter," Sarah said as Agnes looked up astonished. "I know I have not told you enough, but you have been. I love all my children dearly."

Sarah was not an effusive person. She was restrained in her emotions. She loved strongly and deeply, but her passion had always lain just beneath the surface, stifled by pride and expectation. It was a skill honed through a lifetime of living.

Agnes was touched by her mother's words. She had not heard the like often. She loved Sam's praise, but he gave it often. Sarah's was so rare as to be almost unsettling. It felt as though it was a hint of something bigger to come. And that is exactly what frightened Agnes.

Sarah's hand trembled as she picked up her teacup. The woman who had been so strong, so vital for as long as Agnes could remember, sat before her weak and worn. Agnes was sad that she could not stop time, that she was being robbed of the person who had always been her constant. Suddenly she felt ashamed of all the times she disagreed with her mother, all the times she thought she knew better, all the times she mocked the advice, sage in retrospect, but tossed aside at the time it was offered. It tore at her and riddled her with guilt. If only she could do it all over again.

"Thank you for bringing us to Canada, Mum."

It was Sarah's turn to be surprised. She didn't know Agnes still thought about coming over; she had been so young. They had moved such a long time long ago, and it felt as though they had always been in Canada. But they hadn't. Sarah had spent almost half her life in England. She grew up there, got married there, and had most of her children there. Her husband, daughter Elizabeth, parents, and all who came before her were buried in English soil. Sarah and her family had moved to Canada and taken their lives with them, and she was glad for it, but she found herself thinking about what had been left behind. Once they moved, she had only ever looked forward, focusing on the new, but as she began to reflect she thought of those who had gone before her and she couldn't deny that part of her soul was still across the sea.

It was as though Agnes's words opened a door.

"I was very angry with God for taking your father and Eleanor from us. However, it was not my choice. They were God's decisions."

Agnes had not heard her mother speak of Eleanor in many years, nor had she *ever* heard her speak of anger toward God. Eleanor had been her best friend since childhood and her death had broken Sarah's heart. It was with Eleanor's death that the bonds with England had been severed. There was nothing left but memories. Eleanor's inheritance provided passage to Canada, but it was Eleanor's brother, William, who gave Sarah the push she needed, the confidence to take such an arduous and life-changing journey. Sarah never developed another friendship like she had with Eleanor. Sam became her best friend, and she had her daughters for female companionship. She had been content with that.

"You were so young when your father died. He was a good man. I want you to know that."

"I know, Mum."

The birds began to chirp outside and Agnes looked toward the window. The blackness of the night had faded, and the morning sun had begun to illuminate the yard.

"It looks like it will be a nice day."

"Yes, it does."

Dorothy began to stir on the chesterfield. She woke to find her mum and grandma sitting at the table. She rubbed her eyes and sat up.

"Good morning, sleepy-head," Agnes said to her.

Dorothy got up from the chesterfield and went over to the birdcage. She took the cover from it, and Bluey and Queenie began to chirp.

"Good morning, Bluey and Queenie. How are you this morning?" she asked. "Did you sleep well?"

Dorothy opened the cage door and put her hand in. Bluey jumped on her finger right away. She removed her hand from the cage and placed Bluey on her shoulder. Queenie walked out of the cage and climbed to the top. She liked to sit where she had a good view but wasn't far from the safety of her home. She had laid another egg the day before, but it had been removed. She was never to know the joy and sorrow of being a mother.

Dorothy sat at the table and Agnes poured her a glass of milk.

"Do you have to leave, Grandma? You can have my room."

Sarah smiled. "That is very generous of you, my dear. I would very much like to stay longer, but your grandpa has to get back to the shop. There is much responsibility that comes with owning your own business. If you don't pay it care and attention, it will not be successful."

Bluey flew from Dorothy's shoulder toward the bedrooms.

"Bluey needs his morning exercise," Dorothy explained to her grandma. "He likes to fly around the house. You never know where he will land. Queenie doesn't like to venture far."

"I know exactly where Bluey landed today," Art said as he emerged from the bedroom. Bluey was perched atop his head. Art loved the birds and whenever he was home, he would let them fly freely. Bluey always found his way to Art.

Dorothy laughed and reached up to get Bluey off her father's head, but Bluey had no intention of moving. He was perfectly content where he was and Art didn't mind.

Sam joined them and, for the last time, they sat together at a table for a meal. There wasn't the usual conversation. Everyone was deep in their own thoughts.

"Thank you for your hospitality. We have had a wonderful trip," Sam finally said, directing his appreciation to Art.

"Our pleasure, Sam. It was good to have you here."

"Are you at a job today?" Sam asked.

Art hesitated. "No. I will be prospecting today."

"Well, it certainly looks like a nice day for it."

Art hesitated again. "Yes, it does."

A knock at the door brought Mary and Margaret.

"I'll take Dorothy over to my house and will be right back," Margaret said.

"Mum, Pa, let's finish packing your things," Agnes said as she tried to remain cheerful.

When all was gathered and they were ready to depart, Art turned toward Sarah and Sam to say his good-byes. Sarah embraced him longer and with more force than he ever remembered. He loved Sarah. She had always treated him like a son. His own mother's death had left such a hole in his life, and Sarah had helped fill it for him.

"Take care of my girls," Sarah said. "And do not forget to take care of yourself. You are no good to anyone else if you are not good to yourself."

Sarah's words caught Art off guard. Sarah was not one to speak of the verities of life, usually leaving philosophical advice to her husband, but she needed to make peace before she left.

"Yes, of course." Art said. He suddenly felt uncomfortable. *What is Sarah thinking? Is she doubting my ability to care for my family?* Art's thoughts, long embraced by self-doubt, were now amplified by self-consciousness.

Art reached out to shake Sam's hand. Sam took it and grasped it tightly, holding it as he looked Art in the eye. It was a gaze that pierced.

"You know, if you ever need anything, you can just ask. You know that, don't you?"

Art felt as though all eyes were on him and he couldn't hide.

"I do. Thank you."

Art stood at the door, waving as the car pulled away. He walked back in the house, closed the door, and took another pill.

Chapter 35

Sarah stood before her daughters. It was a good-bye no more or less painful for Sarah than the last one. She had done her mourning in private, and as always she faced the challenge as pragmatically as she could.

"My girls, I love you all so much. I will treasure this week. I am blessed to have you, and you are blessed to have each other. It is a gift. Don't ever take it for granted."

"We love you as well, Mum, and we know how blessed we are. We do," Mary said. She turned to face her sisters; each was trying to be strong.

Sarah and Sam embraced each of their girls, but their embrace lingered longer with Agnes. Her fragility begged for it. Agnes didn't speak, fearful words would bring tears. She held her breath and swallowed hard as Sam and Sarah walked onto the train. As they took their seats, they waved through the window. Agnes could no longer hold the tears in. She turned around and walked toward the door as they rolled down her face. She knew final and this was final. Like her mother, Agnes mourned finality before it was so, knowing in her heart when it was whispering in her ear. But the sacred bond of mother and daughter would live on, and her words would become more important than Agnes ever could have imagined.

The children were playing at Margaret's as though nothing had changed. They were children and their emotions were short-lived and fickle.

"When is John due back?" Mary asked.

"Usually about noon. Depends on how full the nets are. He'll only be home to get changed, and then he will go directly to the restaurant."

John had started off by joining a friend's commercial fishing boat here and there for fun, and if he was lucky he would catch a salmon or two for the restaurant. At the start, there was nothing commercial about his activity, but as business began to wane at the restaurant, fishing became a way to earn an income and he was fortunate for it.

"I was happy to see Art was feeling well enough to join us yesterday," Mary said.

"What do you mean? He hasn't been ill," Agnes added, perplexed.

Mary looked surprised herself. "I thought Percy had mentioned that he was going to take Art to meet with a few builders this week so that he could offer his services, but Art was feeling under the weather and declined. Maybe I misunderstood. Percy wants to help. It must be hard that Art hasn't worked in a few weeks. If we can do anything to help, please let us know."

Agnes felt as though she had been kicked in the gut. She tried desperately to appear flat and unaffected, to pretend this wasn't news to her. This made no sense. With the exception of the day before, Art had been out of the house working every day that week. He had told her so.

"Oh, yes. It completely slipped my mind. It has been so busy at home with Mum and Pa staying with us that I forgot. Yes, thankfully he is feeling better. Now look at the time," Agnes said as she looked at her watch. "We should be going."

"I thought you were going to stay for lunch," Margaret questioned.

"Thank you, but it completely slipped my mind that I need to stop at the market. I haven't had an opportunity to shop this week and the cupboards are bare."

"Let me drive you both," Margaret offered.

"No, thank you. It is a nice day to walk, and I will stop at the market on the way home. Dorothy!" Agnes called through the open window.

"On second thought, why don't you let me take Dorothy home with us? You have had a busy week and could use a break. She can stay the night."

Agnes didn't know what to say. She hadn't expected the offer, and her first inclination was to say no, but she could think of no reason why she should deny her daughter.

"Yes, Mum," Dorothy said as she came into the kitchen.

"How would you like to stay the night at your Aunt Mary's house? Your father and I would see you at church."

Dorothy began to bounce with excitement and released the broadest of smiles.

"I don't believe she wants to," Margaret quipped.

Agnes started off toward the market. The clouds had rolled in and the sky was starting to mist. Agnes put her plastic rain cap on her head and tied it under her chin. The mist wreaked havoc on her hair, and if she didn't cover it, it would become a frizzy, curly mess by the time she reached home. Dorothy would giggle and tease her that only grandmothers wore them. That day she felt old.

Is Mary right? Did Art tell Percy he was ill? If that is the case, where has he been? If he hasn't been working, how will we survive? Every possibility began to swirl in Agnes's head and her imagination ran away. A knot formed in the pit of her stomach, the acrid burdens searing a hole into her belly.

Agnes walked down The Drive. Shop after shop had been boarded up, hardworking proprietors' dreams collapsing after the crash. Agnes and Art had faced challenges, as did those close to them, but until that moment Agnes had never truly felt vulnerable. She had only read about the dire state of the world in newspapers. She had seen long lines for social assistance, but she didn't know anyone directly who received it. As she stood in front of the restaurant, she peered in. It was just before noon on a Saturday, and the restaurant was dark and empty. The sign on the front door said "closed for lunch until further notice." *What happened?* Agnes wondered. *Have I been sleeping?*

"Mrs. Craig, how are you today?"

"Mr. Patelli. I am well, thank you. And you?"

"Very well. What can I do for you?"

Agnes reached into her handbag and took out her list and handed it to him. The stores on The Drive remained old fashioned, the owners and their clerks doing the shopping for their customers. Only in the larger department stores to the west, in the downtown core, had shops become "self-serve."

"Very good. I will have your order to your home this afternoon. I will update your statement. If you could, please have your husband provide payment early next week. It would be appreciated. I'm sure he has been busy and it slipped his mind."

Mr. Patelli was a pleasant man with a charming Italian accent that Agnes loved. He was always happy and friendly, but today his charm wasn't enough to lift her spirits.

"Thank you, Mr. Patelli. I am sorry for the delay. We will pay it promptly."

Agnes was sure it had slipped Art's mind. He was always very organized and punctual. He insisted on managing the finances and paying the bills, wanting to spare Agnes the tedium of it. But Agnes was feeling the strain of having no control. She worried about things getting done when she wasn't the one to do them.

The house was quiet when she arrived home. The bustle that filled the house the previous week was no longer, and the contrast was deafening. Agnes enjoyed solitude, but at that moment she felt lonely.

The groceries arrived from the market, and Dorothy placed the statement on the kitchen counter beside the hospital correspondence. There were two statements atop the hospital bill, both still in their envelope and one marked with "urgent" across the front. A portion of the cost was being covered by government funding—they were considered low income—but what remained was still greater than what they had.

It would just be the two of them that evening and she wanted to make a special dinner. They hadn't had a dinner alone in years, and she felt it might do Art some good.

Agnes cut up chuck steak into cubes and added them to a pot with some garlic, canned tomatoes, and fresh thyme and pearl onions from her tiny backyard garden. A little salt and pepper and it was ready for the oven. A few hours on simmer, and then the potatoes would go in.

Agnes set the table, placing her favourite candles in the middle. The only thing missing was flowers. Agnes put on her shoes and walked up the road toward her bench. There were plenty of wild flowers along the edge of the green space, so she took scissors with her and cut some vibrant purple ones. She wasn't sure what they were called, but they were lovely. As she was admiring them, she noticed some bright yellow flowers in the distance. Purple and yellow was her favourite colour mix. They were across the street along the tree-lined edge where she recalled seeing Art that day. Deep in her mind, she knew that Donny had died on the other side of them; but unlike Art, she could not bring herself to go down there. She walked toward the flowers, and a nervous feeling rushed through her body. She prayed a train wouldn't come. She couldn't bear to hear that sound so close. She cut the flowers and added them to her bouquet of purple. She stood there, hesitating, and she didn't know why. But clarity returned, and she hurried across the street and back to her house.

Agnes placed the flowers in a vase and put them on the table. Flowers always brightened her mood.

As the stew cooked, Agnes cleaned her house. She had not been able to do so properly when her parents were there, and it had nagged at her. She had never been one to let things go, instead holding in her consciousness all that she felt herself obligated to do. For Agnes there had never been burden in work. The burden had rested solely atop the reliance upon others.

She removed the sheets from Dorothy and Donny's beds for washing. They didn't own an electric machine, Agnes insisting she could do a better job with her own elbow grease. There were also other things that their money could be better spent on.

The tub in the basement was filled with warm, soapy water, and Agnes scrubbed the sheets against the scrub board until her knuckles were raw. She was only eight when she left England, but she still remembered helping carry boiled water to the courtyard to wash clothing—the courtyard being a small communal patch behind their row house that was covered with heaps of garbage and shared privies. This was heaven compared to that. Once washed, rinsed, and wrung through the ringer, Agnes hung the sheets on the line in the yard. The sky was overcast, and she knew it wouldn't be a quick dry.

Art walked through the door at half-past five. He had been consistent in his arrival for so long that Agnes now expected it. As he arrived, she was waiting for him.

"Hello, darling. How was your day?" She kissed Art as she took his bag from him and placed it beside the door.

"Good." He offered no more detail, nothing to explain why. "Is that my favourite?" he said as he inhaled deeply.

"Yes. It will be ready at six. In the meantime your drink is waiting for you on the table beside your chair. Why don't you get changed into comfortable clothes and relax? I will put the finishing touches on dinner."

"Thank you. You do spoil me. Where is our girl?" he asked as he looked around.

"She is spending the night at Mary and Percy's."

"So it is just me and my beautiful bride tonight?"

Agnes laughed at the glimmer in his eye. "Yes, it is just us."

Art went into the washroom to clean up and Agnes went into the kitchen. The dinner rolls had ten minutes left in the oven, and the stew was still cooling down on top of the stove. Agnes wanted the evening to be perfect. Art had been under such strain and she wanted to be supportive; she needed to be supportive. She couldn't be the reason for any difficulties. If he hadn't worked for the last few weeks and hadn't told her, then he must have been feeling terrible about it, she thought.

Agnes placed dinner on the table. When she looked up, Art was in his chair, sipping his martini. Bluey was perched atop his shoulder and chirping in his ear. To Agnes it looked as though he was speaking to Art.

"Dinner is ready."

Art put Bluey on the top of the cage beside Queenie, and then he sat down.

"Darling, you have outdone yourself. The flavour ... magnifico," he said.

Art's attempt at Italian reminded her of the grocery statement, and she pondered the best time to bring it up.

"How did you spend your day?" Agnes asked with an exaggerated smile. "Did you find any potential jobs?"

"I walked up Clark but had no luck. Will try again tomorrow."

Agnes's face dropped despite her attempt to remain positive.

"Don't worry, my darling, I would never let you down." He reached out and put his hand on hers. She was losing faith and fear was overcoming her, but she would not tell him so.

"I was at the market today, and Mr. Patelli gave me a new statement. He mentioned that the last one wasn't paid. I know your mind has been focused on work, and I would be happy to pay it myself."

"No." His response was abrupt and harsh. "I mean," he said as he tried to soften his tone, "no, you don't need to do that. I don't want you worrying about such things. It is in my pocket and I simply forgot. I'll go to the bank on Monday, and then pay it directly."

Art's reassurance provided some comfort to Agnes, and she allowed herself to relax slightly. She had been tremendously tense since leaving Margaret's and had given herself a rather painful headache, but it was beginning to ease.

Minutes passed without a word being shared between them. Agnes picked at her food as she tried to think away the deafening silence, each moment trying to find something to say but never bringing herself to say anything.

"Did your parents get off all right?"

"Yes, they did. They are both safely on their way. I'm hoping the journey won't be too difficult for Mum. She seemed so fragile. I'm worried about her."

"It was good of them to come."

"Yes, it was. I will miss them dearly. It is difficult to be so far from them, especially as they are getting older."

"I'm sure."

Art's pace had become languid and his responses stilted. Suddenly, her Art vanished.

"You are hardly eating. Are you not hungry?"

Art stared at her blankly. "I guess not," he muttered. "I'm sorry. You went to so much trouble."

Agnes fought back tears. "Please don't be sorry. It will keep until tomorrow. I bought a newspaper for you today. You can read it. I have to bring the sheets in, and then I will make you a cup of tea."

The northerly wind was blustering and threatened to pluck the laundry from the line. It fought the wooden clothespins, but they held strong, doing exactly what they were made to do. And like the sails on a great ship, the sheets danced with the gusts, flapping and snapping with the wind's changing direction.

As Agnes took the linens off the line, she felt the force of the wind on her face. It numbed her cheeks and as she turned into it, it took her breath away. She felt as though it were taking the very life from her. But she remained, holding strong and inhaling deeply to get the air she needed to sustain herself.

Inside Art was asleep in his chair. The lid to the gramophone was up and Agnes lifted the arm from the end of the record and put the needle back to the beginning. She cranked the handle and *If You Were the Only Girl in the World* began to play. She remembered back to her wedding day when Art sang it to her as they danced, his lips pressed against her ear. She melted at the memory. It filled her heart with such joy.

Agnes took the sheets into Dorothy and Donny's rooms and made their beds up. When she returned to the living room, Art was still asleep.

"Art, darling, wake up," she said as she shook his leg. It was only nine o'clock, but Agnes knew when he had fallen asleep like that the evening was over. She tried one more time to wake him up and realized it was of no use. She retrieved a blanket from the closet, turned the light out, angled herself into the side of the chair, and covered them both with the blanket.

She couldn't bear the thought of spending the night apart. They hadn't since the children were babies, and she wasn't about to start. As she lay there, she could feel his beating chest under her hand and its comforting rhythm drew her into the same deep sleep.

Chapter 36

Two weeks after Sam and Sarah left to go back home to Winnipeg, Agnes received the letter. Sarah had died four days before, but she made Sam promise to not let the girls know until after the funeral. He didn't agree with her request, but he couldn't deny her it. Sarah didn't want them to make the long journey to Winnipeg when they had just seen her. She would be gone and nothing would change that.

Sarah's health had not been good, but it had taken a drastic turn as soon as she had returned home, and she died a week later. Sam wasn't sure when it happened. He just knew he woke up and she was gone, her spirit now free to fly through the halls of heaven, her family past to greet her and welcome her in. She was gone and he was never to be whole again, but he rejoiced at the thought of her reunion, of heaven's gain, and of the day he would see her again. His heart was broken, but it wasn't destroyed. He would endure. It was not the end for them; there was no end, only doorways and time.

Agnes walked to Margaret's with her letter in hand. She knew they would have each received one written just for them; Sam was thoughtful that way.

Agnes was sad, but she was not devastated. Her mother had always been such a strong presence in her life and she would miss her, but the distance that had come with the move had already altered Agnes. So much had dulled in Agnes's eyes, the bright, vivid colours that she had always longed for, that she had lived for, were muting before her. She was hardening to the changing tide, and she felt she was one step closer to her own end.

Agnes walked past Dorothy's school. As she stood at the fence looking in, she contemplated stopping and pulling Dorothy from her classes, but she didn't. She wasn't ready to face her daughter. She wasn't ready to console her.

Agnes continued to walk toward Margaret's house. As she stood at the corner of Margaret's street, she stopped. She couldn't bring herself to continue. *What words could offer comfort? They will just be words. They will not alter what has come; and what has yet to come will still come, regardless.* Agnes turned toward Mary's house, but that too felt pointless, so she turned and walked back in the direction that she came from.

At the end of Woodland, Agnes sat the bench. Even home wasn't where she wanted to be, and she could think of no other place to go so she sat down. The afternoon dragged on; what felt like minutes was in fact hours, the sun moving across the sky unnoticed. Eventually the sound of a train brought her out of her blankness. When she heard the first whistle blow, she didn't know what time it was or how long she had been sitting there. When the second one blew, she knew it was time to get up.

As she stood, she was still unsure which way to go. She looked at her watch and saw that it was three o'clock. Dorothy would be home from school in minutes.

The train continued to roll down the track. Dorothy could feel it in the ground beneath her feet. And without thinking, without forethought, Agnes found herself walking across the street and standing at the foot of the path. She had never seen what was at the other end; it was only her imagination that had provided her any picture.

From a distance, there was no discernible entry. The trees offered no obvious parting, and it was only a slightly worn path that guided the way. If Agnes had not seen Art appear in that exact spot she would not have been aware of its existence.

Agnes stood on the path, still undecided if she would continue. The train had passed and its whistle sounded in the distance. Agnes had experienced no desire to see the track, and she was unsure why she found herself standing there. But she did, and her legs continued to carry her forward. As she walked through the brush, she pushed the branches aside. It wasn't travelled enough for the brush to be stunted. It was thick and lush and needed to be pushed back as Agnes walked through it.

The path was short and, if not for the trees, would have been inconsequential. Within a few steps, the brush opened down to The Cut. Agnes had crossed over these track many times from the bridge on Commercial, but she had refused to look. Even when a train was passing under the bridge, she refused to look down.

As she stood at the top of The Cut, she looked toward Commercial. The tail end of the train was moving under it, fading into the distance, and she continued to watch it until it was out of sight. Agnes turned and looked down toward the track. There was nothing extraordinary about it. She wasn't sure what she expected to see. She didn't see anything that would remind her of her son, nothing to offer any window into Donny's world. It was just a track.

As she moved to turn back, something caught her eye under the Woodland Bridge just over from where she stood. She could see a sack on the opposite side of the track and the silhouette of a person standing not far from it. She stepped closer to the edge of the hill to see who it was, but she didn't have to; in her heart she knew. The ground was loose beneath her feet, and she held her arms up to maintain her balance. As she stepped forward, her shoe slipped on a rock and she almost tumbled down the hill, but she caught herself. She stepped backwards to move beyond the lip. From where she now stood, she could no longer see her husband. But it didn't matter; the image was seared in her mind.

Agnes brought her hands to her face and covered her eyes, but it didn't make the image go away. She vacillated between sadness and worry. *How often does he come here*? she wondered. That he was so drawn to that spot tore at her. The situation was far more dire, Art's state of mind more fragile, than she had allowed herself to believe.

Agnes left her husband behind and rushed toward the street. She paused to compose herself; she could not allow Dorothy to see her so distressed. As she passed the end of Woodland, Dorothy appeared in the distance. Agnes quickly crossed over and turned onto their street. Dorothy would come the alley way and Agnes would enter from the front. Agnes had a few minutes on her so she would be able to settle before Dorothy arrived.

Agnes continued her jog up their street. Any faster and her heels would have made the dash a tricky one. As Agnes approached their house, their landlord, Mr. Palmer, was coming down their walk.

"Mrs. Craig," he said as he greeted her.

"Mr. Palmer. How are you today?" Agnes asked.

Agnes walked through the gate toward him.

"Is Mr. Craig home? I must speak with him." His demeanour was serious, and it gave Agnes cause for concern. He had not been so severe and abrupt on any of their previous encounters; in fact, he had been quite the opposite.

Agnes did not like to lie, but she had no other answer to give. "I'm sorry, Mr. Palmer, he is working at present. Can I help you with something?"

Their landlord hesitated, wanting to speak with Art. As he began to tell Agnes what he wanted, his demeanour softened.

"Mrs. Craig, I would be obliged if you would please tell your husband that I need rent payment by tomorrow at ten. He can bring it to my office on Hastings. Mrs. Craig, this is the third notice. I would appreciate his attention to this matter."

"I'm very sorry, Mr. Palmer. It must have simply been an oversight. I'll ensure it is paid tomorrow morning."

"Thank you, Mrs. Craig. That would be appreciated. Good day," he said as he tipped his hat and walked toward his car.

"Mum!" Dorothy called.

In those short five minutes, Agnes had completely forgotten about her daughter. She turned toward her voice as Dorothy walked from the backyard to the front.

"The back door was locked. I tried knocking," Dorothy explained.

"I was speaking with our landlord." Agnes held out her hand to Dorothy, and Dorothy took it happily. Together they walked toward the house. "How was your day?"

Dorothy reached into her schoolbag and retrieved a piece of paper.

"What is this we have here?" Agnes asked as she took it from her daughter.

Agnes turned it over and saw a large, red "90" written across the top.

"I received an 'A' on my test," she said proudly.

"You certainly did," Agnes beamed. "What a hard worker you are, my dear. I am very proud of you." Agnes kissed her daughter's forehead.

"I can't wait to show Dad. When will he be home?" Dorothy couldn't hide her excitement.

Agnes reached into her pocket to retrieve the house keys, and she felt the envelope. It took her only a breath to remember what was inside it and her heart sank.

Agnes handed her daughter the house keys. "Head on in, Dorothy. I will be there directly."

Agnes looked up the street and saw no sign of Art. She contemplated going to him, but she didn't want a confrontation. She didn't want to cause him any more strain than he was under already. She loved him and she wanted him well. She wanted the man beneath all the suffering, the man she knew he was deep down, to come back to her.

As her mind went back to the beginning, she realized it had never been just one thing. It had been so many things, each on their own enough to notice but not enough to fear, but as they began to pile one on top of another, Agnes could see the void was deeper and darker than she had allowed herself to believe.

Inside the house, Dorothy waited impatiently for her father. When the door opened and it was Agnes, Dorothy's face dropped in disappointment.

Agnes held the letter tightly in her hand. "Dorothy, sweetheart, please come sit down."

Dorothy did as she was asked. Her mother's expression was neutral, and Dorothy had no reason to expect the news that she was about to receive.

"I just received a letter from your grandfather. Your grandmother died four days ago."

That was it. That was all she could offer her daughter. She had no energy for anything more, and whatever she had felt herself had been pushed down already.

"Oh," Dorothy said, reacting to her mother's flat expression. "Thank you for telling me." Dorothy walked back into her room and closed her door.

Agnes sat there, alone and empty, the core of her being stung with sorrow and regret, and she longed for relief.

"Lord, please tell me what I have done so wrong. I beg your forgiveness for I know not my sins," Agnes muttered quietly as she closed her eyes and looked down.

The front door opened, bringing Agnes back to the room.

"Darling," Art said, surprised to see her sitting there.

"Art...." Agnes wiped at the corner of her eye and stood up. She ran her hands over the wrinkles in her skirt and greeted her husband with a kiss.

"How was your day?" she asked.

"What is wrong? You look upset." Agnes wasn't expecting him to notice.

"Mum has died."

Art replayed the words over again in his mind. He looked long and hard at his wife, trying to make sure he had heard her properly. She only stared back at him, unaltered in expression. He swallowed hard and tried to keep his emotions from running away from him.

"I am so sorry, my love."

Art embraced his wife. Tears began to roll down her face and she sobbed every last ounce of sorrow. Art rubbed her back as he held her, but his hand soon dropped and his embrace went limp. Agnes pulled back and looked at her husband, her tear stained face awash with a ruby hue. Art's eyes revealed his own sorrow. Art loved Sarah as his mother, and he just lost his all over again. He was that fifteen-year-old boy, the oldest son, consoling his father whose beloved wife had just been taken from him. The anguish tightened across his chest, and he could barely breathe. He broke free from his wife and dropped into his chair. Agnes wiped her eyes and watched the transformation in her husband, frightened by the pace and by the contrast. For a moment, he had been there for her and, in the blink of an eye, he retreated back into himself.

"Mr. Palmer stopped by today," Agnes said, trying to change the subject. "He mentioned that the rent was due and could be brought to his office. I would be happy to do that for you tomorrow," Agnes said with a cheerful tone. "Would you like me to do that for you? I would enjoy the walk."

Agnes continued to offer her inflated smile while Art looked at his wife, his face expressionless. Agnes grew more uncomfortable. His cheeks began to flush and his face contorted in anger. He stood from his chair and Agnes took a few steps back.

"Do you not think I am capable? You, the last person I thought would ever doubt me," his voice rising to crescendo. He stormed past Agnes, close enough that she felt a chill from the gush of wind that followed him. He rushed through the front door, slamming it behind him.

Agnes tried to grasp what had just happened. He had never spoken to her like that before. She was stupefied. She turned to find Dorothy standing a few feet behind her, her test in her hand and tears streaming down her cheeks.

It had been a day of blows for Agnes, one after another striking her when she was not braced for them, and one after another taking her a little closer to the edge of herself.

Chapter 37

Art left the house early the following day. He had apologized again for his behaviour and Agnes forgave him, but she was deeply troubled. It was his sadness more than his remorse that lingered after he was gone. Agnes was floating between fear and despair, unsure where she would land. She hoped that the clouds would part and the sun would come out; but the rain remained, blanketing every surface, everything she held slipping through her fingers.

Outside, as well, the rain continued. It came down in sheets, pounding against the windows, shifting with the wind. Agnes looked out into the wet and dreary world and wondered where her husband was. She had no idea.

She turned back from the window and looked around her tiny home. Everything she possessed she could see from that spot. It was not much, but it was all some part of her. She had never been one to want more than she had, but she found she did want more. She longed for more than could be seen with her eyes.

She didn't know what to do with herself. She felt lost. She had no impulse or ambition to carry her forward. She shivered in the damp chill and sighed. Her mind raced with nothingness, only the sound of her own breathing filling her head. She took her mother's box off the shelf and sat down. She brought it to her nose. The dampness brought out an earthiness in the wood that it never had in Winnipeg. Agnes loved the smell. She didn't know why, but somewhere in the far recesses of her mind the reason lay.

Suddenly Agnes's father's funeral played in her mind. She hadn't thought of it since she was a child, but that day the memories were vivid. He had been buried in a simple wooden box, much like the one she held. There had been no marker to decorate the life he lived. He simply passed from life to death. Agnes remembered the emptiness she felt when his box was lowered into the ground. She felt the same emptiness again.

Queenie began to squawk in the cage, bringing Agnes from her deep and pensive thought. Bluey seemed out of sorts, and Queenie was dancing on her perch trying to rouse him from his stupor.

"Silly birds. What has bothered you so?" Agnes said as she walked by their cage.

Agnes passed by Donny's room first. His door was closed and she left it that way. She didn't have the strength to look inside. Next she walked by

Dorothy's room and noticed the top drawer of her bureau open. Dorothy knew disarray bothered her mother so Agnes was surprised to see it left that way. As she went to close the drawer, her eyes fell inside it. Where Dorothy's journal usually lay, there were only a few pieces of paper. They were jagged on one edge, as though torn from a book. Dorothy reached in and pulled them out. She noticed two shiny coins sitting beneath where the pages had sat—they were dimes. She wondered where on earth Dorothy could have gotten them from. She turned to the pages she held in her hand. Dorothy's handwriting filled the top page, and as Agnes flipped through the other pages she could see they too were covered with her daughter's script.

Agnes sat on the corner of Dorothy's bed. She felt she was being invasive of her daughter's privacy, yet she felt compelled to read what lay on the pages. The first page described the day Dorothy received her beloved journal. Agnes gasped. *Were these pages torn from her journal? Why?* Page by page, Dorothy described her joy and her sorrow. Agnes was stricken with grief over her daughter's silent suffering.

I do not understand what is wrong with Dad. Some days it feels as though he doesn't know who I am. I know he is sad about Donny, but I am still here. Does he not love me? Is it because I am a girl? Maybe he only ever loved Donny.

Agnes clutched at her chest. She couldn't catch her breath. She felt she had failed her daughter. She hadn't seen the pain she was suffering. It was the worst betrayal imaginable.

Dad was out of sorts again tonight and Mum looked so sad. I too am sad and I don't know what to do. I overheard Aunty Margaret say it was because of Donny, but Aunty Mary said that Dad's problems started during the war. I don't know what that means. What happened during the war? They said that we are going to run out of money soon. I don't know what will happen to us. I am scared. But I must be brave. Elizabeth Masters said she would buy my journal for twenty cents. I will keep that money safe until Mum and Dad need it. Please God, please take care of my family.

Agnes suddenly felt anger toward Art. She didn't want to, but she did. Agnes knew this was happening because of him and she couldn't pretend otherwise. *How could he have failed so miserably? What kind of wretched wife and mother am I to let this happen?* They were standing on such thin ice, and she could hear the cracks beneath their feet.

Agnes put the pages back in Dorothy's drawer. Despite her guilt and her desire to console her daughter, she would not speak a word of it to her. She decided, instead, to bake her favourite cookies to cheer her up. A trip to the market was needed to get a few missing ingredients, so Agnes put on her raincoat and boots and grabbed her umbrella—it was raining too hard for her rain bonnet.

As Agnes reached her gate, Mr. Palmer pulled up in his car. Agnes's stomach twisted another turn. There was nowhere for Agnes to go. He had already seen her.

Mr. Palmer leaned over his front seat and rolled down the passenger side window.

"Mrs. Craig, is your husband home?"

"Mr. Palmer, he is working. However, he did tell me he would bring the payment in today."

"He didn't come. I have been there until just a few minutes ago. I'm sorry, but I have no choice but to provide notice to evict."

Agnes started to panic. They would be homeless. She could not let that happen.

"I'm terribly sorry, Mr. Palmer. I may have neglected to tell him the time with your request. The delay is not deliberate, I can assure you. I will bring the payment to you myself. I will have it to your office by end of day. You have my word. I apologize for the confusion and inconvenience."

Their landlord was silent as he decided whether or not to offer another reprieve. Against his better judgement, he offered Agnes some kindness.

"Very well, Mrs. Craig. You have until the end of the day. I will see you at my office then."

"Yes. And I thank you for your patience."

Agnes was distraught at the thought of Art letting things lapse so dreadfully. *Can things possibly get worse?* she wondered. She thought not.

Agnes walked the three blocks to the bank while the rain continued to pound her umbrella. She decided she would no longer take a passive role in the managing of their finances. She allowed Art control because she was the wife and that was what wives did. Art's pride had been more important than her need for control. No more. His gross lapse in management had seen to that.

Agnes approached the counter at the bank. She was relieved it was a teller she knew. She had rarely come into the bank in the three months that they had lived there, but on the two occasions that she had she was helped by Miss Hall.

"Mrs. Craig, how are you today?"

Agnes was impressed that she remembered her name.

"I am fine. Thank you for asking."

"What can I do for you today?" she asked helpfully. She had a cheerful demeanour that helped set Agnes at ease.

"I need to withdraw twelve dollars from our account, please. Our rent is due, and I don't believe my husband has done so yet."

"Of course, please wait whilst I get your ledger."

Miss Hall went to a large file cabinet and pulled Agnes and Art's account ledger. She ran her finger down the list of transactions to the last few and then looked up in Agnes's direction. She smiled and held up her index finger to indicate a short wait. A moment later, she returned to the counter with the manager in tow.

"Mrs. Craig, I am the bank manager, Patrick Greene. Your husband was in here a short while ago, and we informed him that your balance isn't sufficient for that withdrawal. The balance is only three dollars and fifty-four cents at present. Would you like to withdraw that amount, or a portion thereof?" The news was devastating to Agnes, but appeared as a matter of course for Mr. Greene.

Agnes felt as though she had been robbed, but she realized you cannot be robbed of what you did not have to begin with.

"Mr. Greene, can you please tell me when the last deposit was placed in the account?"

"April fifteenth," he said as he looked at the ledger. "It appears it is the only deposit other than the one that was used to open the account."

Agnes tried not to look surprised, but she was unsuccessful. Agnes made no fuss, which wasn't always the case in such situations, and the manager relaxed when he saw there was no threat. His face dropped as Agnes sighed deeply.

"I'm sorry, Mrs. Craig. Is there anything else I can do for you?" he asked.

"No, thank you. That will be all."

Agnes tried desperately to remain strong. She held her head high as she turned to leave the bank.

"Mrs. Craig," the teller called.

Agnes turned back. The bank manager had already returned to his office, and the teller remained on her own. Agnes looked at her, hoping she would speak quickly. Agnes was on the verge of tears, and she didn't want to lose control in the bank. As Agnes stood there, the teller wrote something on a piece of paper.

"I'm certain this is only temporary, Mrs. Craig. You are new here and it takes time to adjust. There is help. Go to the address I wrote down. It is downtown, very easy to get to by streetcar. They can help with your rent. You are certainly not alone; there are so many who are having troubles."

She held out the piece of paper to Agnes. She looked genuinely concerned and it made Agnes feel worse. She could only imagine how pathetic and desperate she must look for her to have shared such information. Agnes only wanted to go back home and hide from the world. She wanted to see no one and talk to no one, but she knew she must. If she didn't act, they would not have a home to live in.

"Thank you," Agnes responded politely. She could no longer make eye contact with the teller. She dropped her head and turned and walked out of the bank.

Agnes knew there was always the money that Sam had given her. The twenty-five dollars would cover a month's rent. They only owed two weeks' worth that day, *but then what?* she wondered. It didn't matter. She was adamant she would not touch Sam's money. She just couldn't bring herself to do it. In her mind, it was an inheritance and inheritances meant the person who was leaving it had died. Sam was still very much alive, and she prayed he stayed so for a very long time.

Agnes stood outside the bank, under the awning and protected from the rain. It was raining as hard as it had been earlier, as hard as she had seen it rain in Vancouver. It was a wall of water coming down from the sky, barely a break in the rush. Thankfully the streetcar stop was a few short steps from where she stood.

As soon as Agnes saw the streetcar, she rushed to the stop. She deposited the coins in the box and took her seat. For comfort's sake, she sat at its front. It was her first time, and she wanted to be close to the driver.

"It is only a three minute walk up Cambie, Ma'am, so unless that streetcar is at your feet when you step off this one, you best use your feet to get you there."

Agnes thought herself silly for being so nervous about something as innocuous as a streetcar ride, especially when she had ridden one so many times in Winnipeg. It was only a three mile journey, but she felt lost as soon as she set foot on it. She felt as though she was heading nowhere, riding into the abyss, somewhere to which there was no return.

The rain had never felt so dreary. The city was awash with a monochrome palette of greys. It was as though colour existed only in her memory. Agnes needed the greens and the reds and the blues, and she found them there. As Art twirled her around the dance floor on her wedding day, she was blissful. The memory transcended time and circumstance. The past was perfect and perfect it would remain, never to change with God's will. It was the last thing within Agnes's control and she was determined to protect it.

The streetcar came to a stop and Agnes tried to get her bearings. She wiped the fog off the window with her hand and saw they were in front of their church. Hungry souls were lined up for its soup kitchen, far beyond the end of the block. They were drenched from the rain, but the nagging in their stomachs kept them in line despite the discomfort of the chill. Agnes felt pity for them before, but that pity only made her stronger as it distanced her from their hardship. Today there was no pity, only an understanding formed of her own misfortune, and now she stood in the line right along with them.

A few moments later, the streetcar came to another stop.

"Ma'am, this is your stop. Three minutes that way," he said as he pointed south.

"Thank you."

Agnes walked off the streetcar and stood facing Cambie. She was closer to the water and the wind had picked up. It lifted her umbrella with fantastic force, threatening to turn it inside out. She held tightly to the handle and angled the top down in front of her as she faced the wind directly. As soon as she saw an opening in the traffic, she darted across the street.

Victory Square filled the block opposite from where Agnes walked. It was lined with towering trees on three sides, and within it paths circumnavigated the park and criss-crossed it from corner to corner. At the north end of the park sat the Victory Square Cenotaph, a war memorial that rose thirty feet into the sky. At its base sat wreaths of flowers many layers deep. With the inclement weather, the square remained empty, no one to pay homage to those who had died for their country nor to appreciate the park's beauty. Agnes had seen it when the weather was more hospitable, and she had thought it looked like a lovely place to sit.

It was only one more block before Agnes stood in front of Vancouver's main relief office. There was a wall of people leading up to the door and no break to be seen inside. It was as though the entire city had come in search of assistance. Suddenly Agnes felt like a beggar, reduced to scraps. She couldn't do it. She lived on scraps as a child before coming to Canada and she couldn't go back. She couldn't bring herself to step back into that world. With what little pride she had left, she turned back toward home.

All she had was Sam's money. When it was done, there was nothing else. They would be destitute. She would have no choice but to seek assistance if Art could not find his way. Agnes turned in every direction, and in every direction she found nothing. It was as though the world was swallowing itself up and there was no escape.

Agnes knew what she had to do. Despite her misgivings, she would use Sam's money to pay the rent. She had no choice. She was grateful for it, but she felt she was betraying herself by doing so.

Agnes had just enough time to get the money from her drawer and take it to Mr. Palmer before Dorothy arrived home from school. It would only be a temporary reprieve and she knew that, but it would get her through the day, through the week, and that was all she knew she had the right to ask for.

As she walked up to her gate, she wondered where her husband was. She turned and looked up the street. She thought of going down to the track, to bring him home if he was there, but she didn't have time for that. She had to pay the rent. She had to be back for her daughter when she arrived home from school. It was all falling to her.

Agnes opened the front door and ducked in surprise. A flash flew by her, and she turned to catch a glimpse of it. Bluey sat on the fence, seemingly pleased with his newfound freedom. Agnes gasped in horror. Art would be devastated.

Agnes began to walk slowly toward Bluey, softly calling his name. He sat there, head cocked, looking directly at her. She thought she might be able to grab him, but as she slowly reached out he flew away, across the street and toward the track. He didn't look back nor did he slow down. He just kept flying.

"Bluey, come back," she called. But he didn't. He was gone.

Queenie?! Agnes stepped inside the house and swiftly closed the door. She couldn't lose both of them.

Agnes heard Queenie straightaway. She was chirping loudly in her cage, as though she was calling out to Bluey. Unlike Bluey, she never left. Agnes closed the door, locking her in safely. She was alone now, no mate for comfort or company, but she didn't know it yet and Agnes was sad at the thought.

Agnes went back to the door and opened it. She stepped out onto the landing and looked as far as her eye could see. She saw no signs of Bluey.

The door must have been left open. *How could this have happened?*

"Bluey!" she yelled. "Bluey!" Agnes didn't care who heard her. She only cared about getting Bluey back.

There was no sign of him and she retreated back into the house. *What will I tell Art?* The thought made Agnes's stomach turn. He was in such a fragile state, and this would surely weaken him further.

As she took her shoes and coat off, she noticed Art's shoes sitting neatly beside his slippers.

"Art? Art, darling, are you here?"

There was no response.

She looked in the closet, and Art's coat was hanging where it always did.

"Art?"

Agnes went directly to the bedroom. There was no other place she could think to look. The door was opened just a crack and she quietly opened it farther. The hinge creaked noisily and she held her breath. She could see his silhouette on the bed. As she approached him she stopped, not wanting to wake him. He was lying on top of the covers, his eyes closed. She remained quiet. One arm was hanging uncomfortably over the side of the bed. As she reached down for it, she noticed a bottle on the floor. It was empty and on its side. She picked it up and placed it on the bedside table. There she noticed a second bottle. She picked it up and it too was empty. Her heart began to beat harder and faster in her chest. Something wasn't right. She felt it in the pit of her stomach and then she saw it. The face that she had kissed. The face that she had caressed. The face that she had loved. It had changed. And like Donny's had, it looked peaceful, as though he were only sleeping.

About the Author

Lisa Brown is an avid genealogist and enjoys writing about the fascinating lives of generations past. She is the author of *The Porter's Wife* and its sequel, *The Seeds of Sorrow*, both of which loosely follow three generations of women in her family history.

Lisa currently resides in Ontario, Canada, with her husband and three sons.

CPSIA information can be obtained at www.ICGtesting.com
Printed in the USA
LVOW12s2031171014

409330LV00004B/15/P